Hope in the Inferno
SP Neeson

Happy Reading :)

SPχ

18 STREET PRESS

Hope in the Inferno

Glamour Blind Book 3

Cover Designed by Natasha Snow Designs
www.natashasnowdesigns.com

Developmental Editing by Tracy Thillmann

ISBN: 978-1-7389875-4-2

Version: May 2024

For Jamie, one of my first readers.
And for Ryan. Always.

CHAPTER 1

When I woke up in the middle of the night, Ronan was no longer sleeping beside me. This didn't worry me since he often kept odd hours as my marshal, the head of my guard. I got up and dressed in black pants, a black shirt, and my black leather jacket and riding boots. Then I let the shadows in the room envelop me and I moved through them from the bedroom directly outside and across the property.

I'd been practicing the shadow-walking magic since my return to the human world from the Sidhe. My cousin, Kai, had been teaching me. Now I understood why he wore all black clothing. Well, maybe for him, it was a style choice to go with his black skin and eyes, but for me, it made it easier to blend into the shadows.

I appeared next to the Way to Winter, where Kai and I had agreed to meet, and stepped out of the darkness, alone for just a second before the guards who had been hidden among the trees surrounded me, weapons drawn.

"What are you doing here?" Ronan asked as he casually stepped into the circle.

"A little melodramatic, don't you think?" I responded, gesturing to the people under his command.

He closed his eyes in a bid for patience—I'd seen the look enough times before to know what it meant.

Then he opened his eyes and said, "My princess, how am I supposed to protect you if I don't know where you are?"

Kai appeared next to me as though from thin air. "Are we going to fight your personal guard?" he asked curiously.

A few of the people gasped and stumbled backward. They must be new, since most people had gotten used to him appearing from nowhere by now.

"I don't think that's going to be necessary," I said, staring hard at Ronan.

He jerked his head in a dismissive gesture, and the guards put away their weapons, falling back. I noticed Ansgar and Mada in the group, as I expected, and they took charge of the others, leading them away. Once we were alone except for Kai, Ronan fixed me with a stare.

"Don't bother trying to tell me this is the first time you've gone wherever you're going," Ronan began, stalking toward me in a way that might be menacing to anyone else. Especially with his naked sword held against his shoulder and how much taller he was than me.

I felt a tingle run down my spine, but it wasn't fear. He was very hot when he was in charge.

"I wouldn't insult you like that."

"So just where have you been going?"

"Well, you know how we've added a few more to our numbers lately and they all look a little…"

"Ragged?" Kai supplied.

"Tortured," Ronan said. "Ancient Mother be merciful. Little changeling, tell me you haven't been sneaking into the Queen's dungeon and freeing prisoners."

"Okay. I haven't been sneaking into the Queen's dungeon and freeing prisoners."

He closed his eyes again, this time to hide the emotions I could always see in them.

"You take too many risks," he said.

"You've said that before. You'd think you'd be used to it by now."

His eyes flew open as he sheathed his sword. "I will never get used to you being in danger," he said, gripping my shoulders, just shy of the point of pain.

And there it was, everything he had been trying to hide. The fear for my safety. The frustration that he couldn't stop me. And the love.

"You know I need to do this," I said, touching his cheek. "After what happened to you, and to the person who failed the flora challenge..." I shuddered as I recalled the man completely broken by the Queen of Winter in a matter of hours for failing a challenge during the Solstice events. His empty expression as she led him around on a leash before handing him back to his family. "Do you really think I can stand by and let that continue to happen?"

He didn't let go of me. "You also have obligations *here* you have to take care of."

I'd certainly been putting a lot of things off lately. All of them big decisions I didn't want to deal with. The responsibility of so many lives weighed heavily on my shoulders. I couldn't run from that responsibility, but I could focus on something else for a while. "I know. I will. But I also need to do this."

"Then let me come with you."

"Without darkness magic of your own, it would slow us down to bring you with us. We're already bringing one prisoner each on our way out. Besides that..." I hesitated, recalling what the Queen had said when I rescued Ronan from her torture chamber. Words he hadn't heard because he was so deep in the abyss that had kept his mind intact during weeks of pain. *You must be careful with your toys. Because next time, I will break him. If only because I now know how important he is to you.* "You've spent enough time in her dungeons."

He leaned his forehead against mine. "You make things so difficult."

The side of my mouth hitched up in a semblance of a smile. "Always."

"If we are to go, it must be now," Kai said. "Or else we will not have the time we need."

I raised my eyebrows at Ronan, waiting.

"You know I won't stand in the way of something you believe you must do. Nor can I stand idly by while you do something foolish just to prove a point." He glanced at Kai, then back at me. Then he let me go and stepped away. "Just come back."

"I will."

I wanted to kiss him, but he never kissed me in front of people. From what I understood, that would be a declaration I wasn't quite ready to make. Instead, I simply stepped away and followed Kai through the Way.

I'd created it a bit more than a month ago, opening a Way directly from my estate to Ronan's ranch to ensure I could come and go between the two without difficulty and in relative safety. To ensure no one tried to come onto his property, I also closed the Way that had originally led from his ranch to a spot just north of Glacia.

Once we were in Winter, Kai placed a hand on my shoulder. He had been to the Queen's dungeons more than I had and knew the shadows there better.

As we slipped into the darkness, I said, "I know. I should have told him where I was going. But I didn't want him worrying. I've caused him enough grief over the years, don't you think? And considering he's in love with me, and I haven't figured out if I'm in love with him, it's hardly the worst thing I've done to him, right? But really, who falls in love with someone after only a few months? It's just not reasonable to think someone could fall in love that fast. Right?"

"Calynn," Kai interrupted my rambling.

I held my breath, waiting for some profound piece of wisdom from the depth of his thousand years of life experience.

"You're asking the wrong person," he said.

"Oh." I paused, considering. "You mean you haven't ever fallen in love? Not even a little bit?"

He shot me a look, one black eyebrow cocked. "I've spent my life as an assassin. My queen turned me into someone to be feared, not loved."

I set my teeth together, adding one more thing Mab would have to pay for to her ever-growing list of debts.

Before I could respond, we stepped out of the shadows into the lowest level of the dungeons. When I'd first brought up the idea of freeing prisoners after a little foray into a dragon's den to free some stolen eggs, Kai had told me about this place. It was where Mab stored the prisoners who she had finished torturing but didn't want to release yet. Some had been there for centuries. They had been left forgotten, not even a guard to watch them, only fed once a week—just enough to last them if they rationed properly.

Tonight was feeding night.

There hadn't been many, so over the last week, we had taken them, two at a time, to my property in Winter then on to Ronan's ranch in the human world. Tonight, we would liberate the final two prisoners before the guard brought food at dawn. Kai took up a spot near the stairs to ensure we weren't disturbed, and I moved to the last cells at the very back of the dungeon. I peeked in through the window but couldn't see anything in the shadows.

"Hello?" I called quietly.

Something rustled inside, but I heard no other response.

"Is anyone in there?"

Still nothing. I cast a glance at Kai, who gave me a look telling me to hurry. I nodded toward the cell, then wrapped myself in shadows, stepping out on the other side of the door so I was inside with the prisoner. After I was inside, it occurred to me I should maybe have been a little more careful. Especially when the prisoner screamed and launched herself at me, fingers extended as though she wanted to claw my eyes out.

Thankfully, I'd been practicing krav maga for the past ten years and I caught her as she attacked and threw her against the wall.

"Now that's not a very nice way to greet the person who is here to get you out of this shit-hole."

It had been easy to throw her. She was little more than skin and bones. Even so, she looked up at me from the floor, murder in her dark eyes. With her back pressed against the stone, she got carefully to her feet. I could feel her calling on her magic. The air crackled with electricity as sparks of it traced through her pure white hair. I called upon the magic from the earth, grounding the lightning before she could hurl it at me, then stepped into the shadows again. She twirled around, seeking me, but I'd learned darkness magic from the best and she had none of it herself. I stepped out of the shadows behind her, wrapping her in a choke hold.

"If you're not going to play nice, neither am I," I said, holding the choke for the few seconds required for her to slump against me, unconscious. I lay her gently on the ground, quickly tying her hands and feet together with the zip-ties I'd packed along in case we ran into a guard. I didn't have time to play games with the prisoner. I found a bandana in another pocket and tied it around her mouth so she couldn't scream, then pulled her with me into the shadows, moving to the other side of the door where Kai waited.

"We are out of time," he said, glancing at the woman. "They are coming down the stairs now."

"You said they bring the food at dawn. That's still another hour."

"They are early tonight," he said with a shrug.

"Son of a fucking bitch."

"We must leave before we're found."

I stood my ground. "I'm not leaving the last prisoner."

"Our only other choice would be to kill the guard. You said you did not want to do that."

"I don't. And I won't. The guard is innocent in this. He's just following orders."

Well, most of the guards, anyway. I wasn't going to take the chance on guessing.

I could hear the steps on the stairs now. He would be here in a few seconds.

"Take the woman," I said.

Kai blinked at me.

"Take her. I'll get the last prisoner and meet you at the edge of the city. I should be able to get that far on my own."

Kai bent to pick up the girl, hoisting her over his shoulders as she started to stir. She was going to be a fight when she came to, but Kai would deal with it.

"Your lover will not like you staying behind on your own," Kai warned me. Then he disappeared into the shadows before I could respond.

I glared at the spot he had been for only a second before I also pulled the darkness close and let it carry me to the other side of the dungeon into the final cell. The guard descended the steps as I looked out, still cloaked in darkness. He carried a couple loaves of bread and a bucket of something that looked like congealed oatmeal. He set the bucket down and went to the door of each cell, collecting the bowls I had made sure were placed at the small flaps where he'd expect them to be. As he came closer to the cell I was in, I held my breath until he moved away, back to a table where he ladled sloppy goop into each bowl. He wouldn't be long. I turned to find the prisoner and almost mistook him for a pile of rags in the corner. He was tiny, his head resting on his knees, eyes closed. As I inched closer to him, I realized he was a child. He was a child like Rhys.

Fagen.

He was thirteen and had been Rhys' best friend. We'd all thought he'd been killed when Queen Mab had tried to eradicate the chalice children from the village. But here he was. Alive.

Every single prisoner I'd helped free had made some kind of noise when I appeared in their cell. I had to somehow get Fagen to come with me, silently, in the next two minutes, before the guard noticed anyone missing.

I eased the shadows away from me, letting myself appear in the room slowly so as not to startle him. Then I crouched in front of him, one finger pressed against my lips in a bid for silence. I touched his shoulder.

He jerked upright with a gasp. But he took my warning and stayed otherwise quiet.

"We have to leave now," I said in a low whisper.

He nodded and stood, taking my outstretched hand. Just as his fingers touched mine, the guard spoke.

"Hey. Come get your food." He rapped something against the door.

I pulled the boy against me and wrapped us both in the shadows, slipping into the corner of the room. Unlike Kai, I couldn't just think of where I wanted to go and have the darkness take me there. I had to see where I was going. Though I could move much faster in the shadows, I still needed a line-of-sight to get there. This dungeon was underground, so there were no windows I could look through to get outside the palace. I needed to go through the main area and get back to the stairs.

The guard opened the cell door, sounding an alarm. People rushed down the stairs. They would check every cell, but they wouldn't be able to see us unless they brought enough light to dispel all the darkness. We stayed huddled in the corner, waiting. Finally, a guard flung the door open, and I could see where everyone stood in the main room. Five more guards, all opening cells, searched for prisoners who were no longer there.

I held the boy tight as I moved through the shadows to the far side of the room, waiting for the set of boots on the stairs to come down before starting up. I wasn't certain if someone bumped into me if they would feel me, so I decided not to risk it. Wouldn't Ronan be proud? Every time I heard more guards coming, and there were a lot of them, I pressed the boy and myself against a wall and held my breath until they passed.

We made it up to the next level of the dungeons—where Mab did all her torturing—but it was underground as well. I had to get up one more floor before I could find my way out. I was about to continue when I heard a familiar voice and Fagen began to tremble.

"What do you mean, gone?" Mab said.

"All the cells are empty, Your Majesty. The doors were closed and still locked. The bowls were at the flaps, just as they should be. But when he opened the doors, no one was inside."

I couldn't see her. She was inside one of the torture rooms, the door standing open. Light flooded out and I could see a couple of shadows, Mab's and whoever was talking to her. A whip cracked and someone screamed. Fagen trembled harder, tears leaking into my shirt, where his face pressed against me. I swallowed as I listened to the consequences of my actions. Mab was pissed. And she would take her anger out on whomever was in that room with her—if not others as well. I clutched Fagen. I had saved him, and another fifteen people. But what would the final cost be?

I forced my feet to move, to carry us—cloaked in darkness—one more level up. It took a lot longer as I did my best to avoid the torches casting light that ate up the shadows I moved through. But I reached the ground level and found a window with a clear sight line to the other side of the river, all the way down the road that would take us out of the city. I gripped Fagen tighter and moved through the shadows faster than I had ever moved before, getting us outside the gate and beyond the small town on the far side. We continued toward the Way, Kai finding us during our sprint. He added his shadows to mine, helping me move faster until we were safely away and back in the human world.

Something Ronan had once said floated back to me through my memory. *Each action has a consequence, sometimes ones that are far more terrible than doing nothing in the first place.* I couldn't believe that was true in this case. But the sound of that scream would haunt my dreams for a very long time.

CHAPTER 2

We stepped from the shadows into Ronan's living room as the first light of dawn touched the sky. Ronan stood from his spot on the couch immediately, but I turned to Kai first.

"Take her upstairs into the spare bedroom and close the door. She can stay tied up until she decides to behave herself."

My cousin nodded and carried the woman, who was now struggling, up the stairs.

I still clutched Fagen, unsure who was holding whom harder. Mab's voice and the sound of her whip followed by the scream echoed in my head.

"Get Rhys," I told Ronan quietly.

He left, and I tried to calm Fagen, who still shook in my arms. "It's all right, Fagen. You're safe now."

"She wanted to fix me," he said, his voice wavering. "But all she did was hurt me. She put me in the deep dungeon when she couldn't figure it out and just left me there. She said she wanted the others, but she couldn't find them."

"What do you mean, she wanted to fix you?" I asked softly.

"She said I was broken. Me and all the chalice children. She said she would fix me, and everything would be okay. But it just hurt. It still hurts."

"It's okay, Fagen. She's not going to hurt you anymore, and I'll figure out how to make it stop hurting."

The back door flew open, and Fagen flinched, burying his face into my shoulder.

"Fagen!" Rhys exclaimed, rushing to us.

The scared boy turned at Rhys' voice, then they were embracing. Ronan slipped past us into the kitchen.

"We thought you were dead," Rhys said. "If I'd known you were alive, I would have done everything I could to get you back."

"The others?" Fagen asked.

"Here. They're safe. I'll take you to them."

Rhys looked at me, asking the question with his eyes. I nodded. "Bring him back tonight. I want to talk to him again. But he can see the others and rest. Get him some food. Ask the brownies. Careful though, too much food at once will make him sick."

Rhys wrapped an arm around Fagen's shoulders and led the other boy from the house.

Once they were gone, I sat on the couch and Ronan pressed a steaming cup into my hands. I could have kissed him for that, but I closed my eyes, breathed in the hot aroma, and took a small sip of rich coffee.

"What's wrong? Did you get hurt?" he asked.

I considered my fight with the woman, but she hadn't landed any of her attempts at hurting me.

"I'm fine," I said.

"You're lying."

I tried to give him a smile, but I couldn't quite manage it. "That's supposed to be my line."

"Calynn."

Fuck. He *named* me again. He only ever called me by my name when he was frustrated or angry with me. I guess he had the right. I'd been sneaking out every night for the past week. To stall, I took another sip of coffee.

He took one of my hands in his and rubbed my fingers.

I sighed, closing my eyes as his touch soothed me more than the coffee.

"Actions have consequences," I whispered. I opened my eyes and turned to him. "On our way out, I had to take a different route than Kai. He left with the woman while I had to wait and take Fagen. I can't move through the shadows like he can because I have to see where I'm going. So we went up the stairs and Mab was on the main floor of the dungeons." His grip on my fingers tightened for just a moment, the only indication he was nervous about what I would say. "She knows what I did. No. Let me rephrase. She knows her lower dungeon is empty. She doesn't know it was me. And she's pissed. I couldn't take the ones from her main dungeon. It's too busy. And now they're going to pay the price for the others being free."

"I know you want to save them all," he said, rubbing his thumb over the back of my hand.

"It's more than that. She's going to take her anger out on them. Anger about something I did. It could kill some of them."

"And the ones you rescued? What would have happened to them if you'd left them there? She was always going to kill some of her prisoners, little changeling. That's what she is."

"She wasn't always this way."

"What do you mean?"

"The Sidhe chooses the Queens. It would never have put her in charge if this was what she was always like. Something must have happened to her and Titania to make them into what they are." I shook my head. "It doesn't matter. They are this way now." I stood and Ronan stood with me. "I'm going to talk to the woman. She attacked me when I tried to get her out, so I'd like you with me."

"Of course."

I set my mug down and wrapped my arms around him, letting the scent of pine and ice wash over me, feeling calmer when his arms came around me as well. He grounded me.

"I should have told you what I was doing."

"You should have. We agreed to no secrets."

I pulled his head down so I could kiss him, loving the ease in the gesture, something I'd never had with anyone else before. "I'll tell you next time," I said.

He sighed, his eyes closed. "Of course there's going to be a next time."

This time, my smile was easier. "I'm really good at bad ideas."

He growled, which I took to mean angry agreement, and I led him upstairs to the spare bedroom.

The woman lay on the bed where Kai set her before he disappeared to wherever he was making his home these days. The murderous look was still in her dark gray eyes.

"I'm going to take the gag off," I told her. "I'd like to have a nice little chat. If you scream, I'll have to put the gag back and return later. I don't need a headache. I'm already running on little sleep and not enough coffee."

I moved toward her cautiously and took the bandana from around her face.

"Now, I understand you're pissed about something, but since I just took you out of the Queen's dungeon, I can't really think what that might be. Would you care to enlighten me?"

"If you think I am going to be beholden to you in exchange for my rescue, you are mistaken," she snarled.

I blinked at her.

"You think I took you out of there so you would swear fealty to me?"

"What other reason could you have to steal me and the others from the Queen if not to use us against her?"

I turned to Ronan, who stood at the door, his gigantic sword resting against his shoulder, his expression impassive. He shrugged. I returned my attention to the woman.

"I don't want anything from you. I don't have fealty from anyone." I paused. "Anymore. I rescinded all my offers. Everyone who's here is here because they want to be."

It was her turn to blink. "You do not make sense."

"I got you out of the dungeon because it's wrong that she was keeping you there. While I guess there could be some people who deserved to be punished for something, everyone I've found so far had been tortured for Mab's whims and pleasure alone. Why were you there?"

"My mother opposed Mab."

I looked at her white hair, falling in a sheet down her back, straight and fine despite being in a dungeon for however long. The only other people I'd seen with hair that white were Rhys and his mother. "You aren't Deardriu's daughter?"

She hissed and moved as though she wanted to strike me again. Obviously, Deardriu was a sore spot.

"My mother was Deardriu's fiercest rival. That vulture betrayed my mother, and the Queen had her killed. I was tortured for so long I could not tell you the length of time. Then she tossed me in the deepest cell in the lowest dungeon and left me to rot."

"How long were you in the cell?"

"As with the torture, time is meaningless down there. It could have been ten years, it could have been a hundred."

"Who was your mother?" I asked.

"Bedelia," Ronan answered for her. "She was my mother's and uncle's cousin. She and Deardriu had similar gifts. If I remember correctly, it made Deardriu jealous that Bedelia was better with the elements than she was."

The woman bared her teeth. "The slime set my mother up to be sent to Mab's torture chamber. I was dragged along. Mother died. Mab kept me alive."

"How long was she there?" I asked Ronan.

"Bedelia was brought to Mab while I was still with her. She'd been there for about a year when I finally left Mab's service. Her daughter had been only fifteen when she arrived in the torture chambers."

I did the math. Ronan was a hundred and three years old now. He'd left Mab's service when he was sixty. The woman had been in Mab's dungeons for forty-three years and was now fifty-eight years old.

I told her this, and she closed her eyes, looking relieved. "You do not know how much just knowing that means."

I took a pair of scissors I'd brought from downstairs out of my pocket and cut her free. She sat up, rubbing her wrists.

"What's your name?" I asked.

"Morrigan."

"Well, Morrigan. You're welcome to stay here and recover. It's early in the day, but you can rest, and we'll find you a more permanent place, if you want one. Or you can go on your way. We're in the human world, but I can take you back to the Sidhe. I've been recommending the people from the dungeon stay here for a while to stay off Mab's radar. But you're free to do what you want. Take some time. Think about it."

She grit her teeth. "I wish to make Deardriu pay for what she did to me and my mother."

"That might be tricky. You'd probably have better success if you take a minute and make a plan." I didn't mention Rhys, Deardriu's son, making a mental note to keep them as far apart as possible. I didn't want Morrigan to get any ideas about using him against his mother. "There's a bathroom over there." I pointed in its direction. "We can get someone to show you how it works if you want to bathe. I'm going for a nap."

CHAPTER 3

I'd like to say I slept peacefully. I'd like to say I wasn't bothered by dreams of broken windows and black holes. Of course, I'd be lying. At least the Ancient Mother no longer showed up. She just sent me a dream with a dirty window, hairline fractures throughout. With a single touch, it would shatter, and the dream would shift, some other entity reminding me of the two paths I could walk. One would lead to a peaceful destruction, if such a thing could ever exist. The other path would lead me to total annihilation. It was not helpful enough to explain what the two paths were, but I figured that had more to do with the fact that it didn't really have a voice.

I woke to the smell of coffee and Ronan climbing into the bed, wrapping his arms around me.

"Why are you here?" I asked, a smile in my voice.

"Because I can be."

"Don't you have work to do?"

"Yes," he said, placing a kiss on the spot where my neck met my shoulder.

I turned, but Ronan had stayed on top of the blankets, so a lot of fabric separated us. I pulled his lips to mine and kissed him. It was deep and languid, and I wanted more. I started picking at his shirt, trying to get the buttons open so I could take it off him. He chuckled darkly against my lips.

"Not now, little changeling. You have visitors."

"Tell them to go away. I'm busy."

"One of them is Arial," he said, and I paused.

"I should see her."

"You should. Cacey is here as well. He's waiting in the office. As for me, I'll be back in this bed tonight if you'd care to join me. And if you decide to stay the whole night and not go off rescuing people, I can make it worth your while."

"You drive a hard bargain, sir. I'll see what I can do."

After kissing him one more time, we got up, and I straightened the clothes I'd worn to the final rescue. I hadn't bothered to change before falling into bed. Then I got the coffee Ronan had brought me and went downstairs.

I smiled at Arial sitting at the kitchen table and Quinn in the kitchen. Ronan touched my hand in a quiet gesture before leaving out the front door. I went to the office, leaning on the door frame, to find Cacey looking through some paperwork.

"You want to join us for lunch?" I asked. "We can talk while we eat."

He looked up, a startled expression on his face. "I don't want to intrude, my lady. I can wait until after you've spent time with your friend."

"Don't be ridiculous. Come eat. Arial won't mind if we talk a little business."

I went to the table where Quinn had already set out three places, anticipating my intention before I'd even come downstairs. I sat at the head of the table—I'd started sitting there because that's where people expected me to sit. This table only seated six, unlike the one at my Winter estate, which sat up to twenty. Cacey joined us and sat down across from Arial.

Arial was as new to all this fae stuff as me. She hadn't known she was half-fae until about a month ago but had been taking it well. She and her half-brother Aiden had become fast friends, and he'd even promised to bring her to meet her other siblings soon.

She and Cacey had been introduced when she'd come to my Winter estate, and I knew she'd been curious about him, so when we sat down, I turned to her. "We are not going to grill Cacey with questions. He's here on business."

Arial pouted and sat back as Quinn brought a lunch of toasted BLT sandwiches and cream of broccoli soup to each of us. When we'd returned to the human world, Quinn took on some of the cooking while Aelwyd, the brownie who used to care for Ronan's house, continued with most of the cleaning.

Quinn lived with Rhys, Aiden, and a few of the guards in a house next door. Only me and Ronan lived in this house, keeping the spare bedroom open in case it was needed in an emergency.

"So, what brings you here, Cacey?" I asked as we started eating.

"I need direction on a few things at your property. Even with people coming to live here, you are still at risk of having more people living at the estate than there is room for. Will you build another place for them? And if so, where? Soon you will need to decide if you will continue to grow wheat. If not, what else would you like to grow?"

"Is there a reason I might want to change from wheat to something else?"

"Whim?"

Arial snorted, and I sent her a brief smile.

"I'm not a very whimsical person, Cacey. You should know this about me by now."

"I do, my lady," he said with a nod. "But you are in charge. As such, I must ask you to make these decisions."

"What would Tavon and Tavia think of me changing their crop?" Tavon and Tavia were the twin half-humans who tended my fields.

Cacey shrugged. "It is not their property, my lady."

I thought back to the maps of my property I had been studying. "We have twelve fields and half are growing wheat while the other half are fallow, yes?"

"Yes."

"When is the wheat harvested?"

"It is winter wheat, so in late summer. It is planted during the Fall Equinox."

I drummed my fingers on the table. "So I have some time to make that decision."

"You do," he said. "Though if you are going to make a change, we would need to know how to prepare for it. Also, you do not have as much time to decide about what to do regarding the influx of people."

"How long?"

"If people continue to arrive at the pace they have been, you will run out of space in less than a month."

I sighed. Word had slowly been spreading among the daoine sidhe that I was taking in people and the ones who had come to me were happy. No one had told my secret of being able and willing to help those with only one gift gain access to their latent magic. But it was only a matter of time before that got out.

I also hadn't told anyone beyond my inner circle about what my supposed destiny was and how there may not be a Sidhe or a Winter estate for people to come to after the Spring Equinox. So far, only the friends who had come with me to the Fréimhe—Quinn, Rhys, and Aiden—and

Ronan and his two most trusted guards—Mada and Ansgar—knew. I was still wrestling with the idea myself.

"I'd intended on returning to Winter in a few days. When I come, I'll have an answer for you." I took a bite of the sandwich and closed my eyes at the taste of the bread. "This bread came from the wheat on the estate, right?"

Cacey nodded. "Daric made a few loaves, which I brought with me."

"We're not changing crops. Not when I have the twins and Daric to work together to make something like this."

"Fair enough. There is one more thing that requires your attention."

There was always one more thing.

He handed me a book. "This is the current list of people who have come to you for assistance." I took it and began flipping through the pages. There were a lot of names. "You will need to return to your estate to accept the bargains."

That was something that couldn't be put off for long. "How many now?"

"Twelve."

"Can I do it when I come with the decision about the new quarters? Or should I do it sooner?"

"A few days will be soon enough."

I nodded, and we finished eating. Arial got to pepper Cacey with questions after all, learning leprechauns did not have a pot of gold they hid at the base of rainbows. Though they tended to have magic that aligned with precious metals and stones, making them excellent with finances.

Eventually, he stood up, gathering his papers.

"It was a pleasure dining with you, my lady. And you, Miss Arial. I look forward to our next conversation."

"Same," Arial said with a smile.

Then Cacey bowed to me and left the house.

Arial turned to me with a grin. "It's so weird to hear people be so formal with you."

"If you can believe it, that was pretty informal for Cacey. I've worn him down a bit over the past few weeks."

Quinn finished tidying up in the kitchen and said, "I'm off to see Aelwyd. She promised to show me some recipes." She set a cup of coffee in front of me. "Remember, you made plans to exercise with Mada this afternoon, and Rhys will bring Fagen back this evening."

"You're awfully bossy, you know that?" I said to her back.

She smiled serenely over her shoulder, then went out the back door.

Once we were alone, Arial turned to me with a quirked eyebrow. "So, with all the *my lady's* and the maid who tells you what to do, I guess you've landed on your own definition of princess?"

I thought about her question for a long time before answering. Had I figured it out?

"Maybe? I feel like I can be the leader they need. But—"

I cut myself off. I didn't want to say it. Because I knew, once I did, I wouldn't be able to take it back. Arial just watched me, waiting.

"I guess, in the first few weeks after I learned about all this, I had these people telling me I had all this power and it made sense, you know? I'd always felt like I had what it took to take care of myself and what it took to stand up to people who needed standing up to. Like I was supposed to be the one to stand up to them. Then I went to the Sidhe and there was this problem and I started thinking maybe I could do something about it. Maybe I was supposed to be the hero. So I went to learn my destiny, but it turns out I'm not the hero. I'm really the villain."

Wasn't that what they would call me? The person created to destroy the Sidhe. People would die. A lot of people. And I would be the cause of it all. The Ancient Mother had told me I would also be the one to rebuild it, but that was after I'd torn it all apart.

The more I thought about it, the more I had trouble breathing. My heart raced, and I felt sweaty. I wasn't sure what a panic attack felt like, but I was pretty sure I was on the verge of having one.

"Calynn." Arial's hand covered mine, drawing my eyes down to where we touched, easing something in me. "Everyone is someone else's villain. You don't have to be the hero in anyone's story but your own."

"I'm not sure I'm even that." My breathing evened out, but my heart still felt heavy in my chest.

"What is a hero other than someone who stands up for people when they can't stand up for themselves?"

"But what I have to do—"

"What you have to do is not who you are. And who you are is not a monster. You'll figure out a way."

I huffed a laugh. "Why is everyone so confident in me and my ability to figure things out when I feel like I'm making it all up as I go along?"

She patted my hand and stood. "It's because we're all smarter than you."

I laughed and stood as well. She gathered her things. "I have to get going. You'll be all right, though?"

"Yeah. You're right. I'll figure it out." Probably. I was just running out of time.

CHAPTER 4

Rhys brought Fagen into the house with Tarian, the third oldest of the chalice children. Rhys and Tarian stood on either side of the boy, holding him as they walked slowly. Fagen looked pale and sick, his gold eyes dull and sunken. He looked worse now than he had this morning. What had she done to him? Was it just his age? Or was it something more?

"Hey, Fagen," I said as he sat on the couch between his two friends. "How have you been today?"

He shook his head.

"He's been unable to speak for the last couple of hours," Rhys said. "We weren't sure if it was because he's now in the human world."

"You could have brought him sooner," I said.

Rhys grimaced. "I know. But he seemed stable, and we didn't think it was urgent enough to come earlier. Then he seemed to suddenly get worse."

I sat on the table in front of Fagen. "May I see what she did to you?" I asked him, holding out my hands.

Fagen looked from me to Tarian, then to Rhys, his eyes wide and scared.

"It's okay," Rhys said. "She won't hurt you. Calynn only wants to help."

He reached his hand out to mine slowly, shaking with effort. I caught his fingers, careful not to squeeze tightly for fear of bruising him.

Then I looked at what damage had been done. Looking into his magic, I found that same empty space that had been in Rhys until we'd brought down the barrier separating him from his gifts. But this empty space had been filled with water that threatened to pull me in. I came out of Fagen's magic quickly, afraid I might drown if I didn't.

"Evander," I said, gasping for breath. "I need Evander."

But I hadn't needed to say anything because Ronan was already coming in the back door with the brownie. The foreman on Ronan's ranch, and an excellent healer, Ronan told me he'd noticed Fagen's state as Rhys and Tarian brought him in and went to fetch Evander right away.

"Something's been done to his magic," I said as Evander knelt in front of us, checking the boy over. "I think there's too much pressure."

Evander nodded and pulled something out of his bag of supplies. It was a small vial of amber liquid which he placed a drop of into Fagen's mouth.

"What's that?" I asked.

"A reconciliation tincture. It restores equilibrium in magic. Reconciling what is there with what is supposed to be there."

He sat back, and we waited.

My knee jumped in impatience as I waited to see a change in the boy. "Is there nothing else we can do?"

"I am afraid not. I have seen this before and do not know of a way to reverse what has been done."

After a moment, Fagen took a deep breath and seemed to relax slightly. He was still pale and looked like a soft breeze would knock him over, but he could sit without support, and what was more, he could speak again, murmuring, "I'm okay."

"Can you tell me more about what she did to you?" I asked.

"She kept me locked up for a long time," he began, his voice quiet. "At first, she didn't do anything. Then, a couple weeks ago, maybe—it's hard to know how time passes in those dungeons—they brought me to the upper level again. I heard the Queen arguing with another woman. The woman asked where the rest were, and the Queen said they had been stolen before she could capture them. That I was the only one available."

I caught Rhys' eye. We both understood. They'd been talking about the other chalice children. Rhys, the oldest of them, had given them the moniker because they were empty, but still valuable—like a chalice. I'd taken them in before Mab could remove them from the Winter village.

Fagen continued. "Then the woman came toward me and told me everything was going to be okay. She didn't seem right, though. She felt too warm or too bright. Then she started pushing her magic toward me—or more like into me—and there was all this pressure. For a while, I couldn't breathe or see. Then it eased, and they put me back into the dungeon."

"Do you know what they did to make it ease?"

He shook his head.

"Okay. You rest now."

I stood and went to the kitchen, where Ronan had waited out of the way while we worked. He poured me a cup of coffee and I smiled at him gratefully before smelling the strong brew and taking a sip. I immediately felt calmer and more in control, which was something I would need in order to figure out what to do next.

Evander and Rhys followed me into the kitchen while Tarian remained on the couch with Fagen.

"You said you'd seen this before," I said to Evander, my voice low.

"I have," he said, looking down at the floor. "To my great shame, I admit I assisted in the creation of the technique used."

Shock ricocheted through me. I had always known Evander to be a kind and compassionate person. Doing something like this to people didn't fit with his personality at all. I wanted to demand answers. Instead, I waited for him to offer them himself. It didn't take long.

"When I came into my magic, I realized I had a rare gift among brownies for healing. Around the turn of my first century, one of the Summer high healers, Anstice, asked if I would be interested in working with her. I agreed; I wanted to learn, and she was the best. After I'd been working with her for a few months, she brought me in on a special project. She was attempting to fix the daoine sidhe with only one gift. She'd been experimenting for about two hundred years at this point. There had been some deaths, but she was certain she was coming close to a solution." He paused, his eyes shifting to the ground.

"She was not. Though the fae she experimented on no longer died." He shuddered out a sigh. "Mother forgive me, I helped her. I was never certain if we were doing the right thing, but I wanted to learn. And people were not dying. I convinced myself it was for the best. If we could find a solution—if we could help these people—it would all be worth it. We worked together, creating a procedure where I would build a construct in the space where the latent magic should be using my earth and flora magics. Then Anstice would fill the construct with water magic."

"Why water magic?" I asked.

Evander glanced at me, head tilted to the side as though this was a silly question. "That's the only magic she has."

"Right."

"I noticed a difference between the patients she had done the procedure on without me compared to those for whom I had created the constructs. Fewer of them descended into madness."

"Madness?" I asked.

He nodded. "But I could see their pain. Only one thing ever helped ease it. A reconciliation tincture." He took the vial from his pocket, where he'd stored it after giving Fagen a dose, setting it on the kitchen island. Then he took a deep breath and continued. "About fifteen years ago, a girl was born. This child—this infant—had no magic at all."

My eyes shot to Rhys. He was also fifteen years old and had been the first child born in Winter with no access to magic.

"Anstice brought the girl to our laboratory and started running tests. I knew what she would do. And I knew the procedure would kill the infant."

"So you told her you wouldn't do it?" I asked.

"If I had said I wouldn't do it, Anstice would have found a way to force my hand. Instead, I stole the child, burned the laboratory and all the notes we had taken, and left the Sidhe. I left the child with some people I knew who lived in the Summer village. Since the day we left, I have regretted not bringing her with my family to the human world. I feared what being here, in a place without magic, would have done to her. And I feared they would search harder for me had I brought her with me. I have wondered every day since if she was still alive."

"She is," I said quietly, remembering hazel eyes flecked with gold and long, iridescent hair. "I met her when I was in Lumina. She ran into me, just like you did when I first walked through the Winter village." I looked at Rhys.

"How can you be certain it was her?" Evander asked.

"I can't. I just know it."

"Do you think the woman who did this to Fagen is the high healer you worked for?" Ronan asked, bringing the subject back around.

"I believe so. He said she felt too warm or bright. How would *you* describe people from Summer?"

"How do we undo it?" I asked.

Evander looked back at me. "We cannot. We never bothered to learn how the treatment could be undone. We gave the tincture if the pressure became too much. But to remove it?" He shook his head. "I know no way to do that."

"There has to be a way," I said. "He can't remain like that. It's causing him pain and he can't use the magic that was put into him."

"What did you see?" Ronan asked.

I explained the water that filled up the space where his magic should live, taking up all available room.

"Couldn't you give him access to his magic like you did me?" Rhys asked.

"I don't think that's a good idea. If his magic is separated from him the same way yours was and I remove the barrier that keeps them apart, the water will flood into whatever magic he has, drowning it. I don't understand why they thought this would work."

"Because they were unaware there was any magic there that could be drowned," Ronan said. "They—we all thought there was no magic at all. But if there could be a way to give a person magic, even if it wasn't their own, it makes sense to try."

"So you're condoning the experimentation?" I asked sharply.

"Of course not," Ronan said. "I'm saying I understand it. You've never had to live without magic you know should be yours. I wouldn't even be surprised if a lot of the people Anstice experimented on volunteered. Not the infant, and not Fagen. But the others."

Evander nodded. "We had no shortage of volunteers. I admit, not all of them were willing, but most were. No one believes the magic is there, hidden away. Everyone thinks there is just nothing. So it matters not if we fill the empty space."

"The empty chalice," Rhys whispered, looking at his friends.

"What do you propose I do, then?" I asked. "We can't just leave him like this."

"I haven't worked for Anstice in fifteen years," Evander said. "And the data from the previous experiments were all lost. She would have had to start again. I don't know how the experiments have changed. However, I've seen you do things no one thought possible, so if anyone can fix this, it would be you. First, you would need to learn exactly what magic was used."

I straightened, setting aside my coffee, half-finished. "For that, I have to go to Summer."

I started toward the stairs, intending to go up and pack what I thought I might need, even though Quinn would scold me later for not letting her pack for me.

"There is one more thing, Miss Calynn," Evander said.

I turned at the foot of the stairs.

"I know you sent Aiden to find out if the Queen was kidnapping the Summer children and he said they were not."

"That's right."

"But Anstice made a special trip to Winter to perform the experiment on Fagen. She had intended to do to all the Winter children what she did to him on a single trip. In Summer, she would have no such time restriction. She could capture a child, do the experiment, and release them back into the village."

"What are you trying to tell me?" I asked, though I was certain I already knew.

"If she came to Winter to do the procedure on Fagen, she will already have started on the children in Summer."

CHAPTER 5

A year ago, I would have left the human world and gone straight to Summer without hesitation. I would have found the kids and gotten them to a safe place and not cared about who might worry or be left adrift without me. A year ago, there was no one to worry or leave adrift. Then again, a year ago, I hadn't known this world existed.

As much as I wanted to go to Summer now, I knew I had to do things in the right order. So I made sure everything was ready and went to bed while Ronan and Quinn prepared for us to leave.

We left the human world the next morning and went to my Winter estate. Ronan had stationed guards everywhere he thought best around the property. So many guards, in fact, that I'd had to appoint lieutenants for the guards at Ronan's property, the Winter estate, and my personal guard. We'd chosen Sorcha and Andras for the properties, two fae who had come to me from Ronan's uncle Anant. We'd chosen Mada as the lieutenant of my personal guard. She and Ansgar had wanted to remain together, or else we would have appointed him as a lieutenant as well.

As I neared the house, I felt something ease in my chest. I loved Ronan's house, but it was his. This one was mine. Cacey greeted me as soon as I arrived and introduced me to the twelve new people who had come to seek shelter. I told them what I could do and accepted bargains with all of them. After that business was concluded, I was set to discuss the new barracks with Cacey when my housekeeper, Ethna came into the library.

"Daric has lunch prepared in the dining room. And you have a visitor waiting in the solarium."

"A visitor?"

She nodded. "By the name of Ryleigh."

"I'll see them now and we can discuss the property after, Cacey." I turned back to Ethna. "Is there enough that I can invite them to lunch if I think it's necessary?"

She rolled her eyes and didn't answer, leaving me and Cacey alone again.

"Most liege lords do not allow that kind of insolence from their people," he said.

I shrugged a shoulder. "She's good at her job. I shouldn't ask stupid questions."

He struggled with a smirk, then let it go. "As you say, my lady."

I grinned at him, then stood, leaving the library and starting toward the solarium. Ronan, who had been waiting outside the library, and another guard followed me to meet my guest.

Ryleigh waited, looking out the floor to ceiling windows at the barracks I'd had built on that side of my house. I'd met them during the Solstice challenges when they had competed with me in the earth challenge. They hadn't been happy about us both succeeding at the third, and most difficult, task but eventually, I must have said something right and they'd decided I wasn't so bad.

Ryleigh was an androgynous beauty with shoulder-length black hair and dark brown eyes. They wore charcoal gray pants that looked similar in style to the ones I wore and a baggy green shirt that looked easy to move in. Their strong hands were clasped in front of them tightly, belying the seemingly comfortable stance in which they stood.

"Ryleigh," I said as I came into the room. "I wasn't expecting you, was I?"

"Princess, it's good to see you again. I apologize for my rude intrusion."

While their first sentence was true, their apology was a straight-up lie, buzzing in my ear as loud as any lie I'd ever heard.

"Why don't you tell me why you've come?"

Ryleigh took a deep breath, and I waited. Finally, they said, "I heard a rumor."

"I see."

The fae were typically difficult to get information out of. Especially when they wanted something from you. I knew this could take a while, and I was starving.

"Why don't we go to the dining room and discuss this rumor you heard? Would you like some lunch?"

After they agreed, we went into the dining room and got settled. Daric served the food and set a steaming cup of coffee in front of me.

"Did you make this?" I asked him.

He nodded.

I smelled it and took a sip. Then I smiled at him. "It's perfect."

He smiled in return. "If you're not careful, you will start saying things that put you in my debt."

"For coffee like this, I wouldn't find it a hardship." I looked at Ryleigh. "Did you want some? It's not the magic-infused coffee you get here. It's from the human world."

They looked confused for a moment. "I suppose I would try some."

I nodded at Daric, who went to make another cup for my guest. Then it was time for business.

"Okay, Ryleigh. You heard a rumor, and you had to come here, even though you know it's rude to arrive unannounced without an invitation. Yet, you're not really sorry you did. Tell me. What's the rumor you heard?"

Ryleigh looked over at my guards, Ronan and a man I had recently met named Kavan.

"If you think you can trust me, you can trust them as well."

"I'm not sure you want your guards to hear this rumor," they said quietly.

"If it's what I think it is, they already know."

Ryleigh's eyes went wide for just a second before they closed them in a gesture meant to keep me out but maybe also to pray. They swallowed before they opened their eyes again.

"Is it true? Are you able to find a person's missing magic?"

I considered what I wanted to say. On the one hand, I hadn't wanted people to know too quickly. I was already getting more people asking for bargains than I thought I would be able to help before the year and a day was up. That was something I'd have to discuss with Cacey. On the other hand, with the children being experimented on and the Spring Equinox looming over my head, I wanted all the people who stood the risk of losing their lives to come to me before that happened.

"Can I trust you, Ryleigh?"

"Yes."

I was never more relieved to have the ability to know when someone lied when I didn't hear it in that statement.

"It's true. I've already helped a number of people. I have many more on a schedule. Ronan was the third. Kavan is the next." I pointed to each of them.

"If I bring someone to you, could you find her missing magic?"

"I can, but she'll have to wait. I can't move people to the front of the line. And there's a bargain to be made before I put her on the list."

"Of course. I would expect nothing less."

"Do you want to know what the bargain is?"

"Whatever it is, you are getting the short end of it, I'm sure."

I laughed. "You're probably not the only one who thinks so." I considered Ryleigh for a moment, realizing I had an opportunity here I shouldn't pass up. "This person who you want me to help is important to you. Maybe you can make the bargain for her."

"What would you have me do?"

Daric returned with coffee for Ryleigh, then retreated to his kitchen. It allowed me a moment to eat and time to think through an idea.

"There are a lot of people in Glacia who I could help. Many of them are finding their way to me already. But there are some whose fealty terms aren't up yet and so they can't just leave. I haven't exactly endeared myself to many of the nobles. If I ask for these people to be let go, no one is going to consider it. But if you do it..."

"I can try," Ryleigh said, lifting their mug of coffee. "I know others who may have better luck than I might. How many people would you consider for this bargain?"

"How many are there?" I looked between Ryleigh and Ronan, then to Kavan.

Ronan said, "I've not been part of Glacia for a number of years, my princess. I'm afraid I don't know the answer."

Ryleigh said, "I never paid that close attention to how many daoine sidhe have access to only one magic, let alone when they pledged allegiance to their lords."

Kavan shrugged, looking slightly nervous. "I don't know, Princess."

"That's a problem I'll have to solve." I looked at Ronan again. "Do you think my friend will be able to answer the question for me?"

I hoped he would understand who I meant since I didn't want to mention I had a spy, nor that he used to be the Queen's best assassin.

"If he does not know the answer, I'm certain he would be able to find out."

"When he returns, we'll need to ask him." I looked back at Ryleigh. "For now, we have to settle the bargain." I took a deep breath and closed my eyes, searching my magic for what I believed would be fair. I believed my magic had been created specifically to help these people. Since I believed that, it wasn't much of a stretch that I should instinctively know how many I needed to help. I considered the question for a while and decided on the number.

"Twelve," I said. "One person for each month your friend should be in service to me."

"It's a bargain," Ryleigh said. Then they started to laugh. "You know, bargains are supposed to be equal. This feels like I'm getting more than you are. You could have asked for anything. Yet you choose to ask to be able to help more people. You are not like other fae."

I grinned. "I've heard that a lot. But in this case, I think you're underestimating how important this task is to me." I touched the antler necklace I wore. It had been a gift from the White Stag, the protector of the forest and a bringer of change. He had said I was also a protector and a bringer of change. Helping these people was part of that. "There's one other thing. I know there are other changelings in Glacia. I assume not all are treated as kindly as Bridget."

Bridget Cleary was the oldest changeling in Glacia. She was around a hundred and fifty years old and had helped me figure out Nialas, who had recently changed her name to Niall, had been the one to put in motion the events that led to the selkie Meriel's murder. Niall and I had recently worked our way to a truce, and she had fallen in love with a half-human, Andras, the new lieutenant of my Winter guard. Andras' father was human, and a changeling living in Glacia.

"This is true. Many are treated quite poorly. They are human, after all." Ryleigh spread their hands as though to say, *what can we do*?

"What is their relationship to the daoine sidhe they live with? Is there any way they can leave the people they're with and come here?"

"You want to bring the daoine sidhe with only one magic as well as the changelings?" They chuckled. "You want the mongrels, too?"

"I don't like that term. But yes. If they want to come. All of them."

Ryleigh regarded me blankly. "All right. In answer to your question, it depends on the changeling. Bridget made a bargain with my parents. Each bargain will be different, so you would have to find out individually."

"Fuck."

"I can look into this if you want me to."

"What will it cost me?" I asked.

Ryleigh shook their head. "I will look into it as part of the bargain. I'm certain Bridget will be happy to help. But I cannot promise to bring any with me."

"Fair enough. Twelve daoine sidhe with access to only one magic and information about the changelings in Glacia. In exchange, I'll help the person you want me to help."

"You're not going to ask who this person is?"

I took a drink from my coffee. "What business is it of mine? You made the bargain. How you deal with that is between you and your friend."

"You're not even slightly curious as to why a noble daoine sidhe wants so badly to help one of the lesser daoine sidhe with only one magic?"

My eyes went, involuntarily, to Ronan. I traced his body with my gaze from the top of his head to the heavy boots he wore. His long sword was in its scabbard instead of resting on his shoulder, an indication he saw no threat here. His dark emerald eyes gave me the smile he wouldn't allow on his lips.

"No, Ryleigh. I'm not curious at all."

CHAPTER 6

After Ryleigh left, I remained at the table for a long time, thinking. Finally, I got up and went back to the library where Cacey was still at work. He moved to get out of the seat I usually sat in when I was here, but I waved at him to sit back down.

"This won't take long," I said. "I've made a decision about the accommodations."

"Oh?"

"We're going to take over two of the fallow fields and build housing on them."

"Two?" He dropped the pen he'd been holding and sat with his mouth open. After a moment, he recovered, picked up the pen, and said, "Do you think that's really necessary?"

"I do," I said, sitting in one of the chairs across from him. "I'm going to try to have all the people with only one magic come here within the next few weeks. As many of the half-humans and the changelings who want to come as well."

"That could be a large number."

"I expect it is."

"How do you plan to feed these people?" he asked, scribbling some notes.

"You said we have a decent amount of money saved, yes?"

"Yes. But—" He took a deep breath. "You wish to spend the money the estate has made on taking in these other fae?"

"I do."

"Do you know how many people that is?"

I steepled my fingers together in front of my face, looking at my hands instead of at my house manager. "Not yet. I hope to have an estimate in the next few days."

He shook his head. "I do not like this. With the number of people already here, we will be lucky to last until the Summer Solstice. With an unknown number still remaining to arrive, that date will shrink greatly. That does not consider what the twins will think when you take away two of their fallow fields."

"I know Tavia and Tavon will be upset. But this is what's going to happen. You're going to buy stores of food and anything else you think we'll need to last as long as we can."

Silence grew between us as Cacey took in what I was saying.

"You want me to prepare for a time when we might be cut off from the rest of Winter?"

"I do. And I'd like it all to be prepared by the Spring Equinox."

"What about beyond?" I could hear the fear in his voice, though he tried hard to hide it.

I finally looked at him again, then said quietly, "I won't be making any plans beyond the Spring Equinox until we get there."

The sentence hung heavy in the air. Neither of us spoke for a long time.

Finally, Cacey nodded. "I understand, my lady. I will do my best to prepare for as many eventualities as I can before the Spring Equinox. And I will pray for what is beyond."

***

Once I'd sorted out all the details at my Winter estate, it was too late in the day to leave for Summer. I went to my room that night and paced the floor, agitated that I couldn't move on to the next stage of my plan. But Ronan had insisted, correctly, we leave at first light when he'd be better able to defend me if someone tried to kill me on the trail.

I knew both Queens wanted me dead. They had to be searching for a way to slip past my defenses, but Ronan kept me and my properties too heavily protected. He wasn't taking any chances, and I was trying to listen to his suggestions. Except for when I snuck out to free prisoners, but if my marshal didn't know about that, neither did the Queens.

I was still pacing when Ronan came into the room late that night.

"What are you still doing awake?" he asked, unbuckling his sword belt.

"Can't sleep. I want to go now."

"You know how dangerous the forest is at night. We have excellent night vision, but it'll be safer during the day."

"I know you're right. I don't have to like it."

He chuckled as he sat to pull off his boots. "Welcome to the club. I'm the president. You can be vice president if you want."

"As the princess, shouldn't *I* be president?"

"As the person who hates at least half the shit you pull, no."

He stood again and came toward me, wrapping me in his arms so I couldn't pace anymore. Now that he was surrounding me, I didn't feel the need to.

"You know," I said, "you had promised to make it worth my while if I stayed in bed last night, but by the time you got there, I was asleep."

"You were."

"So maybe you could make it worth my while tonight to go to bed?"

I looked up at him, a sly smile spreading over my lips.

"I could find it in me to be persuaded."

I rose onto my toes to kiss him, our lips meeting softly for a moment before his hands slid down to grip my ass and lift me off the ground. I smiled at the angle change, deepening the kiss as I wrapped my legs around his waist and he carried me to the bed, lowering me onto it until I knelt in front of him. He caught the bottom of my t-shirt and pulled it over my head.

His hands on my skin felt like lightning, desire sparking off his fingertips as they drifted over me, pulling me closer until my pelvis was pressed against his, grinding his erection into me.

"Fuck, Ronan," I gasped. "We're wearing too many clothes."

My fingers fumbled with the buttons on his shirt for a second before I gave up and just ripped it open, sending the buttons pinging around the room. I shoved the shirt off his shoulders and skimmed my hands down his arms, pulling him closer to me.

"You're always so impatient," he said, scraping his teeth along my jaw as he worked on pushing my pants down.

I sat, and he pulled them off before climbing on the bed between my legs. I felt hot, my body throbbing for him. I pulled him toward me and growled.

"You're still wearing pants."

"Patience, little changeling," he said, a smile in his voice.

He pushed me down and gripped both my hands in one of his, as his mouth traveled toward my breast and his other hand slid toward my pussy. I glanced up at where my hands were trapped above my head.

"You do that a lot. You know, if you're into bondage, we could get some ropes or a silk scarf or something."

He lifted his head to catch my eyes, a grin on his perfect lips. "I like it this way. I like feeling you trying to get free because of how much you want to touch me."

"I think you're letting it go to your head too much."

"You're pulling your hands right now," he pointed out.

I looked up, stopping them from moving immediately. He laughed, lowering his head to capture one of my nipples between his teeth, flicking his tongue over the tip, creating the perfect mix of sharp and sweet sensations.

Then his other hand began to move again, sliding over my stomach and down. His fingers reached my wet folds, making me moan and strain against his hands. My eyes closed, and I fell into a world of nothing but Ronan and sensations and pleasure. His lips on my breast, his fingers strumming me like an instrument only he knew how to play.

I continued to strain against him, pulling at my hands and lifting my hips toward him, but he held me still, pressing me into the mattress.

"Ronan," I said on a sigh. I could feel his thrill at hearing his name in the way he bit down a little harder, moved his fingers a little faster, sending me a little higher, until I broke with a shuddering cry. I saw stars. They flashed across my vision, blocking everything except him and how he continued to stroke me higher.

Exactly when the pressure became too much, he eased off just enough to drag the orgasm out even further.

When the aftershocks subsided, I gave him a lazy smile, and he kissed me.

"Was that distracting enough?" he asked against my lips.

"It was a good start. Are you going to take those pants off now?"

He laughed, kissing me again. "You are insatiable."

"For you? Yes."

He climbed off the bed and I watched as he undid his belt, unbuttoned his pants, and pushed them down. His eyes on me the whole time. My heart felt like it expanded in my chest at the look of desire in them. When he revealed his erection, I got up and went to him.

"My turn," I said, reaching for him.

"I don't think so." He gripped my wrists, holding my hands away from him, capturing my lips in a deep kiss.

I moaned into his mouth as our bodies pressed together. Then he was moving closer, forcing me to lie back on the bed.

"If you're not going to let me give you a blow job, are you at least going to fuck me?"

"I'm going to ensure you are sufficiently distracted from the thoughts causing you distress, my princess."

His hands moved from my wrists to twine our fingers together, holding my hands down while he positioned himself over me. His hard length found my entrance and slid in with ease, like that was where he belonged.

"Fuck, little changeling," he groaned into the side of my neck. "You are so perfect."

I wrapped my legs around his hips and held him close in the only way I could. Then he began to move, long smooth thrusts that kept me on edge. I'd get close, and he'd slow for a moment before continuing with the steady rhythm.

He pressed my hands down into the mattress regardless of how much I wanted to touch him. I strained against the pressure, trying to make him move faster, let me have use of my hands. He was implacable, completely in control. His lips began a trail from my jaw and down to my neck. His steady movement never wavered, and the pleasure built higher and higher.

"Ronan. I need—"

He laughed darkly against my skin, sending a shiver down my spine. "Need what, little changeling? What can I give you?"

I couldn't think. I couldn't do anything more than submit to him, and I couldn't think of any reason why I might want to.

Somehow, he seemed to understand and finally started moving faster, driving me toward an abyss. My fingers tightened around his, twining us together. Pleasure tightened within me, the pressure growing until it crested, and I began trembling, the orgasm shaking me and the world around me. I distantly felt Ronan following me into bliss, calling my name as he did so. I couldn't say how long I floated there before I became aware again. Ronan had collapsed over me, favoring one side so he wasn't crushing me. Though I wouldn't mind if he did. His face was turned toward me, settled in the space between my jaw and shoulder, his lips touching my neck, but not kissing me.

"Did you feel that?" I asked. During my climax, it felt like the whole world had shifted with us. Thinking back, it was startling to consider because it had felt like a physical shift, not an internal one.

The ground had shaken.

Ronan nodded into my neck.

"Do you think anyone else did?"

He lifted his head, and I was struck by how open his expression was, his beautiful features relaxed and happy. He grinned like a man who knew he had done a good job. A little bit arrogant, a little bit mischievous, a little bit playful. I loved it when he was like this.

"I doubt it. But we could go ask."

He started to shift away, and my fingers gripped his where they were still intertwined, my leg wrapped around his, keeping him in place.

"If you leave me now, I am liable to react violently," I warned.

"We can't have that."

He settled down again, his weight half on me, half on the bed. One hand dislodged from mine to drift over my hair.

"I've never felt that before," I said.

He twitched in a shrug, unconcerned. "My latent magic is bedrock."

"So you're saying I shook your magic?"

"You shake many things, little changeling. You turn my life upside down and inside out."

"And you still think I'm perfect?"

He pretended to consider the question, and I bit his shoulder.

He laughed. Then he kissed me, slow and lazily. I loved this, too. The simple pleasure in each other's company. The simple desire for each other.

I loved *him*.

I felt like I had been splashed by icy water. I was in love with Ronan. When had that happened? It felt like something that had crept up on me a little at a time. But also something that had happened all at once.

I hadn't realized we had stopped kissing until he said, "What's wrong, little changeling?"

I searched his green gaze. I couldn't catch my breath. I loved him. If something were to happen to him, I would be crushed. The sheer terror at that thought, the idea that I could lose him.

The enormity of it all crashed down on me and I couldn't speak. I couldn't breathe.

And he knew. Like always, he knew.

"Calynn? What's wrong?"

But I couldn't answer him. I couldn't do anything but bring his mouth back to mine and kiss him with a fierce desperation. I knew he was confused. I knew I should tell him. He'd already told me he loved me. He deserved to know I felt the same. But I couldn't say it.

So I kissed him. I rolled us so I was on top. He could have easily removed me. He could have insisted I tell him what was wrong. But he let me have my way.

"I've got you," he whispered. "Whatever it is, little changeling, I've got you."

Then he pulled me back toward him.

And I loved him even more.

CHAPTER 7

When I woke up the next morning, Ronan was gone, but his side of the bed was still warm. I got up and dressed quickly, even though the sun hadn't risen yet and we wouldn't be leaving until it did.

I made my way downstairs where there was a bustle of activity of people getting ready, Ronan and Quinn orchestrating it from the foyer. I went to them, touching Ronan's hand instead of kissing him good morning like I would have preferred. Even after last night's epiphany, I wasn't ready to make our relationship public.

"Breakfast is ready for you," Quinn said. "We should be ready to leave in the next hour."

I went into my library to stay out of the way, letting her do her thing. No one could organize people the way Quinn could. She'd really grown in confidence over the last couple months. Daric brought me in breakfast and coffee, and I went over some paperwork until it was time to go.

I was about to leave the library when someone knocked softly on the door frame.

"May I speak with you?"

Niall stood there, the woman who had been changed with me as an infant. She was completely human and, other than our eyes and style choices, we looked identical. Our relationship had improved over the last few weeks when she'd changed her outlook on a lot of things and given herself a new name. Previously, she'd been called Nialas, which was an

Irish word that meant nothing. She'd repaid her debt for her part in the selkie Meriel's death and then some, by bringing a family of wyverns to the property and helping me defeat the dragon that had been stalking the wyverns.

"What's up, N? I was just about to leave."

"You're going to Summer, right? To see Mother?"

"Among other things." I paused, looking at her. "Did you want to come with me?"

"No," she said, resolute. "What Father believes, Mother follows. Plus, I'm happy here with Derecho and Andras. But I hoped you'd convey a message?"

"Yeah, sure. What is it?"

"Tell her I'd like to see her, if she would like to see me."

I regarded the woman I thought of as my sister for a moment, catching something sad behind her eyes. "I'll tell her. And when I get back, what do you want me to tell you?"

She gave me a wavering smile. "Tell me she loves me, but doesn't have time to see me."

I nodded.

She started to turn away.

"Hey, N?"

She looked back.

"I know it's easier said than done, but they're not worth your time. You can build your own family."

This time, the smile was real. "I have. And I'm glad you're part of it."

We left the library together, and I watched, somewhat jealous, as Niall walked right up to Andras, who was talking to Ronan, and kissed him before continuing on. It was stupid, since I was the one who had to make the move. I knew that. But as I watched Ronan, in charge of the surrounding chaos, the panic from last night started to rise again.

I loved him, and there was no taking it back. I was certain I didn't want to, but I also didn't want to be hurt. Not that he ever would. But what if someone hurt him? What would I do to keep him with me? The panic rose higher until I was struggling to breathe, my heart racing in my chest.

He looked over at me, concern on his face. Then he strode to me and I grabbed his hand, needing at least this contact.

"Are you all right?" he asked.

I managed a nod.

He lifted a brow in an expression that told me clearly he didn't believe me.

"I will be. Are we ready to go?"

"Yes."

The plan was for me and a small group of guards to go to Summer today to speak with my mother and gain control of my Summer estate. Then the rest of the guards who would be accompanying us would come and I would find the children and bring them all to my estate.

I should have known the plan wouldn't last much longer than walking into the Summer village.

The party consisted of me, Ronan, Quinn, Rhys, Aiden, Mada, and Ansgar. It took us about three hours to reach the edge of the village from my Winter estate. Immediately upon entering the village, a teenager ran straight into me.

I caught the same girl that had run into me the last time I came to Summer by the shoulders and grinned. "We have to stop meeting like this."

She looked up at me, startled for a moment, before recognition dawned.

"Are you going to let me go again, or are you going to keep me this time?" she asked.

"I think I'll keep you. I'm actually here to help you."

"Right," she sneered. "A noble helping a child with no magic. I'm certain I don't want your kind of help."

I shot a look at Rhys. He didn't say anything in response to her statement.

"I know you're not going to believe me," I said, turning my attention back to her. "But I know something about what's been happening to you and your friends. I know I can help you, if you'll let me. What's your name?"

She didn't answer.

"I'm Calynn. These are my friends." I introduced them all.

She snorted. "Friends? You're friends with a mongrel, a child, a pixie, and your guards?"

"Yeah, I am. And if you call Quinn that again, I'll have to take offense."

The girl blanched and gave me a swift nod. We stood like that for a while until I sighed and let her go. I couldn't make her talk to me. I couldn't make her trust me, so I took a step back.

The girl turned as though to go, then hesitated.

"You really think you could help?"

"I helped him." I nodded toward Rhys. "He decided my help had been enough that he's been following me around ever since."

She considered us for another moment, then nodded. "My name is Lorna. If you want to try to help, you can follow me. But I won't owe a debt."

"I never asked you to. Lead the way."

She took us through the streets of the village, casting looks around as though worried she'd be followed.

"You have someone who's after you?" I asked.

"The guards are always trying to keep the streets clean."

Her tone told me exactly what she thought about how they did that.

"My princess," Ronan said. "I know you like to deviate from plans when it suits you. But perhaps we should see your mother before we meet the other children? So you have somewhere to bring them."

"I know that was initially the idea, but you don't think it's interesting she literally ran into me? Just like the first time I was here, and just like Rhys did when I entered the Winter village for the first time."

"I can't argue with that."

"As much as you'd like to."

He cast me a sidelong glance I interpreted as saying I was right. We continued on for about five minutes when Lorna, looking around one last time, opened the door to a beautiful house made from a tree with fluttering green leaves.

We went inside where it was completely dark, Ansgar and Mada remaining outside to ensure we weren't disturbed. Lorna led us further in, winding around the furniture unerringly even though we couldn't see it. I only knew it was there because I tripped over a couple of things before I started following her footsteps exactly. She took us down into a basement, then found a match and lit a candle.

"How is he doing?" Lorna asked.

I stumbled to a stop when the room came into view. Children sat on the floor all around the room. Most of them looked like they were five or younger. Behind me, Rhys also stopped.

"The chalice children," he said under his breath.

I squeezed his shoulder before I moved into the room.

"What happened?" I asked Lorna.

"The Queen happened," she spat, fishing a small vial from inside one of her pockets. "For the last couple months, she has taken the littles, one at a time. She keeps them for a few days or a week. Then she releases them, and they return to us like this." She gestured to the child in front of her.

The boy's skin had been leeched of almost all color, just a hint of green that matched his lank green hair. His brown eyes looked muddy and dull and he was barely more than skin and bones. As I looked around, I saw a few others who had similar looks to them, dark circles under eyes that should be bright with mischief and curiosity.

"Do they all recover?" I asked.

Lorna motioned to the others. "Do they look recovered?" She unstopped the vial and pulled a dropper out. The child opened his mouth and accepted the medicine on his tongue.

"What's that?" I asked.

"A concoction of a few herbs and some magic. I'm not sure what kind of magic. But I've found it's the only thing that helps. It's expensive and hard to steal. I've gotten a few doses from some of the vendors in the village. They're not as good as the ones in the city. But they're easier to steal."

A reconciliation tincture, like Evander's.

She finished with the boy and moved to the rest of the children, putting a drop or two on each of their tongues.

"Do you know what happens to the children when they're taken?"

"Not exactly. She's always taken the littles. They can't explain as well as the older children might. But I know she's messing with them, trying to give them magic or something. We have none. Why can't she just leave us alone?"

She hadn't lied. I would have heard it. But she was wrong. Every child in the room had magic. I could feel it all simmering, seething, wanting to be unleashed to help the person it was connected to. Just the thought of helping them all access their magics had me feeling exhausted, the ghost of a headache starting in the back of my head.

I could do something else right now, though.

"May I see what they did?"

Lorna shot me a look.

"I won't hurt them. I just want to see what happened. I can see magic."

"How?"

I shrugged, trying to avoid a whole long talk about my abilities. "I just do it. May I?"

I held out my hand. The child looked from me to Lorna until the older girl nodded. He reached out his hand, barely able to hold it steady. I caught his fingers, holding them gently.

Then I looked at what damage had been done. A river had been carved into the space, flowing from no where to no where. I left his magic and went to the next child.

Each one had water in the empty space where their magic should be. Some had water filling the space completely, like Fagen. Others had rivers carved into the space, like the first boy. One child had a steady drip into a single spot, wearing a hole. That child seemed to be doing the worst out of them all, a slightly crazed look in his young eyes.

Like with Fagen, I was certain I couldn't give these children access to their own magic because the water would drown it.

"Well?" Lorna asked after I had looked into the magic of all eight children who had been taken.

"You all have a space where your magic should be, and it isn't. Someone has put their magic in that space instead. That's what's causing the illnesses and not allowing the children to get better."

"Can you fix it?"

I shook my head. "Not yet. There's a boy in Winter who had this same thing happen to him. I got the other children out in time before it happened to more of them. I'd like to move you all to my estate north of the city, but I need to talk to my mother first so I can get access to it. Then I'll look into what I can do for these guys."

Lorna blinked at me, her head tilting to the side. "You'll... look into it?"

"Of course I will."

"Why?"

Startled, I looked around the room. Most people in Winter accepted it when I said I was going to do something now. They'd stopped questioning why I tried to help people. Here, all the Summer children were looking at me with a strange curiosity. I remembered a conversation with Ronan what felt like so long ago. He'd asked why I was going to investigate Meriel's murder. No one cared about exiled fae. If I'd asked, I was certain Lorna and Rhys would tell me no one cared about these chalice children either.

I found Ronan near the bottom of the stairs, and our gazes locked. He knew why I was doing this.

"Because what happened to you is wrong and someone needs to put a stop to it. It's the right thing to do and no one else is going to do it."

CHAPTER 8

There was no way Ronan would agree to let Ansgar or Mada remain with the children and not come with me. But since I didn't want to leave them unprotected, I left Rhys and Quinn with them. Him to help if someone tried to abduct anyone. Her to help get everything prepared for them to leave the Summer village. I also left Aiden so he could come find me if anything went wrong.

We exited the children's house and started toward the gates of Lumina. Ronan walked next to me, Ansgar and Mada a couple steps behind.

"I have told you I will support you no matter what," Ronan said. "But I want to ask you a question. Are you doing this—helping these children—because you need to do it? Or are you doing it to put off doing what you know you need to do?"

I sighed. It was a good question. Something I'd been asking myself for the last day and a half.

"The thing is, I don't know what I need to do. I know the big picture. But I don't know how I'm supposed to do it. I need more time to figure it out." I knew I was supposed to kill both queens and take over their role. I'd also figured out, in order to not throw the whole Sidhe into chaos, I needed to kill them at the same time. The only problem was—other than the fact I didn't want to kill anyone, regardless of how much someone might deserve it—they were never in the same place at one time. "Besides,

I have this feeling that if I don't do this now, if I try to wait until after the Equinox, I won't be able to help these kids at all."

Ronan didn't respond. He just continued walking with me to my mother's house.

Calling it a house might be a little misleading. It was a small palace. Small because it was right next to the Queen's palace, which was larger and grander than anything else in Lumina. And, as Glacia was carved from a glacier, Lumina was carved from trees. Living trees grew clustered together, carved inside and out to create elaborate homes for the daoine sidhe who lived here. The leaves above created a canopy that allowed sunlight to filter in, dappling the ground with shadows and green-tinted light.

I had to admit, it was gorgeous. Everything here was clean and beautiful. Who wouldn't be happy in a place like this? But that happiness was a lie. People here were just as scared of their dictator as they were in Glacia.

I stopped at the door of my mother's home and opened it like I belonged there, even though I felt a little awkward. First rule of breaking into a place: act like you belong. I figured it was a good rule to follow here as well.

"Your Highness." One of my mother's staff stumbled to a stop in front of me, bowing. "Your mother was not expecting your arrival."

"I know. I'd like to speak with her. Now, if possible."

"She's in her courtyard. Shall I see if she's available?"

"No need. I'll go myself."

"May I take your... jacket? And should I prepare your rooms?"

"No and no," I said over my shoulder as I started toward my mother's garden. My guards followed me, looking imposing, which helped me find the confidence to open the door to the courtyard with the same air of I'm-supposed-to-be-here as I had when opening the front door.

My mother, Eilidh, sat among some flowers, touching a leaf here, a bloom there. A fragrance filled the air, and my steps faltered for just a second. I recognized it.

Hyacinths.

Arial had flora magic, specifically attuned to the spring flower. It was her favorite. When I was here last, during our first conversation, I'd told my mother it was mine as well, even though I didn't really have a favorite flower. To have one, you'd have to think about them more often than never.

Eilidh was a beautiful woman with long, golden brown hair and olive skin. Today she wore a simple blue dress the color of the sky on a summer day. The dress had a white collar and hem.

"Hello, Mother," I said as I made my way toward her.

"My love. You have arrived in time to see the first blooms of spring."

"Isn't it a little early for that?"

"Not in Summer. Would you care for some tea?" She motioned toward a tray with a pot and a cup laid out.

I'd come here to speak with her the same way I'd dealt with Queran, but as I stood in her garden, with her offer of tea, I realized she was very different from him. Of course, I'd known that before, but I'd barely spent any time with her before leaving for the Fréimhe and I hadn't been back.

And yet, she'd remembered the flower I'd said was my favorite.

"Uh, no. I don't really like tea. But I'll take a coffee if you have any."

A maid dipped into a curtsy and rushed away.

My mother motioned to the bench we had occupied the last time I was here, and I sat down. She picked up her cup of tea and sat next to me, looking over at Ronan, Mada, and Ansgar.

"You brought guards with you this time."

"I'm no longer under the Queen's protection. I need to protect myself now."

"So I heard. I admit, when your father told me about your showing in the Solstice challenges, I was hard pressed to believe him."

"Believe it. I'm still learning different ways to use each element, but they're all there. He told you I set up my own house, and he gave me control of my estate?"

"He did."

The maid returned, interrupting us, and handed me a steaming mug of magic-infused coffee. I'd gotten used to drinking the regular stuff and fought not to wrinkle my nose at the smell. I still felt Ronan's humor as he caught my distaste.

I drank the coffee anyway.

"I would like control of my Summer estate as well," I said. "What would you bargain for?"

"Why would I bargain? Why would I not simply give you the property? It is set aside for you, after all."

"Queran made me bargain for it. He wanted something from me. I assume you do, too."

She flinched slightly when I called my father by his name, but she didn't remark on it. "Your birthday is merely a few weeks away, my darling. Why not simply wait?"

"I want it now. Do I need a reason?"

"You do."

I set my teeth together, then took a quiet breath. "My reasons are my own."

"I could make it part of the bargain that you tell me."

"You could." I waited. Instinct told me she wanted something from me, and in order for me to be able to do what I needed to do, I had to gain control of my Summer estate similarly to how I'd gained control of my Winter estate. To maintain balance.

After a long moment, Eilidh finally answered. "I will not make that part of the bargain. Instead, I will ask you for your time."

"Time?"

"Yes. I want a relationship with you. You are my daughter and I do not know who you are."

I bit my tongue over the *whose fault is that?* retort. I could be diplomatic when I needed to be. I also knew the deal she was offering was very vague, and it needed to be of similar weight as the one I'd made with Queran.

"Queran made me participate in the Winter Solstice events. Three parties lasting about four hours at each one and the three days of trials, about four hours for the first two days and one hour for the last. Plus, two hours at each party after the trials." I did some quick math. "That's twenty-seven hours. That is how much of my time you have. You can use it at any time you want, but must use all of it before March first. We can meet here or at my Summer estate. For my part, I gain access to the estate today."

I glanced at Ronan, seeking reassurance I hadn't missed anything. His nod was almost non-existent, but I caught it.

"I agree to these terms," Eilidh said.

"Then it's a bargain. Do you have an idea when you want the first... meeting to occur?"

"How about now? You can tell me about your plans for this estate. You must have some." Eilidh took a sip of her tea and waited for me to respond.

I hadn't anticipated my meeting today to go longer than it needed to. I wanted to get out of here and get the kids to my estate before anything else happened to them. But I felt the rules of the bargain—that I had set—close around me. I had done this to myself.

After a deep breath, I focused back on my mother, figuring out how to tell her the truth without letting her know my real plans.

"For now, I just want to know what goes on here. I want to understand the differences between Winter and Summer."

"You traveled to visit the Ancient Mother recently to seek your destiny. Did she offer you wisdom?"

"She offered me something," I muttered. "My destiny includes understanding the differences between Winter and Summer. Understanding the balance between the two."

I didn't want to tell her about my plans for my estate, and I wanted to tell her my destiny even less. I changed the subject.

"Did Queran also mention what happened with Niall?"

"Niall?" she asked, her head tilting to the side.

"My sister. She doesn't want to be called Nialas anymore. She wants to be called Niall."

Eilidh shook her head as though she didn't understand. Then she said. "Your father mentioned, yes. I wish she had let us know what she was feeling before she took it too far."

"You know she's living with me now. In Winter. I've forgiven her for everything that happened. She said she'd like to see you."

Eilidh pursed her lips, eyes straying to one of the flower beds. "I do not believe that will be possible. Your father's decision to cast her out was the correct one. I will not go against his wishes."

"How can you say that? She's your daughter, too, isn't she?"

"She is only my daughter because of you. She was a constant reminder I could not have you with me. I would look at her and see what you would look like, not at all like what you should have looked like. My poor child.

You could have been taller than the Queens." She reached her hand out as though to caress my face. "Instead, you look so human. Like her."

I flinched away before her fingers could make contact with my skin. "I look like her because you and Queran decided to change me. Niall had nothing to do with that decision. None of this was her fault."

"Tsk. This is not the kind of thing I meant when I said I wanted to get to know you, my love. Tell me more about the things you like. The things that bring your heart joy."

Anger burned within me at the injustice of it all. No wonder Niall had hated me before. If this was how she'd been treated, I didn't even blame her. And if this was not what Eilidh wanted to discuss, then I doubted she really wanted to get to know me. Because this was who I was. The person who tried to make things right, no matter the cost.

My eyes found Ronan's, and I felt a sudden, deep calm; I realized, even if my mother and father couldn't see me, he did.

Eilidh and I chatted for an hour about flowers and trees. I told her about my private investigator business back in the human world and I knew she didn't understand any of it. She asked if there had been any Winter nobles I had found interesting, and I wondered if she was asking if I was sleeping with anyone. I looked at Ronan again, my heart squeezing in panic for just a moment, before I told my mother about my friend Ryleigh. *Friend* might have been stretching our relationship a bit, but they were as close as I had found so far among the nobles.

I hesitated to mention Arial since she was half-human, and I wasn't sure what my mother's feelings were about people like that. I didn't want to disturb the uneasy peace between us just yet. Plus, if she had a problem with half-humans, I wouldn't be able to fulfill my end of the twenty-seven hours' worth of time.

"Actually, speaking of meeting with nobles," I said into a lull in the conversation. "I wouldn't mind if you could introduce me to some. I feel like I don't know anything about Summer or the people who live here."

In truth, I wanted to meet Anstice and get a read on her.

"It can prove difficult during Winter's reign. Most of the nobles have retired to their country estates. They will begin to return after the Equinox when the power begins to shift back toward Summer. You could meet everyone then."

"I'd like to meet people now, if possible."

"What rush, love?" she asked, her head tilted in confusion. "The Equinox is only a matter of weeks."

I took a sip of coffee to give myself a moment to think. She didn't need to remind me of the approaching Equinox. The date felt like the zero moment of a bomb and the time ticked away in my mind every second we got closer to it. But I couldn't tell her about that or about what the Ancient Mother had tasked me with. Instead, I said something that was not quite the truth, but not quite a lie, either.

"I've felt the pull of my Winter and Summer heritage. I've spent time in Winter and feel like I've made some roots there, met some people who I can form relationships with. But I don't have the same in Summer. I feel a little unbalanced."

"Of course. I never considered how your heritage would pull you from both sides." She held her teacup and tapped a short fingernail against the side of it, considering my question. "I could host something. There are a few people still in the city. Others may return for a revel. Not all, of course, but a good portion."

"I would appreciate the assistance."

She smiled at me and I was suddenly dazzled by her beauty. She glowed with happiness, literally. A nimbus of light surrounded her completely.

It wasn't glamour. I'd see through it if it was. It was simply her joy. "It would bring me delight to be able to help you in any small way you need."

And the funny thing was, she didn't lie about that. She really would find joy in simply helping me. I wondered for a moment if she was being sincere. Suddenly, I wanted to tell her everything. She was my mother. She was the one person in all the worlds who was supposed to have my back in all things. The one person I was supposed to be able to trust over all others. That's who a mother was.

Who a mother was supposed to be.

But I didn't really know this woman. And I'd be a fool to think otherwise.

CHAPTER 9

The sun was still high in the sky when we left my mother's home. Aiden hadn't come to find me, so I had to assume the children were still safe in hiding. The streets of Lumina and the village were quiet, almost no one around. I found my hand drifting to the sword at my side as I scanned the area uneasily.

"You feel it, too," Ronan asked, walking a little closer to me, his sword coming from its sheath in a smooth draw. He leaned it against his shoulder in its resting position.

"A little too quiet. There were more people around when we went in."

He nodded. Ansgar moved to the other side of me, and I felt Mada right behind. They both drew their weapons as well.

As we exited the city gates, I felt it, the presence of the person who waited for me. He stepped into the road as if from nowhere, but I knew it had just been a trick of the light which he'd bent around him to make himself invisible.

"You do not leave your fortress very often, child," Gavyn, Queen Titania's top spy, said as he blocked my way down the road, flashing me a smile with those startling black teeth. He took a step toward me, closing the distance, but staying far enough that none of my guards moved just yet. "Now that you finally have, you have been smart and surrounded yourself with guards. But you will not always be so careful. I will be waiting. My Queen has requested your death, and no one is more loyal to my Queen than I am."

I arched a brow and after a quick glance around to ensure we were alone, I said, "You mean no one is more loyal to your mother."

I had to give Ansgar and Mada credit. They didn't react to my statement any more than a small shift in posture. Their reactions were less than Gavyn's.

He stopped breathing, his eyes going wide and his grip on his sword loosening. I used the moment of shock to disarm him with a swift move I'd been practicing with Ronan. In less than two seconds, I'd moved toward him, drawn my sword, and used it to knock Gavyn's to the ground.

"How—" He broke off, and I knew he was more interested in how I'd learned his secret than how I'd disarmed him.

"I know a lot of things. I've been piecing facts together over the past few months. My instincts are pretty good. I know who you are and why you feel you need to do this. But I'm telling you, she's using you and she's wrong."

He stood a little straighter, a sneer coming to his face. "You know nothing about it."

"Maybe I don't know anything about your relationship with your mother. But I know someone else who has a strained relationship with their mother."

"Who, you?"

I shook my head. "No Gavyn. I barely have any relationship with my mother. But I know someone who was in a very similar position to yours. I managed to change their mind. I hope you'll let me change yours."

"Not today."

"I expected nothing less." I picked up the sword that had fallen—not taking my eyes off him as I did so—and handed it behind me for Ronan to take. "I'll see you again."

We continued on our way, moving around Gavyn, who stood in the middle of the road like he wasn't quite sure what he was supposed to do next. I knew Ansgar and Mada kept watch on him to ensure he wouldn't follow us. I still took a circuitous route back to the chalice children's home, extra conscious of how the guards had found us when we'd taken the Winter children. Quinn answered the door when we arrived.

"We've been waiting. Is everything okay?"

"Yeah. Everything's ready to go?"

She watched me with concern but nodded. We both knew I'd tell her about everything that had happened later, when we were no longer in danger.

Aiden hovered nearby, the orange light that usually spilled off him brighter than I'd seen it in a long time. Likely because we were finally back in Summer, his home domain.

"I'm going to be asking you to do a lot of flying, if you're up for it."

He grinned. "It will be nice to get some air in my wings. What would you have me do?"

"Fly ahead to my estate and tell them the owner is coming. I want a wagon brought down to meet us. These kids won't be able to walk that far very quickly."

He took off in a shower of sparks, heading north while the rest of us started walking. Ronan, Mada, Ansgar, and I formed a group around the children as we left the village, heading toward my estate. We made our way toward the river. I knew my estate was next to it, and if Summer was really a mirror image of Winter, there wouldn't be anything else between the city and my land. No other villages, settlements, or homes. On the way, I spoke with Lorna, who carried one of the children who had been tampered with, a little two-year-old girl, the youngest of the group.

"I want to find a way to help you," I said. "You mentioned the reconciliation tincture. Where do you get it?"

"There are a few apothecaries who make them. Two I found in the city. One in the village. The one that worked the best came from Tidal Blossom Remedies on the east side of the city. The other two are Meadow Glow Apothecary in the city, and Ivy Leaf in the village."

I made note of the names, intending to check them out later. I was certain Ronan would have something to say about that, but I felt confident the Queens wouldn't openly attack me. Especially Titania. She had cleared the streets to allow Gavyn his shot, and he'd missed. They would have to regroup. She was all about making her city seem beautiful, making it look like everyone was happy. Killing one of her subjects openly would call that facade into question. She would strike at me from the shadows.

That didn't make it easier to counter her, but at least I felt like I could walk the streets of Lumina and investigate this tincture and what had been done to the children without worrying about someone trying to murder me.

"When did it all start?" I asked her.

"Just after the Winter Solstice. It started with Owain, the boy your friend Rhys is walking with. He came back to us and said someone had hurt him but couldn't exactly explain who or what they did. He became more and more sick for a week before I figured out something that helped him."

"How did you do that?"

She looked at me for a long moment.

"I don't care that you stole things, Lorna. You did what you had to do to survive."

She hesitated a moment longer. "I stole a bunch of medicine from the apothecary in the village. I tried each one and waited to see if there was any change. None of the things I tried helped except the reconciliation tincture. Then I stole a vial of that from each of the three apothecaries who sell it and found out which was best."

"Did you keep a list of the other medications you tried?"

She nodded.

"I'd like to see it."

"Why? They didn't work."

"True. But someone who knows what they're looking at might be able to tell me why they didn't work and why the reconciliation one did. It'll be useful information in helping me figure out how to cure them." I didn't say it, but I also put Lorna and the five other children who hadn't been experimented on high on the list of people to help gain access to their missing magic, as I had done for Rhys. If they had their magic available, Anstice's experiment wouldn't work on them.

I asked a few more questions about how long the tincture helped and what the symptoms were, intending to write it all down when we got to my estate. I wanted Evander to help me figure this out, but I had a feeling he'd need someone else's help as well.

We'd been walking for about an hour when a wagon came toward us, driven by a small humanoid creature. She was black and about the size of a vulture. I recognized she was a puca, a kind of fae who loved to make bargains.

The wagon pulled up to us and stopped, Aiden flying out to greet me.

"Calynn, this is the house manager, Idelisa. Idelisa, your mistress, Calynn."

The puca hopped out of the wagon and dropped into a curtsy. "Greetings, Mistress Princess. We did not expect your arrival. The house is ill-prepared to receive people."

"We'll get it sorted out. For now, I want the children loaded up and brought there. Aiden." I indicated a spot a small distance away while everyone except Ronan got people organized. Aiden, Ronan, and I stood off to the side. "Now that I have control of the estate, can you go back to Winter and tell the other guards to come through? Will they have trouble?" I asked Ronan.

"They should be fine. They might need a bit of time to adjust, but it shouldn't take long."

"You, Mada, and Ansgar didn't need that time."

"Our connection to you is stronger. We've also had our latent magic the longest of all your guards."

"All right." I turned back to Aiden. "Go back. Lead them to my estate." He nodded and took off on his next mission. By the time he was gone, everyone else was ready to continue. I climbed into the wagon next to Idelisa and we started back the way she had come.

"Tell me about the estate," I said.

She explained it made decent money and was entirely self-sufficient. I apparently raised goats and sheep used for their fleece. We produced a large amount of wool and fiber the Summer city used to make clothes and blankets. We also had hay fields which we used to feed the animals and to trade for grains they needed.

"There are two brownies who look after the house," she continued. "As well as two mongrels who take care of the goats and sheep and a daoine sidhe who only has one magic who sees to the stables."

"Good. I'll meet the stable master as soon as we arrive. And I'd like it known that word isn't allowed on the property anymore."

"Which word, mistress?"

"Mongrel is offensive, and I won't tolerate its use."

She shot me a worried glance. "Oh. I will ensure everyone knows."

"Good. Now, I assume the brownies have decided to live there because they like the house. What about the... shepherds?"

"Yes. They are called shepherds. They arrived because they wanted to leave the city. I suppose they chose your property because there was no lord. They are pixie and human. Their own kind would likely not have kept them as they cannot fly."

"I see. And are they related?"

"Oh no. They are a mated pair."

"And our stable master?"

"He came to us broken. He did not share his story. When healed, he stayed."

"And you?"

"I made a bargain with your father. He is better at bargains than I gave him credit for."

So all the people on the estate were loyal in similar ways to the people who had come with the Winter estate. That didn't surprise me. The most surprising thing was the puca had bargained with my father and lost.

"I'm in need of builders and guards, Idelisa. I'd first like to take on daoine sidhe who have only one magic. Do you know how I can find them?"

"I would probably be able to find some," she said, considering. "Barden might know more. He never said directly, but I believe he was originally from Lumina."

"Barden is the stable master?"

"He is."

We fell into silence as the gates of my property came into view. We crossed through and I caught my first glimpse of the house. Like the buildings in Lumina, it was made from trees growing together. It looked like it was laid out exactly opposite of the house in Winter, and I felt my heart pull when I saw it. Mine. My place to protect and shelter.

There would be a lot to do to make this place feel like my home, the way Winter already did. But I knew I would get it there. Only a few short months ago, I had one friend and was barely holding on to my home. Today, my problems were bigger, but I felt more stable. Part of that was the two places I could call my own.

CHAPTER 10

We got the wagon sorted, and I left Quinn to organize the furniture placement while Rhys and Lorna took the children inside. Ronan insisted he, Mada, and Ansgar stay with me. I rolled my eyes but didn't argue. He was probably right.

"I want to talk to Barden alone, though," I said.

Ronan watched me with a raised eyebrow. He didn't like the idea, but he nodded. "We'll be right outside."

I touched his hand and went into the stables where Barden was singing while he worked.

He was a deep baritone and sang a song in a language I didn't know but somehow understood. He sang about a lover who had gone to seek his glory and the person he had left behind. The lyrics and melody pulled at my heart, making me want to cry.

I leaned against the door of the barn and watched as Barden finished feeding the animals. As he did, he started a new song. This one a slow lament about a lover who had drowned.

When he finished, he turned to face me. He had to have known I was there, and I wasn't sure if I should be impressed he hadn't stopped because of his commitment to his task or offended because of the lack of respect for my station. I decided to give him the benefit of the doubt, since I hated people pandering to me, anyway.

"You have a beautiful voice," I said.

"I have had a long time to practice," he replied.

"Do you know who I am?"

He glanced behind me at Mada, who stood just outside the barn, watching him closely. I knew Ronan and Ansgar had moved off somewhere, checking the area for potential threats, or perhaps deciding where to post guards. Or both.

"I assume you are the lady of the estate. And my cue that it is time to move on."

"You don't have to. In fact, I'd like you to stay. I think you found some peace working here. And I think I can offer you more, if you let me."

He took a towel from where it hung on a door handle and wiped his hands. He set the towel aside, then started toward me. "The noble daoine sidhe do not care for people like me."

"I'd like the chance to prove you wrong. Idelisa told me about how you arrived here. It's not the way anyone should be treated."

He stopped across from me, head tilted to one side. "You're different."

I nodded. "I am. I'm a changeling. Grew up in the human world. I see the flaws of both worlds and I'd like to try to make this one... better."

He shook his head. "That is not possible."

"I know you don't think so. You're not the only one. For now, if you'll agree to stay, I can offer you something no one else can. Though there's a waitlist."

"What can you offer me?"

I touched his hand and felt his magic, the air, clear and bright in a morning sun. It helped him when he sang. And I felt the direction of his latent magic humming deep within him. "Can you feel it, too?"

He gasped, his eyes widening. He continued to stare at me, shaking his head slowly. "It—It was there the whole time?"

"It was. And I can help you get it."

He gripped my hand painfully. I tried to tug away, but he wouldn't let me go. Mada took a step forward, partially drawing her sword before I held up my other hand to stop her, preferring to try to diffuse the situation before things got out of hand.

"I can't do it now. You need to let me go."

The fire in his eyes burned a little brighter for a moment, making me feel foolish and a little scared. I'd specifically not told people about my abilities for fear they would force me to use them and not give me any choice. I could see in his eyes, Barden wanted to do just that. Then he seemed to come back to himself. "You're right, of course."

He breathed heavily and loosened his grip on my hand, but still didn't let go.

"Barden," I warned.

He looked down to where he held my hand, as though he didn't realize he did. Finally, he stepped back.

"I have other bargains ahead of you I have to fulfill. But I will help you. If you agree to remain my stable master."

"Anything."

"All right then. The bargain is for a year and a day of loyal service. In exchange, I swear to give you access to your latent magic before the year and a day is up."

"I must wait a year?" he exclaimed.

"Probably not. But I built time for myself in case something happens. I can't make myself an oath breaker with my own bargain."

He glared at me. "Fine."

I could tell he wasn't happy with the details, where everyone else had just been glad to be on the list. To know they would have their latent magic soon.

I nodded and left the barn, Mada following closely behind.

"I don't like him," she said.

"I know." Now that we were away, I rubbed the wrist he had gripped and looked down to see the bruise already forming. "Don't tell Ronan about what happened."

Mada shot me a look. "I won't keep information from my marshal."

"I wouldn't ask you to. Just. Let me tell him."

She watched me as we made our way to the house. "Fine. Just make sure you tell him today or else I'll tell him tomorrow."

I'd already intended to tell him tonight when everything had calmed down. With the amount of activity, that would probably not be until later in the evening. We sorted out furniture, then ate dinner. After dinner, Aiden returned with the rest of the guards from Winter. When I finished confirming the crossing was easy enough for everyone, I retired to my room while Ronan sorted everyone out.

I sat up in bed, waiting for him, rubbing my wrist absently. It didn't really hurt, and I wouldn't be surprised if the bruise was gone by morning. I usually healed quickly.

But the covetous look in Barden's eyes when I told him what I could do had left me feeling uneasy.

Ronan came into the room about an hour after me and removed his sword belt and boots, like he always did. He watched me the whole time.

"Are you going to tell me now?" he asked.

"How do you always know?"

He lifted a shoulder in a half shrug as he sat on the edge of the bed. I held up my hand to show the bruise.

"Barden was a little overexcited when he learned I could help him."

He stood and went back to where he'd set his boots, stepping into them.

"What are you doing?" I asked.

"Going to have a word with him. I won't be long."

I scrambled from the bed, placing a hand on his arm. "I took care of it. It's fine."

He halted what he was doing like I had frozen him to the spot. He hadn't sworn fealty to me. He hadn't made a bargain. He didn't have to listen to a word I said. When he did what I asked, it was because he wanted to, because he trusted me.

"The bruise isn't what's making you uneasy," he said.

I shook my head. "I'm not sure I trust him."

"Is there something in particular?"

"No. Just a feeling. I should have waited to tell him about his latent magic. I should have waited to trust him. Two months ago, I would have."

"You've had a lot of people come to you lately, people you could trust. You've opened up and allowed them into your life. That's a good thing. There was bound to be someone we'd have to watch. And we will. I'll make sure we keep an eye on him."

"Don't let him know. I don't want him to feel unwelcome if I'm wrong."

Ronan tipped my chin up so I would look him in the eyes. "I'll try. But my first priority is always you. Your safety. Your happiness. Nothing comes before that. Do you understand?"

I nodded, caught in the emerald-green depths of his eyes.

"Should we go to bed then?" he asked. "Or do you need to brood some more?"

I felt a smile tugging at my lips. "Well, it's not like I could stop you if you made the decision for me."

He grinned, stopping my heart for a second with the perfect way he looked at me. Then he stooped and threw me over his shoulder. I squeaked, a rather undignified sound I would swear I never made if anyone asked, then laughed as he dropped me unceremoniously onto the bed.

He leaned over me, kissing me before pulling back to whisper over my lips, "Do you need some more distracting, little changeling?"

"I think so," I said as somberly as I could, trying to keep the smile contained. "At least a few hours' worth."

"That can be arranged."

CHAPTER 11

My dreams didn't let me sleep for long. Visions of destruction, of all the people I loved, hurt or worse, danced through my mind. I dreamed of a world torn apart, everything in chaos, an inferno raging, consuming everything. Mada sobbed over Ansgar's lifeless form. Quinn screamed as she held Aiden's small body, his wings shredded. Rhys lay crumpled on the ground, blood flowing from him like a river. Ronan wasn't anywhere to be found. What had happened to him?

Within me, a voice whispered, *You hesitated too long*.

I woke, my heart racing, my body heavy. I stared around the room, refusing to close my eyes for fear of seeing that horrific tableau again.

"Another dream?" Ronan asked.

I got my heart rate under control and shook my head. "Not a dream. A nightmare. Just a regular nightmare."

He pulled me to him, and I calmed.

"You want to tell me about it?"

I didn't really, but I found myself speaking just the same, telling him about the chaos and fire. "You weren't there. I didn't know where you were."

"I'll always be there with you, little changeling. That's not something you need to fear." He stroked my back as I lay on his chest, listening to the sound of his heart. "Who do you think sent you this dream? The Ancient Mother again?"

She'd sent me so many over the past few months, it wasn't a stretch to think she had caused this one as well.

"No one sent it." I huffed a humorless laugh. "It's not bad enough I get dreams of destruction sent from the Ancient Mother and some other unknown entity. My subconscious is doing it now, too."

"You're worried," Ronan said. "You keep the worries away during the day by keeping yourself busy. When you're asleep, your subconscious is free to show you what you've been trying so hard to avoid."

"It would be nice if my subconscious would come up with a solution instead of just telling me I'm hesitating too long."

He kissed my forehead and my eyes drifted closed again for a second. But the scene was still there, right on the other side of my eyelids. It was maybe a little too early to wake up, but I knew I wouldn't be able to sleep anymore. After resting for a short while wrapped in Ronan's arms, I got up and he followed me to the practice ring, where I took out my stress in the form of exercise.

When we were done, I had another plan to keep myself busy that Ronan hated. But I convinced him three guards had been enough to deter Gavyn, and I didn't want to draw too much attention while interviewing the apothecaries. Plus, the Queen had already made her shot. She would have to regroup and come up with a new plan before coming after me again. It was a risk, but I felt confident about it. So after breakfast, we returned to the barn and took four of my six horses. Ronan didn't say anything to Barden, but I certainly noticed his chilly demeanor toward the other man.

When the horses were saddled, we left my estate. I hadn't ever ridden a horse before, but Ronan promised it wasn't difficult as long as we kept the pace slow. He also promised to give me riding lessons so we could go faster in the future.

"I just want my motorcycle. I don't need to learn to ride that."

He didn't respond. A couple months ago, I'd noticed the Triumph Bonneville had a strange kind of sentience, like a tree. Or at least the trees in the Sidhe. Ronan and I were sure I had given her the magic, but neither of us understood how it could have happened.

For now, though, we rode horses in what Ronan called a trot. It felt very slow, but at least it was faster than I could walk. As a result, we arrived back at my mother's home in one hour instead of three. We stabled the horses there and went to the village on the other side of the gates of the city.

"Why are we going there?" Ansgar asked. "I thought Lorna said the best one was in the city."

During our ride, I'd told him and Mada about what had happened to the children and what they'd been using to help them.

"She did," I said. "But I want to know why that one is the best. To figure that out, I need to know why they're different."

Ronan and I entered Ivy Leaf Apothecary with a little ring of a bell when the door opened. Ansgar and Mada took up spots just outside. A small man turned toward the door with a smile.

"Good afternoon," he said.

I found myself grinning back at him. He was only about three feet tall and dressed in all shades of green and brown. A pointed hat and a pointed beard framed his ruddy face above and below.

"Hello," I said. "I'm looking for a reconciliation tincture."

"Ah. Of course, of course. Come in. I have just the one." He turned back to shelves lined with vials, containers, jars, and pots. He selected a small vial and met me at his counter.

"Here it is."

I took the vial, stamped with an ivy leaf, and examined the gold liquid within. I could feel magic humming inside it as I turned it in my fingers.

"What's in this?" I asked.

The man chuckled. "I cannot tell you that, now can I? Trade secrets." He winked at me, and I grinned again.

But then I remembered the children. "I have a friend who's sick. They said this tincture is the only thing that helps, but I don't know why. They also said there are three reconciliation tinctures they've tried, and they work to varying degrees. Could you help me figure out why that is?"

The smile slipped from his face as I spoke.

"I haven't sold this tincture to anyone in over five years. But it has been stolen. Ten vials in the last two months."

Fuck. I thought Lorna had purchased a few vials. If she had, she hadn't purchased any from this apothecary. Which made sense. If she was as good at stealing as Rhys, she would have had little issue stealing from a vendor in the village where the security wasn't as strict.

But at the same time, I believed the man wasn't malicious. He was angry someone had stolen from him, rightly so. Ten vials was a lot. I pulled out my purse and set a few gold coins on the counter.

He crossed his arms over his chest and lifted his eyebrow at me.

I set out a few more gold coins.

He swiped them into his palm and the coins disappeared.

"You may leave now," he said, his jovial manner gone.

"But I—"

He turned and left the storefront, heading into the back. Ronan and I left the shop, and we all started into the city again toward our next destination. I slid the vial into my inside jacket pocket.

"Let's go to the next apothecary," I said. "And not mention the sick children this time. You think she stole from all of them?"

"Absolutely," Ronan said. "I know you don't know her well yet, but you know Rhys. What do you think he would do?"

"He'd probably go in to buy something cheaper to give himself a reason to be in there. Then, he'd swipe what he was really after when the proprietor wasn't looking."

Ronan nodded his agreement. When we arrived at the Meadow Glow Apothecary and went inside, a tall, willowy woman greeted us with a small smile, her shimmering golden hair swaying around her hips as she turned. A daoine sidhe, but not one of the nobles.

"Hello," she said. "How may I help you?"

"I'm wondering if I could get some advice."

"Of course, my lady. I'm happy to be of service."

I held my smile in place. I knew I wouldn't be able to hide the fact I was a daoine sidhe noble since I was traveling with three guards. But I didn't want people to figure out exactly which noble I was. No one in Lumina knew me yet, and I wanted to keep it that way for as long as possible.

"A friend mentioned a tincture to me. They said it might help me and I'm not sure if they were actually trying to help or if they were insulting me."

"What tincture did they mention?"

"A reconciliation tincture. You see, I don't know what it's supposed to do."

Her smile slipped for just a second at the mention of the reconciliation tincture. I wondered how many vials she'd had stolen in the past couple of months. But, ever the professional, she turned and selected a small vial of golden liquid from the shelf and set it on the counter between us.

"A reconciliation tincture is meant to ease pressure and restore equilibrium. Its base is almost always water from the sea, and it is bound together with a balancing charm, an alleviation charm, and a consistency charm. But from there, of course, each apothecary will have their own recipe. Mine has been handed down for three generations."

Given how long the daoine sidhe lived, that was a long time. And the way she said it told me she would not be giving me the recipe any more than the last apothecary had.

"Wow. That's impressive. I guess my friend wasn't trying to insult me, after all. I'll take a vial."

We exchanged a couple coins for the tincture, then I left the shop, heading toward the final apothecary on the other side of the city.

I huffed an annoyed breath. "I need those recipes," I said. "There's something about the tinctures that makes one more useful than the others, and I need to know what it is."

"We could always break in and steal the recipe," Ansgar suggested.

I cast him a glance. "That sounds like something Rhys would say. Have you been hanging out with him?"

Ansgar grinned. "He's a fun kid. And his skill with a bow is incredible for one so young. He just needs a little direction. Besides, given the disparity between the people who live in the city to the people who live outside its walls, I wouldn't lose much sleep over stealing from them."

"A regular Robin Hood."

"What is that?" Ansgar asked.

"It's a story about a guy who steals from the rich to give to the poor. I think you'd like it."

"I do love stories."

We crossed the bridge separating the west side of the city from the east, walking underneath the Queen's palace and making our way to the outer ring of the city where the shops were located.

"Even if we get the recipes, I'll need the help of a healer to understand what makes this last one more effective than the other two. Too bad I don't know anyone in Lumina I can trust."

"It is tricky," Ronan said. "If we went back to Glacia, we could speak to my uncle. But with his age, I wouldn't recommend bringing him to either Summer or the human world."

"It takes hours to get back to Glacia. If we have to, we will, but I'd like to find someone here. Besides, the children are from Summer. Someone from Summer needs to help with this."

"And Fagen?"

"Once we figure out how to help the Summer kids, we'll take that to Anant. See if he can figure out if there's something we'd need to change to make it appropriate for Fagen."

We subsided into silence as I opened the door to the final apothecary, Tidal Blossom Remedies. Immediately, I knew what made this apothecary different from the others. As the owner greeted us with a warm smile, I knew, unlike the other two shops we had visited, this man had water magic.

He was tall, his skin a greyish-blue like the color of the ocean when it stormed. His navy hair was cut short around his ears, and a little longer on top. His dark gray eyes reminded me of storm clouds. While he had some other magic that reminded me of the first two apothecaries—flora magic of some kind—his main magic was certainly water-based.

"Good afternoon, my lady," he said.

"Good afternoon," I said, moving toward the counter. "I'm in search of a reconciliation tincture. I've heard yours is the best in the city."

The man chuckled and reached behind him, taking a vial from the wall, this one silver instead of gold like the previous two.

"Indeed, a young girl has been purchasing this from me in great quantity for the past few weeks."

Interesting. Lorna had purchased from this store while she had stolen from the other two. I could guess why. If this was the one that worked best, she wouldn't want to get banned because she was caught stealing.

"I can't say many people have had much interest in reconciliation tinctures for the past..." he paused, thinking. "Let us just say, a long time."

"Why do you think that is?"

He shrugged. "It restores equilibrium in magic. Reconciling what is there with what is supposed to be there. People believed it might help those poor souls who have only one gift, but alas, it did not. You cannot reconcile what is not there."

I bit my tongue against the urge to say it was there. It was just... hidden. He wouldn't believe me. Or if he did, he'd want to know how I knew. Which would probably be worse. Barden's reaction to learning what I could do was still fresh on my mind, and this man was a stranger in a world where loyalty tended to be bought more than earned.

"But there's a girl who's found a use for it," I said, bringing us back to the topic at hand.

"Yes. She comes in once a week and purchases a vial. She always has exact change. Alona, over at Meadow Glow, has been complaining her reconciliation tinctures have been going missing. The girl may have stolen from me as well. One vial went missing a while ago, before she started coming in regularly. I have not told Alona about her. Though I probably should."

"How many vials do you have in stock?" I asked.

"Ten, including this one."

I set a gold coin on the counter for the vial Lorna had stolen. Then I set one down for the vial I had intended to purchase. A stack of nine coins went next for the remaining stock. Finally, I emptied the remaining coins from my purse, about fifteen of them, onto the counter and looked up at him, meeting his eyes.

"That girl won't be returning," I told him. "So there's no reason to tell anyone about her, is there?"

He looked from the coins to me, then placed all ten vials on the counter between us.

"I see no reason to stir up trouble, my lady."

I slid one vial into my inside pocket and the rest into the purse that had held my coins, before leaving the apothecary and starting back the way we'd come, toward the west side of the city and the village beyond. I wanted to get the nine vials to Lorna before night fell.

"You still need the recipes," Ronan said. "But I think that went well."

"Yeah. I really don't want to have to go all the way back to Glacia. If only there was someone here who could point me in the right direction."

I stopped as I looked up, right before stepping onto the bridge that would take us beneath the Queen's castle. A slow grin spread across my face.

"Ha. There is someone. Come on."

CHAPTER 12

"This is an unbelievably bad idea," Ronan said as I cloaked us both in shadows and brought us into the Queen's dungeon.

I grinned. "You say that like you think it's going to change my mind."

When I'd told my friends my plan, all three of them had tried to talk me out of it. We couldn't all go traipsing into the palace and hope to come out alive. But I hadn't been practicing shadow-walking with Kai for nothing. That said, I could only bring one person with me at a time. So, with no argument whatsoever, we decided I would bring Ronan while Mada and Ansgar waited for us at my mother's estate.

"I know how much you love a good bad idea," Ronan said. "But this is ridiculous."

"Quiet. Just because no one can see us doesn't mean they won't be able to hear us."

He didn't say another word, but I knew he wanted to. Even if everything went right, I'd probably hear more about it tonight when we were alone again. Thankfully, when we were alone, I had ways to distract him.

I saw Deegan before we reached the level he was on. He was hard to miss. His bulking frame filled up the space at the bottom of the stairs, and I grinned, stepping out of the shadows.

"Deegan," I said. "It's nice to see you."

Unperturbed by my sudden appearance, he gave me a look some people might find intimidating because of the massive tusks, but I knew was a smile that echoed my own. He still wore only a mossy loincloth draped around his hips and nothing else, leaving his thick gray skin bare, reminding me somewhat of rhinoceros skin. He held a club in his hand, but today it rested against his shoulder instead of menacing toward me.

"Miss Calynn. You survived, after all."

"My enemies have found me notoriously difficult to kill. But I made it into the Sidhe. Found some answers."

"You are smart as well as stubborn."

The way he said it made stubborn sound like a high compliment.

"This is my..." I hesitated, stumbling over what to call Ronan, "friend, Ronan," I said. "Ronan, you didn't get to meet Deegan before. He's the Queen's dungeon master."

Deegan made a pensive, rumbling sound. "Friend, you say. I am uncertain who you are trying to fool, me or yourself."

I snorted. "Myself, obviously."

He laughed, a rumbling sound that reminded me of rockslides.

"You got a new club," I said.

He swung it around as though showing it off, his grin widening. "It is a much better club than my previous one. The weight is better. And it is hickory instead of oak."

"That's great," I said, no clue why hickory was a better wood than oak.

"I owe you a debt for breaking my last club. This one is far superior."

"Perfect. I came to ask you for some information. Do you think that would make us even?"

He grinned again. "What information would you seek?"

I pulled one of the vials from my pocket. "I'm looking for someone—probably a healer—who can tell me what's in this and why it would be helping someone."

"There are many healers in Summer. If you want the best, you'll want one of the high healers."

"That's probably exactly what I want. But I want someone I can trust."

He nodded sagely. "There are two high healers in Summer. Anstice, of course. She works directly for Queen Titania. She has a lab in her home where she does much work and even sees patients."

"I've heard of Anstice," I said.

Neither of us mentioned our feelings on that particular healer, but given both of our tones, I was certain we were on the same page.

"The other high healer is Gwanwyn. She and the Queen have had some differences. So if you want to know which one you can trust, I am certain you know which one to choose."

He didn't say it. He didn't have to. Even though he had attacked me a few months ago, my instincts had told me then, as they were telling me now, that I could trust Deegan. That his loyalty to Queen Titania was not as complete as she believed it was. He followed her orders to the letter. But there was a difference between following the directions as they were stated and following the intention behind them.

"Your advice has merit, Deegan. I certainly know who I will discuss this issue with. Will I see you around?"

"Likely not, unless you search me out, but I am usually here in the dungeons. If you ever have need of me, you have but to ask. And if you wish to spar, I will be happy to throw you into the dirt."

"That sounds awesome."

Ronan made a strangled noise behind me, but I ignored him.

"Your lover does not agree," Deegan said.

"He disagrees with me a lot."

Deegan made a pensive sound. "It is a good relationship when the two people challenge each other."

"He is often challenging."

Ronan spoke for the first time. "Yes, my princess. I am the challenging one."

This time, Deegan laughed. "You have chosen well, Miss Calynn."

I grinned, casting a glance over my shoulder at Ronan, who stood with his usual impassive look, though his eyes sparkled with humor. "Yeah. I guess I'll keep him around." I turned back to Deegan. "My mother is going to throw me a party to meet some of the noble daoine sidhe here. Maybe when she does, you can come by before and we can do a little sparring. Ronan's got me practicing the sword more than hand-to-hand, so it'll be nice to do some real fighting for a change. I'd love to see if I can throw a mountain."

He rumbled out another laugh. "Let me know when and I will be there. It will be a delight to watch you try. But I must ask. Why would you seek me out for this information and not ask your mother?"

I considered the question. I didn't have to answer it. We didn't owe each other anything. But I liked Deegan, and it was a good question. "When you fight someone, you get to know their character really fast. You can tell if they're honorable or not based on the moves they make, when they choose to move forward, and when they choose to hold back. I've never fought my mother."

Deegan nodded, understanding, as I knew he would. Ronan probably also understood, though I didn't look back to check. So would Ansgar and Mada. We were all fighters.

I said goodbye to Deegan and wrapped shadows around me and Ronan again before urging them to take us out of the dungeons and to my mother's estate. Outside the palace, I had to drop the shadows since it was so bright there weren't many to work with. Maybe Kai could have maintained them, but I couldn't.

"It might be safer for you to move around the city at night," Ronan said as we made our way through my mother's property to where Mada and Ansgar waited for us near the stables. "If no one can see you in the shadows, no one can try to kill you. No one knows you have the shadow-walking ability."

"True. But I can only take one person with me. You prefer me to have a full contingent of guards."

"We're here today with only three. I can compromise when I think it's warranted."

I turned to him with a raised eyebrow.

"I can," he insisted.

"Sure, but you certainly complain a lot when you do it."

"I do not complain."

I snorted but didn't respond because we met up with Ansgar and Mada and went inside to find my mother in her garden, as usual. I wondered if she spent time anywhere else in the estate.

"I did not expect to see you," she said as I sat on the bench behind her. Ronan stood beside me while Ansgar and Mada took spots by two of the four entrances to the courtyard. Eilidh looked at each of them in turn. "You think you are unsafe in my home?"

"My marshal is ever vigilant," I told her.

She gave a tight nod and pulled a weed out of the ground, dropping it into the bucket beside her. I already knew Queran had wanted to keep me and Ronan apart. Though I wasn't sure why. My mother's expression made me wonder if she had similar feelings. Before I could ask her about it, she said, "In fact, I meant to send you an invitation today. I am planning a revel three evenings hence."

"I appreciate it. I wondered if I could also invite someone over for tea tomorrow?"

"Of course. My house is your house."

"I'd like to invite Gwanwyn."

"The healer? Whatever for?"

"Someone mentioned I might find a…" I hesitated over the word ally, "friend in her."

"All right. We can send her an invitation immediately."

"There's one other thing," I said. This was going to be the most difficult ask. "Do you have any people who might want to change fealty from you to me?"

"Whatever would you need people for?"

"I need guards for my Summer estate. All the guards I have currently are from Winter." I hadn't mentioned this to Ronan yet, so I felt his surprise and relief. I was taking my safety seriously. It maybe didn't seem that way to him all the time, but I was. And if I could kill two birds with one stone, so much the better. "I'm looking specifically for daoine sidhe who have access to only one gift."

She glanced up at me from her place among the flowers, a look of confusion on her face. "That is a very specific ask."

"I've found a good deal of talent among them," I said. "Talent other people have let go to waste." I didn't offer any more. I just waited for her to decide.

Finally, she said, "There may be a few here who would do for you. I will look into it."

"Great. Since I'm here, did you want to eat lunch together? Maybe we could chat?" And if it struck another hour off the time I owed her, so much the better.

She lit up again, like she had before, the nimbus of light surrounding her, showing everyone how joyful she felt. "That sounds like an excellent plan."

For just a moment, I wondered if I'd been wrong to go to Deegan instead of her. Maybe I should trust her. Maybe I should let her in. Why was it so difficult to do so?

CHAPTER 13

We rode back to my estate. When I got there, Quinn had the next person I was supposed to help gain access to his latent magic already waiting in the library. He was one of the guards from Winter. I created a path from his main magic of fire to the air magic that had been too far to reach. Thankfully, I didn't get burned or soaked, something I was getting better at, and so when he left the library, I sat in my desk chair and unfolded the maps I'd brought with me from Ronan's house.

One map was of his property and the other was my Winter property. I'd asked Idelisa to bring me one of the Summer estate and I'd already spread it out on the desk. I was staring at them when the library door opened.

"How are you feeling?" Ronan asked as he came in carrying a tray.

"A little tired," I said, looking back down at the maps.

"That's all?"

He set the tray down to one side. Soup steamed in a large bowl with a roll slathered in butter. I picked it up, dunked it in the soup, and shoved it into my mouth. Then I swallowed and took a long drink of coffee. Quinn had brought the good stuff from Ronan's ranch, so there was no taste of magic polluting it.

"It's getting easier. I'm thinking of switching from every three days to every two days."

"If you're certain." He sat in the chair across from me as I took another bite of the roll and soup.

"You're not going to argue? Tell me I'm pushing myself too fast?"

He shook his head. "You'll know when that happens. And so will I. When I do, that's when I will argue with you." He nodded toward the maps. "What are you looking at?"

I had them set side-by-side. I shuffled them around and stared at them while I ate.

"There's something I'm missing," I said. "I'm sure there's something here I need to see."

When I'd been working as a private investigator, I'd used my magic without knowing. It steered me in the right direction when I was looking for something. Some feeling within me told me when I was on the right track. I felt that now.

Ronan and I sat together in comfortable silence while I tried to figure it out. I shifted the maps again and again, trying to see whatever was just out of reach. I ate the soup and drank my coffee. When they were gone and the tray was empty, I still hadn't figured out what it was. Finally, I sighed.

"Maybe it's nothing."

I stood up and as I did, I accidentally pushed the map of Ronan's property so it was half above the map of my Winter estate and half beside it, Winter on the left. I noticed how a stream ran through Ronan's ranch and split, exiting on either side of the property. Where the map sat, the stream could connect to the Winter river bordering the far side of the land. I sat back down.

"Shit."

"What do you see?" Ronan asked, leaning over the desk.

I moved the map of Ronan's property higher and moved the Winter estate half underneath it, pulling the Summer estate to touch it. Together, they formed a triangle.

"How big is this place?" I asked, pointing to his property.

"250 acres."

"And these?" I asked again, pointing to my estates.

"The same. 250 acres."

I stopped as it all fell into place. "That's it. They're all the same."

"What?"

I stared for a while longer. When moving the three maps into these positions, I'd inadvertently made a miniature version of the Sidhe itself. Except Ronan's property wasn't the Fréimhe. But somehow, I understood that wasn't as big a problem as I thought it should be.

"I need to connect them." I stood and left the library, then the house. Ronan followed me outside.

"Wait. Now? It's getting late."

I lifted one shoulder in a shrug.

"You gave someone access to their magic only a couple hours ago. It usually exhausts you."

"I feel fine," I said, not stopping. He continued to follow me.

He was right, it was getting late. And I had lied, I was getting tired. People were starting to think about going to bed or were just relaxing before heading that way. No one was outside except a few guards on patrol.

"Are you sure you want to do this? It can't at least wait until morning?" Ronan said.

I stopped near the three trees standing in a triangle off to one side of the house near where the new barracks were going to be built. Construction was to start in the morning. A similar stand of trees grew on my

Winter property where I'd created the Way from Winter to the human world.

"I'm sure. I need to connect them. It makes sense so we can go from one to the other without needing to leave the property, which you should like since you can keep me safer on my properties than you can off them. But it's more than that. They're all mine. They need to be touching somehow."

"I'm not saying you shouldn't do it. I'm just saying maybe you shouldn't do it right this second."

"You said you didn't think I was pushing myself too fast."

He rolled his eyes. "I said if you switch from every three days to every two days, you wouldn't be pushing too fast. But this is not the same."

I touched his hand, and he turned it to entwine our fingers.

"I think I can do this now. What's more, I think I have to. The sooner they're connected, the better. I wish I'd done it a month ago."

"You didn't have your Summer property a month ago," he pointed out.

"I should have. As soon as the Winter Solstice stuff was over, I should have come straight to Summer and gotten my Summer estate. I keep putting things off and I need to stop. After I'm done, you can take me to bed and I promise to sleep in tomorrow morning."

He snorted and gave me a disbelieving look. "I'm sure you will."

I smiled, loving how he could be so sarcastic without sounding like it at all. Then I let go of his hand and stepped into the center of the trees. Ronan stayed outside, watching me. I closed my eyes and breathed deeply a few times, twisting the Ring of Creation—a gift from the Guardian of the Space Between that made it easier to create Ways, though wasn't exactly necessary. Then I concentrated on the place I wanted this Way to open to. I thought of the stand of trees on my Winter property, a mirror image of these three trees. I'd spent a lot of time there, memorizing the pattern of the bark on each tree, the exact color of the leaves and needles. I'd eventually used that memory to create the Way from Ronan's ranch to that spot. Now I would use that memory again to connect it to this place, two Ways, side-by-side.

I took a deep breath, focusing on the magic that created paths, and breathed out as the Way opened, forging the first connection. A new cat sidhe sat in the Space Between, cleaning its paw as though it hadn't a care in the world. As though it hadn't just winked into existence.

"Guardian," I said to her.

"Princess," she replied.

"That was much easier than the previous Ways," I said to no one in particular.

The cat looked up at me, pausing her grooming. "That is because you connected two spots meant to be connected. It is easy to create a Way between balanced places." She went back to licking her paw and using it to wash her face, completely ignoring me once again.

I stepped back and focused a second time, this time on the space on Ronan's ranch next to the Winter Way. It didn't connect quite as easily as the last Way. It felt like the two spots were further apart and I had to drag them together. When they finally met, I felt the click, and the Way was created.

I stepped back and stumbled, feeling lightheaded. Ronan was there immediately, catching me before I fell.

"I'm okay," I said.

"The fuck you are. You're pushing too hard."

I shook my head. "Ways aren't as difficult as helping someone with their latent magic."

"No, but you're still about to pass out. Are you finished now?"

"Yes." I leaned into him as he started helping me back to the house. But I stopped us when I felt a familiar presence.

"Way Finder."

I turned to find the Father of the Guardians, a cat about three times bigger than any of the ones who guarded the Ways. His gray and brown fur was so long I could lose my fingers in it. Of course, I felt confident if I touched him without his permission, I'd be missing a hand within seconds.

When I'd seen him before, he was always casual, usually sitting or laying down with his tail tucked around him. Tonight, he stalked toward me with purpose, sitting before me, his tail twitching behind him.

"Is something wrong? Did I make a mistake with the Ways?"

"No mistake. You are becoming a better and stronger Way Finder as you create and close more of them. I am here on other business."

"The princess has had a long night and needs rest," Ronan said, his arm still around me.

"Would you walk with us?" I asked. "I can be moving toward rest, which will make my marshal happy, but you can tell me what business has brought you here."

"This is acceptable."

We began a slow walk, the Guardian keeping pace beside me.

"What's your name?" I asked suddenly, realizing I'd never asked before.

He blinked up at me as though the question didn't make sense.

"My progeny call me Father. The White Hart calls me Guardian. I do not converse with many others."

"What about the other Way Finders?"

"They also called me Guardian."

"Well, that's not your name. That's a title. We should come up with a name for you."

"My princess," Ronan cut in, "I don't think he arrived to discuss names."

"Right. I'm a little tired. What brings you here, Guardian?"

"You opened a Way just now. There is a Way Finder on the other side."

I stumbled to a stop. "How do you know?"

He growled low in his chest and Ronan shifted so he could move me away if the cat made any threatening moves. Looking at him, I knew I had insulted him and while the fae almost never apologized because of the implied debt, the Guardian deserved one.

"I'm sorry. I didn't ask because I thought you were wrong. I asked out of ignorance."

He narrowed his eyes at me, but then nodded and we continued.

"So someone on the ranch is a Way Finder. I created a Way from my Winter estate a while ago. Why didn't you come to me then?"

"The Way Finder was not there then," he said. "I should have noticed if they went through the Way, but you brought a few through cloaked in darkness. I could not see those, so it could have been one of them."

The people from Mab's dungeon.

"So it's someone who's come to the ranch between when I opened the Winter Way and this one. Could it be an exiled fae? We've had a few people come to us from parts of the human world who've heard about me."

"It is possible. I have noticed a few Way Finders who have left the Sidhe in the past, but once they are in the human world, there is nothing I can do about it."

"Why not?"

"I cannot leave the Sidhe."

"Oh. Well, I can help you find whoever it is. I'll have Quinn or Cacey draw up a list of all the people who have arrived during that time and we'll find them."

The cat nodded. We had reached the back porch, and every guard posted there watched the Guardian carefully. We stopped at the bottom of the stairs, turning toward each other.

"It's important to find this Way Finder?"

The cat looked away into the distance. "There used to be many. They would find me when they passed through the Space Between and I would teach them. Ways were opened and closed all the time. It is one way the magic refreshes itself. You are but one person. You have little need of Ways other than the few you have created so far. Some of my progeny are exhausted and wish to be returned to the Sidhe. Yet must all Ways be guarded. More Way Finders will help restore the balance among the guardians. They do not find me anymore."

When I'd closed the Way from Winter to Ronan's property, the Guardian had told me whenever a Way was closed, one of the guardians would return their magic to the Sidhe. Essentially, they'd die. I hadn't been happy about it, but the Guardian told me it was necessary. If I'd cried a little bit, or a lot, that night, no one but Ronan knew.

"I'll find whoever it is. Is there some way I can know?"

"If you looked into their magic, you would see it. Also, all Way Finders who have been born in recent years have had access to both of their gifts. The magic of Way Finding has allowed it to be so."

Idly, I wondered what "recent years" meant to a creature who was likely well over five thousand years old. I assumed he meant in the last thousand, since that was how long people had been born with access to only one magic. Regardless, his information gave me a place to start in eliminating potential possibilities.

"Could the Way Finder be someone who is not daoine sidhe or be half-human?"

"Of course."

"You make it sound like the rest of the fucking realm doesn't think those people are worthless."

"What the people in the Sidhe believe and what is true are not always the same thing. As one who is glamour blind, you should understand this better than anyone."

He made a good point.

"I'll let you know when I have the list."

He faded into nothing without acknowledgment. Then I allowed Ronan to help me up the stairs and into the house. By the time we reached the bedroom and got my boots off, I was too tired to do anything other than climb into bed and descend into sleep.

CHAPTER 14

I slept as late as I could, which wasn't as late as I wanted to. I woke with all the things I needed to do running through my head and couldn't get back to sleep. I changed out of the clothes I'd slept in into ones that looked pretty much the same and went downstairs.

Ronan had gotten up a couple hours before me and met me in the dining room where Nainsi, the cook here, had served me a breakfast of sausages, eggs, and fresh fruit. I was busily shoving it down my throat as Ronan sat next to me.

"If you don't slow down, you'll choke," he pointed out.

"My stomach feels like it's collapsing on itself. I haven't been this hungry since after the Solstice challenges."

Quinn came in carrying a tray with two cups on it.

"Oh, Quinn. I need a list of people who arrived at the ranch between the time I opened the Way from there to Winter and last night. I need it as soon as possible. Could you work with Cacey on it? There's a Way now that leads to Winter, so you can go whenever, and it won't take hours."

She blinked at me for several seconds.

"What?" I asked.

"A Way to Winter?" she asked.

"Yeah. I made it last night."

She shook her head and smiled at me. "I will talk with Cacey," she said, setting one of the cups she carried in front of me.

"This isn't coffee," I said, staring into the clear depths, genuinely confused.

"It's water. You need to stay hydrated if you're going to continue pushing yourself as you apparently did yesterday. Caffeine is the opposite of hydrating. Drink."

I scowled. "I remember when you were very timid and would never think to tell me what to do."

She gave me a sympathetic look. "Unfortunately, someone taught me I have a voice, and I am allowed to use it."

I rolled my eyes. "That was rather shortsighted of her."

"It truly was."

I downed the glass of water. Partly because I could smell the coffee in the other cup she had, and I knew she wouldn't give it to me if I didn't do as she said. Partly because she was probably right. She smiled as I drank the last of it, then switched the cups around.

I picked up the coffee and inhaled the steam, letting the rich scent of the brew settle me in a way the breakfast hadn't.

Quinn started back toward the kitchen. "From now on, a glass of water before every cup of coffee."

I choked on my drink. "You want to drown me?"

She smiled at me over her shoulder. "Drink less coffee and you can drink less water."

Without waiting for my response, she disappeared back into the kitchen.

"I've created a monster."

"You wouldn't have it any other way." I turned to find Ronan smiling, a genuine, actual smile. He really was beautiful when he smiled.

I picked up my fork and started eating again, slower this time, still looking at him.

"So what's first today?" he asked.

I looked away at that question, unsure what he was going to think of what I had planned.

"I want to go to the ranch and get my bike."

He was silent for so long I finally glanced at him again to see a look of confusion on his face.

"Why?"

"I just feel like I need to. Like she belongs here with me."

"What about fuel?"

"I've been testing a theory. I haven't filled her up in the last four weeks."

"Not once?"

I shook my head. "And she's still going. She doesn't seem to need fuel. I've noticed a complete lack of exhaust lately *and* she seems to be running better. Smoother. Like now the fuel is out of her system, she's not congested anymore."

"That doesn't make sense. She's a machine. Motorcycles need fuel to go, just like any other combustion engine."

"She doesn't. She's magic."

He scrubbed a hand over his face. "Magic still makes sense. Cause and effect. All of it."

"We can create fire from nothing. How does that make sense?"

"It lives within us. I have no fire within me. I cannot make fire. Ansgar has no air within him. He can't make air."

I rolled my eyes. "So whatever she needs to run lives within her. Also, I've decided to call her Bonnie."

"You named her. After her model."

Bonnie was a Triumph Bonneville. I never claimed to be good at naming things.

"Do you have a problem with that?"

He shook his head, a bemused smile on his face. "Not at all. I do want to point out, we still don't understand exactly where her magic came from."

I lifted my coffee to my lips. "It came from me." I took a sip and set the cup back down. "I don't know how I did it," I said. "But every time I've touched her lately, now I know the magic is there, I feel this echo inside me. Like I gave her the magic, and she's thanking me for it."

He stood up to pace. "I know it's the only logical thing, but it doesn't make sense. We cannot give life to inanimate objects."

I shrugged helplessly. "There's a few impossible things I can do that most people can't. I don't know how to explain it. Anyway, I want to bring her here so I can ride to Lumina instead of riding a horse."

He continued to pace. I continued to let him while I finished my breakfast. Eventually, Mada tapped on the door and entered.

"Are we going to Lumina today?" She watched Ronan pace and turned to me. "What did you do this time?"

"What makes you think it has anything to do with me?"

She just looked at me, one eyebrow raised.

Ronan stopped. "She's bringing her motorcycle to the Sidhe. You and Ansgar get ready and head there now. We'll be at her mother's estate in an hour or less."

Mada nodded and left. I watched Ronan as he slowly turned back to me. "Let's go get Bonnie, then."

I jumped up, grinning and hugged him, realizing after I'd done it that we were in a room in the house where anyone could see us. We tended not to have any kind of public displays of affection if people could walk in. But that was because of me. Because I wasn't ready to declare him as my potential anam cara. My soul mate. Maybe it was something I should change?

We left Summer and went back to his ranch, where Bonnie waited for me. I'd always been very safety conscious while riding her before on the streets of Vancouver. It was illegal to ride without a helmet, after all. But since returning from the Sidhe and learning about her magic, I'd stopped wearing it. I only ever rode her on the ranch land since Ronan couldn't protect me as well if I left his property. And now that I had my magic, I felt confident if I were ever to be in an accident, I could keep myself safe. Plus, Bonnie seemed to want to keep me safe as well.

When Kai had shot me, before we became friends, I rode her from North Vancouver all the way back to Langley. I'd thought she'd run out of gas before making it to Ronan's property, but the truth was, she had just stopped. As though she knew I wouldn't be able to hold on any longer. I'd walked the last little bit and been fine, or as fine as anyone who had been shot. If she hadn't stopped, I probably would have fallen off, been knocked unconscious, and later found dead from blood loss on the side of the road.

Since our first ride together, Ronan had come with me on a few others, and he was a good passenger. So we climbed on and I started her up, simply placing my hand on her gas tank.

"Where's the key?" Ronan asked.

"Oh, I don't need that anymore, either."

I could feel Ronan's exasperation as we rode out of the garage and toward the Way. For the first time, the cat there stopped me.

"What is this?" he asked, head tilted to one side.

"My motorcycle. She's coming with me."

His nose twitched as though he smelling the air. "I have not seen a magic like this before."

"She's special. One of a kind. But she belongs in the Sidhe with me."

I waited while the guardian considered. I had a feeling, Way Finder or not, if he decided my motorcycle couldn't come with me, she wouldn't be.

"You are correct. She belongs with you. I will let it be known this new creature may be seen through Ways and the Space Between."

Just like that, we were through. I could still rev the engine, and so I did. She growled happily as we rode through my property, drawing the eyes of everyone outside. We made it to Lumina in fifteen minutes instead of the hour it would normally take us, parking in my mother's stable with the two horses Ansgar and Mada rode.

People had watched as I rode through the streets of Lumina, making me wonder if I should have drawn so much attention to myself. If I could have done any glamour, I would have made her look like a horse. But I had none whatsoever, a side-effect of being a fae changeling. I was glamour blind, which meant I could hear lies, see through other people's glamour, and could do none of my own. Most of the time, I didn't care, but it would have been pretty handy at the moment.

A maid led me to the solarium, where coffee, tea, and snacks had been set out for me and one other person. Mada and Ansgar were already there, one on either side of the solarium door on the outside.

"Is my mother not joining us?" I asked the maid.

"No, Your Highness. She thought you might wish to speak to Lady Gwanwyn on your own. However, she requests you meet her in the courtyard after your tea."

I nodded, and she left, returning a few minutes later, followed by a daoine sidhe noble who had to be Gwanwyn.

She embodied the term statuesque. If someone had told me she'd been carved from blue veined marble, I wouldn't have been surprised. Her long hair hung straight down her back like a waterfall and I could see many shades of blue in it, from a dark blue that was almost black to white and every shade in between. Her eyes were like two black stones that seemed to look straight through me with ease.

I rose to greet her, and she ignored me completely as she took her seat across from me, sitting like she was royalty, shoulders square, back straight, a slight look of disdain on her face.

"Good afternoon, Lady Gwanwyn. I appreciate you coming."

She looked at her empty teacup, which the maid hurried to fill. When she was done pouring tea and coffee and handing out a few biscuits, she stepped back from the table, but Gwanwyn said, "Leave us," and the girl scampered out of the room. Gwanwyn cast a glance at Ronan standing behind me, but said nothing to him.

"Now. I am an old woman, nearing the end of my years. I have no patience for games. You have called me here to discuss something. Let us discuss it."

"I wish more daoine sidhe were like you." I pushed my plate and coffee cup aside—it was the shitty magic-infused stuff anyway—and leaned forward. "I'm looking for some advice. I found some people who have been...." How to describe what happened to the children? "Tampered with. Magically."

Gwanwyn's black eyes filled with rage. "I know of what you speak. These people, where are they now?"

"Out of harm's way. But I need to figure out what was done to them and how to help them."

She scoffed. "You have no healing magic. I would know it if you did."

"I don't heal the body the way you do. I heal something else." I let that hang there. Waiting for her to understand.

It only took her a second to look at me with less disdain and more interest. She tilted her head to me.

"You are not what I expected."

I smiled ruefully. "I hear that a lot." I pulled the three vials of the reconciliation tincture from my pocket. I'd given Lorna the rest of the ones from Tidal Blossom. "The people who were harmed have found these ease the pain they're in." I tapped the silver one. "This one works the best. I want to know why."

I hesitated. I needed help, someone who was actually a healer, who could tell me what had been done and how to reverse it. But in order to help me, she first needed to know what had been done. For that, I would need to trust her. I could ask. I would know if she was lying. Or I could just trust her. I'd been deciding to trust a lot of people lately—not something that came naturally to me. Then again, Deegan had said she and Queen Titania didn't get along and that was exactly who I would need.

"The people who were harmed are children who have no access to their gifts at all. When I looked, someone had put magic that didn't belong to them into the space where their gifts should be. Specifically, water."

Gwanwyn leaned back in her chair, her fingers steepled together. "I know the people of whom you speak. And I have a guess as to who did this heinous thing."

"I assumed it was Anstice, under Titania's orders," I said bluntly. She was the one who said she didn't have time for games.

She inclined her head.

"I would have to see one of the children to know for certain. But who did it and why are secondary questions. You say these tinctures ease their pain?" She picked one up, examining it. "Reconciliation. Interesting. I will take these back to my home lab and see what I can discover about the three. Perhaps from there we can come up with a solution as to how to undo the damage done."

"I also know someone who used to work for Anstice. He chose voluntary exile rather than continue to help her. He can't come to Lumina for fear she might try to punish him for how he left. But if you think it would help, I'm sure you could come to my estate north of the city, and he could come there."

"I will look into these first. Then we can discuss if I should meet with the brownie."

"You know him?"

"I did. He showed promise as a healer. By the time I noticed him, he already worked for Anstice. Then suddenly he was gone. I assumed he had been killed." She paused, taking a sip from her tea. "I will get started examining these tinctures. I will let you know what I find."

"What will you require as payment?"

She considered me for a long moment. "What are you asking the children for your part in helping them?"

"Nothing. They need help. I can help them. So I am."

Gwanwyn continued to watch me. "For now, I too, will help these children without requiring payment. If that changes, I will stop work and we can discuss what arrangements must be made."

"May I ask why?"

She sighed. "There was a time when Anstice and I were friends. She came to me about five hundred years ago and told me what she had been researching in her labs. I told her our magic would never be able to help the poor souls who had but one gift. She believed she could help them and ended up doing harm instead. I am a healer. I owe a debt for not stopping her when I should have."

She stood as though to go, then stopped and turned back to me. "You say you are able to heal something besides the body. Yet, no one knows of your abilities to do this."

"A few people do. But I'm trying not to let it be common knowledge. I worry someone might try to take advantage of my abilities. Others might try to stop me."

"It is ever so that the strong wish to keep the weak as they are for fear of losing their positions of power."

"Not me."

"Then you know what they do not. When the weak are brought up, they only add to the power of the strong. I will reach out when I have information."

She started toward the door, and I stood to walk her out.

"You don't want to eat? Or finish your tea?" I asked.

"I have much to do and I no longer have thousands of years to do it all. I begin to understand the rush of humans. They have but a hundred years stretching ahead of them and waste the first twenty too young to do anything. I have almost three thousand years behind me, child. Yet now I feel as if it were not enough."

We reached the doors that exited out into Lumina, and I said goodbye to Gwanwyn.

"Out of curiosity," she said before she left, "who told you to seek me out?"

"I've had the privilege of being punished by the captain of the Queen's dungeons. Deegan said Anstice worked with the Queen. He also said you do not."

"Ah, Deegan. He is an interesting fellow. Until later, Princess."

I still hated the title most of the time, but sometimes, like now, it felt like a compliment.

CHAPTER 15

I found my mother where I usually found her, sitting among her plants in the courtyard.

"I wondered if I could ask you some questions," I said as I sat down with her.

"Of course, dear. What do you want to know?"

"Why does Queen Titania favor Anstice over Gwanwyn? She seems like a very capable healer."

"She is incredibly capable. Possibly the best healer in all the Sidhe. Though I'm certain those in Winter would argue." She rolled her eyes as though it was a stupid argument. It probably was. "She and Titania had an argument some years back. I'm trying to remember how many." She considered. "Could it have been as long as a thousand?"

The way these people talked about time kept startling me. As though a thousand years was like a decade instead of a millennium.

"Titania asked for Gwanwyn and Anstice to assist her in some project. I believe it had to do with those poor souls who only have a single gift. I think they were trying to figure out what happened to them and how to stop it from continuing."

"She wanted to experiment on them," I said.

"Oh no. Nothing so obscene. She just wanted answers. For the good of the Sidhe."

Sure. That's what she said. But I'd seen enough lies in Lumina to know this would have been another one.

"Gwanwyn refused to help. Many thought her selfish. If she had only worked with Anstice, they might have come up with a solution to the problem by now. Instead, the problem has gotten worse." She leaned forward, conspiratorially. "For about a decade or so, children have been born with no magic at all." She leaned back again, relief plain on her features. "I am just grateful you were not so afflicted."

I didn't correct her that it was fifteen years ago and not ten. She didn't need to know how much I understood the problem.

"When Anstice started her research, did she... speak to any of the daoine sidhe who work here?"

"Of course. She has spoken to most of them, I'm sure."

My heart raced at the implication. How many people had Anstice actually tampered with? I wouldn't be able to help any of them until I figured out how to reverse the experiment.

I had to change the subject before I said too much, or she started to wonder why I was asking these questions. I told her my motorcycle was in the stables if she wanted to understand what it was, and we went to see it. She was just as confused after seeing the bike as she had been from my description. She also thought it was far too loud.

All the while, my mind was already on my next task. After about an hour, I told her I would stay for dinner, and she returned to her garden. I turned to Ronan, Ansgar, and Mada.

"I need to talk to people who work here," I said. "Daoine sidhe with access to only one gift." I told them about how I was worried about how many people had already been experimented on.

"That shouldn't be difficult," Ansgar said. "There are plenty who work here."

"What might be difficult," Mada countered, "is getting anyone to talk to you. People don't fear Titania like they do the Winter Queen. But they are still scared. At least the lesser fae are."

"The ones she experimented on, you mean. We should split up, talk to as many people as we can." I held up my hand before Ronan could protest. "You're coming with me, obviously. Mada and Ansgar can go on their own to try to talk to people. They'll probably have better luck than I will, anyway."

He gave me a tight nod, and I sent them on their way, hoping at least one of us would be successful. Ansgar started outside with the groundskeepers and animal handlers. Mada went to talk to the guards. I went inside to talk to the kitchen and housekeeping staff.

After a few hours, I hoped Ansgar and Mada were having more luck than I was because no one said more than a few words to me. Mostly, "Hello, Princess," and "Goodbye, Princess." I couldn't exactly tell them I wanted—and had the ability—to help them. Not without possibly being forced to help them all. So no one talked, and I eventually headed back to my rooms to come up with a new plan and hopefully hear better news from the others.

Outside my door, a woman waited. She looked nervous.

"Your Highness," she said when she saw me, snapping to attention. Her eyes darted between me and Ronan behind me, and she seemed to get even more nervous.

"Hello. Who are you?"

"My name is Airleas, Your Highness. I wondered if I could have a private word with you."

I arched an eyebrow, but nodded. Given her clothes, I could see she was part of the guard.

"Come in," I said, opening the door and letting her follow me and Ronan inside. She closed the door behind her.

I went to the sideboard and made myself a cup of coffee, more to give me something to do with my hands than because I actually wanted to drink it.

"So, you sought me out. What do you want to talk about?" I asked as I prepared the elaborate contraption.

"I wanted to offer you some advice," she said. "Some questions are dangerous to ask."

Ronan tensed, but I turned to the woman. "You didn't come here to threaten me, did you, Airleas? Because if you did, I don't think we can be friends."

Her eyes widened and her mouth dropped open. "I—Your Highness, I would not—you misunderstand."

We were silent as the coffee finished brewing. I picked it up and went into the sitting area, settling on the couch, indicating Airleas join me. She hesitated, looking at Ronan, then back at me. While I waited, I breathed in the brew's aroma. Today's magic smelled like pine trees. I took a sip. It wasn't as bad as some of the others I'd tasted. Still not coffee, but at least it didn't make me grimace. Eventually, Airleas sat down in the furthest corner from me, perched on the edge like she was ready to bolt up if necessary.

"Are you afraid someone will hear us in my private suite?" I asked.

"No, Your Highness."

"Cut the Your Highness. It's unnecessary. If you're not comfortable calling me Calynn, just don't call me anything."

"I—all right."

"So if you're not worried about being overheard, you must not want to be direct because you're worried about my reaction. I swear, I won't punish you for telling me something I don't like to hear. Not now. Not ever."

She watched me carefully, trying to gauge my sincerity. I let her come to her own conclusions in her own time. She had come to me, after all. And she was the first daoine sidhe in Summer who had offered me more than cordial pleasantries.

Finally, she took a deep breath. "People who ask the wrong questions disappear sometimes."

I nearly dropped my coffee. "My friends."

"They're all right. I asked a couple of the guards I trust to look out for them."

"Why would you do this for me?"

She swallowed. "I remember when you were born, Your Hi—I mean—I... remember. A few of us felt drawn to you immediately."

I looked at Ronan. He'd felt the same, which is what led to him being exiled when he changed me with Niall almost thirty years ago.

"We've waited for your return," Airleas continued. "Now you are here, we want to ensure you are safe."

"I'm looking for some answers."

"Those answers are dangerous ones. Not worth risking your life in pursuing."

I set my teeth together. "I will be the one to decide what answers are worth pursuing."

She paled at my tone. "Of course, Your Highness. I mean no disrespect. It is only that what has been done is done."

"It's done for you. But what about the others?"

"There are no others. The experiments stopped fifteen years ago. When Anstice's lab burned down."

"They've started back up again. About a month and a half ago, apparently. On children who have no magic."

She shook her head at my statement. "That can't be true."

"It is. I've met the children and seen the damage done to them. A few of them are in so much pain they can't speak anymore."

Airleas pressed a hand to her mouth. But after only a few seconds, resolve cleared the horror from her features.

"What do you want to know, Your Highness?"

I set my coffee down on the table and leaned forward, arms resting on my knees. "What happened to you? Start from the beginning."

She thought for a moment, then began. "You learn quickly if your child will have two gifts or only one. When that happens to a family, it used to be they could enroll their child in a program offered by Queen Titania. The child would be removed from the home around age fifteen. They never performed experiments on the children. We were kept under observation until our magic manifested. Then the experiments began. Anstice had pages and pages of notes on how to accomplish the end result she desired. I was never quite sure what she did or what the result was she aimed for. But by the time I reached my fortieth year, she had finished with me and released me."

"Then her lab burned down, and the experiments stopped," I said.

"It is all rumor, you understand. There was speculation, whispers, her research had been destroyed in the fire."

"What did Anstice and Titania say about all of it? Anything?"

"Oh, certainly there was an official statement. But no one in Lumina believes a word of any official statement. They said the fire had been an accident. Then they said the experiments had been concluded and found to be unhelpful, thus they would no longer be continuing. Two separate statements spaced some time apart."

"Right. Wouldn't want people to connect those dots." I lifted my mug again, taking a sip of the coffee and tapping a finger against the side.

"Airleas. Would you mind if I look at your magic, see what was done to it?"

"If you think it will help the children who now suffer," she said

"It might. It might not. But I won't know until I look."

I held out my hands and Airleas came closer, setting hers on top, palm to palm. I found my way into her magic and immediately saw the water magic that didn't belong to her. Except this time, instead of filling the space and creating pressure and pain, or dripping through the space creating agony bordering on insanity, it was contained in structures. I searched my memory for the term. Aqueducts. Someone had built aqueducts into her magic so the water could flow into then out of it. It had likely been incredibly painful to have built, but now it was here, it would just be an old ache she didn't notice much anymore. I also understood I would not be able to give her access to her latent magic while the aqueduct stood. It would imbalance the structure, causing it to collapse.

In order to help Airleas, and a lot of other daoine sidhe in Summer, I would first need to figure out how to undo this. I would need to create a new bargain with these people, since they would require more help than the others and I still didn't know the first step in helping them. Add one more thing to my list of things to do.

What it really all came down to was, I needed more time.

CHAPTER 16

Before I left Lumina, I reminded my mother about needing guards for the Summer estate and mentioned I'd met Airleas and we'd formed a rapport. My mother said she would talk to the guard and would have all who were interested in coming to me ready to leave after the party in a few days.

Then, Ronan and I rode my motorcycle back to my house while Ansgar and Mada followed on horseback. When I got back, I asked Aiden to invite Cacey to Summer since I had something to discuss with him and Idelisa. By the time he arrived, I'd already eaten dinner and was sitting in my library where he and Idelisa met me.

I introduced them then explained to my Summer house manager what I could do and how I'd set up the bargains.

"I've previously been bringing daoine sidhe to their full power every three days, but I'm going to switch it to every two days now. And we're going to switch back and forth between Summer and Winter. The number of people I have is very unbalanced and I need to at least stop that from getting worse. Tomorrow, I'll make the bargain with Barden and give him access to his latent magic." I still felt uneasy about Barden and his reaction, but I hoped giving him his latent magic would help the situation. Maybe he'd just overreacted to the news that it was possible to have something he thought he never would. "In three nights, I'll be getting more people from my mother, so I want you two to coordinate the lists."

Cacey nodded. He'd already been helping me with this for the last few weeks. But Idelisa stared at me in shock.

"Do you know what this ability means?" she asked, breathlessly.

"I do. I also know how dangerous the information can be. Which is why very few people know about it." Well. Very few people in Summer. "I'd like to keep it that way."

She nodded rapidly. "Of course, Princess. I won't say a word to anyone."

At least she hadn't lied about that. My ability to hear lies was even less well known than my ability to help people. It wasn't something people needed to know, and I'd rather they tell me the truth for its own sake than because they knew they couldn't lie.

I was in the dining room eating breakfast when Idelisa came in with Barden, looking slightly uneasy.

"You told me to bring him today," she said. "But you didn't say what time."

I waved for them to come in. "Now is fine. Would either of you like breakfast? I'm going to eat before I do anything."

Idelisa declined, saying she had to get back to work while Barden sat down next to me at the table. Ronan joined us a few minutes later and Nainsi brought them both food. Barden didn't touch anything. He just sat there, fidgeting. His leg jumped and his fingers tapped against the table. I tried to ignore it, but he knocked the table with his knee and spilled my coffee, which I hadn't even sipped yet because I was still finishing the required glass of water.

"Barden, calm down. I understand you're nervous, but I'm trying to eat."

"How can you sit there and eat when I am waiting like this?" he asked. "I feel like I stand on the edge of a cliff. Your stalling is about to push me over the edge."

Ronan was halfway to standing before I held up my hand for him to stop.

"That was awfully rude, Barden," I said, setting down my fork and folding my hands in front of my plate. "I offered you assistance in exchange for your service for a year and a day. I'm going to give you that assistance. You haven't even waited that long."

"I've waited my whole life."

"How old are you?"

He blinked and his fidgeting stilled. "Excuse me?"

"How old are you?" I asked again.

He tried to bring back his ire and sneered at me. "Older than you."

"Of course you are. But that's not what I asked."

He looked between me and Ronan, who I was sure was not hiding his anger at Barden's rudeness. I could feel it rolling off him, and I wasn't even looking at him. Finally, Barden said, "I'm 97 years old."

I picked up my fork and began eating again. "So older than me, yes. But not older than Ronan. Who waited a long time for his magic. Or older than Sorcha or Mada or Ansgar. None of them have ever been rude to me." I took a bite of my breakfast, letting Barden wait while I chewed and swallowed. "Now, I moved you forward because you're the first person in Summer to bargain with me and I need to balance out my bargains. However, you are in no way the next person who should be helped. I have plenty of people from Winter who bargained with me weeks ago. They've been waiting patiently for their turn. So, while I understand your impatience, I will not tolerate your rudeness."

He at least looked contrite, but I could also see he was still upset. I hadn't encountered anyone else as impatient as Barden. Everyone so far had been grateful they would soon have access to all of the magic they were supposed to. I hoped the rest of the Summer people I was going to help weren't as annoying as Barden. I also wondered if he would remain in service to me after the year and a day was up. I kind of hoped not.

I finished my breakfast, and we moved to the library. Ronan followed but remained outside, closing the door behind us. I could tell Ronan didn't want to leave me alone with Barden. I was certain I could handle him, but I also understood. Barden made me slightly uneasy as well.

We sat in the two chairs in front of the desk and I held out my hands. Barden looked at them suspiciously.

"You need to give me your hands so I can help you."

He hesitated, his rudeness and impatience forgotten in the wake of the nervousness that always seemed to catch the person I was about to help.

"This isn't some trick?" he asked.

"I showed you before that it's there. I need to go into your magic and lay a path so you can reach it."

He set his hands on top of mine and we descended into his magic together. We stood together in the clear fresh air of a bright morning. Air and light surrounded us, but I could feel the latent gift further away.

"What do I do?" he asked.

"You wait. I'll do my job." I set out toward the magic. It was difficult to see when I transitioned from one into the next because they blended together seamlessly. The bright morning light from his main gift glittered here still, but the air was no longer clear and crisp, filled instead with the scent of wildflowers. As I began to lay the path back toward Barden, the flowers followed me, springing up on either side.

When I reached him, I was tired, but no more so than usual.

"Where is it?" he asked.

"It's here," I said, pointing to the flowers that had grown all the way back to his main magic.

"Flowers?"

"Yes. Flora magic. I'm sure there's more than just flowers, but I didn't spend a long time looking. Flora magic usually comes with an intuition for all—"

"I don't have flora magic," he interrupted. "My mother was a healer and my father has fire and earth."

"I'm not sure what you want me to do about that. I don't choose what the magic is. I just show you how to get to it." I began to leave his magic, but he grabbed my wrist, holding me in place.

"You did it wrong."

A spike of fear sliced through me, and I felt a pull toward that red, sticky magic. It would be very easy to use it here, already inside his magic.

"I didn't. You may be unhappy about what your latent magic is—though I don't understand why—but that doesn't mean I did it wrong. It just means you don't like it."

"Neither of my parents have flora magic. Or air or light. Where did my gifts come from?"

"How should I know? I didn't give them to you. The magic was there the whole time. I just gave you access to it. I don't have any more answers for you than that."

"You do. I know you do."

I looked down to where he still grasped my wrist, the threat increased since we were in the heart of his magic. "Barden. Let me go or I will take all of your magic away." That red magic came to me, slippery and oily, spreading as visible lines on my skin.

I guess he could feel it too, because he dropped my wrist like I'd burned him.

I moved out of his magic again and he called after me, "This isn't over."

When I returned to myself, he was still slumped in the seat across from me, eyes closed. I stood and left the room, finding Ronan right outside. He looked me over as though checking to make sure I was okay. I heard Barden begin to stir, so I motioned to the solarium, and we went there, closing the doors.

"Barden's going to be an issue," I said, sitting down on a small couch.

I noticed Ronan's hand twitch like he wanted to reach for his sword, but he sat in the chair across from me. "What do you want to do?"

"Nothing for now. You already had people watching him. Just continue that. He's angry and thinks I gave him the wrong magic."

"But you don't give people magic. You just help them find what's already there."

"He doesn't believe that," I said, rubbing a hand over my face. "I'm worried he'll do something he shouldn't."

"I'll let the guards know. They'll keep an eye out."

"I don't want to kill him." My head dropped back against the couch. "I don't want to kill anyone. It feels wrong. That magic is within me. And it feels bad."

Ronan's hand wrapped around mine, and I gripped it without looking at him, taking the strength he offered.

"You will do what is necessary to keep yourself and your people safe. Sometimes bad things must happen for the right reasons."

I recalled something similar I'd said to Queran a while back. He'd told me everything he'd done had been to keep me safe. I'd said he'd done the wrong things for the right reasons. That still made them wrong. How was what I had to do any different?

CHAPTER 17

After another night plagued by nightmares sent by my own lovely subconscious, I went down to breakfast, and Quinn placed a glass of water, a mug of steaming coffee, and a piece of paper in front of me.

"What's this?" I picked up the paper, scanning a list of names.

"The people who have arrived at the ranch between when you opened the Way until when you asked for it. I have much to prepare for the party tonight. Do you need anything else?"

I was already lost in the list, shaking my head and reaching for my coffee. Quinn slapped my hand, and I looked up at her.

"Water first. I'll know even if I'm not in the room."

She narrowed her eyes at me, and I scowled, picking up the water instead. "Go before I have you beheaded or something."

She snorted and left the room.

I went back to the list, thinking of the Guardian. I didn't look up when he appeared in the seat next to me. Somehow, he always appeared whenever I needed him.

"Is that because I'm a Way Finder?" I asked out loud. "You appearing when I think of you."

"It is. I cannot go to them if they do not know it, but once they have learned, we have a connection that will allow me to appear if they have need of me."

I glanced at him. "Handy. About that name thing. Do you want one?"

His tail twitched before it wrapped around his front toes. "I do not know if it matters."

"Well, think about it. In the meantime..." I picked up the pen Quinn had left with the paper and started crossing out names. "These are all people who came to the ranch lately. The ones I'm crossing off have only one gift." The list of thirty-three names dropped to sixteen.

"This is a good list."

"Yeah. Eleven of them came from the Queen's dungeon. Those are the ones I had cloaked in darkness. The other five are exiled fae. If it's one of them, it'll be tricky. I can invite them to the Sidhe, but they can only stay as long as my invitation holds. You know this as the one who enforces the exile."

If an exiled fae entered the Sidhe, they needed an express invitation or the key to the realm. The key that was almost always in one of the Queens' possession. If they had neither, the guardian at the Way would execute them. Ronan had been exiled when he changed me as an infant. I still needed to ensure I was with him every time he went from the human world into the Sidhe. I'd explained to the Father of the Guardians my invitation stood regardless of how often we went from one realm to another, but I didn't trust a mistake wouldn't be made if I wasn't there to stop it.

"Would you be able to just let them through?" I asked.

"Like you, I do not have the authority to rescind an exile. I am bound by my magic to uphold the exiles set in place by the Queens of the Sidhe. It is understood exile is not a punishment doled out lightly."

I snorted. "Maybe that's how it's supposed to be, but that's not how it is. Otherwise, I wouldn't have a list of almost a thousand exiled fae living in the human world."

I'd asked for the list a few weeks ago. The head of the Diaspora Corporation—the company that took care of exiled fae living in the human world—in Dublin had sent it to me. We'd agreed to meet after the Equinox. I hadn't told him why it had to wait until then, but I hoped—if I was in charge—I could rescind some of those exile terms.

"Regardless, I cannot allow an exiled fae to enter the Sidhe without an invitation. But if you bring them before me, I will know which of these people is the Way Finder."

I nodded. "I'm going back to Winter tomorrow for part of my bargain with the ones with a single gift. I'll bring these people over. You'll know who it is as soon as they cross through the Way, won't you?"

He dipped his head in a nod.

"Meet me on my property by the trees. How do we find the rest of the Way Finders? Do you know how many there are?"

"Indeed. But how to find them, I know not. If I did, I would have tried to find them long before now. In years past, they would find me when their magic matured. For daoine sidhe, when they reached their third decade. Other ages for the other fae. I noticed some centuries ago no one came to find me any longer. I was left to find them myself if they crossed through the Space Between, which happened less and less frequently."

His voice was tinged with sadness and frustration. I placed a hand on his back, just over his shoulder blades. It was the first time I'd ever touched his fur, and it was softer than I could have imagined.

"We'll figure out how to find them."

He gave me a hopeless look, then disappeared.

I was left to think about all he'd said, listening to the rest of the house as my people busied to get me ready to leave for Lumina. The Guardian had no name and no one to talk to. I couldn't imagine how lonely he must have been. And he was certainly the oldest creature I'd come across.

Possibly as old as the Sidhe itself. And like all the other people I'd met who'd needed my help, I wanted to help him. I added "find Way Finders" to my internal list of things to do. I might not be able to focus on it until after the Equinox, but I would do it.

Someone knocked on the door frame, drawing my attention away from the list of people in my hands. Ronan stood there.

"We're ready to leave if you are."

I nodded and stood.

"What's wrong, little changeling?" he asked softly.

"Is it really that obvious?"

"To me it is."

I sighed. "I just met with the Guardian. I'm just... sad for him."

Ronan opened his arms, and I went into them, letting the smell of ice and pine envelop me. He was so strong and patient, his careful consideration the complete opposite of my brash recklessness. I didn't want to think about what my life might be like if I had to live it alone, specifically without him. I'd probably go completely insane.

We left my house practically as a convoy. I was in a carriage with a bunch of guards as outriders. Inside, Ronan sat across from me and Quinn beside while Aiden sat on the window ledge, happily watching the forest pass.

He seemed happier than he'd been in a long time. I wondered how much of that had to do with him being back in Summer where he belonged.

"Does it bother you guys to be here?" I asked suddenly. "And you, Aiden. Does it bother you to be in Winter?"

Everyone turned to me with looks of surprise.

"What do you mean?" Quinn asked.

"I mean, you're from Winter. Does it bother you being in Summer?"

"Not terribly. I'm half human and humans don't have affinities for one or the other. My Winter half is uncomfortable, but not a lot. It exists more like a consciousness that I'm in the wrong place. There may come a time when it becomes overwhelming, but if it did, I would let you know."

I nodded and looked at Aiden.

"Winter is far colder than here, but as long as I am in liege to you, a princess of Winter, I can survive there."

"But you prefer to be here."

"The human world also. I like going there to meet with Arial. And in Winter, when I get too cold, I just start a fire."

He did spend a lot of time in the fires while we were in Winter. He had a special affinity for flames.

"If it gets too much, you'll let me know as well?"

"Of course."

Finally, I turned to Ronan.

"Being in Summer doesn't bother me at all."

"But you're fully Winter. It doesn't feel weird? Or uncomfortable like Quinn?"

"No," he said. "My connection to you is very different from Quinn's or Aiden's. I barely notice the difference between Winter and Summer."

"How is that possible?"

"*You* feel no difference between Winter and Summer."

That was true. They didn't feel quite as right to me as the Fréimhe and the Space Between. But I felt no difference between Winter and Summer.

"I'm from both, though. You're from Winter."

He shrugged and relaxed back into his seat. And for the first time in a long time, I felt the tingle of a lie coming from him. His posture was not at all how he was feeling. He was trying to tell me something. He didn't feel a difference *because* I didn't feel a difference.

Aiden had returned his attention out the window and Quinn had relaxed and closed her eyes. Ronan still sat back in that faux-relaxed state, watching me. Somehow, I understood he was waiting for me to understand what he had said.

Now that I was thinking about it, I understood his thoughts and emotions a lot better lately. I could feel it when he was frustrated or happy. I'd always been able to find the emotions in his eyes, but now I knew them even without looking at him. Sometimes when he wasn't even in the room. I hadn't questioned it, just accepted his presence within me. I'd even felt his magic giving me strength when Mab had tried to kill me on the Winter Solstice.

I felt that same panic rise within me I'd been feeling ever since I realized how much I loved him. And there he was, offering me calm reassurance. I held on to it, feeling like I was holding his hand, squeezing it to keep myself grounded. I fought the urge to move to sit next to him so I could make physical contact until I realized Aiden and Quinn were two of my best friends.

Public displays of affection announced intention. I wasn't completely certain I was ready for that. But my friends wouldn't hold it against me.

I got up and switched sides, gripping his hand. Quinn and Aiden had to have noticed me moving, but neither turned to us. The overwhelming feeling of Ronan's presence within me had me pressing closer to him, lifting my hand to turn his face toward me, and kissing him softly. I curled into him, his arm wrapping around me.

I love you, I thought, really hard.

I wasn't sure he would be able to hear the words. Mada said it had taken her and Ansgar a long time before they could hear each other's thoughts. But I felt his happiness as a thought came back to me.

You don't need to shout, little changeling.

CHAPTER 18

We reached my mother's home and Ronan had me completely surrounded by guards on the way from the stables to my suite. Since this was the first time when it was common knowledge I would be coming to the city and we didn't know who might be working for the Queen or not, he wasn't taking any chances. He said it would be better if I just shadow-walked, but it was the middle of the day and there weren't enough around for me to do it.

I'd asked Deegan if he could meet me for a sparring session, but he'd had to decline, stating he had another engagement he had to attend to outside of Lumina.

As soon as we were in my room, Quinn started the party-readying routine. I'd decided to wear the short dress I'd worn on the Winter Solstice. It was red with a black lace overlay on the bodice and red and black tulle for the skirt ending just above my knees. The colors fit well in Summer and Winter, unlike some of my other dresses that looked distinctly Winter. I also felt it was a sort of lucky dress since Queen Mab had tried and failed to kill me while I wore it. Plus, I could wear it with my motorcycle boots and leather jacket, and it looked awesome and edgy. It made me feel like myself.

I got to this party early, which was a first. But since I'd asked my mother to host it for me, I figured I should. Ronan and Quinn followed close behind me while eight other guards took positions at various doors around the ballroom, though my two friends wouldn't leave my side during the event.

My mother found us and as people began filtering into the space in pairs and groups—all looking beautiful or terrifying or both—she began to introduce me. I remembered the first party I'd attended with Queran when he'd introduced me to the entire Winter court. After the first few people, I'd stopped cataloging names because I just couldn't keep them all straight. Tonight was no different, though I tried very hard to pay attention, keeping close track of the people who seemed hostile and the ones who seemed friendly.

Eventually, I met Anstice, and I took a long look at her. She had water magic, like all healers I'd met so far. Both her main and latent gifts were water-based, but that was as far as I could tell just by meeting her. Her skin was a lovely teal, her eyes a bright gold. Her hair was a lot shorter than most and framed her face in a riot of pure white curls. Like Gwanwyn and Anant, she was much older than any other daoine sidhe I'd met, but not quite as old as the other two. If I'd been looking at a human, I would have guessed her to be in her late sixties to early seventies, whereas Gwanwyn and Anant looked in their eighties.

"Lady Anstice. It's such a pleasure to meet you," I said. And for what it was worth, I was telling the truth. I'd wanted to meet Anstice more than anyone else. "I've heard about some interesting things you've been researching and wondered if we could discuss your findings."

Her golden eyes burned into me, and I knew she didn't believe me for a second.

"I fear I do not discuss my research with anyone but my queen."

"Of course. I've just been so interested in the healing arts, and I know you're one of the best in the Sidhe. Possibly *the* best."

I'd hoped the compliment would soften her, but I was wrong.

"How was your tea with Gwanwyn?" she asked.

Fuck. How did she know about that? Was the gossip mill in Lumina really that fast? If she thought I was allied with Gwanwyn, she probably wouldn't trust me with any of the information I needed. Too bad. I guess I'd have to get her notes the hard way.

"It was lovely," I said. "We discussed some very interesting things. It's unfortunate you and I won't get to have a similar conversation."

"Hm." She looked down her nose at me. An easy feat since I was almost a foot shorter than everyone in the room. Then she stalked off, head high, posture ramrod straight.

The evening continued. I was introduced to so many people they became a blur. Gwanwyn arrived and said hello then went on to mingle with some others. As the number of people arriving dwindled and I was considering going to circulate among the guests, a man strode up to me.

I was taken aback by the ragged scars all down the right side of his face, reaching into dark hair cut close to his scalp, the better to see the scars which reached the top of his head. He was also huge, potentially the biggest daoine sidhe I'd met. I recalled the size of a person was supposed to be in direct correlation to the amount of magical power they possessed—except in my case because I was a changeling and looked identical to the human woman I was changed with. In this man's case, I wondered if he had more magical power than the queens.

"Princess. Long has your mother mourned your absence."

He bowed over my hand and kissed it while I performed a practiced curtsy, a movement made easier thanks to the boots that steadied me.

"Sir."

"I hear from a mutual friend we may have some ideas in common. I look forward to learning more about you in the coming weeks and to seeing just exactly what you think you can do."

His eyes found mine, startling in how very black they were, and I was struck by the questions there. I hoped he was talking about Gwanwyn. That would make him a potential friend. Because I did not want this man as an enemy.

"You have me at a disadvantage," I said. "You know who I am, but I don't know who you are."

"I am called Conroy. My aunt advised me to seek you out. I heard your mother would host a fete for you, so I came to see what my aunt mentioned. I must say, I am not yet impressed."

"You haven't seen anything yet. I've noticed when people in the Sidhe get to know me, I tend to attract one of two reactions. The person either decides they like me, and I can't get rid of them, or they want to kill me."

"You would want to get rid of these people who like you?"

"Nah. It's just weird. I was alone a lot in the human world. Humans react weird to magic. The people here, though?" I cast a glance at Quinn and Ronan behind me, the first waiting to see if I needed anything, the second waiting to see if anyone tried to harm me. "I like having them around."

"But they've sworn fealty to you. So they must act respectful."

"Actually, I rescinded all offers of fealty I held." I hooked a thumb behind me. "Neither Ronan nor Quinn have fealty terms. They're just here because they want to be."

Conroy stared at me for a very long time until I grew uncomfortable with his scrutiny.

"You brought a contingent of guards with you. None of them have fealty terms?"

"Nope. All of them are serving a term of a year and a day of loyal service in exchange for something. But I know a few intend to remain once that year and a day is up, and I won't force fealty on them if they decide to."

"Why?"

I felt Ronan caution me and spared a second to wonder how deeply he could hear my thoughts. It was something I'd have to discuss with him. For now, I sent him a reassuring, if exasperated, *I know.*

"Your aunt. It's Lady Gwanwyn?"

"Would your answer change if my aunt was someone else?"

"My answer won't change. Whether or not I tell you might."

He grinned. "My aunt is Lady Gwanwyn. Now that you know, does this mean I get an answer, or I do not get an answer?"

"You can know. I hated the idea of having that much power over a person. It made me uncomfortable. I don't have to have a fealty agreement in place to offer my protection. Quinn has been loyal to me since I arrived in the Sidhe. If someone hurts her, I will take immediate action. I won't hesitate or hold back. Ronan has been loyal to me even longer. He can take care of himself, but if he were to ever need me for anything, he knows I'd be there, just like he's always been there for me. They offer me their loyalty freely. And I offer mine in return."

"That is a very pretty notion. But how can you be certain they will not betray you?"

I shrugged. "I can't be. That's the nature of trusting someone. It's not supposed to be something you control. It's supposed to be something that just is."

"Perhaps my aunt is not wrong about you. She requested I give you a message. She has preliminary findings on what is in each tincture, and some initial thoughts regarding why they work. However, to understand fully, she would need to know what was done to cause the malady."

He hadn't lowered his voice. In a room full of people who could snatch sounds out of the air with magic, eavesdropping would be easy.

And lowering your voice would ensure people's interest in eavesdropping.

"I'll see what I can figure out. Perhaps she would do me the honor of coming to my estate in three days? We can discuss the matter further."

"I will let her know. Until later, Princess."

"My friends, or most of them, call me Calynn."

"Is that what we are? Friends?"

"I sure as fuck don't want you as an enemy."

He tipped his head back and laughed, drawing looks from around the room. Some people smiled in response. Others just openly stared. I had to admit, it was a nice laugh, and I found myself grinning.

"I look forward to seeing more of you," he said with a smile. "And seeing if my aunt's assessment was correct."

I dipped my head in a nod, and he strode off into the crowd.

Titania arrived at the party with her consort, Oberon, and completely ignored me. I wondered if it was because of the number of guards I had with me or if it was because she wasn't the type to get her hands dirty. I figured it was most likely the latter.

Eventually, my mother found me, greeting me with a smile. "My love. The night has been such a success. Everyone here has been delighted with you."

Well. That wasn't exactly true. I knew Titania was not delighted. Nor was Anstice. But I didn't mention that.

"You spoke with Lord Conroy. Did you know he is the youngest person to open his own house in the last five hundred years?"

"Well, until this past Winter Solstice," I said.

My mother stared at me blankly for a moment.

"Until I did it. I doubt he opened his house when he was twenty-nine."

"Oh. I suppose you are correct." Her smile returned. "He was about a hundred years old. It was only a couple decades ago, so he is still quite young."

"That's great for him." I was confused why she was telling me all this until Ronan sent me a thought.

She wants you to consider him for a lover.

"What the fuck?" I accidentally said out loud. Thankfully, I didn't shout it, so only my mother looked at me. "Are you trying to set me up with him?"

"I merely thought you might enjoy one another's company."

"I'm not on the market for anything like that."

"Why not?"

Yes, little changeling. Why not? The thought he sent me was laced with amusement.

Shut up.

"I'm just not. I mean, he seems like a nice enough guy, but I just met him, and I'm not interested. Can we just leave it there?"

I'd only just started to come to terms with my feelings for Ronan. I was in no way ready to share them with my mother. Or anyone else, for that matter. It was enough that he knew how I felt.

"I hope you will at least consider it. Your father mentioned to me you have not seemed interested in forming many relationships with the people of Winter. I hoped you would change that here in Summer."

"Wait a second. Forming relationships or getting into one? Because I made some friends in Winter. And I believe I'm making friends here in Summer. Seems to me, you and Queran want more than that. You want me to start fucking every noble I meet."

"You need not be so crude, my darling."

"Or are you just trying to pimp me out to further your own ambitions? I know Queran has them, but I didn't think you did."

"I do not know this word, pimp."

I huff and roll my eyes. "It means you're trying to sell me to someone so you can gain from the interaction. But, just to remind you, I have my own house. So nothing I do is yours to claim. My actions are my own. My friendships are my own. My relationship status is my own. You and Queran have no say in when I start one or who I start one with. I could start a relationship with one of my guards if I wanted to."

"Do not be ridiculous. Guards are fine for the occasional roll, but they are below your station and thus not fit for forming a lasting relationship like the one I have with your father."

While I would love for our relationship to be out in the open, don't let her goad you into saying something you don't want to say right now.

Ronan's thought stopped the words that had been on the tip of my tongue.

It doesn't bother you that I haven't announced us yet?

I know where we stand, little changeling. Whether you claim me publicly or not doesn't change how we feel about each other. Our ability to communicate this way proves that.

Movement behind my mother drew my attention. Titania was watching my conversation with interest. Suddenly, I was terrified. If she knew about me and Ronan, she would know she could hurt him to get to me. But what really made my blood run like ice was the idea that, if she knew, Mab would know.

I returned my attention to my mother.

"I'm going to mingle before I say something I'll regret."

I turned and stalked away, clenching my fists to keep them from shaking. If people saw, they would just think I was angry.

CHAPTER 19

I could have left in the night. Ronan and I had discussed it. He and I could have used the shadows to return to my Summer home and no one would have known. The rest of my guards and Quinn and Aiden would have followed in the morning.

In the end, I'd decided to wait. I'd asked my mother about guards, and I wanted to know if she'd found any who wanted to come with me. I also figured, despite our fight, I should probably say goodbye before disappearing.

Fucking Ronan in her house was just an added little bonus.

In the morning, when we were ready to leave, I found my mother in her courtyard. For once, she wasn't sitting on the ground weeding or planting. She was sitting on a bench, happily watching her flowers.

"Good morning, Mother," I said.

"Good morning, my love. Are you going to stay today?"

"I can't. I have some obligations I need to take care of. But I should be back soon." I sat next to her. "I wondered if you'd given any thought to the guards I might take with me."

"Yes. In fact, I was going to seek you out before you left had you not found me first. There are eleven waiting for you in the stables. All but one is a daoine sidhe with only one gift. The last person is a mongrel. Since you have others with you, I assumed you would not mind another."

"I wish you wouldn't use that term," I said. "It's really offensive. And there are a few half-human people who I've become friends with."

"Like your maid?" she asked, rolling her eyes. "Honestly, dear, you cannot be friends with the help."

"Actually, I can. Quinn has been kind and thoughtful and she's helped me navigate a world I didn't really understand. But it's more than just Quinn. My best friend is half human and half pixie. She's the only one who was ever nice to me in the human world."

"That's different."

"How? She's still half human. She would still be considered a mongrel by you and almost everyone else in this world. Why is she different, but Quinn isn't?"

"Because she didn't grow up here." She said it like that explained everything. And I guess to her, it did.

I knew I wasn't getting anywhere with this argument, so I just stood and said, "Goodbye, Mother. The party was lovely. I'll see you again soon."

She didn't try to stop me from leaving. I wasn't sure if I wanted her to or not.

In the stables, I found Airleas waiting with ten other people.

"I hoped you would come with me," I said to her as I approached.

She smiled. "When Princess Eilidh mentioned your need for Summer guards, I knew exactly who to invite. We look forward to serving you, Princess."

She dropped to a knee, and I knew she was about to offer me her fealty.

"Not here. Let's get back to my estate, then we can sort out all the details. You've all had your fealty rescinded?"

After a round of nods, we got everything loaded into the carriage. The guards didn't have much beyond a pack each that they all carried. My mother had sent word ahead to the stables to loan me a wagon and driver, so we left Lumina in an even larger convoy than I'd arrived with.

During the hour-long drive, I considered exactly what I wanted to tell them, Barden's reaction to both my ability and his magic weighing on me. I still hadn't decided when we arrived at my house, and they stood in front of me in a line. That's when I noticed something.

Eleven people. Ten daoine sidhe and one half-human. Exactly the same numbers as the first guards who came from Sir Anant in Winter.

"Who speaks for the group?" I asked.

Airleas stepped forward. "I do, Your Highness."

"I figured you might. Why did you decide to come to me?"

"We all have differing reasons, but mainly because we believed it to be the right choice for us."

"Fair enough." I stood in front of the half-human. She looked frightened. "You weren't asked to come, were you?"

"No, Your Highness."

"You're welcome, anyway. I'll speak with you separately."

"As for the rest of you. You were asked to come because you have access to only one gift. I have the ability to help you gain access to the latent magic you're missing. However, some of you have had something done to your magic. I'm working right now to figure out exactly what was done and how to undo it. Until then, I can't help you. But if you offer me a year and a day of loyal service, in return I will figure out what happened, undo it, and grant you access to the latent magic you've been missing."

Gasps and murmurs broke out among the line until Airleas turned to them all with a hard look and everyone quieted.

"I also want you to understand something about living here. Other people like—" I turned toward the half-human.

"Firtha, Your Highness."

"Firtha live here as well. You will not be disrespectful toward them or anyone else you might consider *lesser* fae. That includes using derogatory words to describe them. Is that clear, or do I need to spell it out?"

"It is clear, Your Highness," Airleas said. "And I cannot speak for everyone on this, but I will accept your bargain."

In only a few minutes, everyone else had accepted the bargain, so I dismissed them, asking only Airleas and Firtha to stay.

"Obviously, you don't need the same bargain as the rest," I said to Firtha. "I also don't hold fealty for anyone. If you choose to stay, do so because you want to. As long as you offer me your loyalty, freely, I'll offer mine in return."

She nodded rapidly, and I sent her off with the rest of the guards. Finally, I turned to Airleas.

"Do you know Ronan?" I asked her, gesturing to where he stood behind me.

"No, Your Highness."

"I'm pretty sure I told you that wasn't necessary. Calynn would be best. Miss Calynn is fine. Some people insist on my lady." I rolled my eyes. "Anyway. The reason I asked you to stay was because I'd like to offer you the position of lieutenant of my Summer guard. Ronan is my marshal, so he'd effectively be your boss. But you would be in charge of the safety of the Summer property."

Airleas' mouth dropped open. "Are you certain? I have only just arrived. Surely there is someone else who might be more appropriate."

"You're the first of my Summer guard, Airleas. You came to speak to me when you didn't have to. You joined me when you didn't have to. You also seem to have the respect of those who came with you. You're it."

She looked between me and Ronan for a long moment. "In that case, I accept. It would be my honor."

I turned to Ronan. "You should stay here and get her situated."

I knew immediately he didn't like the idea of me returning to Winter without him. I held up my hand to stave off any protest. "Ansgar and Mada are coming with me, along with all the others of my personal guard. You can stay here for a couple of hours, then meet me there. I won't be leaving the ranch or the Winter property. And the Guardian will be with me."

"He doesn't protect you. He protects the Space Between."

"I feel like he'd defend me if he's right there. I'm currently the only Way Finder." I placed my hand on his arm. "You know this is your job. If you'd rather I appoint a different marshal, I can do that. Then you can follow me around as my personal bodyguard. But I'd prefer having you in charge of all my security."

He glared at me for a long moment. "All right. You sure know how to lay it on thick."

I grinned, then turned back to Airleas. The look in her eye told me she suspected my and Ronan's relationship was more than the label, but she didn't comment.

"Ronan's in charge. I'll be back tomorrow." I touched Ronan's hand before I left, a soft gesture of fingers brushing fingers, then went to find Mada and Ansgar.

When we stepped through the Way to the ranch, Evander had all the people I'd requested waiting right there. I looked them over, wondering which one might be the Way Finder. For all I knew, a couple people could be. The Guardian had said there was someone here, but could there be more than one?

Some of the people who had come from the Queen's dungeons were there. The former prisoners looked like they'd been eating well and had started to put some weight back on their bony frames.

"Hi," I said. "We're going to go for a little trip into Winter for the day."

Everyone looked around at each other as though confirming they'd heard correctly. Some people were nervous. Others were excited.

"I know a few of you are exiled fae. I'll extend an invitation to all of you to come into the Sidhe. I don't recommend any of you remain given your statuses as exiles and escaped prisoners. I can't guarantee your safety inside the Sidhe."

"So why are we going then?" Morrigan asked.

I turned toward the woman. She looked a lot better than she had the last time I'd seen her. She'd replaced the rags with tight, black leather pants and shirt. Her hair had been braided to keep it out of her way. She had weapons strapped here and there. Throwing knives attached to her arms, daggers to her thighs, and if I wasn't mistaken, those rings on her right hand were actually some kind of brass knuckles. She gave new meaning to the term *dressed to kill*.

"A friend of mine wants to meet at least one of you. But he can't leave the Sidhe. If you come through and want to remain, you're welcome to. I have no say in what any of you do. However, other than on my Winter property, I will not offer any kind of protection. Even on my property, I can only do so much. If you draw the Queen's attention, I'll have to ask you to leave for the safety of the others who live there. Are we clear?"

I looked right at Morrigan, staring into her stormy gray eyes. They weren't as dark now as they had been when I'd first met her.

She nodded once, and I returned the gesture.

I had everyone step through the Way one at a time, inviting the five exiled fae as they went through. The last one through, besides me, Ansgar, and Mada, was Morrigan, and I nearly walked into her back as she stopped in the Space Between, staring into the branches where the Way's guardian sat watching us.

"You can see her, can't you?" I asked.

"She is gorgeous," Morrigan breathed, reaching a hand toward the cat. I caught her hand before she could lift it.

"They're not the friendliest of creatures. I'd be careful if I were you."

Morrigan turned, blinking at me as though coming out of a trance.

"Come on," I said. "I'll explain on the other side. And the Guardian will be waiting for us."

We really needed to come up with a name for him to differentiate him from the other guardians.

As I suspected he would be, the large cat sat among the trees on my Winter property, waiting for us. His tail tucked around his body, but the tip twitched in impatience. No one else looked at him except me and Morrigan.

"I hoped there would be at least two," I said to him. Then I turned to the people who were not Way Finders.

"That's it. Morrigan is going to stay with me. The rest of you can do what you want. If you'd like to return to the human world, the Way is here. If you want to stay here for a while, that's up to you. You're all welcome."

Everyone dispersed. Ansgar and Mada took up positions on either side of me.

"Is he going to show himself?" Mada asked.

I looked at the cat, eyebrows raised in question. He stood and stalked toward us, and I knew as soon as he made himself visible to Ansgar and Mada because Ansgar's sword came out of its sheath about an inch before he shoved it back in. Mada had more control over her actions, but just barely.

"Morrigan, I'd like to introduce you to the Guardian of the Space Between. The father of the guardians of the Ways. We're working on a name."

She dropped to one knee, bowing her head, and I wondered if I should have done the same when I'd first met him. Oh well. Too late now.

"My Lord," she said with reverence.

"Way Finder," he responded.

"My mother told me such stories of you and your kind. I never thought to be granted the gift of meeting you."

"Bedelia," he said with such sadness. "She was the last until I found Calynn."

"You know when the Way Finders die?" I asked.

"I do," he said, dipping his head in a nod. "The connection between us tells me when their magic has been returned to the Sidhe, then later when the magic has been reborn into someone new."

"What about the ones who you didn't meet yet? You said the connection happens after you meet them. Can she get up now?"

He looked at Morrigan, still bowing. "You may stand, Way Finder Morrigan. To answer your question, Way Finder Calynn, if the connection is not forged, I will still know when the magic is returned to the Sidhe. However, if a fae dies in the human world, their magic cannot be returned to the Sidhe."

"Fuck." I thought of all the exiled fae. Thank fuck the Diaspora Corporation existed. Hopefully, they would be able to tell me who had died in the human world and how I could bring them to the Sidhe so their magic could return to it. Just another thing I needed to do.

Morrigan stood and continued to stare at the Guardian. "My mother used to call you *an cosantóir*. She said you are the defender of the Fréimhe."

"Morrigan," I said, turning her attention back to me. "I know you want to get revenge on Deardriu for what she did. I assume that was your plan until Evander asked you to wait for today." I gestured at the weapons covering her outfit. "Instead, I hope you stay so you can learn how to be a Way Finder. The Guardian and I will help you. But if you leave on some revenge journey, we won't be able to."

She shook off the awe the Guardian's appearance had caused. She bared her teeth and her hands drifted toward the daggers strapped to her thighs. Beside me, I noticed Mada's hand rested on the hilt of her sword.

"Deardriu must pay for her role in my mother's death."

I had to say something to diffuse the situation.

"I can't help you with that right now. But what if I could help you get revenge on the Queen?"

Morrigan scoffed. "There is no getting to the Dark Queen. She is untouchable."

"Untouchable by most. But not by me."

"You will bring her to her knees?"

"I will bring her to justice. All her debts are about to come due."

CHAPTER 20

Morrigan agreed to stay and went off somewhere to train with the Guardian. She seemed mollified by the idea that I would be going after the Queen, but I thought the real reason she decided to stay was because she wanted to learn to be a Way Finder, like her mother. She would remain on the Winter estate while she learned what to do. I helped the next person from Winter access their latent magic, but mostly spent the day in the library going over details and business regarding the estate. Quinn brought me coffee and water. Daric, the cook, made me an amazing meal. Ronan came to check on me as soon as he came from Summer. I waved him away, focusing on what Cacey and I were discussing, something about irrigation in my wheat fields that demanded all my focus just so I could understand what he was talking about.

The next day, I returned to Summer and went over similar things with Idelisa. She also brought me a message Gwanwyn had sent. She would arrive the next day with her nephew. I sent Aiden to the human world to request one more person join us.

By the time I got up in the morning—early, I might add thanks to more nightmares—the housekeeper, Moina, and Quinn were already hard at work getting everything ready for my guests, who would arrive shortly before lunch.

I went to train, finding Ronan in the ring with the new Summer guards.

"Shall we show them how it's done?" I asked, joining them.

"You are still a novice compared to all of them, my princess."

I grinned. "I can still throw you in the dirt. Maybe we can do hand-to-hand instead of swords today. You know, so I don't look like a complete newb in front of people who should respect me."

"We all respect you, Your Highness," Airleas said, a worried expression on her face.

I waved her off. "It was a joke, Airleas. You'll get used to it."

She looked confused, but backed away as Ronan and I squared off. We started fighting, because that's what it was. Neither of us bothered to pull punches, since neither of us landed any. The interesting thing about our bond, while training, I knew exactly what he was planning as soon as he did and vice versa. Our fight became an intricate dance of just missed punches and kicks. My heart was beating fast, partly from exertion, partly from exhilaration. It was *fun*. I'd always loved sparring—which was one reason I'd chosen to practice krav maga prior to starting my training with Ronan—but with him, now, it was almost better than sex.

His step faltered for a second when I had that thought and I broke out in laughter, doubling over. He took my distraction as an opportunity to grab me from behind.

"*Almost* better," I said, through my laughter.

"You still thought it," he murmured into my ear, sending a shiver through me.

I adjusted my stance, and he moved with me, knowing exactly what I was thinking. But I'd learned how to distract him. So I brought up an image in my mind of him as I remembered him last night, kissing my neck, pressing my hands into the mattress, making slow, languorous love to me as I completely went insane with need.

This time, when I adjusted my stance, he was too distracted to notice, and I flipped him over my shoulder, following him to the ground and pinning him.

"You win," he said, quietly. "But you realize two can play that game."

I got up and held out my hand to help him up. He took it and when he was standing, I leaned a little closer.

"I'm looking forward to it." I wanted to kiss him so bad.

He touched my hand. "You should probably go eat before Quinn drags you in to get ready for your guests."

I nodded, and we turned away at the same moment. Mada followed me back to the house while Ronan and Ansgar began the training session with the Summer guards.

"You know," Mada said conversationally once we were far enough away, "Ansgar and I don't practice together anymore." She paused. "Well. In front of people, anyway."

"Is that so?"

"It became a little too obvious to the other guards that we meant more to each other than we were telling people. Now, I would just fear what we would do if we forgot people were watching."

I snorted a laugh, then caught myself. "I don't know what you're talking about."

"Sure you don't. No clue." She'd been practicing sarcasm and was getting good at it. She nudged me with her shoulder. "You can fool people who don't already have an anam cara, and who don't regularly fight with them. But you can't fool me."

I scrubbed my hands over my face. "We haven't—I'm not—"

Mada grabbed my arm, pulling us both to a stop.

"Calynn. I kept my relationship with Ansgar a secret for fourteen years. You don't have to explain anything to me." She shrugged. "But I'm here if you want to talk."

"It's just…" I glanced back toward the practice ring where Ansgar and Ronan were leading people through a series of warm-ups. As soon as my gaze landed on him. Ronan turned toward me. His eyes found mine across the distance and I felt his concern, asking me if everything was all right. I tried to send him reassurance back, but I wasn't sure if I really managed it. "It's the idea that I could lose him." I rubbed my chest, trying to ease the panic already starting to claw its way from my heart up my throat.

"I know. It's terrifying." We started walking again. "In the Sidhe, you know death is just a renewal. But when it's your anam cara…" She shook her head. "Nothing can ease the fear of losing them."

"It's more than that, too. What if something happened to *me*? He'd be devastated. And I wouldn't be around to make him feel better."

She grinned at me. "Maybe you should start being more careful. A little less reckless?"

"Now you're being ridiculous."

She laughed as we went in through the back door.

"There you are!" Quinn said, rushing toward me. "We have to get you ready. Your guests will be here soon."

She dragged me upstairs and told me to bathe while she moved around the room, tidying things that really didn't need to be tidied. I rolled my eyes, and Mada smiled from her place by the door.

I did as I was told and was rewarded with a steaming cup of coffee when I emerged, freshly scrubbed. Quinn immediately got to work on my hair. The makeup they had in the Sidhe was more like paint than what you found in the human world. It was difficult to remove and easy to smear. Human makeup only reinforced my human-seeming appearance. As a result, we'd decided not to use any makeup unless I was going to a party.

She had me dress in a pair of black, flowy pants that almost looked like a skirt, a ruby-red blouse made by Evander's daughter Bidina, and my leather jacket. She had washed and shined my boots and given them back to me to put on.

"We really should get you a second pair," she lamented. "Maybe something with some embroidery."

"That's not a bad idea," I said. "Then you won't have to clean these every time I need to do something fancy."

"I didn't mean—I don't mind cleaning them."

"I know. You weren't thinking about how much work you do, but I do. You do so much for me, Quinn. If I can make your job easier, I want to."

She flushed and looked down, but I caught the pleased smile.

Then someone knocked, and Mada opened the door to admit Ronan. He opened his mouth to speak, then just stared at me with open appreciation.

"I look good then?" I asked, moving toward him.

"You always look good, my princess," he said with a bow, offering me his hand so he could escort me. "Today, you look radiant. Also, your guests have arrived."

I snorted and took his hand. Quinn tried to repress her smile and failed. Mada just gave me a knowing look and fell in behind us.

"Evander was seated in the solarium, my princess," Ronan said as we made our way down the stairs.

I nodded as Gwanwyn and Conroy came into view. She was as intimidating as ever, especially flanked by Conroy, huge and menacing with his display of scars.

"Gwanwyn, it's my pleasure to welcome you to my home," I said.

"You have pretty manners, child, but we can dispense with them now."

"Cool. Let's go to the solarium, where we'll be comfortable for our talk."

"Lunch will be ready shortly, Your Highness," Quinn said quietly beside me, her eyes cast down.

I hated she did that when other people were around, but I didn't say anything about it. Instead, I led my guests into the solarium where Evander waited for us.

"Gwanwyn, I'd like to introduce you to Evander. Have you guys met?"

The brownie stood when we came in and bowed to Gwanwyn.

"Briefly, Miss Calynn," he said. "Many years ago."

"Well," Gwanwyn said as she took a seat in one of the chairs. "This is already more interesting than I thought it would be. You met my nephew at your mother's revel."

I nodded to Conroy, who also took a seat.

When we were all settled, I said, "Conroy mentioned you had some information about the tinctures. And some theories as to why it works."

"Yes," she said. "As you know, it is a reconciliation tincture, meant to ease pressure and restore equilibrium. The base magic is the same for all three, a balancing charm combined with an alleviation charm and a consistency charm. After that, the recipe depends on the manufacturer." She set the three vials out on the table in front of us, two gold and one silver. "All three include extracts from lavender and peppermint. This one includes extract from olive leaves." She pointed to one of the gold tinctures. "These two include extracts from feverfew and lemon balm. But what makes this one most different from the others," she lifted the silver vial, "is that it was created with water magic, whereas these two were created with flora magic."

"The magic that was forced into the children, and the daoine sidhe with access to only one magic, had water magic inserted into the available space."

Conroy leaned forward, his eyes glittering with interest. "What do you mean, *access* to only one magic?"

Shit. I looked at Evander, then to Ronan who stood just inside the door of the solarium.

It's your choice, little changeling, he thought. *You've decided to trust them to help you with this. It's up to you whether you trust them with that as well.*

I took a deep breath. I shouldn't have trusted Barden, but other than him, everyone else who had come to me in good faith had been worthy of my trust. My instincts were telling me Gwanwyn and Conroy were here to help.

"The daoine sidhe who everyone thought had only one magic, actually still have both. The second is just hidden from them in one way or another. I've been able to help them find their latent magic and give them access to it. I've only helped one person in Summer so far, but I've helped many in Winter. The trouble is, because of these experiments, I can't give the affected people access to their magic. I have to remove the magic that was put there first. That's why I asked Evander to come." I turned to the brownie. "You helped put it there. Can you tell us what the procedure was? Maybe together we can think of a way to undo it."

CHAPTER 21

L unch was served. While we ate, Evander explained the overview of how the procedure worked. Like most fae with water magic, Anstice could look into a person's magic, then she would slide water magic into it. When Evander worked with her, he built the aqueducts.

"She needed someone with earth and water magic. And brownies' earth magic is some of the most careful and quiet of all earth magics. There are also not many of us who have water magic."

"So she probably doesn't have anyone helping her now," I said.

"It is possible she has found someone new to assist her," he said. "But it is unlikely. If she has, that person does not seem to have the control to create the works I created, as we noticed the children have none. It took me half a century to perfect the technique. And I burned all the notes regarding how I did it."

"Could you still do it?" I asked. "Without the notes."

He looked around the dining table, alarmed. "I—Perhaps. But I chose to leave that behind. I vowed never to touch another person's magic again."

I drummed my fingers on the table next to my plate. "If the water magic is already there, could you create something to ease the pain? I saw inside the children's magic. And inside Airleas'. Hers is little more than a persistent ache. The children have no structures to protect them from the pressure of the water. Could you do something that would help them until we can find a way to remove it entirely?"

"I might. I always created the works before Anstice added the water. It may not work for all the children since her water is already there."

We discussed it further and Evander said he'd try it after we finished eating lunch.

"In the meantime, I would like to hear more about how you give access to the latent magic," Conroy said, breaking into the conversation for the first time. "We now have an idea how to help the children, at least temporarily. But there are many who need help."

"You're right." I explained how the magic was too deep within the person and they needed my help to build a pathway to it. Once the path was laid, they could reach it and would have full access to it. Then I explained the bargain I'd made with everyone so far, but that it was a tiring process and so I had a schedule I'd been sticking to in order to pace myself.

"This path magic. It seems like the same principle as what Anstice is doing," Gwanwyn said.

"It does. But my magic isn't putting something there that shouldn't be. It's leading them to what's already there. Also, I go into the person's magic. I don't push something in from outside."

We continued to eat, and they asked me more questions. I answered them as best I could. We had just finished eating and were drinking coffee—the good stuff, not the crap they could find in the Sidhe—when Conroy leaned back in his chair and fixed me with an assessing glare.

"I would like to see this for myself. Evander will help the children if he can. But I would like to see you help someone with no latent magic."

"I don't usually do that for an audience. I have someone I'm supposed to help today, but I'd like to clear it with them before I make it public."

"Why?" Gwanwyn asked.

"How would you like it if your magic was laid out in front of everyone? It's private. What if it isn't as strong as you hoped it would be? What if it isn't there? It always is, and it's always plenty strong enough. But if you've lived your whole life without it, you have doubts. It's scary."

My guests returned to the solarium while I had Idelisa gather the children and Ainthe, one of three Summer guards who had never had their magic tampered with. The rest of them would have to wait until I figured out how to remove the aqueducts before I could help them. I asked if she would mind having an audience. She looked more scared than she really had reason to be, but she agreed.

We started with the children. Evander and I found the child who was the worst off—the one with the steady drip of water in a single spot within his magic, reminding me of Chinese water torture. I sat next to them as Evander held the child's hands.

"This may hurt initially," he said, "but my hope is it will make the rest hurt less overall."

The boy nodded.

With a subtle exertion of his magic, Evander pushed earth magic into the empty space, shaping it into a trough. The boy cried out, squeezing his eyes shut. I put my arm around him, trying to offer him comfort.

After a few minutes, Evander released a breath, sagging in his seat.

"There is nothing more I can do without causing more harm than good, I'm afraid. I created a basin to catch the water so it will no longer drip into his space. The water is invading the area I would have used to create the aqueduct. Without that, I cannot create a way for the water to flow out."

The boy slumped against me, asleep. But his breathing was easier than I'd seen it since I'd met him.

"How long do you think it'll be before the basin is filled?" I asked.

He shook his head. "It could be a few weeks, it could be a few days. At the rate the water is dripping, I am hopeful you will have a couple of weeks."

Evander couldn't help any more children today. He was exhausted as well so he left to rest, and I turned toward Ainthe.

She was shaking by the time I reached out my hands toward her. My guards were stationed on the outside of the solarium doors to ensure no one came in. The audience was small, consisting of only Gwanwyn, Conroy, and Ronan, who absolutely refused to leave me alone with anyone, even people I mostly trusted, while I did this.

I understood. I was pretty out of it afterward. Even if I was getting better and my recovery time was getting shorter, I was still very tired for at least ten minutes, enough that I wouldn't be able to defend myself from attack.

Ainthe and I sat facing each other.

"Are you ready?" I asked her.

She swallowed and stared at the hands I held out to her like I was about to burn her. "This won't hurt?"

I shook my head. "Not at all. If you're too nervous, we can wait, and I'll find someone else willing to do it in front of an audience."

"You won't tell what you find in there?" she whispered.

"I won't say anything." I motioned to the people surrounding us. "They won't know what's there, just that it *is* there. What we find will be between me and you."

She licked her lips and held out her hands to mine. I felt the sweat on her palms as our hands touched.

I nodded to her, and she nodded back, and we began the journey into her magic together.

Immediately, I understood why she had been so nervous.

"You're growing a life in here," I said, staring around the fire magic flickering and blazing around us, at the separate entity that grew but had yet to take shape. Right now, the life wasn't exactly what I would call a baby, but I couldn't think of what else to call it. I also had no idea how it had come to be here as it occurred to me, I didn't know how babies were created in the Sidhe.

"It's almost ready to come forth," she said. "I think during the Equinox."

I saw the connection from her to another. A connection I doubted she even understood was there. "You're in love with someone."

"Yes. She has a few days left on her fealty term. I told her you allow guards to have relationships and to come as soon as she could."

"Is she with my mother?"

"She is. She's a maid there. We didn't mean for this to happen."

I stared at the magic growing within her own magic in wonder. I could see little bits of the person who Ainthe loved in it. And I felt the love Ainthe already felt for this new life. Tears pricked behind my eyes. If any fell, the heat from her fire magic dried them immediately.

"Your baby is beautiful."

"You won't make me give him up?"

Just like that, the wonder turned to grief and horror. "Who would do that? No. Don't answer. Ainthe." I took both her hands in my own. "Your child is welcome. And I will make sure you and your child are cared for. You don't need to be afraid. Now, let's do what we came here to do."

Her latent magic was easy to find. It was a stark difference to her main magic, and it stood out clearly. I found my way down into it and shivered at the abrupt change in temperature from the heat of her fire to the frozen wasteland of her ice magic—a very rare Summer ability. I laid the path back toward her so she could find it and noted as I did that the baby was growing here as well. It didn't make logical sense that the baby was growing throughout her gifts. I was still thinking of pregnancy like a human. The baby wasn't a physical thing yet and wouldn't be until it was born. Or brought forth, as Ainthe had said. It was pure magic right now, built on what lived within Ainthe and what had been left behind when she and her lover had come together. As I returned to Ainthe, I realized the "birth" would occur in a similar way to how I bring forth an element from within my own magic, creating light or fire or earth from nothing but what lived within me.

When I reached Ainthe again, she was crying happy tears as she felt the gift that had been inaccessible to her and the baby that grew from it.

"Stay here as long as you need. You won't be disturbed." I moved out of her magic and opened my eyes in the solarium. Ronan stood next to me, a hand on my shoulder, offering me his strength.

I looked up at him and a wave of anxiety washed through me, but I pushed it away. I still needed to deal with my guests.

"So?" I said to the people who had been watching. They were leaning forward, watching intently.

"It is a miracle," Gwanwyn breathed. "I did not believe even as I felt it happen."

We left the solarium so Ainthe could come out of her magic in peace.

"I'm hoping to gather any who need my help. I already have someone in Winter working to let people know about what I can do. Secretly, of course."

"Of course," Gwanwyn said. "You would be persecuted should this become common knowledge. If not to force you to work this magic, then to prevent you from creating stronger fae the Queens would have less control over."

"You say that like I'm not already persecuted." We walked into the great hall where another sitting area had been set up and took our seats. I'd held on to Ronan's arm. It looked like he had simply been escorting me, but really, I wasn't sure I would have been able to make it on my own. My legs felt weak, and I gratefully sank into a chair.

"I can help you in this endeavour," Gwanwyn said.

"There'll be some who have time remaining on their fealty vows."

She nodded. "We will get as many as we are able. I do not foresee too much difficulty in convincing most liege lords to release them early from their vows if we begin with them."

"What of the mongrels?" Conroy asked. He said the word without malice, but I still gritted my teeth.

"I prefer not to use that term. The half-humans have access to all the magic they can, but they're still treated poorly. I've taken them in, and I'm happy to. My maid is one. My best friend is one. The most I can offer them is a safe place."

"What is your goal here?" Conroy asked. "Why do this?"

I took a moment before I answered, looking at them for a long time before finally turning toward Ronan, who went to the doors and locked them, ensuring we weren't disturbed.

"You came here today for a number of reasons, I'm sure," I began. "Curiosity at what I could do. Interest in what I'm doing. Desire to help those who need it. But I think one of the biggest reasons you came is because you recognize what I recognize. The Sidhe is out of balance. The magic is broken. It's important for the people who have been tampered with to be healed. It's important for the people who don't have full access to their magic to be brought to it. But that's a Band-aid on a much larger problem."

"I'm not certain they know what a Band-aid is, my princess," Ronan cut in.

"Fuck." I shook my head. "It's a short-term solution for a long-term problem."

Conroy leaned forward, his arms on his knees. "And the larger problem is difficult to speak of."

"Without resorting to treason, certainly," I said.

"You mean to solve this long-term problem?" Gwanwyn asked. "How?"

"To begin, I don't intend to buy people's loyalty for certain lengths of time. The year and a day of loyal service is appropriate compensation for what I'm giving in return."

Conroy snorted. "A year and a day is a pittance compared to what you offer. But if you think it is fair compensation, then so be it."

"I've heard that, but I find it fair. After the year and a day is up, they are free to leave. I had a few people who offered me fealty, and I accepted, but then rescinded it. Thirty years is too long to force someone to be in your service. If they want to leave, they should be able to leave."

"The thirty-year rule was brought in by the Queens," Gwanwyn said.

"Auntie?" Conroy asked.

"Was it a millennium ago? Perhaps a bit less?" She shook her head. "No matter the length of time. It was not always thus. The Queens decreed the initial fealty term should be thirty years. Barely a blink of time to those who lived thousands. You see, people had been swearing service, then leaving immediately because the people who they swore to were terrible lords. They sought to find people who would take care of them. Of course, most of these people were those who had access to only one magic or other lesser fae."

"It would have been less than a millennium, then," I said. "I know the first two people who were born with access to only their main magic. They're around a thousand years old."

"You have helped these two?" Gwanwyn asked.

"One of two. I'm still working on getting the second one to trust me."

"And do you know why it started?" she asked.

"Not exactly. But I have some theories. Do you know what makes a Queen?"

"They are born to it," Conroy said. "At least our Queen was."

I took a deep breath. I'd never said this out loud to anyone. Not even my friends. "A Queen, like the Ancient Mother, is not born. They're created. They're given a mantle of power. That's why, in Winter, Queran can't challenge Mab for her seat. Even if he killed her, the mantle of power wouldn't necessarily go to him. It has to go to the person who it's meant for."

"The Ancient Mother," Gwanwyn breathed. "You've met her."

"I have. And I must say, I'm not entirely fond of her. My theory is, the Queens have done something against the nature of the mantles, and it started a cycle of the magic breaking. Every time it breaks in one domain, a corresponding break must happen in the opposite. The magic is still trying to balance, but it's balancing in a downward spiral."

"If the spiral continues?" Gwanwyn asked.

"There will be no coming back. The brokenness must be eradicated completely. The mantles must be stripped from those who wear them and healed." I paused, swallowing back the fear and desperate anger threatening to engulf me. Ronan's steady presence offering me a sliver of calm. "And we're running out of time."

"How long?" Conroy asked, quietly.

"Weeks before the spiral is irreversible."

Gwanwyn looked at Conroy, who gave her a slight nod before she turned back to me. "We will stand with you."

CHAPTER 22

My guests remained for dinner, then returned to Lumina. I walked Evander to the circle of trees that included the Way back to the human world.

"How was it being back in the Sidhe?" I asked.

"Feeling the magic again is incomparable. Though the idea of Anstice finding me is somewhat concerning."

"I think you helped that boy. Hopefully, you can rest and help one of the others who is really struggling. I appreciate you coming."

We were at the Way and he looked up at me with a smile. "It is my job to do as the leader of the property requires. Such is the condition of my position there."

"I'm not the leader of the property. Ronan is."

"Is he now? I will see you again, Miss Calynn."

He turned and disappeared through the Way, back into the human world, leaving me alone to figure out what he meant.

I turned to find Ronan waiting for me.

"You have something you need to do?" I asked.

"I need to check on a few things."

"I'm going to go up to bed. I'll see you in a bit?"

He nodded and walked me back to the house, touching my hand before going off on whatever task he needed to do.

I went upstairs and began to pace. I kept thinking about Ainthe and her baby, how it grew within her magic instead of within her body. How had that happened? How were babies created among the fae? I'd never considered it before. I remembered Ronan saying you needed to have love between two people in order to have a baby, but I hadn't exactly asked what that meant.

Ronan and I had love between us. That was pretty obvious given the connection and our ability to communicate via thought. And we'd been having a lot of sex lately. Usually, once a night. Sometimes more. Sometimes less, if I was really tired. Did you even need to have sex to create a baby? Was it something else? You apparently didn't need a man and woman like humans since Ainthe was having a baby with another woman.

I paced for an hour—unable to stop moving, my body vibrating with tension—before Ronan finally arrived. I paused for a second, then kept moving.

He just stood at the door, closing it gently behind him, and watched me, waiting.

"I'm not ready to have a baby."

That wasn't how I had intended to start the conversation. He looked at me, alarmed.

"What are you talking about, little changeling?"

"Babies. They don't grow in my body. They grow in the magic. There's no birth control for that."

"Of course there isn't. Fae do not procreate quickly. We do not prevent children."

"How would I even know if I was pregnant or not?" I asked, hysteria edging the question.

"You're not."

"But how would I know?"

"We would feel it," he said. "The same way you can feel my magic and I can feel yours. We would know."

That made sense and my immediate panic eased, but the idea that I could become pregnant and not be able to prevent it was terrifying.

He came toward me, catching my shoulders between his hands, stopping my pacing.

"I should have told you before now, but I sometimes forget how little you know. The daoine sidhe don't reach child-bearing age until we are closer to three hundred years old."

"Is that certain? Or is that like our magic doesn't manifest until we turn thirty and mine manifested at least five months early?"

"I suppose it's possible you could break the rules that every fae believes is fact. You are pretty good at that. But it's very unlikely. Even if you could break the rules, I doubt I could. I'm also not yet three hundred years old." He gave me half a smile. "Unless you're sleeping with someone else?"

"Don't be stupid." I wrapped my arms around his waist and laid my head on his chest. His arms came around me and his hands swept up and down my back.

"It's not that I don't want to have a baby with you," I said, my heart pounding as I said words out loud I never thought I'd say to anyone. "It's just, with everything going on... I have too much to worry about. I want to be able to focus on any child we have. When we get to that point."

"I agree. You have a lot on your mind right now. But I don't think it's anything we need to worry about for a while. If something happens, we'll deal with it."

I nodded into his shirt. "I just got all in my head about it. I'd been still thinking of pregnancy like a human and for that, you just need sex. But you said before you need love, and... I love you."

There. I said it. The words were out there in the open. For real and not just in my mind.

Ronan lifted a hand to tilt my chin up to look at him.

"Say it again?"

I swallowed. But it was easier the second time. "I love you."

He leaned down, brushing his lips across mine in a soft kiss.

"One more time."

I bit back a smile. "Greedy?"

"Incredibly."

I didn't fight the smile anymore, my hands drifting up his chest to slide around his neck. "I love you, Ronan."

"I love you, too."

He said the words against my lips before crushing them beneath his. He lifted me and I wrapped my legs around his waist.

"I love kissing you from up here," I said as he took me to the bed. "It's such a nice angle."

"You're ridiculous," he said, our lips never parting more than a fraction of an inch.

"You're the ridiculous one. *You're* in love with *me*. I am a fucking handful."

He slowly lowered me onto the bed, letting my body slide along his. "That's true. But I have very strong hands."

Then he used them to pull my shirt over my head.

I went to work on his belts. First the sword belt, letting it clatter to the floor. Then the belt on his pants, opening it and undoing the buttons, sliding my hands inside to find his hard cock ready for me. I squeezed gently, watching his face as he closed his eyes and groaned. The connection between us allowed me to feel his racing desire, and it danced with mine, stoking higher.

I knelt on the bed, finding his lips with my own, nipping his bottom lip as I slipped buttons free on his shirt. His calloused hands slid along the skin of my back in a feather-light caress, up to my shoulders, then back down to my hips, pushing my pants down and gripping my ass.

I shoved his shirt off and tugged him onto the bed.

I knew his favorite thing was to hold me down and watch as I came apart in his hands. He loved when I said his name, knowing he was the one to bring me that pleasure. I even understood how I knew all this.

But tonight, I wanted my favorite thing. So once we got rid of our pants, I said, "Lie on your back."

He obliged immediately, stretching out on the bed. I climbed onto him, resting my hands on his chest, his erection resting against my ass. "I am going to do things to you now and you're going to lie here and take it."

His hands stroked up my thighs in a light caress, sending shivers through my body.

"How long?" he asked.

I leaned down, pressing a light kiss to his lips. "Until you can't. Hold on to that control, Ronan, until I make it snap. Hands under your head."

He did as he was told. His self-control was something to behold. He'd had over a hundred years to hone it, use it as a shield against all those who wanted to own him. He still always held on to that control, even in the bedroom. So I loved setting fire to it and watching it burn away.

"Little changeling, I can feel the direction of your thoughts."

His eyes closed as though he already needed to grapple with the hold on his self-control.

This was going to be fun.

I kissed him again, dragging my breasts along his chest, creating some delightful friction that tightened my nipples. I trailed my kisses along his jaw to the spot just under his ear, lingering for a moment before drifting down the column of his neck. I licked and bit and sucked on the skin, breathing in the scent of pine and ice that wrapped around me. All the while, I kept the mental replay of past sex going in my mind, moments of him driving into me, me sucking him down my throat.

"You realize, two can play that game," Ronan said, his voice husky.

"You told me not to move. You can't make me not think."

Then he inundated me with memories of his own. Him licking my pussy and nipples, his fingers tracing my body, learning my curves, me unravelling under his touch.

"Fuck," I said as the thoughts swamped me. The memories were so clear it was like they were happening now. "You keep those in HD or something?"

He chuckled. "Or something. I pay close attention to you, little changeling. Always."

I looked down at him, my heart hurting from how much I loved him, from how much I could feel he loved me. Tears sprang to my eyes from the force of it.

Bending back to my task with a new, single-minded determination, I licked and kissed my way down his body, letting my pussy graze over his cock as I slid down. My hands traced his body the same way his had traced mine in the memories he'd shown me. My fingers bumped over the hard ridges of muscle on his belly and through a smattering of coarse hairs around his thick erection, then down to the velvety skin of his balls.

As I stroked them, I thought about licking the underside of his dick a split second before I did it. He jerked in response, settling down quickly, the reins of his control clearly in hand, but not for long.

I thought of everything I was going to do right before I did it so he felt everything twice. My mouth lowered onto him, sucking his entire length into me until he hit the back of my throat. I swirled my tongue around him, delighting in the heat radiating from him.

But I could feel his thoughts just as easily as he could feel mine. And his were now consumed with the pleasure I was giving him, which added to my own until my pussy throbbed with need. His hands, his mouth, his dick. I didn't care. I just needed something of him touching me there.

What had started as a game of his self-control became a game of my own. I kept my mouth on his dick, my tongue stroking him while I sucked, my hands on his balls gently stroking, giving him every part of me I could while denying myself anything. When his cock swelled in my mouth, he said, "Calynn, I—"

He lost the ability to form words, but I understood.

It's up to you. But if you touch me, I'll stop what I'm doing. I sent him the thought without stopping my motions, bobbing my head up and down on his shaft.

He thought back, *If you stop, I'll just flip you over and fuck you senseless. I'm fine with either option.*

His desire had grown so much that I felt his control slipping. Pleasure raced through him, consuming us both. I felt my body tightening along with his. Then his control broke, and he grabbed me. Instead of flipping me over, he pulled me roughly up his body until my pussy aligned with his cock, then he pushed me onto it, gripping my hips so I couldn't move myself, pumping up into me. In a matter of seconds, I was trembling, my orgasm tingling along my spine, tightening my pussy around his cock. I moaned his name as he thrust into me one more time, shouting my name as he came right with me.

I collapsed onto his chest, but my pussy still ached. It needed more. I'd come so hard that my body shook, but it had barely had a single touch.

Ronan rolled us over without me saying a word, drawing my legs along his sides, then began moving within me.

"How are you still hard?" I asked. "That was one motherfucker of an orgasm."

"You still ache, so I still ache," he said, pressing his lips to my neck. "Your desire feeds mine just as mine feeds yours."

I moaned as he thrust hard into me, then slowed his pace again.

"Note to self," I said, my voice breathy. "Teasing Ronan will only lead to teasing myself." I met his lazy pace, not in a hurry yet. "Not that there's anything wrong with that," I amended. "Just need the warning."

He sat up, pulling me hard against him, lifting one of my legs to his shoulder to get a deeper angle. My eyes fluttered closed as I moaned again.

Then his fingers found my clit and began slow, easy circles around it.

"Fuck, Ronan. Yes. That's it."

This time, my orgasm started as a flash of heat that washed through me, but he didn't stop, his movements still slow and languid as though now we'd both come, the frenzy had died down. As he moved, it built up again in both of us. My body trembled as he moved faster and harder, sliding so deep inside me while still rubbing soft circles around my clit. I moved with him, meeting his thrusts as they ramped up until we crashed together over and over. His pleasure increased mine until it overwhelmed me. If I broke now, I would fly apart and never come back together.

"It's too much, Ronan," I breathed, shaking my head. "I can't. It's too much."

"Look at me," he growled.

My eyes shot open, latching onto his dark green gaze, anchoring me to the world and to him.

Then I shattered. I cried out, my eyes still locked on his. He leaned down and kissed me, muffling his own shout as he came right after me.

I held his face, keeping his lips on mine until the last of the aftershocks had worn off. I felt like a puddle of jelly, unable to move a muscle.

He gathered me against him, kissing the top of my head as he pulled blankets around us.

"I love you," I said again. Now that it was out there, I wanted to tell him over and over. As many times as he wanted to hear it.

"I love you, too, little changeling. I'm glad you finally got around to saying it."

"What do you mean?"

"I mean I've been waiting for weeks now. You sure took your time."

"Weeks? But I only just..." I cut myself off. I'd only just *realized* I was in love with him. But, by the time I figured it out, I'd known it had been there for a while. "Do you mean to tell me, I've been terrified to tell you I love you and all this time, you already knew?"

"Yes." I could hear the smile in his voice.

"Since when?"

"Since the moment it happened. Or at least from the moment you accepted it."

I raised up on my elbow to look down at him. "When?"

"The night before the first Winter Solstice challenge. You said you chose me. I felt it then."

So had I. And ever since then, I'd been able to feel his presence on a deeper level than before. I hadn't questioned it.

"You brought me coffee."

He quirked a brow in question.

"You said I grimaced whenever I drank the coffee from the Sidhe. So you brought me regular coffee from the human world. Just because you knew I wanted it. You see me. Better than anyone has ever seen me. You support me, even when you think I'm doing something insane, even

when you don't like it. You're steady when the ground feels like it's
shifting beneath me. You're calm when I'm crazy. You knew so long ago.
It shouldn't have taken me so long to get here."

He gave me a small smile and pulled my head down to kiss me. "You
got here. You just like to do things the hard way."

I laughed. "Always."

I settled against him, feeling calm.

A storm was coming to the Sidhe. A storm that I had to do something
about. I had a list of responsibilities a mile long. Dozens, if not hundreds
of people, were counting on me. Yet somehow, I felt at ease. Like maybe
everything was going to be okay.

CHAPTER 23

There are those scenes in movies where the actor or actress has a bad dream and sits up in bed with a gasp. I'd always thought it never happened in real life. Well, apparently it does when a daoine sidhe breaks a bargain with me in the middle of the night.

I sincerely woke up gasping, my heart pounding, sweat pouring down my spine.

"Calynn?" Ronan asked. "What's wrong?"

He was already reaching for his sword, still half asleep, ready to defend me against my enemies. I put my hand on his shoulder to stop him.

"Nothing that sword will solve," I said as I began to shudder.

My breath became ragged as my heart continued to race. That red, sticky magic I hated had started working without my say so. I could feel it pulling magic away from someone, dragging it into my own. It felt awful, like tar rolling across my skin.

"What's wrong?" Ronan asked again, sitting up.

"Barden's left us."

"But he bargained. He can't break that."

"He must have thought I hadn't fulfilled my end of the bargain, so he didn't have to fulfill his."

"But you did. His magic will be ripped from him. He'll lose it."

I nodded. "It's already started. I can feel it." I looked down at my hands. The nail beds were such a dark red, they looked almost black.

Spikey lines stole down my arms, past my elbows. Why was my magic doing this? Barden wasn't the only person to ever break a bargain or an oath. Was it simply because he broke the bargain he'd made with me? But that didn't make complete sense either. No one else had this tar-like magic. So what happened when a bargain was broken with someone else? After a moment, the thoughts fled as I started to feel sick. "I want to shower."

I left the bed, but we were in Summer and there was no shower here, only baths, and I didn't want to sit in it. I needed to wash this feeling away. I started getting dressed, and as soon as I did, Ronan did, too.

"What did he do?"

"I don't know. But he betrayed me. If I were to guess, I would assume he went to Titania."

"If he told her what you said you can do, the people who are coming here will be in danger."

I nodded as I finished pulling my boots on. "I'll have to send a message to Gwanwyn and Ryleigh. They'll need to be careful." I gasped again, doubling over in pain. Ronan was by my side in an instant, his hand hovering over me, unsure if he should touch me or not. When I could, I straightened. Then continued in a strained voice. "Once Titania knows, it's only a matter of time before Mab finds out."

"What does this mean going forward?"

"Nothing changes." I slipped into my leather jacket and started for the door. I needed to get into a shower. I needed to wash away the tar coating my skin before it made me sick. The magic was building. I worried I wouldn't be able to move fast enough. I left the room, moving quickly toward the Way back to the human world and glorious indoor plumbing not created by magic. Ronan would follow after he gave some direction to the guards standing sentinel around the house.

Quinn always followed me to whichever world I was in, but I left her to sleep. Ronan caught up to me as I stepped through the Way. We were alone, for which I was grateful when I bent over and started gagging.

This time, he didn't hesitate when he put his hand on me, offering me strength and comfort in the simple gesture.

"I told Aiden to go to Gwanwyn first," he said softly, rubbing my back. "Then he'll go to Winter and let Ryleigh know."

I kept heaving, but nothing came out. I dropped to my knees, trying to keep the sobs in.

"It feels awful," I said, my voice hoarse.

"Can I lift you?"

I nodded and suddenly my world shifted as he picked me up and carried me, bridal style, toward the house. We went right up the stairs and into the bathroom, where he set me on the lid of the toilet so he could turn on the water. I reached over and turned the cold water off and started removing my jacket. I'd put on entirely too many clothes, and it felt like they were pressing the sticky magic closer against my skin.

Fat, ugly tears streaked down my face. I hated crying, but I couldn't stop. The magic was thick and wrong and filled me up and stuck to me like oil. I managed to get my clothes off and get into the shower. Then I sobbed again. I don't know why I'd thought the hot water would work, but, of course, it didn't. The magic wasn't on my skin, it was inside me.

I continued to gag and sob as the water pounded on my body, hot and turning me pink, but it didn't stop the feeling of the red magic consuming me and getting worse. I scrubbed with soap and a loofa, but it did nothing to wash away the feeling of being coated in tar. Red lines spiked along my arms, across my torso, and down my legs. The magic ate away Barden's magic, pulling it from him into me where it didn't belong.

I didn't know what was happening to his body, but I was certain it was nothing good.

"What can I do?" Ronan asked.

I couldn't speak past the sobs and the heaving. I just shook my head. After another few moments, he kicked off his boots and climbed into the shower—fully clothed—reaching for me.

"Don't touch me," I screamed, flinching away, but he grabbed my shoulders tightly.

"Stop it," he said. "You're not going to hurt me." Then he pulled me into him.

I clung to him, gripping his wet shirt in my fingers, letting the hot water splash around us, soaking everything, but doing nothing. Waiting for my magic to finish consuming Barden's, feeling every single moment of it.

CHAPTER 24

I spent the day in bed in the human world. I didn't want to touch magic if I didn't have to. I didn't want to think about magic. But of course, I did. I thought about the children a lot. All the other people I had to help.

And I thought about what the Ancient Mother wanted me to do. I'd been ignoring my destiny as best I could for the past few weeks. Shoving it to the back of my mind, letting my subconscious mind stew about it, while I tried to do as much good as I could. Maybe, if I helped all the people who needed it, it would balance out the destruction I was going to cause later.

But after Barden's magic had been literally torn away, sucked into the red magic within me, consumed and destroyed, I began to wonder if there was any amount of good I could do.

By the time night rolled back around, and I was sure everyone was asleep, I got out of bed and dressed in black pants, a black shirt, and my black leather jacket and riding boots.

If I was going to make the good and bad balance, I'd have to work faster.

"Just what do you think you're doing?" Ronan asked from where he'd been laying with me.

"If you're coming, you better get up and get ready," I said.

"Exactly where are we going?" he asked as he pushed the blankets aside and found some black pants and a black shirt, changing into them.

"Anstice's lab. I need her notes on what she did to… everyone." I'd intended to say what she did to the children, but it was so much worse than that.

"Why now?" he asked as he finished strapping his sword belt back on.

"I figured we could go in the shadows. You said yourself I'd be safer going into and out of Lumina via the shadows than any other way. And the deepest part of night holds the most darkness."

"Let's go then." He sounded resigned.

"You're not going to argue?"

"You're going to do it either way. At least you told me and are letting me come with you. We're already better off than when you took the prisoners from the dungeons."

"I took Kai with me then," I said, slipping my hand into his and pulling him with me into the shadows.

The journey to the Ways was one I had taken many times before, so we were there in a matter of seconds. We went through to Summer then started toward Lumina, the trip taking only a few minutes.

"Do you even know where you're going?" Ronan asked as we passed through Lumina's gates.

"Of course I do. Gwanwyn told me the other day."

"So you've been planning this for a while, then."

"It was more of a back-up plan," I said. "For your sake, I'm trying to refrain from enacting my bad ideas until they're a last resort."

He snorted. "Sure."

We stopped in front of one of the large estates that stood next to the palace. It was on the far side of the river from my mother's home. I had to consider where I was going to enter from. Gwanwyn had said the lab was on the ground floor, with a separate entrance.

"If it's in her house and you've never been invited, you'll have no magic once you cross the threshold."

I nodded. In Winter, I'd received an invitation to every noble house, so it had never been an issue. But since most people in Summer were away, no one had invited me over. And I doubted Anstice would. Just because I wouldn't have access to magic, didn't mean I wouldn't be able to physically break in. Kai had done it once when I'd still lived in the human world. He hadn't been able to kill me since he'd not had access to his magic and I'd slept in the light. He still hadn't been able to exist without darkness and shadows back then.

"I'm hoping her lab, which is attached to her clinic, won't have the same magical threshold on it. Since it's kind of a business and not a home."

I found the entrance to the clinic, and it had a window on the door, so we remained in the shadows as we went through. However, inside, the door to the lab, which was handily labeled, had no such window.

"We'll need to step out of the shadows and open that door. I need to be able to see where I'm going for the shadows to take me there."

"It's a risk. There could be some kind of alarm set up."

"We'll have to take it. The notes are on the other side of that door. I know it." I brought us right to it and let the shadows fall away. I tried the door. It was locked, but I made quick work of picking the lock, a handy skill leftover from when I was a private investigator. "You take that side. I'll check here."

We split up, looking through every desk, drawer, and shelf we could find. As I searched, I noted things within the room. Jars filled with various concoctions and preserved... things. A small cauldron hung over an empty fireplace. A chair with straps on the arms and legs. My blood ran cold as I thought of all the people who had been strapped to that chair and had their magic messed with.

When I reached a desk at the back of the lab, I knew immediately I was in the right place. I'd find what I was looking for here. I didn't know why I knew, just that I did. But then, while I'd been working as a private investigator, this feeling had been pretty common. So I listened now and searched every inch of the desk. A few vials sat on the top, golden and silver, with stamps of two of the local apothecaries. Interestingly, she didn't have anything from the one in the village. I pocketed them, then searched through the drawers. From the top one, I lifted out a worn book.

I flipped it open to the first page and froze.

We must start again. So close to a cure, and my assistant burned the lab—and all notes on our process—to the ground. I pray he returns to the Sidhe so I can properly express my displeasure.

I read through a bit more, my heart pounding in my chest.

"Ronan, I think I found it."

He came over to me, reading over my shoulder.

"This looks promising, but does she include her new process?" he asked.

I flipped a few pages. After a few minutes of reading, I snapped the book closed. "She wrote about everything." I searched through the drawer some more, finding another book and some papers. I didn't bother to read these. I just took them. I took everything. In the next drawer down I found folders and pulled every one out, stacking all of it on top of her desk. Once I'd gathered every piece of information she had, I found a small crate with jars in it and upended it, sending the jars crashing to the ground, not caring a bit as they smashed.

I placed all the documents inside and called some fire.

"What are you doing?"

"Setting her back a bit," I said, lighting her desk on fire.

We returned to the clinic as the flames began to lick up the walls of the lab. I watched for a moment as the fire grew, consuming more and more of the space, finding its way to the chair and melting the straps before moving on. The nice thing about a city made from trees was that it was easy to create a bonfire.

I took Ronan's hand, intending to step into the shadows and start back to my house, when I felt something.

"Someone's here," I said, stopping and looking around the clinic. But I couldn't see anyone, only feel their magic. A familiar magic. "Gavyn?"

My mind raced through what to do. I could step into the shadows and get us out of there, but I didn't know enough about Gavyn's magic to know if he'd be able to follow us.

"You stupid girl," he said from everywhere and nowhere. "Did you think I would not know you returned to Lumina? I have been watching for you."

"I'll keep that in mind."

"You will not need to. You die this night."

I felt it the split second he stopped bending the light around him, making him invisible, and moved to stab me. That's the only thing that saved my life, because I flinched just before the dagger he held plunged into my back. I screamed and staggered, dropping the crate of notes and falling against a wall.

Before Gavyn's attack was even finished, Ronan's sword was out and flying toward the other man. Gavyn fell back, dodging the strikes, but only barely. I watched the fight in a daze as Gavyn tried to pull his own sword from its sheath, but Ronan advanced on him too fast to allow it.

I'd seen Ronan fight once before when we fought a dragon with Niall and a bunch of others. That time, I'd been busy fighting along-side him so hadn't been able to appreciate the sheer beauty of his sure and precise movements, honed after years of daily practice. In the training ring, he was amazing. When he was really fighting, he was magnificent. His arms were a blur, and I realized he had borrowed some of my air magic to allow himself to be faster, while also using his earth magic to keep him grounded. And he did it all soundlessly, keeping his emotions ruthlessly in check, just like he constantly told me I had to do while fighting.

He pushed Gavyn back toward the lab, now engulfed in flames, beginning to lick out into the clinic. Just before Ronan pushed him into the blaze, Gavyn pulled up his light magic again and disappeared.

Ronan stopped and took a quick step back, looking around the room. "Where did he go?" he asked.

"He's gone," I said, hoarsely. In an instant, Ronan was by my side, helping me upright again. "I guess he figured his job was done, anyway."

"His job is not done," Ronan said, a firm edge to his voice as he looked at my back. "The dagger is still there. We have to leave it."

"I know about stab wounds. Get the crate."

"Fuck the crate," he said harshly.

"I'm not leaving without those notes."

He stared at me for two full seconds, letting me feel his anger, frustration, and fear. I stared back with all the righteous stubbornness I could muster. He could have picked me up. He could have ignored me and gotten me out of the clinic. There wasn't anything I could do to stop him. Instead, he thrust his sword into my right hand, since the left wasn't working at all anyway, and grabbed the crate of notes. Then he wrapped his arm around my waist, and we moved into the shadows. I wasn't sure if I had done it or if he had used my darkness magic to do it himself.

"We should go to your mother's estate," he said as I took us out of Anstice's clinic and toward the palace and the gates on the far side of the city. "She's closer and can get Gwanwyn to you faster."

"No. I don't want anyone in Lumina to know I've been wounded. And I want those papers somewhere safe immediately. Evander healed my gunshot wound. He can heal my stab wound, too."

The good news was that I was far closer to help than I'd been the last time I'd been this wounded. When Kai shot me—before we became friends—I'd had an hour-long motorcycle ride before I could reach help. Today, I just had one fifteen-minute shadow jump. The bad news was that my magic stuttered out when we reached my Summer estate. Ronan and I fell out of the shadows, and I stumbled from his grasp, falling to my hands and knees with a yell.

"Fuck," Ronan said, dropping the crate and picking me up. A couple of guards rushed toward us. I thought I saw Airleas, but my vision was darkening. "The princess has been hurt. You, go through the Way and tell Evander we're coming. I'll continue bringing her." He turned to the other person. "And you, take this crate to the library. Ensure it is safe. No one touches it until the princess returns."

The first guard was already running through the Way as the second one picked up the crate and carried it back to my house.

"Thank you," I said as Ronan carefully lifted me into his arms and carried me toward the human world.

"Don't thank me. That crate nearly cost you your life. If I never see it again, it'll be too soon."

"You know, you're really hot when you're fighting."

He glanced down at me, an exasperated expression on his face. "You're going into shock."

"Almost certainly, but it's still true."

I leaned my head on his shoulder, closing my eyes as I concentrated on working through the pain throbbing in my shoulder and arm. Had the dagger gone all the way through? There was so much pain in my back, I wasn't sure if it was radiating from there to my front or if there was another wound on my chest. My jacket would need to be patched again. I wondered if Bidina would be able to fix it like she had last time.

"For fuck's sake, Calynn, your jacket will be fine."

Had I been speaking out loud? I hadn't intended to. I didn't think I even had the strength to speak anymore.

"You're not speaking out loud," Ronan said. "You're just telegraphing your thoughts to me as though you're shouting in my mind."

Oops. I didn't mean to do that.

He opened a door, and we stepped through. I opened my eyes to look around a cozy living room with a couch and a table, both of which had been shoved back against a wall, a few blankets laid out on the floor by a crackling fire. That was good since I was very cold. But also, this wasn't Ronan's house.

"This is Evander's house," Ronan said.

Then I saw him. He was setting out instruments from his regular black case. I appreciated that he always kept it stocked. He always took care of me when I did stupid shit and got myself hurt. Ronan set me down carefully on the blankets.

"She wants you to know she appreciates you keeping your medical supplies stocked and for taking care of her when she gets hurt," Ronan said.

He and Evander shared a long look I didn't quite understand. Then the brownie knelt next to me.

"Miss Calynn, I have a draught for you. It will put you to sleep while I remove the dagger and patch you up." He looked up at Ronan after he was finished talking.

That was fine. I trusted Evander. He wouldn't give me anything I shouldn't have.

"She trusts you," Ronan said.

Then Evander opened my mouth and poured the draught in. After only a couple seconds, I was asleep.

CHAPTER 25

At some point during the night, the drugged unconsciousness gave way to sleep, and the dreams found me again. Nightmares from my subconscious about my friends hurt or dying. Windows shattering and black holes sucking worlds away courtesy of the Ancient Mother and whatever entity wanted me to be cautious. It was a full night.

I woke terrified and in pain, heart pounding, fear clogging my throat so I couldn't breathe. I hated feeling scared.

I hadn't bled as much with the stab wound as I had with the gunshot wound, so I sat up and barely felt dizzy at all.

"What are you doing?" Arial asked from where she was curled on one of the chairs from the loft, a book in her hands. Someone must have brought the chair down for her.

"What are you doing here?" I asked, my voice cracking.

"Ronan called me. He said you'd been hurt, and he wanted someone to stay with you since he had to do his job. Apparently, he's very busy shoring up all your defenses."

"He would. One little stabbing and he freaks out."

The truth was, I was also freaking out. I'd instinctively known the next meeting with Gavyn would end badly. The third meeting with Kai had ended in me getting shot, and it seemed Gavyn and I were following the same pattern.

But I'd almost died last night.

I mean, I'd almost died when Kai had shot me. But back then, I didn't have all these people counting on me. My world had exactly one person in it: Arial. Well. Ronan, too, even if I hadn't admitted it to myself back then.

Now there was Quinn, Rhys, and Aiden. Ansgar and Mada. Cacey and Idelisa. Niall and I were finally on good ground. Dozens of people were counting on me. I had two estates to run. Maybe three, if you counted this one.

Then there was my destiny. I'd been putting it off because I wasn't sure I really wanted to do it. I certainly didn't want to kill the queens. But even though I didn't want to, I knew I would when it came time if I had no other options. However, if I died, I wouldn't be able to do anything. Which meant the Sidhe would remain unbalanced, and eventually it would be destroyed.

But mostly, there was Ronan. Now I had a clear mind—and didn't have a dagger sticking through my shoulder—I thought back to the moment I was stabbed and the absolute terror he'd felt at the thought of losing me. If I hadn't moved when Gavyn dropped his magic, his blade would have pierced my heart, and that would have been the end. Ronan had known it, too. He'd fought Gavyn back until it was safe again. Then he'd gotten me out of there and even brought back the notes because they'd been important to me.

And all I did was get stabbed.

I could have died last night, and the enormity of that thought was at the crux of my fear.

So I did what I usually did when I was scared and hurt. I covered all those feelings up with righteous anger. A little voice in my brain reminded me the last time I'd done this, I'd sent Ronan away to be tortured, but I ignored it.

I stood and found some clothes. Someone had changed me into one of the over-sized t-shirts I liked to wear to bed, which made me angrier for some reason. How dare someone look after me when I got hurt? How dare someone make me feel loved when I made a mistake?

Yes, it was irrational.

"What are you doing?" Arial asked.

I pulled on pants and a shirt. "I need to go. I'm so angry. I need to exercise."

"That's the dumbest thing I've ever heard you say. Can you even move your arm?"

I shrugged, looking around for my leather jacket only to remember I'd been stabbed. It wouldn't be here. Which just made me angrier.

"You're going to hurt yourself," Arial said, following me out of the room and downstairs.

"I'm already hurt," I said, stepping into my boots and lacing them up.

Quinn was in the kitchen, cooking, but I didn't say anything to her. I didn't want to talk to anyone. I didn't want to be nice. I wanted to hurt something. I wanted something to hurt as much as I was hurting, physically and emotionally.

I could have died last night.

The practice arena was full, as it usually was at this time of day, on all three properties. I knew Arial and Quinn had followed me out of the house, but I didn't spare them a glance as I climbed over the railing and stalked to the middle where people were going through a training sequence.

Everyone paused what they were doing and looked at me. I couldn't say what they saw, but everyone backed away except for Ronan, who met me head-on. Someone brought him two short swords. I didn't know where mine was at the moment since I hadn't brought it with me to search the lab. It could still be in Summer or Quinn might have brought it when she came over.

"You're going to fight me?" I asked him as he handed me one of the swords.

"In your present humor, I figured I would be the best choice."

I got into the proper stance, and we faced off. "You think I'm dangerous to the people here?"

"I think you could be," he said as we began. "So you would hold back." Our swords clashed, and I spun around him, looking for another opening. "You don't want to hold back, so do your worst, little changeling."

He almost never called me that nickname when other people were around, so I faltered a step and he took advantage, pushing me toward the edge of the ring. I knew people were watching us. I didn't care. I fought like my life depended on it.

"You don't think I'll hurt you?" I asked.

"You can't. I know every move you're going to make before you make it. Just like you know every one of mine."

He was right. We danced around each other, swords clashing together or missing entirely. My arm and shoulder throbbed. I wondered if I might tear my stitches. I should probably not be doing this.

"You need to remember to keep your guard up," Ronan said. "And when you're truly fighting, you need to keep your emotions in check."

It wasn't the first time he'd given me that admonishment while we trained. I took an opening, but he blocked me at the last second. We'd drawn quite a crowd by this time, no one else training. People sat on the railings or stood around watching as we fought.

"That's better," Ronan said after a bit.

Fifteen minutes later, my arm became too tired to hold the sword, so I dropped it and threw a weak punch at him instead. He dropped his sword as well and blocked my punch, twisting me around so my back was to his front. I bent and threw him over my shoulder. He landed on the ground with a thud, and I moved to pin him, but he rolled, getting to his feet in a fluid motion and turning back to face me.

I switched my motion as soon as he started to rise, so his turn was greeted with a kick. He caught my foot, spinning me again until I was trapped against him. I couldn't flip him this time since I was standing on one foot.

"Ready to stop, or do you want to keep going?" he asked, breathing as hard as I was.

I shifted, trying to get free and continue, but he just knocked my single foot out from under me, gripping me tighter so I didn't fall to the ground.

"You're exhausted. You should be able to get out of this hold. And you've torn your stitches. It's time to stop."

"I don't want to."

"You want to keep going until you pass out?" he asked.

One foot was still caught between us, but the other was back on the ground. I twisted my shoulders and kicked with the foot Ronan held. He'd known the move was coming and let me go before I could connect. As a result, I stumbled forward, catching myself and rolling back to my feet, turning toward him.

My body felt heavy, like I couldn't hold it up anymore. It begged me to stop, but the anger just kept building, raging into an inferno I couldn't seem to bank.

"What's making you so angry?" Ronan asked, still far calmer than he should have been.

"I could have died!" I shouted, clenching my hands into fists.

"I know that," he said. "I was there, Calynn. I watched you get stabbed. You know what that did to me."

I did. In the moment, I had felt all his emotions, even if I'd been too out of it to notice. While he'd pushed Gavyn back, he'd shut everything down, but underneath, he'd been screaming.

All my anger evaporated as though it hadn't been there at all. I practically ran to him, wrapping my arms around his waist, pressing my face into his chest. His arms came around me, holding me tightly while I shuddered.

"I'm sorry," I said, tears stinging my eyes. I couldn't let anyone see. "I'm sorry. I don't want you to hurt like that. But there's so much dangerous shit I still have to do. I don't want to hurt you. I don't want to die. I want to live for a thousand years with you."

A small chuckle rumbled through his chest. No one else would know he'd laughed, but I did.

"Three thousand, little changeling."

I looked up at him. "Forever."

He nodded, his emerald-green eyes burning into mine. "Forever."

I'd been hiding our relationship from everyone out of fear. But the fear that we would be separated trumped everything else. I wasn't scared if everyone knew anymore. I wasn't scared of how official this act would make everything. I pulled his head down and kissed him.

My hands curved around the back of his neck as he leaned into me, giving me everything I asked for and more. His tongue met mine in a sweet caress. Everything disappeared around us as I kissed him, my exhausted body pressed against his and he held me up, like he could hold me forever.

The kiss came to a slow, lazy end, then I heard the cheering. I thought I heard someone say, "It's about time."

My face heated. Ronan linked our fingers together as we left the arena. Ansgar smirked at us, clapping Ronan on the shoulder as we passed. Other people offered congratulations and smiles. It felt weird but also nice that everyone seemed happy for us. Of course, it was likely everyone had already known for a long time.

He led us away from the arena and toward a small house.

"Where are we going?" I asked.

"Evander needs to stitch you up again. And I figured you'd like to ask Bidina about your jacket."

"I'm a mess, aren't I?"

He glanced at me. "You are who you are, little changeling."

"And you love me, anyway?"

He pulled me to a stop, turning us toward each other. "No. I love you *because* of who you are. Do you doubt it?"

"I don't doubt you at all. But this morning when I woke up and realized how close I'd come to ruining everything, I doubted myself."

"I don't understand why. I'm not the only one who believes in you. Look around you. Everyone is here because of you."

I took a moment to do as he said and looked around the fields. They looked a little different from when I'd first arrived back in October. There was snow on the ground, for one thing, something that never occurred in the Vancouver area, but apparently always occurred here because of this land's proximity to the Sidhe. The biggest difference, though, was the people everywhere. And they all looked happy. The guards were obviously vigilant, but they also laughed and smiled. Conversation. Something I'd noticed a complete lack of in Queran's estate and even at my mother's.

Maybe I was doing something right after all.

CHAPTER 26

After I went to Evander's house and he clucked and tsked me while stitching me up again, I returned to the main house. Ronan had insisted I go eat and rest. I had a visit with Arial, a much more pleasant one now that I wasn't so angry. She congratulated me on getting my head out of my ass where Ronan was concerned. Quinn made us food and after we ate, Arial went home. As she was leaving, Killian arrived.

"Hello, Killian," I said as Quinn helped the dwarf remove his jacket. "What brings you here?"

"Ronan asked me to come check you over. He mentioned you have found yourself injured. Again."

"Don't sound so surprised," I said, my voice laced with sarcasm.

He laughed. "You are something of a constant, child. If I can expect anything in this life, it is that the sun will rise from the east, set in the west, and you will find yourself in trouble."

He made his way to the living room and sat across from me. He held out his hands, and I placed mine in them. After a moment, he nodded and said, "You will be fine. As I suspect we both knew."

"We did. But it was good of you to come. Ronan worries."

"It is like that when someone you love is hurt."

"How—" I'd only just made it public a few hours before.

Quinn brought Killian his tea and left us.

"Evander mentioned it. Before he rendered you unconscious, you were speaking to Ronan with thoughts. There is only one way that can be possible among the fae. And only the most connected anam cara can do so."

"Really? I thought it was pretty common. M—" I cut myself off. Maybe Mada and Ansgar didn't want people to know about their bond.

"It used to be. But the magic within the Sidhe is failing. You know this."

"I do."

"And that means *all* the magic. Anyway, Evander mentioned it to me only because he knew I would be checking the status of your magic. He wondered if it would make a difference."

"Does it?" I asked.

"Of course it does. But not for my purposes. You borrow of Ronan's magic when you have need of it. He borrows from yours."

"He did that when he fought Gavyn. He borrowed my air magic to make himself faster."

"It was likely unintentional."

"I don't mind. He can take everything if he needs it." I blinked, realizing what I'd just said. "I mean." I paused. But there was nothing I wanted to change about that statement. He could take everything.

The idea of someone else having access to as much magic as what lived inside me should have been terrifying. But I wouldn't have fallen in love with him if I didn't trust him. He wouldn't abuse the magic any more than I would.

"It's not a big deal that you know. I kind of made it official this morning. I was a little bit angry about the whole almost dying thing. Put a few things in perspective for me."

"It usually does."

I nodded in agreement. Then I looked toward the old dwarf to say something else, but the thought fled as I was suddenly distracted. I stared at his face for a long time, trying to figure out what I was seeing. His beard covered the lower half of his face and most of his chest, just as it had the last time I'd seen him. His nose was still crooked where it had been broken and not healed properly at least once in his long life. His dark hair fell around his ears and merged with his beard in coarse waves. But what drew my attention was the magic around his eyes. I was certain I hadn't noticed it before, but I'd also been using my magic a lot lately to see other magic.

"Killian, may I ask how you were blinded?"

He startled and turned his head in my direction. "What do you mean?"

"Not the circumstances around why. How? Did the Queen do something to your eyes?"

"No. She simply took my sight from me."

"I don't think she did. I think she put darkness in front of your eyes. And you can't see through it." I reached my hand toward his face to touch the magic. It felt cold, like ice. "I think I could remove it. Though I'd recommend doing it in a dark room, then slowly allowing more light in to allow your eyes to adjust over a few days. We could go to your home, and I could do it there."

He gave me a smile. "Child. You have just been stabbed. The knife certainly held magical properties, thus your magic must heal just as your body must. I am grateful you want to help me, but I am the least of your concerns at present."

"But you could see again."

"I have lived without my sight for many years now. If you are able to help me, I can wait a bit longer until you have less responsibility."

I laughed. "I don't know if that will ever be the case. But I will help you. After the Spring Equinox, I'll know better about when that will be."

"Good enough." He leaned back in his seat and drank more tea.

"I have to return to Summer," I said.

"You rush about a lot these days."

"I'm pretty sure I've always rushed about. I just have people in my life now who notice."

"It is good to have people in your life. Though I also understand how they can sometimes be...."

"Annoying?" I supplied.

"Overbearing?" he offered.

We sat together in companionable silence for a while, finishing our drinks. When I was done, I stood. "I appreciate your coming so quickly, Killian. It was good to speak with you again. Stay as long as you like here. I'll be leaving, but you don't have to."

He nodded, and I turned to leave but paused, realizing I had just given him permission to remain here even though it was technically Ronan's house.

"Something else on your mind?" Killian asked.

"Something Evander said to me. I said this property belonged to Ronan. He asked me if that was really true. Is it?"

Killian stood and reached for his shillelagh, a black walking stick with a lot of mean looking spikes going down the length of it. "The person who leads the exiled fae has always been the strongest of us. Before Ronan arrived, it was me. When he was exiled, the responsibility passed to him. Now, he is no longer the strongest person who has decided to make this place their home." He patted my arm. "Do not hesitate to call on me again if and when you need more assistance. I am happy to aid you in any small way I am able. Princess."

Then he turned and made his way to the front door, navigating the furniture as though he wasn't blind.

CHAPTER 27

Ronan kept to his word about refusing to look at the crate of notes again. He even refrained from coming into the Summer library since that's where I kept them. Over the next week, I poured over them, sorting through the ones that might be useful and the ones that certainly would not be.

I sent a note to Gwanwyn asking if she would come to my estate to look over the information with me. She sent a note back with her nephew saying she was feeling poorly, but Conroy would be able to help.

He'd also brought along the group of daoine sidhe with access to only one gift, as we'd discussed.

"Is this everyone?" I asked.

Conroy nodded. "Everyone who still had time remaining on their fealty terms. The rest can request to leave on their own. And they should all be granted that leave."

I considered the fact that, when Ronan had requested to leave Mab's service before I was born, she'd said no, then tortured him for six months. I couldn't do anything about liege lords breaking rules. I could only bring people to me who needed protection.

Ronan and Idelisa took the new people to get settled, while Conroy and I went to the library.

"Word is spreading quickly now about what you can do. I do not believe Lumina is a safe place for you anymore."

I huffed a laugh. "It was never a safe place for me. Why do you think Ronan insists I walk around with guards on pretty much every side of me?"

We got started combing through the information I'd thought would be useful.

"According to this, she started her research over almost immediately after Evander burned her last lab down," I said, pointing to a page in the notebook. "But she didn't start experimenting again for another ten years."

"So she's only been tampering with magic for five years this time."

I nodded and turned to another page. "And she only started with the children a couple months ago. With the daoine sidhe with one gift, she waits until their magic manifests. But with the children, she's been starting much earlier. I guess because she believes there's nothing there to break."

I clenched my hand into a fist to try to relax the anger coursing through me. But every time I thought of that poor kid with the water dripping into his magic, driving him slowly insane, I wanted to tear Anstice's heart out. I wanted to do to her what she'd done to him and see how she felt.

I took a breath and shook my hand out.

"Something I've been thinking, and I want your opinion," I said. "And maybe you can return to Lumina and ask your aunt her opinion, as well. I might also ask Anant in Winter."

Conroy turned to me. "What is it?"

"I have the ability to go into magic. And I have the ability to remove magic, bringing it into myself. What if I tried to do that? Would that solve the problem?"

I'd hesitated to offer this as a solution, thinking of how Barden's magic had filled me up—and a few weeks ago, a dragon's—but I'd thought of it in the quiet day after Barden's demise. In those cases, though, the red magic had consumed what was inside them and destroyed it. Their magic had been corrupted, Barden's when he'd broken his bargain and the dragon's so long ago, I didn't know what had happened. I hoped this situation would be different.

"My aunt and I have discussed this as an option. We wondered the same thing. You can certainly try it. Our fear is what it will do to you. Bringing that much magic into yourself will be a lot. We think you may need a place to release that magic again."

Considering what I had felt in those previous two cases, he was probably right. I drummed my fingers on the desk, considering. "I'll have to think about how I would do that. Even if it hurts, I need to be able to help them all."

***

Now the properties were all connected, I wanted to spend an equal amount of time at each of them, so I spent the next day in Winter. I sent Aiden to ask Anant if he would mind coming to visit me at his convenience, so when I heard that visitors approached, I assumed it was him. Instead, I was surprised to find Ryleigh entering the solarium, where I'd had coffee and tea and some food laid out.

They came in with a lovely woman in a pale green dress that exactly matched her skin tone. Ryleigh looked huge next to her, though I knew they were not that big. The woman was just that small. Ryleigh had brought more people, but the rest remained outside the solarium. I ordered refreshments for them to be served in the great hall, while Ryleigh and I discussed our business.

"How did you do?" I asked.

"All twelve," Ryleigh said, taking a seat. "And it was more difficult than I thought it would be. So I've changed my mind. This *is* a fair bargain."

The woman with Ryleigh didn't sit. She seemed to not know what to do, and her eyes cast around the room as though looking for an escape.

"You can sit, my love," Ryleigh said. "The princess is not our enemy."

"How can you be sure?" the woman whispered. "What bargain did you make for me, Ryleigh?"

"Sit, Breonna," they said. "I will explain."

When she finally sat—primly on the edge of her seat, as though ready to stand up at the slightest hint of danger—Ryleigh explained the terms of our deal. When it came to the part about her latent magic, she looked at me with a combination of eagerness and trepidation. A look I had become accustomed to by now.

Then she said, "And where will I stay while I wait for my turn and after? I cannot return to Glacia. Your parents and your brother—"

"You're welcome to stay here," I said. "Or my home in the human world. I suppose you could go to Summer, but I doubt you'd want to."

"Why are you being this nice?" she asked. "You don't know me. Or any of the people who are here. Why are you helping us?"

I sighed. I was starting to get tired of this question. "Because I can. And because it's the right thing to do."

"I don't know if I trust you," she said.

"I don't blame you. There haven't been many people in my position who have been deserving of trust. But I assure you, I mean you no harm. While you're here, you can talk to anyone you like about what I've already done. Get settled in. Decide if you trust me. Then, when you're ready, I'll add you to the schedule."

She regarded me for a long moment, then said, "Ryleigh trusts you. Ryleigh made the bargain. So I will trust Ryleigh's judgment. I will do whatever I must in order for us to be allowed to be together."

I gave her a nod before returning my attention to Ryleigh. "My sources tell me there were eighteen who still had time remaining on their contracts. You brought me twelve." Kai had brought me the information a few days ago.

"I did. I couldn't retrieve any from the Queen. She will let go of her pets when you pry them from her cold, dead hands."

"Ryleigh!" Breonna said, aghast.

"I'll take it back if it's untrue."

They stared at each other for a second before Breonna nodded slightly and Ryleigh continued.

"Deardriu was also difficult. She had three people. Two had terms with mere months remaining, so she relented when the right person asked."

"The right person was not you, I take it?"

Ryleigh grinned. "She and I are not compatible." The smile fell from Ryleigh's face. "Deardriu had one other who still had some years remaining. She would not part with him. Even though he would have made my number thirteen, I did try. She wouldn't negotiate with so much time remaining."

"I understand. But you managed to get the other twelve people. That's more than I could have done without your help."

Ryleigh fidgeted, their fingers unsettled in their lap. "I must admit, I fear for those who remain behind. Glacia is... altered."

Breonna nodded sadly. "Since around the time of the Winter Solstice."

I wondered why. What had happened to alter Glacia? Except to take the prisoners out of the Queen's dungeon, I hadn't been back there since the Challenges.

"Altered how?" I asked.

"People are more violent. They beat those who they believe inferior. The mongrels—" Ryleigh shot me a glance. "The half-humans have it the worst. I—"

They hesitated. Breonna reached over and took Ryleigh's hand, squeezing it slightly. "If you trust her with me, you can trust her with this."

"I hoped you would take some in. They were servants of my parents. I've known many of them my whole life. My parents see what is happening and agree it is not safe for them in Glacia at this time. Nor even for Bridget. You had already asked for the changelings, and I brought all I could. I brought the half-humans as well."

"I'll take in any who come to me for refuge. I'm already planning to build more housing. But I'll take in everyone if I have to."

"I must return to Glacia for some time," Ryleigh said. "While I'm there, perhaps I could tell the others who I meet about this place."

"I would appreciate it if you did."

"And perhaps I could come back here? When my business is concluded. My parents were blessed with my older brother and so had always intended to gift him with an estate of his own. They are nobles, but not so wealthy as to be able to gift two estates. As such, I have none of my own."

"You're always welcome here, Ryleigh. I won't turn anyone away who means no harm to me or my people."

It was my turn to hesitate. I wanted to trust Ryleigh. If Ryleigh came to my estate, I was certain I could keep them safe from what was going to happen, but what about their family? From what Ryleigh had said, and from my own brief visit to their home a couple months ago, though they weren't my allies exactly, they were good people, even if they had kept Ryleigh and Breonna apart.

How did I decide who to save and who not to save?

In the end, I decided to trust Ryleigh. They were my ally, the same way Gwanwyn and Conroy were. They'd been receptive to what I'd said so far, what I'd been doing. But how receptive would they be to outright treason?

They had trusted me with the most important person to them. I would trust them to know who else to spread my news to.

I lifted my cup of coffee to my lips. "There's a storm brewing in the Sidhe," I said before taking a small sip, not looking at my friend.

"I feel it on the horizon," Ryleigh responded, their gaze sharpening.

I set my cup down. "I'm afraid I don't know what places will be able to weather the storm. But I'm certain Glacia will not."

They nodded slightly. "Do you have a suggestion for safe harbor?"

"For now, the only place I know will be safe is here. But I'm also hoping to figure out more places."

"And you will truly take in anyone who asks?"

I nodded. "As long as they mean me and mine no harm. I won't turn anyone away who asks in good faith. Though I warn you, I will know if they don't. And I'll respond accordingly."

No one spoke for a long moment. I noticed Breonna had gone very pale. Ryleigh sat forward in their seat, their elbows braced on their knees, fingers steepled in front of their face. Finally, they nodded again. "I will see to it those who should know, do."

I walked Ryleigh to the front door. "I'll let you say goodbye. It was a pleasure to bargain with you, Ryleigh." I started to go to the great hall to speak with the new arrivals, but stopped at the door. "Just one more thing. Equinoxes are a good time for balance."

Ryleigh nodded their understanding. "I agree with you. Good luck, my friend."

CHAPTER 28

The next morning, I prepared to leave Winter when a messenger arrived to tell me someone was approaching my Winter estate. I finished gathering what I needed and went to meet my guest. Again, I hoped it would be Anant, but when I got downstairs, Cacey told me otherwise.

"The Queen approaches with a retinue of a dozen others."

"The Queen? As in Mab? What is she doing here?"

My mind played out a bunch of scenarios. That she had come to kill me was, of course, number one. But her and a dozen others didn't seem like enough considering we were on my land and surrounded by a few dozen guards, with more just in the human world, though she didn't necessarily know that. I wondered if she'd learned I was the one who stole the prisoners from her, though who could have told her was a mystery.

"I could not hazard a guess, my lady," Cacey said. "Where would you receive her?"

"Outside. I'm not inviting her into my home."

Cacey looked at me, startled for a moment. "That is not usually proper. Especially considering it is the Queen."

I shrugged. "Don't really care what's proper. I didn't ask her to come. I'm not inviting her past my threshold until I have no other choice."

He bowed his head and rushed off to get things set up.

I met the Queen in front of my house, flanked by Ronan on one side and Andras on the other. Mada and Ansgar stood near as well. Twelve other guards stood at various points around me. I even had two fucking wyverns, dragons who stood on two legs instead of four, watching my back from near the doors, one young scarlet wyvern named Derecho, and a mature gold one called Cyclone. Niall had named them both.

Mab came toward me with all the fanfare I expected of her, twelve people following behind her, wind blowing her hair and dress around in a show of authority on an otherwise windless day. It was all a bit pretentious if you asked me, but she was a queen.

"What brings you here, Aunt Mab?" I asked, sounding as bored as I could, my arms crossed over my chest.

"Will you not invite me inside, niece mine?"

"No."

We stared at each other for a long moment, her gaze hard. I didn't flinch.

Eventually, she said, "I heard a rumor. I came to see the veracity of it." She turned her attention from me to Ronan, her gaze sharpening, and I knew the moment she felt that he had full control of his magic. Lust filled her features as she took him in, but I wasn't sure if it was lust for him or for his magic.

I set my teeth together.

"So it's true. You have found the magic that has been lost to us."

I had figured she'd hear about what I could do, but I hadn't expected her to come to me to find out if it was true. I thought about denying it. I thought about telling her to get the fuck off my property, especially for the greedy way she looked at Ronan. But she was still the Queen of Winter, and I was technically her subject, since I owned land in her domain. And it was still too soon to take her off her throne. I was stuck between lying outright—which she would absolutely know given Ronan was standing right there proving the lie—and telling the truth.

"I have."

She came closer, still staring at Ronan, and when she reached one hand up to touch him, I lost it. My sword was in my hand before I realized I had even drawn it, the tip touching her neck, which caused all her guards to draw, which caused all my guards to draw. There was a lot of sharp metal being pointed around. Even the wyverns had taken up attack stances, their barbed tails poised to stab anyone they thought a threat.

What no one noticed, not even me for a moment, was I'd also drawn on that red, sticky magic and this time, I was willing to use it.

"You do not touch him," I snarled. "He belongs to me."

Her gaze flicked from Ronan to me, eyes glittering with the knowledge I'd just given her. She already knew I cared enough about him to rescue him from her dungeon. Her threat hung in the air between us. *You must be careful with your toys. Because next time, I* will *break him. If only because I now know how important he is to you.* Now I'd just revealed he'd become even more important.

What would she do with that knowledge? Today, she simply took a step back, and I lowered my sword. The tension dropped about ten degrees, but no one else put their swords away.

I also let the magic go, though the feeling of it lingered on my fingers. I knew, if I looked down, my fingernails would be stained red. I struggled not to wipe my hand on my pants since I didn't want to appear nervous and it wouldn't help, anyway.

"I mean you no harm this day, niece mine. Send away your people so we can talk freely."

Since I knew she told the truth—and through our bond, so did Ronan—he nodded to Andras and Mada and my guards and the two wyverns fell back. They didn't go far, but far enough they couldn't hear.

Linden, the man I'd fought in Winter when I'd brought the chalice children here, took the Queen's guards away. Then it was just me, Ronan, and Mab.

"My marshal will remain," I said. "We can speak freely in front of him."

"You wish to have a guard remain while I do not?"

It was more his wish than mine, but I didn't say that to Mab. "If you have a guard or advisor you trust enough to stay and overhear our conversation, you're welcome to have one."

She said nothing, but all her retinue remained gone.

"Well then," I said, motioning toward her and crossing my arms again. "You came here to talk. So talk."

"How do you do this magic?" she snapped.

"I don't have to tell you anything." I kept my voice calm and unconcerned, noting how my demeanor seemed to make her more angry.

"You are my subject. You must tell me."

"Or else what? If you take my lands, I'll no longer be your subject. So what, exactly, are you going to do if I don't tell you?"

She took a step toward me. "You push too far. What is your goal? To take my throne? I would like to see you try."

I tilted my head to the side. "No, Auntie. You wouldn't."

"You presume...."

Everything suddenly got darker, the air a little thinner. I easily countered her magic with my own, delighting for just a moment in the expression of shock that crossed her face before she controlled it.

"You came here, uninvited, to my home," I said, uncrossing my arms and setting one hand on the hilt of my sword. "You ask me to tell you my secret. Well, I don't have to tell you anything. Unless you would like to bargain with me for the information. Except you have nothing I want."

"Not even the remaining daoine sidhe who could use your help?"

That stopped me. I wasn't certain we would be able to get them all. I would give her the truth if it meant I could save more people. At this point, she already knew I could do it. It didn't really matter if she learned *how* I did it.

"I might consider bargaining for them. How many do you have?"

"A fair few."

I smiled. "If my spies are correct, you have five."

I could tell she was pissed. She wanted me backed into a corner, but I kept moving into the open. She couldn't pin me down.

"Fine. I have five. You have managed to steal all the rest. In fact, another reason I came here today was to ensure you have not overburdened yourself with fealty terms. I could take a few off your hands if you've already reached the maximum number."

Her eyes strayed to Ronan again, who didn't flinch.

"I haven't."

"You do not know what the number is. How can you be certain?"

"I have no fealty terms at all." I gestured to Ronan and my guards still standing nearby in case they needed to rush to my defence. "Everyone is here because they want to be. Some have bargains with me that require loyalty, but only for a short time. Also, you don't have all the rest. Deardriu has one more she's holding on to. So, here's the bargain. You give me the five you have and get me the one from Deardriu. All arrive here unharmed in any way. When you've done that, I will tell you how I can do what I do."

"That is too high a cost for one piece of information. I need more for all six. Especially Deardriu's one."

"What more information did you have in mind?"

She lifted her chin, looking down at me imperiously. "You will tell me how you can do what you can do. And you will tell me what you have done with my Dark."

And for the first time, I saw behind the facade she showed everyone. If you didn't know Kai was her son, you would have missed it entirely, especially with that look she was feigning. But I knew, and I saw the instant of worry for her child. In that moment, I realized she was more than just the mad Queen of the Winter fae. She was also a mother who didn't know what had happened to her son.

"Bring me all six," I said, "free of their fealty obligations, unharmed. I'll tell you what I can about him."

"I will return this evening."

I watched her leave and when she and all her guards had left the property, followed in the air by Derecho to ensure no one doubled back, Ronan said, "Should you tell her what happened to him? I thought you wanted to wait until he was ready."

"I said I'd tell her what I *can*. I'll talk to him about it. If he says I can't tell her anything, then that'll be the truth. I'm sure he and I can figure out something. But he's her son, Ronan. She should know if he's alive or not."

CHAPTER 29

A nant arrived while I waited for the Queen to return. Like Ryleigh, he brought people with him, all half-humans he didn't feel would be safe in Glacia any longer. With regards to the children, he agreed with my assessment that I could bring the magic into myself as long as I had somewhere to release it after. Now, I just needed to figure out where that would be.

When I offered him the guest room for the night, he refused, saying he was retiring to his estate by the Winter sea.

"I'm not sure how safe the Sidhe will be after the Spring Equinox," I told him.

He sent me a sharp look. After a moment, he sighed. "I understand, child. But that is where I belong. I should be with my people. We cannot bring everyone here. I will, however, take your warning to heart and bring the rest of my staff from Glacia to my estate."

I scrubbed my hands over my face. "I know everyone can't come here. I just don't know what else to do."

He patted my knee. "Your magic has a similar quality to it that the Queen has. Your magic calls people to you, urges them to want to serve you. Just as Mab's magic does."

"I'm not sure how much I like being compared to her," I said haltingly.

"Ah, but there is quite a difference between you as well. Your magic draws them to you. But it is your *humanity* that makes them want to stay. The way you care for them. The way you treat them. Your desire to see them safe. I pray to the Sidhe you never lose that humanity, Miss Calynn. For if you do, I fear for the fate of the Sidhe."

After that dire warning, I walked him to his carriage. Ronan met us outside to see his uncle off. He moved toward me, then his step faltered as he looked between me and his uncle, unsure.

"You going to come over here?" I asked.

"It's one thing among your people. But my uncle is one of the highest nobles of the court."

I rolled my eyes as I stalked to him, grabbing his shirt in my fists. His hands settled on my hips, almost hesitantly. "I'm done hiding, Ronan. Now kiss me in front of your uncle, so he knows where we stand."

He dipped his head, a smile tilting up the corners of his lips. "As you wish, my princess." Then he pressed a light kiss to my lips.

I turned back to see Anant watching. "Anything to say, old man?"

He shook his head, a small smile on his face. "Nothing at all, Your Highness. Nephew. You have become consort to the Princess then?"

"No. I am still her marshal."

"Wait," I said, looking between the two men. "Do you want to be my consort? Can you be my consort *and* my marshal? Because if I tried to make anyone else marshal, I feel like you'd just micromanage them to death."

Anant snorted.

"I am happy with whatever role you give me," Ronan said. "Especially now you've started telling people about us."

We said our goodbyes to Anant, and when he was gone, I went back to my library, looking over the map of the ranch in the human world. An idea had floated into my mind, barely more than a wisp of smoke I couldn't quite grasp.

As I considered the elusive thought, I felt a shift in the magic and Kai stepped out of the shadows.

"Cousin," he said, settling into one of the chairs across from me. "You wished to speak with me."

"I did." I set the papers down with a sigh and looked up at my cousin. He tilted his head to one side. "You have had a visit from Queen Mab."

"How did you know?"

"I always know where my mother has been."

"I made a bargain with her. She wants to know how I can help people access their latent magic. She also wants to know what happened to you. I told her I'd tell her in exchange for the five remaining daoine sidhe she has who have sworn loyalty to her and the one Deardriu has. Before I tell her anything, I want to know what exactly you feel comfortable with me saying."

He sat in silence for a long time.

I continued. "I could tell her only that we'd met, and you decided against killing me and left. It's true. It would be enough to resolve the bargain."

"No. She has waited a long time to hear from me. And she knows what you can do. You should tell her you helped me and that I live."

"I know you've had some problems with her. I know she's done some unforgivable things. But, you should know, I saw a look of worry on her for just a moment. She's worried about her son."

He gave me another of his brief smiles. "What is it the humans say about a pot and a kettle?"

I laughed. "You have a point there. But I'm working on my relationship with my mother."

"Not with your father."

The smile fell from my lips. "No. Not with my father. He knows where I am if he wants to have a relationship. He's always known and has never tried."

We sat in silence together for a time. I wondered if he was thinking of his own relationship with his parent like I was thinking of mine.

"I would like to be there when you meet her," he said.

"Of course. She said she's coming back tonight. Are you going to speak to her?"

"I do not know."

I nodded, and Kai stood up and disappeared into the shadows of the room. I was left alone again with my maps and books and accounts and thoughts of parents who failed their children.

***

Mab was as good as her word. She returned that evening with none of the retinue that had come with her that morning, but with all six of the people I'd not been able to get, including the one from Deardriu. With these six people, I had all the Winter daoine sidhe who only had access to one of their gifts. I felt an immense weight lift off my shoulders as my guards led them away.

I'd decided to keep Mab outside, but had my housekeeper set up a sitting area by my front door. Mab looked at the chairs with a raised eyebrow but didn't comment, simply taking a seat while I took the other.

"Well," she said. "I have upheld my end of the bargain. Tell me what I want to know."

Ronan took up his spot behind my seat. Somewhere nearby, Kai stood, hidden in the shadows. Since his magic was so much stronger than Mab's or mine, neither of us would be able to notice him if he didn't want us to. As it was, I knew he was somewhere, but couldn't have found him if I'd tried.

I steepled my fingers in front of my face, elbows propped on the arms of my chair. "There's a special magic in me. It's not an elemental magic at all. Or maybe it's all of them together. It helps me find things that are missing. When I lived in the human world, I used it as a private investigator to find the answers I was looking for. But I can also use it to heal magic and to create pathways to the latent magic that's too deep within a person to be able to access."

"So it is the deficiency of the person, not the deficiency of the Sidhe, creating this problem," she said, relaxing into her seat.

"I think you're deliberately mishearing me. The deficiency of the Sidhe is what's causing the deficiency in the people."

She waved her hand as though this wasn't something she was interested in. And it probably wasn't. She'd learned what she wanted to learn, even if it wasn't exactly true. "Next. Where is my Dark? What did you do with him?"

I didn't answer right away, making her wait.

"I helped him," I said. "Just as I helped Ronan."

She went completely still. "I wondered. So why did he not return to me?"

"I don't have the answer to that question." And that was the complete truth. I'd never asked Kai why he hadn't gone back to Mab after I'd helped him, and he'd never offered me the answer. "Perhaps you should ask him that yourself when you see him next."

"But I have not seen him!" she said, slamming her hands on the arms of her chair, a blast of air blowing my hair back. "He has not returned since he was sent to kill you."

"I gave you the information you asked for. As much of it as I'm able to give. The rest is for you to figure out on your own."

She stood. "This is not the end, child. I will find out what you are holding over him to ensure he does not return to me. You do not know the connection we have. He is loyal to me and to me alone."

I sighed and stood as well. "I'm not holding anything over him to prevent him from returning to you. Maybe he just needs a little space from the one person in all the worlds who was supposed to protect him and instead is the one person who hurt him. More than once." I shook my head.

She slapped me. It came out of nowhere and stung more than I could have imagined. I would probably have a handprint on my face for the next week. I wondered absently if she had used any magic to make it sting more. Ronan was already moving, his sword coming up to defend me. I stopped him with a motion of my hand.

"It's fine," I said. "She's angry. But she also understands that she is a *guest* here. As such, she will abide by the rules of hospitality. Our business is concluded, Mab. You were just leaving, right?"

She seethed. The anger behind her eyes would have burned me if there was any magic in it. "Do not think this is the end, child," she repeated.

"I don't."

She turned on a heel and stalked away to the carriage that had brought her. When she was gone, Kai appeared from the shadows.

"She should not have hit you for telling the truth," he said by way of apologizing on her behalf.

I waved away the concern from both him and Ronan. "It's fine."

"I do not think I will return to visit her," Kai said. "I do not know what I would say that she would hear."

I nodded my understanding. "You're always welcome with me. We're family, Kai. I kind of like some of my family. It's nice to have you around."

"I find I enjoy having you around as well," he agreed. "Even when you are being stupid."

"I haven't done anything stupid in a while."

Ronan cleared his throat.

"In a couple days," I amended.

A brief smile split Kai's face. "Yet you have a stab wound still healing next to the bullet wound I gave you."

"I said a couple days. Fuck. One little stab wound, and everyone makes a fuss."

Kai chuckled as he faded into the shadows once again and the magic took him away.

"You should sleep, little changeling."

Ronan came up behind me and I leaned into him. Today had been a win, but I still felt exhausted.

"There's still so much to do," I said as his arms came around me.

"You can do more tomorrow. Tonight, you must rest or else you won't be able to do anything."

I started inside, taking Ronan's hand and pulling him with me. "I don't know. I'm pretty good at running on coffee."

CHAPTER 30

The next day, I went to the human world again. I had things I needed to check on, people I needed to talk to, and lunch with Arial. After our visit, I went out to the training fields to get some exercise. While I was running through a routine with Ansgar, he stopped suddenly and I turned to see what he was looking at, surprised to find Cacey waiting to speak with me.

My heart stopped for just a second as I worried what could have brought him from Winter. Mab couldn't have come to visit again, could she?

Ansgar and I made our way to where Cacey waited for us. When we arrived at the fence, Cacey said, "My lady. Your father awaits you at your home in Winter."

I exchanged a look with Ansgar who shrugged.

My father awaited me. He was pulling a power play, and I had to turn it around on him. He expected me to drop what I was doing and go to him, so I would make him come to me instead.

"If he wants to talk to me, he can come here. I'm not changing my plans to suit his. Especially with no warning. If he doesn't want to come to the human world, he can wait until I return to Winter in a couple days."

I caught Ansgar's smile from the corner of my eye. Cacey didn't allow the smile to reach his lips, but I knew he approved of my decision.

"Very good, my lady. I will tell him so. And if he should come here, where shall I lead him?"

"I'm training with my people today, Cacey. You can lead him to the practice field."

By the time Queran arrived, escorted by Cacey, Ronan and Mada had joined me and Ansgar. The practice field was full of people training, but the four of us were waiting at one end while everyone else was at the other. A few people looked up as Queran approached, but no one stopped what they were doing. I was practicing with Mada while Ronan and Ansgar watched, and I didn't stop when my father entered the practice field and stood next to Ronan. I didn't acknowledge him until my set was done.

Mada and I were both breathing hard, and she grinned at me before giving me a short bow—which she normally wouldn't—then winked and moved off to give her weapon to one of the people who now took care of the swords. I sheathed mine, then, finally, turned toward Queran.

He looked pretty much the same as when I'd last seen him. His black hair was slicked back in an elegant style, as it usually was. His clothes fit his slim frame impeccably. He looked every inch the prince he was.

He hadn't once thought to visit me in the two months I'd stayed out of Glacia. I couldn't imagine he was here for a friendly chat, and the look in his eyes, usually so happy to see me except when I was causing him trouble, told me I was right.

I felt a twinge of disappointment. This man was supposed to be my father. Granted, he'd never really practiced that role. My two siblings had been killed within the first year of their lives. Then I'd been changed, and my parents had raised Nialas instead. But because she was human, and a constant reminder that their child couldn't live with them, they'd both treated her poorly.

I shoved the disappointment away. It wouldn't help anything, anyway.

"Queran," I said. "What brings you here?"

"I heard a rumor," he said, without preamble.

I figured that was why he'd come. He'd had enough time to examine a few of the people he'd known, so by now, he should have already been able to ascertain for himself that the rumor was true.

"I've been hearing that sentence a lot lately," I said. "Would you care to spar?"

I motioned to the swords behind me.

"I do not spar," he said.

"I guessed not."

"What is that supposed to mean?"

"I just figure you've delegated your safety to others. There's no reason for you to have to train yourself."

He stared at me for a long moment. "I am not sure if that was supposed to be a compliment or an insult."

I just smiled. "So you heard a rumor. What might that have been?"

"There have been a few, as a matter of fact. First, you have stolen all the daoine sidhe who only have one magic and many of the mongrels as well."

"I haven't stolen anyone. They came to me of their own free will. I also dislike the term mongrel and would appreciate it if you don't use it while on my lands."

He sneered and looked at my guards. We all looked back at him in stony silence and the sneer slipped. Then he blinked and moved on. "I have also heard you have been giving magic to those daoine sidhe who have but one."

"That's not exactly accurate. I've been giving people *access* to magic they already had."

He looked again at Ronan, Mada, and Ansgar, who stood next to me.

"Any other rumors you wanna talk about?" I asked, resting my hand on the hilt of my sword in its sheath at my side.

"Some people have expressed the idea that you mean to challenge the Queen for her throne."

"Hm. I wonder where that one came from." I looked toward Ronan.

"I would guess it to be a logical next step, my princess, after your accomplishment of the previous two things your father has mentioned. Added together with your performance in the Winter Solstice challenges. You know how stories can grow."

I arched a brow at his use of "my princess." He'd almost completely stopped using it except when specifically trying to tease me. I'd told him I was done hiding. Anant knew we were together. But this was my father, who had actively tried to keep Ronan away from me my entire life.

I pursed my lips. "I see."

"So it is not true then?" Queran asked.

"I didn't say that."

"So it *is* true?"

"I didn't say that, either."

"If it is true, I would know, daughter. You cannot believe yourself capable of being Queen of the Winter Sidhe. Someone older, with more experience, must be called upon to lead."

"Someone like you?" I asked.

He straightened, lifting his chin. "I am most qualified, you must admit. I have stood at my sister's side for these many years. I can take the throne and the crown and lead our people to a better future."

"Why not someone else, then?" I asked, curiously. "Deardriu, perhaps, or Sir Anant is older than even Mab. Why not him?"

"They do not have what it takes to lead the whole of the Winter Sidhe. You have no idea what is involved."

"But you do."

"I do, yes. And if you intend to stand against my sister, you must also intend to stand against your mother's sister. Your mother would be an amazing queen."

I raised my eyebrows at him. "So you can rule both the Winter *and* the Summer Sidhe?" I tapped my fingers against the hilt of my sword, considering exactly what I wanted to say next. "I will never get the crown for you, Queran. You don't understand the magic. You will never be king of the Winter Sidhe." I said it without malice or uncertainty. Even if I failed, the mantle of power would never go to him. I didn't have any say in that decision.

His previously calm demeanor disappeared, and he bared his teeth. "You dare tell me I do not understand the magic? You are but a child. And a child who has only known of the Sidhe for the last few months. How could you presume to know more than I?"

"You want to throw in my face that I haven't lived in the Sidhe? Do I need to remind you whose fault that is? That aside, do you know how to give the daoine sidhe access to their missing magic? Do you understand the anam cara bonds? Do you know how the Queens are chosen? No? Okay. Here's an easy one: do you know how to command loyalty for loyalty's sake from your people? These are things I've learned in the last few months you haven't learned in a couple thousand years. If you can't learn those things, you don't deserve a crown. I may not be the best person to lead *our* people, but I'm a better choice than you."

"Your people are not loyal to you for loyalty's sake," he said, derisively. "You have their pledge of fealty, just as I do."

"I don't, actually. I rescinded the pledges of fealty I accepted. I have bargains with most of the people I've helped, but only for a single year of service. Many, including the three here, are under no obligation to stay with me whatsoever."

I could feel the magic rolling off him. He wanted to push out with it, swamp me with molten heat, but he'd met my own magic before and failed. That had been in private, with only Niall as a witness. Now, we had an audience. And it was a larger audience than just Ronan, Mada, and Ansgar. People who had been training on the far side of the practice field had stopped and were looking over at us.

Then his magic stuttered.

"What do you mean you understand the anam cara bond? And the way queens are chosen?"

I shrugged. "I learned. The queen thing I learned when I went to seek my destiny from the Ancient Mother. The other…" I looked from Queran to Ronan. He didn't let the stoic expression slip from his face, but I could feel the love for me radiating from him. "It helps that I have one."

"You—This? You have chosen *this* as your partner?" He indicated toward Ronan.

My grip tightened on my sword hilt. "You're going to watch your next words very carefully," I warned.

He turned his attention back to me. "In all the years I spent trying to keep him away from you, trying to keep him from attaching himself to you, I never expected this to happen." He drew himself up to his full height. "I forbid it. And if you push me on this, I will do whatever is necessary to ensure it ends."

Rage flared within me. I drew my sword, slowly, deliberately, from its sheath.

Calynn. Your fingers.

I heard Ronan's thought and didn't need to look down to know my nail beds had turned red. I didn't even care at the moment.

"The only way to sever an anam cara bond is to kill one of the people who have it," I said, my voice cold. "If you even *think* about doing something to hurt Ronan, I will kill you. I don't care that you're the Prince of Winter or even that you're my father. You will die."

I didn't point my sword at him. I didn't have to. From the fear in his eyes, I knew he believed me. He covered it fast, and he covered it well, but I'd still seen it. In half a second, the fear was replaced with a haughty disdain.

"Honestly, daughter. You are far more dramatic than you need to be. I would never threaten your..." He trailed off, turning toward Ronan who now stood next to me, having moved when I'd drawn my sword. "Lover. Regardless of my feelings on your choice. However, you will regret not agreeing with me on the other matter."

"I don't think I will," I said, still holding my sword.

"You have no hope of standing against the Queens without me. This is your last chance. Stand with me."

He'd changed the subject neatly, but the veiled threat to Ronan still hung in the air around us. My heart pounded in my chest as my magic urged me to stop this threat before it could go any further. I took a breath and tried to calm myself.

"I don't think you understand," I said. "You're not doing anything. I'm doing something. This is *your* chance to stand with *me*. Either way, you'll never get the crown."

He sneered again. "You presumptuous infant."

I huffed a laugh. "I'll take that as a no. If that's all, you can find your way back to the Winter Sidhe. I have work to do."

I turned my back on him, sheathing my sword, and walked away to where we kept our weapons, keeping my back straight and my steps confident until I was out of his sight. Then I sagged against the wall. I looked at my hands. The red on my nail beds was pink now. Ronan followed me, watching as I dragged in a ragged breath.

"That was how he was always going to react, right?" I asked. "To me standing against the queens. To being with you."

"Yes," Ronan said.

The building usually had constant traffic, but right now, it was quiet. I wondered if Ronan had set Ansgar and Mada outside to keep people from coming in.

"He's not going to hurt you," I said, straightening. "He's not going to take you away from me." Now that we were alone, the rage that had filled me gave way to the fear it had been hiding. Ronan came to me, crushing me in his embrace. I held him back just as tightly.

"I'm right here, little changeling."

"Promise me you won't go anywhere. Swear it."

I'd made him swear something like that once before, when he was trapped in the void, waiting for me to take him out of Mab's dungeon. He'd sworn then, but this time, I felt him shake his head.

"You know I can't swear that. But I will swear to always do everything in my power to come back to you." He pulled back to look down into my face, wiping away the tears streaking my cheeks. I hadn't even realized I'd let them fall. "I would appreciate it if you promised the same."

A choked laugh escaped me. "I swear. I will do everything in my power to always come back to you." I said the same words, binding me to the same promise.

CHAPTER 31

When I arrived at my Summer estate the next day, Idelisa mentioned people had been arriving to see if the rumors were true or not. Some came because they wanted my help. Others were just nosy. I told her the ones who were looking for help could stay. The rest could be sent away with as much prejudice as was required.

I went to my library while I waited for the one visitor I'd been expecting. After the news of my abilities broke, I'd sent my mother a message asking if she would come to my estate for the remainder of our bargained time together. I'd mentioned how I didn't think it would be safe for me in Lumina. She agreed, and we'd scheduled our last hour for today.

In the time since we had made our bargain, my mother and I had gotten to know one another. I'd told her more about my motorcycle and about Arial and growing up with the humans. She'd told me about her garden and how she'd met my father and even opened up about the children she had lost. I wouldn't say we had become friends, but we were friendly. I was actually happy to be waiting for her to arrive. After today, when we got together, we wouldn't be doing so because of a bargain but because we wanted to.

I had everything ready in the solarium when my mother came in. My staff had outdone themselves with food, tea, and coffee spread out on the table. I sat in one chair while Ronan stayed as my only guard. I'd asked him to be the one to stay with me today, since I wanted to make sure my mother knew about our relationship as well. Usually, he'd have had someone else with me while he did his other tasks.

My mother sat down, looking out of the windows instead of at me. She reached for her tea and took a sip before she'd added the cream and honey she usually did.

"Is something wrong?" I asked her as she doctored the tea to her tastes.

She sighed and set her cup down. "Your father is very upset."

I snorted. "What else is new?"

She reached across the space separating us to grip my hand. "Calynn, my darling, you must stand with your father."

I removed my hand from hers. "I don't need to stand with him. I asked *him* to stand with *me*. He decided he'd rather not since I wouldn't give him what he wants."

"He only wants what's best for you."

"He wants what's best for himself. If what's best for him coincides with what's best for me, that's an accident. In this case, they don't coincide. What did he tell you?" I asked, taking a sip of my coffee to cover the unease I already felt at this conversation.

She looked around the room as though ensuring we were alone. Her gaze landed on Ronan and stopped.

"It's safe to talk here," I said. "No one can hear us except Ronan. I don't have secrets from him."

"I heard about that as well. Your father does not approve." From her tone, I understood she didn't approve either. Finally, she leaned forward and whispered. "He said you are set to oppose the Queen."

"I never actually told him that. But yes. And it's actually Queens. I am going to oppose them both. I mean to make them answer for the imbalance plaguing the Sidhe."

The color drained from her face. "Both? My darling, you cannot think to do that and survive. You cannot think to challenge *one* and survive."

"I can and I will. What else did Queran tell you?"

"He said he wanted to stand with you, but you wouldn't meet his terms."

"Did you ask what his terms were?"

The lack of an answer told me as clearly as if she'd said *no* out loud.

"He wants me to make him king. He also wanted me to make you queen. He intended for you to rule the Winter and Summer fae together. Or more likely to rule them both himself. Is that what you want?"

"Absolutely not," she said primly.

"I didn't think so."

I let my mother consider what I'd said as I leaned back and sipped my coffee. I knew she didn't want to be queen. I think she also knew my father would make a poor king, even if she would never admit it out loud. After a long silence, she spoke again.

"Who do you intend to rule if not your father? Do you mean to correct the Queens and allow them to continue?"

I stared into the black depths of my coffee, considering what to tell her. I figured the Queens already suspected the truth. They had always suspected my parents' child would oppose them even before Queran and Eilidh had any, hence killing my two siblings born decades before me, and my subsequent changing. I had no reason now not to admit what I intended.

"I do not intend for the Queens to continue their rule. They are the cause of the imbalance. If they continue their rule, the Sidhe will be destroyed forever."

I didn't look up at my mother's sharp intake of breath.

"Do you mean to rule yourself?"

This was a trickier question to answer. I could tell her no, but she wouldn't believe me. Especially since I would have to for a time. But she wouldn't believe I would give up the throne any more than she would believe I didn't want to rule. So I gave her the only answer she would accept. I looked up at her from my coffee and tried to sound certain even though I was anything but.

"Yes."

She set her teacup down with a clatter.

"I cannot believe you would want to do this."

"Why not? You see the imbalance, don't you? I've been here for only a few months, and I felt it right away. You know this can't go on."

"It is not your place to fix it," she cried.

"If it's not my place, whose is it?" I asked, standing and moving toward the windows she'd been looking out of earlier. "Look at the people out there. They need someone to look out for them. They need someone to stop this before their home is gone forever."

"The Sidhe will not be destroyed. You are overreacting. You are young and impetuous."

I turned back toward her. "The magic is broken. You can feel that, can't you?"

"The magic is slightly out of balance."

"Slightly?" I scoffed. "People have been born with access to only one magic for a thousand years. That should show you right there that something is wrong. But no one did anything about it, and for the last fifteen years, there have been kids born with no access to magic at all."

"Titania and Anstice have tried to fix that problem," she countered.

"Fix it by shoving magic into people where it doesn't belong. I've seen their work. I know what they've done. It hasn't fixed anything. If anything, they made it worse. Everyone keeps doing the wrong thing for the right thing's sake and it just keeps making everything worse. The whole world is swinging so far out of balance that I—"

Calynn.

Ronan's internal warning was the only thing that stopped me from spilling everything to my mother. But then, maybe I should. Maybe I should tell her exactly what was at stake. I'd been building a relationship with her over these past few weeks. Surely, she'd stand with me.

"You cannot beat the Queens," she said. "They are far too strong. Why do you think your father has never challenged his sister for the crown?"

"You're right. They are strong. And I'll be challenging them together. Which will make it even more difficult. But I will stand against them, and I will win. You can count on that."

My mother stood and came to me, taking my hands in both of hers. "I lost you once, my love. I cannot lose you again."

"You won't," I assure her. "Will you stand with me?"

She hesitated, and in that moment, I knew the answer. Whatever she said next wouldn't matter. Even if she said she would, I couldn't count on her.

"I think it is unwise to attempt this," Eilidh said. "I cannot support it. And I cannot stand against your father."

I took my hands from hers and moved back to my seat. "We have thirty minutes left on our time together. Would you like something to eat?"

CHAPTER 32

After Eilidh left, I went about my duties. I helped someone gain access to their latent magic. I discussed the house and property with Idelisa. I went through accounts. I read books on the Sidhe and the magic, something I'd been doing lately to better understand my role.

All the while, my chest hurt, like my heart was physically broken.

After dinner, Ronan leaned against the library door. "Why don't you call it a night? Do something else."

"Like what?"

"What would you normally do if you were upset about something?"

"I would go over to Arial's house, and we'd drink alcohol and watch movies. I mean. I never really paid attention to the movies. But she would put something on."

The thought warmed something in me. All day, I'd been thinking about how my family wouldn't stand with me. How my mother and father—the people who should have my back in all things—were choosing to stand against me.

But as soon as I mentioned Arial, I realized I had other family. Better family. People who I'd chosen and who would support me. I stood from my desk.

"I want to go to Arial's house."

Ronan blinked and straightened. "You know it's dangerous to leave the estates. I have everything in place to protect you here."

"I know. I also want to go by myself."

He closed his eyes in a bid for patience. "Calynn. What if Gavyn finds you again? Or someone Mab sends? She hasn't sent anyone after you yet. It's making me nervous."

"I'm not worried about Gavyn."

He stalked toward me, eyes pinning me to the spot. "He nearly killed you last time."

"I know. Just like Kai nearly killed me. So, according to the laws of balance, the next time I meet Gavyn, I'll be giving him access to his magic and turning him into an ally."

"Just because that's how it went with Kai, doesn't mean that'll happen with Gavyn."

"I know. But I'm fairly confident it will."

He scrubbed a hand over his face. "Fairly confident is not the same thing as certain, little changeling. And you still ended up hurt when you helped Kai."

I waved the concern away. "That was just because I grabbed the coals instead of laying a path. I'm better at this now. I know what I'm doing." I moved around my desk and took his hands. "I want to ride my motorcycle and go to my best friend's house and be normal for just a little while. Mab hasn't been able to find me at Arial's house yet and she was looking for me before. You said yourself her house has protections on it."

"It does. But you still need to get there. If you had left that Way open in her house, you could have at least gone through that."

I'd opened a Way from a spot near the Ancient Mother's domain to the middle of Arial's living room. It had been the first Way I'd ever created, and I'd done so to get to Ronan, who had been a guest of Queen Mab's torture chambers.

"I wasn't going to leave a Way open in the middle of my best friend's living room. I'll be safe."

He was silent for a long time, searching my face. "Don't make me regret this."

I grinned and kissed him. Then I rushed out before he could try to change my mind. I knew what I was doing was dangerous. I knew it was reckless. And I knew it was a bad idea.

I got on my motorcycle and rode it across my land, through the Way to the human world and onto the road, stopping for only a moment to grab my helmet from the garage. I may not need it anymore now that I knew I could protect myself with my magic, but that didn't make it any less illegal to ride without it.

It had been a while since I'd ridden my bike on roads. I'd forgotten how annoying stop lights could be. Then I turned onto the highway and picked up speed. Bonnie's engine growled, and I felt the magic reverberating through her. I grinned as I raced through a tunnel, revving the engine just to hear it echo off the walls, and emerged on the other side. I slowed as I drove into Vancouver, traveling down a busy road loaded with traffic, before turning onto the cramped streets of Arial's neighborhood.

I pulled up in front of her house and placed my hand on Bonnie's gas tank, letting her know she could turn off. She did with a little purr. I chuckled as I climbed off and removed my helmet, starting toward the red door. As I passed the rowan tree that grew in her yard, I reached out an arm to touch, intending to just brush my fingers over the bark, when I felt something beneath my fingertips and stopped.

I pressed my hand more firmly to the tree, feeling the magic there. I'd known it was there before. Ronan had even told me so. Her father had planted the tree before Arial was born. Now that we knew he'd been a pixie who'd grown too big for his wings, we understood he'd done it to offer his daughter and the human woman he'd cared for some measure of protection. The tree's seed had come from the Sidhe itself and Arial's father had woven his own protection magic into it.

But there was more magic living within the tree. Familiar magic.

I went back to Bonnie and placed my hands on her, feeling the magic I'd accidentally given her. I'd loved her so much I'd given her life. I returned to the tree. My magic imbued the rowan from roots to leaves. The tree showed me exactly what had happened every time I touched it, and I touched it every time I passed it. Without knowing what I'd been doing, I'd offered it magic to keep the protection spell fresh. My love for Arial matched the love her father had when he'd planted the tree. Like called to like, and I'd helped it grow.

"Calynn? What are you doing?"

I turned to find Arial standing at her front door, watching me.

"Communing with nature," I said, pressing my hands to the trunk once again, offering the tree as much of my magic as it wanted to take. Anything I could give it to ensure Arial remained safe from whatever might cause her harm.

Arial snorted. When I turned back to her, she was leaning against the door frame. I was about to go to her, let her know why I was there, and explain what I'd been doing, when I felt magic ripple in the air around me. Instead, I strode quickly to my bike and drew my sword from one of the saddlebags.

"Arial, go back inside."

"What? Why?"

"Just go. Stay on the inside of your threshold."

Dark laughter came to me from everywhere and nowhere. "You realize, even though I cannot use my magic on her, I could simply walk into her house and snap her neck."

"Try it, Gavyn. I dare you. I'll gut you before you get close enough."

"How can you gut me if you cannot see me?"

His voice came from closer to the house, but I knew he was playing me. He hadn't come here for Arial. But without being able to see him, I knew I'd only have a split second between when he showed himself and when he tried to stab me again. I couldn't let him do that.

I closed my eyes.

I didn't need to see him. Like Killian, I could see the magic. Just like I had with the cu sidhe all those months ago. Just like I'd been doing when I reached into people's magic to help them access their latent gift.

And there he was. Coming toward me from my left, sliding closer, the light bending around him so he was completely invisible to sight.

"Will you run from me this time?" he asked. His voice came from my other side. He was throwing his voice somehow, a neat trick, especially for one who could make himself invisible.

"I don't run from people."

"You should." He was close enough now to strike me. I felt his dagger in his hand as it swept through the air toward my neck. In a move I'd practiced hundreds of times, I dropped my sword, grabbed his hand with one of mine and used the other to grasp his elbow. I used my entire body strength to bend him down and twist his arm behind him. I twisted his hand, and he dropped the dagger, which I kicked away. Then I reached into his magic with my own and held on tight.

"What are you doing?" he asked, an edge of panic in his voice.

I switched my grip from his elbow to his other hand, getting a tighter hold on his magic. He could have easily gotten out of my physical hold, but with his magic under my complete control, he didn't move.

"Stop. What are you doing?" he asked again.

Then I dragged us both into his magic.

"How—" He looked around, the light almost blinding in his main magic. "How are we here?"

"I brought us here. Usually I'm a little more gentle about it. But you've been pretty determined to kill me so, desperate times and all that. You want access to your latent magic?"

He shot me a sharp look. "I have heard the rumors. I did not believe them."

"You should." I crossed my arms over my chest, trying to look as bored as possible. There was nothing to lean on, so I just had to stand there. It kind of killed the look.

If he'd had my glamour blind ability, he'd know the nonchalant stance was a lie. I *needed* to give him access to his latent magic. I *needed* to turn him from enemy to ally. Something inside me insisted, some instinct I didn't like to ignore.

"What would you ask in return?" he asked finally.

"Well, first of all, stop trying to kill me."

He narrowed his eyes. "I will not ally myself with you against my queen."

"I didn't say that. I said stop trying to kill me. Surely your *mother* would rather you whole than me dead."

He stilled, his breathing stopping for an instant before he said, "Who told you of my relation to her?"

"No one. I figured it out for myself. Look. Do we have a deal or not?"

It was risky, giving him access to his magic with only the bargain that he'd not try to kill me anymore. But as with Kai, it was the right thing to do. Gavyn wasn't a bad person. He was a spy. He'd tried to kill me, more than once. But he wasn't a bad person. I was certain of it.

"Lay out the terms of the bargain," he said.

"I give you access to your latent magic. In return, you'll never deliberately try to harm me or my people in any way."

He gave me a tight nod, and the bargain was struck. Here, deep within his magic, it would prove even more binding than if we'd sworn in blood.

Finally, I turned away from him, searching for the magic I knew was here. I admit, I was curious. I knew Gavyn was Kai's opposite, and I wanted to know what the opposite of coals and embers was. I was so busy looking for something that fit that description, I tripped over the latent magic before I realized what I was seeing.

A light breeze played through a decimated forest. Trees had fallen all over the place and become dry logs. I shook my head as I looked around, confused. I had been sure Gavyn's latent magic would be opposite to Kai's. The breeze lifted my hair and blew it across my face.

"Not the opposite," I said out loud. "The fuel. Combine them and they become stronger."

I began laying the path back toward Gavyn, all the while thinking about the two men. I'd known they were connected. They were both my cousins. They had exactly opposite main magics. And their latent magics would be stronger if combined. I found my way back and completed the path, ending it where Gavyn stood. He had a look of awe on his face as he felt the magic that lay within him that he'd never known about before. He moved to start down the path, but I stopped him.

"I have someone I want you to meet."

CHAPTER 33

I ended up not being able to stay at Arial's house. When I left Gavyn's magic, I gave her a hug and told her I'd be back later, but I had to go.

"Is everything all right?" she asked.

"Yeah. He's not going to hurt anyone. We have a deal."

She looked between me and Gavyn with doubt and trepidation, but she nodded, and I went back to Ronan's ranch.

Gavyn met me there. I didn't know how he got there so quickly, but I didn't ask. Ronan met me when I pulled into the garage.

"What happened?" he asked.

"Everything is fine. I need Kai."

It didn't take long for my cousin to arrive, either. When the four of us stood in Ronan's living room, I introduced Gavyn to Kai, not really knowing what to expect. It seemed like sparks flew between the two of them. Metaphorically, of course, since in this world, it could just as easily have been literally.

"Kai, this is Gavyn. Gavyn, Kai. You two have a lot in common."

Kai turned to me, an eyebrow lifted in surprise. He understood immediately what I meant. It took Gavyn a little bit longer to figure out he and Kai were both sons of the Queens.

"You're also exact opposites on the surface. But deeper down, you complement each other."

Kai turned back to Gavyn with new interest. He assessed the other man. "I believe we have much to discuss... Gavyn." Then he flicked me a glance, one corner of his mouth tipping up in a hidden smile. "Fear not, cousin. I will ensure he knows everything he needs to know."

Gavyn's eyes shot wide, assessing us both. When his gaze landed on Kai once again, he regarded him warily, but nodded. Then he turned to me. "Our bargain stands, but I still will not ally myself with you against my queen."

"I wouldn't expect anything less."

Then, for the first time since I'd known him, Kai left through the back door instead of taking the shadows, Gavyn following.

When they were gone, I sat on the couch in front of the empty fireplace, the same spot I'd sat in the first time I arrived at this house only a few months ago. Felt like a lot longer. I sat on the couch, staring into space, connecting ideas. Bonnie's sentience came from me. I'd added protection to Arial's tree. Somehow, after I destroyed the Sidhe, I was supposed to be able to rebuild it.

I glanced toward the front yard. Arial's tree had shown me how I'd added to the protection her father had begun. Maybe the tree in Ronan's yard could show me more.

I'd noticed the rowan tree immediately the first time I'd come here. I'd known it was special. Back then, I hadn't known anything about this world. Now, I knew rowan was sacred in the Sidhe. Now, I'd been to the Ancient Mother's home and seen the huge rowan tree that grew there.

I touched the trunk, looking up at the branches, covered in dark green leaves and bright red berries like always, despite the recent winter.

"I don't know what I'm doing," I said to the tree. Ronan would laugh at me, but talking to Bonnie had helped bring her to life, so I kept talking. "I know after it's destroyed, I'm supposed to rebuild the Sidhe. It stands to reason I can create some piece of it now, here. A place that will remain stable after everything happens. I need some help figuring out how to do that."

Just like Arial's tree, this one showed me how I could use my magic to create. It reminded me I had the power of creation at my fingertips. I had every single element that existed in this magical world. There was a reason for that.

I started with the tree. In addition to the elements, I was also a Way Finder, so I used that magic, along with the Ring of Creation, to open a Way to the Ancient Mother's rowan tree, bigger than any Way I'd created before. It opened seamlessly, as though it had always been meant to be here. The bigger rowan from inside the Fréimhe seemed to superimpose itself over the smaller one on Ronan's land. As though one lived on top of the other. And with the tree came the dragon who protected it.

"Mother be merciful," someone said from behind me. A crowd had gathered, watching what I'd been doing, and the two trees that seemed to stand in the same space.

When the dragon sauntered out from behind the tree like she owned it—which she kind of did—a collective gasp went up in the crowd.

She was about the size of a large lion, her golden scales glittering in the dim light of day, her tail twitching back and forth like an annoyed cat. She cast her gaze around the people and when she saw me, she stalked toward me. I knew some people here were my guards and they would mistakenly want to defend me, so I held up a hand to stop them from getting themselves killed.

"I apologize for disturbing you, my friend," I said to the dragon.

She moved around me, rubbing her side against my hips until my hand rested on her back. I smiled down at her. "It's nice to see you, too."

She moved back to the tree and stretched before curling around the trunk. I turned to the others who had gathered around. "She won't hurt anyone as long as you stay away from the tree. Her job is to keep it safe."

"You're friends with a dragon?" Ansgar said.

"Uh..." I looked back at the dragon, who already had her eyes closed. "Yeah. I guess."

Someone gasped again.

"She won't hurt you," I said again. "You can go back to whatever you were doing."

No one moved. I rolled my eyes and turned to Ronan, who had come out onto the front porch at some point while I'd been working the magic. "I have more I want to do today," I said. "I need to send a message to Ryleigh, Anant, Conroy, and Gwanwyn. I know how the nobles can create safe places. And I need the people who had their magic messed with brought here."

"How many of them?" he asked, coming down the stairs toward me.

"All of them."

***

I went to the river. Or rather, the stream. Because, for right now, that's what it was. However, it was running water in the human world that would form the base for what I wanted to create in a new section of the Sidhe.

Based on maps I'd seen, the river started in a land beyond the Sidhe. The magic from the other world flowed into the Sidhe, spreading outward. So that was how I would create the new space.

I waded into the stream—it came up to my knees at the center—and thought of the river in the Sidhe. I'd spent days walking along its bank to reach the Ancient Mother's home. I'd drunk its water when I'd been cut and poisoned by a redcap. When I had the river's image firmly in mind, I called the first person to join me in the stream.

It was the boy who had water dripping into his magical space. Lorna and Rhys came with him, steadying him as he waded into the water to stand with me. Once I had his hands in mine, I jerked my head to tell the others to leave us.

"I don't know if this is going to hurt," I told the kid as Lorna and Rhys went back to the shore with the others. "But I hope you'll feel better once I'm done."

He nodded, his bright golden eyes fearful.

I made my way into his magic and started to pull the water magic into me. Evander had created a bucket to catch the water, so it no longer dripped into the empty space. I pulled from the bucket first, emptying it before pulling the rest of it into me. It filled me up. Given how powerful I was, I should have had room to spare, but this magic felt different. The experiments had been done with good intentions, but they had been conducted without care, making this magic feel wrong, sharper and bigger than it should have felt. The last thing I did was pull the bucket into me, then I left the boy's magic.

I came back to my consciousness doubled over in the stream, my arms wrapped around my middle. Pressure from the water filled my whole body. The boy held my shoulder, keeping me balanced. His face was clear of pain for the first time since I'd found him. Because I'd taken all the pain into myself. I wanted to scream with it, but I couldn't make a sound. I forced myself to focus. Now that I had the water within me, I could release it into what would be the start of the new section of river.

I thought of all I had taken in. I thought of the river flowing through the Fréimhe. Then I let the two thoughts become one, releasing all that water into the start of the new river. As it flowed out of me, I fell to my knees, tears streaming down my cheeks from the pain of it. The Ring of Creation warmed on my finger, helping me create the new river. Suddenly, I realized it had never been meant to create Ways, though it could help, thus why Morrigan hadn't been given something similar. *This* was the Ring's true purpose. To create new land belonging to the Sidhe.

After the magic was gone, flowing around me, sort of superimposed over the original stream, Rhys and Lorna came into the river to take the boy away. I didn't look up. I sat on my knees in the water, panting, staring down at the beginning of the new river.

"Come, little changeling," Ronan said quietly. "We'll get you something to eat and some rest."

I shook my head. "Bring me the next."

I watched his boots in the water as they stayed by my side. "Calynn."

I looked up at him. My head felt heavy, but I met his eyes. They shone with concern. He didn't want me to do another. He wanted to argue, to physically lift me and take me back inside and force me to sleep.

I climbed to my feet, still feeling the ache of all that pressure. "I've felt what they feel for the last twenty minutes. They've been feeling it for the last few months. Some of them for hundreds of years. Bring the next one."

Through our bond, I knew he'd also felt the pain, the exhaustion, just as I could feel his reticence, his desire to have me safe. But beneath that, I also felt his love and pride and support.

Very slowly, he nodded. "As you wish, my princess."

Another child entered the stream, one of the ones Evander hadn't been able to help. I'd tasked Lorna with ordering the children from the ones she thought needed help most to those who could wait the longest.

Over the course of the evening, I went through all of them, one at a time, going into their magic, pulling out all the water that had been forced into them and releasing it into the river.

I worked almost blindly, no longer seeing the people or the river around me. My head throbbed with the worst headache I'd ever felt. My body felt like it would split in two with all the pressure I kept forcing into it and releasing. I felt like a balloon after it had been blown up, then had all the air let out of it.

At some point, Ronan came to me and pressed a hot cup into my hands. I drank the coffee, letting it scald the back of my throat before asking for the next person and the next and the next. Until Ronan placed a hand on my shoulder.

"That's all the children," he said. "The rest can wait. You need to eat and sleep."

I knew he was right, partly because I could no longer get to my feet, partly because I couldn't see anything, my vision gone completely dark, and partly because the Ring of Creation now burned my finger, telling me it, too, needed a rest.

"I need to undo what was done."

"The river has already begun to flow, little changeling," he said, softly. "We can all feel the magic radiating from it. You've done enough for one day."

Someone else came over and I thought they crouched in front of me, but they were little more than a shadow among the other shadows.

"The marshal is right, Your Highness," Airleas said. "You have helped all the children. They were the most important. The rest of us have lived with this intrusion for so long, it no longer hurts us. We can wait."

"You're shivering," Ronan said. "Your body can't take much more before you pass out. You can't hide what you're feeling from me to try to power through it. Let me take you inside."

"I probably couldn't do much to stop you at this point," I said. I wanted to lift my arms to him, but they refused to answer my command. It didn't matter. Ronan knew, and he picked me up, carrying me into the house and up to our bedroom.

I smelled food and my stomach tried to leap out of my body to consume it. I nearly cried at the idea that I wouldn't be able to eat it because my arms were too tired to lift, and my jaw was too tired to chew.

"I'll feed you," Ronan said, setting me on something and undressing me. "And Quinn made soup, so there's no chewing needed."

"I hadn't meant to send you those thoughts," I said as he pulled warm, dry clothes over my head.

"I know. But you're very tired so your walls are down. And the closer we are, the easier it is to hear what you're thinking."

The shadows started to part, and I could make out shapes again. My body warmed now the wet clothes were off, and Ronan lifted me, setting me in the bed, covering me with blankets before putting something on my lap.

"Can you see yet?" he asked.

"How did you know I couldn't see?"

He tsked at me but didn't respond.

I smelled the soup as he brought it closer, and my stomach told me how much it hated me for letting it get so empty.

"Open," he said.

I opened my mouth, and he slid the spoon between my lips. "I don't like being treated like an invalid," I said after I swallowed.

"Then stop doing things that make you into one. Open."

I did as he commanded again. After the fourth or fifth bite, my vision cleared and I could see him, the concern etching his features as he fed me soup. My arms still felt like lead weights. He kept feeding me, focusing on the bowl and my mouth. When the soup was gone, he picked up a large glass of water with a straw and ordered me to drink.

I continued following his orders as he helped me feel better. Finally, he took a small vial and told me to open my mouth again. I did as he asked, and he placed a couple drops of something sweet on my tongue.

"What was that?" I asked.

"Reconciliation tincture," he said, capping it and setting it aside again. "Evander thought it might help and said it wouldn't hurt either way."

He moved to get off the bed, but I quickly set my hand over his. "Ronan?"

His eyes found mine, searching, asking me what else I needed so he could get it for me.

"I love you. I wish I didn't have to cause you so much concern."

He rolled his eyes. "You are who you are, little changeling. I wouldn't have it any other way."

He stood and leaned over me, pressing a kiss to my lips. My eyes drifted closed and when the kiss was over, it felt like I had to drag them back open.

"I love you, too," he said. "Now go to sleep."

"You're not going to stay?"

"I have a few things to take care of, then I'll be back."

The pain had eased a bit from the moment the tincture hit my tongue and I lay back on the bed, relaxing into the pillows.

"Would you stay until I'm asleep?" I asked, my eyes drifting closed.

From far away, I heard his laugh. "Little changeling. You're already asleep."

I felt his lips on my forehead and the blankets pulled up over my shoulders. Then I proved him right.

CHAPTER 34

I t took two weeks, but I got all the magic out of the people and into the new river. And, as I suspected would be the case, it brought magic into the world with it. I kept working until new land lay superimposed over all of Ronan's property until people were again living in the Sidhe, specifically in the Fréimhe. The ranch now existed in both the human world and the Sidhe simultaneously. Eventually, once all the upheaval was over, I would remove it from the human world entirely.

Every night when I went to bed, I dropped into a deep sleep almost as soon as my head touched the pillow. And while I knew Ronan had been sleeping next to me, I didn't see him in the bed much. He would stay with me until I fell asleep, but he was always up and gone before I woke.

I sent notes to my allies, explaining what I hoped would hold pieces of the Sidhe against what was coming: if they stayed on their estates, if their estates had none of the imbalance that plagued the realm, if they were strong enough to host those who lived there, providing protection to those weaker than they were, they should be able to hold their piece of the world against what I had to do.

After I finished my tasks, I returned to my Winter estate. I hadn't been to either Winter or Summer in the entire past two weeks. I'd fallen into bed right after we'd arrived and slept hard, exhausted.

I woke in the morning with a start and looked around my empty room. I couldn't place my finger on exactly what had woken me, but my heart raced as though I'd just been having another nightmare.

I tried to shake off the feeling. I'd had enough nightmares lately it should have been easy, but the feeling lingered. Something was wrong, but I couldn't place what. I tried to remember my dreams, but all I could come up with was a flash of pain and darkness.

After getting dressed, I made my way downstairs for something to eat. My body felt stiff, like I needed a good stretch, so after I ate, I went out to the training arena, finding it empty. It was much earlier in the day than I'd thought it was, but I didn't mind. I stood for a moment, stretching muscles that hadn't been exercised in two weeks. The amount of magic I'd been using had taken all my mental and physical energy.

I moved through the steps I'd learned to warm up my sword arm and my body before I began the routine of the sword practice. By the time I was finished, I had a sheen of sweat on my skin and people had begun to join me in the ring and the other practice field beyond. Including Rhys.

"Hey, kid," I said as I finished my set. The nightmare persisted in keeping me uneasy, so I hoped a conversation with Rhys would help. It was just a dream.

"Hey," he said from his perch on the fence where he'd been watching me.

"You come out to practice?"

"Yeah. I was going to shoot a few arrows before I get back to the little ones."

"How are they doing?" Rhys had taken over his role as the guardian of the Winter children. They tended to stay in Winter. Occasionally, they went to the human world, now the Fréimhe, and visited with the

Summer children who spent most of their time on my Summer estate under Lorna's care.

"Well enough. They've settled in nicely and Fagen has already regained his strength. He and some of the other older ones have started training with the guards."

"I bet none are as good with a bow as you are."

He grinned at me. "*No one* is as good as me."

"Those are some pretty big words. You want to prove it?"

"Against you?"

"Sure."

He jumped down off the fence and we went to the archery range where targets were set at distances of thirty, forty, and fifty yards.

"Can I tell you a secret?" I asked him when we'd arrived, and he began inspecting his arrows.

"Of course."

"I have no idea what I'm doing."

He grinned at me again. "I know. I've never seen you pick up a bow. You want me to show you?"

I nodded, and he turned to choose one of the extra bows set out for practice. While he wasn't looking, I rubbed my chest, trying in vain to soothe the feeling that something was desperately wrong. But what?

I dropped my hand and pulled up a smile when Rhys returned to me, handing me the bow.

"Judging by your sword fighting, I'd guess you're right eye dominant," he said. "So you shoot right. This one isn't too heavy."

I took it and weighed it in my hand. "Not nearly as heavy as my short sword."

He laughed and shook his head. "Not the weight of the bow itself. The weight of the string. How much weight you have to hold when you pull it back. This one is about twenty-five pounds. A good weight for you, I think."

"How much is yours?"

"I'm up to fifty pounds now," he said, pride shining in his eyes. "I'm hoping to get up to sixty by the end of this summer. I met another archer who has his bow set to a hundred pounds."

"Fuck. And you have to pull that back?"

He nodded, excitement dancing in his eyes now. "With only the tips of your fingers."

He proceeded to show me the correct stance and how to hold the bow and how to nock the arrow. When I pulled back on the string, he showed me how to hold my arms and where to pull the string back to.

"When you're ready, let the string roll off your fingers."

I let the arrow fly, and it hit the bottom of the target. "I swear I aimed at the middle."

"Arrows don't fly in a straight line," he explained. "They fly in an arc. So you have to know where to aim in order to get the arrow to hit where you want it. It's based on a lot of factors. The weight of your bow. The distance of your target. The wind or lack of it. Even the temperature and humidity can come into effect."

"How do you know all this?"

He shrugged one shoulder, standing in a spot that would allow him to shoot at all three targets without moving his feet. "Instinct."

He nocked one arrow and pointed toward the thirty-yard target. While that arrow flew, he nocked the second, then the third. All three arrows landed in the exact centre of the targets seconds after each other. He moved faster than my eyes could track. He grinned at me when he was done.

"Show off."

We set our bows down and walked out onto the range to retrieve our arrows. We approached the thirty-yard target, and I pulled my arrow out, so much below his. "I think I'll stick to the sword," I said.

Rhys laughed and went to collect his other two arrows.

We went back to the shooting line and Rhys didn't pick up his bow again. Instead, he handed me the one I'd been using and an arrow. I stood in front of the thirty-yard target.

"I aimed right at the centre last time, but it ended up low. I guess this time I should aim higher?"

"That's right."

I did as he said and raised the tip of the arrow above the bullseye, pulled back on the string, and let the arrow fly once again. This time, it hit much closer to the mark, though still not exactly on it.

"Ha!" I said, with a huge smile on my face. It was stupid, but it felt good.

Rhys grinned back at me. "Great. Just be careful about your elbow. If you turn it in, the string will hit your arm when you release, and that's not pleasant. You want to try forty now?"

I nodded, and we moved down the shooting line. Rhys handed me another arrow.

"So if you had to aim just slightly above at the thirty, what should you do at forty?" he asked.

"Aim higher," I guessed.

Rhys just smiled at me.

I thought about where I had aimed before and went up a few notches. The arrow hit the target low. I took another arrow from my friend and nocked it, aiming higher still, and this time hit the target only slightly off.

"Fifty," Rhys pronounced, and we moved down the shooting line.

I looked at it for a moment. It seemed much further than the other two targets had, even though it was only another ten yards. "I'm going to have to aim really high," I said.

"Yep."

I got ready and considered where I'd had to aim for the forty and also for the thirty, the difference in space between the two. I'd need to go that far for this target as well. "I can't see the target if I aim that high."

"Sometimes you can't see the target. Sometimes you just have to feel it. Trust your bow. Trust your arrow. Trust your instinct."

I took a deep breath and aimed high. I went through Rhys' other instructions about my arms and stance, then trusted my instinct. I let the arrow fly, and it hit the target slightly left of center.

"Shit!" I said, staring.

Rhys grinned. "I'll make an archer of you yet," he said.

"How…"

He took my bow from me, setting it down before we went out onto the range to collect the arrows. "Our magic helps. Archery is all about human physics. And physics is based on gravity and the air. Both of which are tied to our elemental magic. I knew you'd be good at it if you wanted to learn."

"I think I'm more suited to the sword."

"You probably are. You prefer to be right in the thick of it. You'd make a terrible thief. But for me? Thievery and archery are connected, I think. They both require a lot of patience."

I laughed. "Which I don't exactly have."

He grinned at me. "I wasn't going to say it. You could still be good at archery, anyway. You just have to remember to trust your instincts."

"It's been hard lately to trust myself."

He gave me a sympathetic look. "I've noticed. But I trust you."

We collected the arrows and before we made our way back to the shooting line, I turned to him. The fae didn't thank people for things. A simple phrase would put us into another person's debt. But this was a lesson I'd sorely needed, and I wanted Rhys to understand.

"This was a fine lesson, Rhys. You're an excellent teacher. You gave me a lot to consider."

"It's my pleasure to help you in any small way I can, Calynn. My debt to you is great."

"You don't owe me any debt, Rhys."

He gave me a patient smile. "All of us owe you a debt, Calynn. Even if you don't think so."

Something behind me pulled his attention away, and the smile slipped away, replaced with an awestruck look. If he'd been an emoji, he'd be the one with the heart eyes. Naturally, I turned to see who had so captured his notice. Then I took a step in front of him when I saw the look of murder on Morrigan's face. I handed Rhys my bow and rested my hand on my sword.

"Rhys, go put the bows away," I said.

"But—"

"Don't argue. Just go."

I didn't turn to look at him, but I knew he was doing as I'd said when Morrigan's eyes tracked him as he walked away.

"I came to tell you I finished my training and was considering being on my way. Now I see you have my enemy's progeny living right here."

"Just because Deardriu is your enemy doesn't mean Rhys is. She was terrible to him. Threw him out when he was a kid. He's my friend, and he's under my protection."

Her eyes burned with hate. I knew he hadn't left entirely because she wasn't looking at me. She was staring hard at a point behind me where I was certain Rhys had stopped. He really had very little self-preservation instincts. I would have to talk to him about that.

My hand wrapped around my sword hilt. "Morrigan."

Finally, her eyes found mine.

"You cannot have him for your revenge. You'll have to find another way."

The hate still smoldered in her eyes, but she nodded. "Not that I believe Deardriu's son deserves any more mercy than the woman herself. But because of you, I will ignore his existence."

I rolled my eyes. "Whatever. So you're going to leave?"

My heart clenched in fear, but it didn't make sense. Why would I be afraid of her leaving?

"Yes. I am going to continue practicing making Ways outside of the safety of your estate. And I will begin to construct my plan for revenge away from..." she turned to look toward Rhys again, but since the murderous rage no longer gleamed in her eyes, I had to assume he had gone. "From people who might take issue with it."

The fear built in me, making my heart race. I had loosened my grip on my sword, but now I tightened it again, wanting to draw it and fight whatever was terrifying me. There was nothing to fight. I thought of the dream that had woken me this morning. The sense of dread I'd been unable to shake.

"I appreciate that," I said, distractedly, trying to keep my mind on the conversation and not on whatever this bizarre reaction was.

Suddenly, I gasped as pain shot through me, lighting me up from my head to my toes. I doubled over, clutching my stomach.

"What's wrong?" Morrigan asked.

I couldn't speak from the pain roaring through me, filling me up. It was coming from somewhere deep within my magic, and I closed my eyes to figure out exactly where. I scrambled within the magic, searching until I found the source.

"Ronan," I gasped. Now that I understood where the pain came from, I sent strength back through the connection and it eased. "Take as much as you need," I said. "And stay alive. I'm coming for you."

I had no way of knowing if he could hear me. We usually couldn't send thoughts over long distances. But I'd said the words directly to the connection between us, so hopefully at least the sentiment would come across to him.

I emerged from my magic to find Morrigan still staring at me. I straightened and drew my sword.

"Someone has Ronan," I said. "I'm going to get him back."

When had I seen him last? I'd been practicing all morning, trying to dispel that sense of dread, but if I'd thought about it, I should have known. If I hadn't been so tired, I probably would have. He was always near. Now that I knew he was gone, I understood it hadn't been a dream that woke me. It had been him being taken.

"I'll come with you," Morrigan said.

I didn't really care if she came or not. All my thoughts focused on Ronan and getting to him as fast as possible.

I held out my hand with the Ring of Creation on it and concentrated on the path magic, thinking of Ronan and who he was, what he meant to me. Then I slashed the air, creating a Way leading directly to him.

"What's on the other side of the Way?" Morrigan asked.

"Murder and mayhem," I said, setting my teeth together and drawing my sword.

She grinned. "What are we waiting for, then?" She drew her twin daggers, spinning them in each hand before nodding and we stepped through the Way.

CHAPTER 35

We rushed into a dank room I recognized, though it registered distantly. I rushed the first of two guards, slicing through him with my sword like he was paper, noting the man I killed was Linden. His blood spilled on the ground, but I was already stepping over him toward the Queen, where she stood next to Ronan's prone form. The other guard fell to Morrigan's daggers.

I gripped the Queen's blood-soaked shirt in my fist—Ronan's blood—the point of my sword pressed into her belly. I shoved her against the wall as rage colored my vision red. The sticky magic filled me, urging me to dig the sword into her, spill her entrails onto the floor where she'd hurt Ronan. Far at the back of my mind, I recalled I wasn't supposed to kill her, but I couldn't remember why. The red magic rode me.

"You thought I wouldn't come for him?" I yelled. "You thought I wouldn't gut you for this?"

"You can't kill me," she said, her voice firm. "I am the Queen of Winter."

"You don't know how little that matters to me," I snarled.

Every single atom in my body wanted to plunge my sword into her to prove how wrong she was. In the split second before I made the decision, Ronan made a noise. A sound between a groan and a protest.

"Calynn," Morrigan said. "We must get him out of here. He bleeds fast."

"You live today," I said to Mab. "But don't think this is the end. You've crossed a line you shouldn't have crossed."

Then, with all the speed and strength I'd gained, I spun her around, dropping my sword and pulling her into a choke hold. She struggled against me, but I had it locked and after only a few moments, she slumped. I let her fall to the ground.

"Is she dead?" Morrigan asked.

"No. And she'll wake up in a couple minutes, so we need to get out of here now."

I lifted Ronan, pulling one of his arms around my shoulders. Morrigan took his other side, and we carried him back through the Way I had created. I turned and closed it as soon as we were back on my estate so no one could follow us.

"What happened?" Ansgar said. He was right there, taking Ronan's weight from Morrigan. When Mada tried to take his arm from me, I bared my teeth and she backed away.

"You doubled over, then you straightened and disappeared," Ansgar continued when I didn't answer.

"Mab took him," I said. "Sometime this morning."

Aiden flew up to me, waiting for instructions. "Get Assana," I told him. "And send for Anant and Evander. I want all our best healers here. Now."

Assana had arrived when Anant brought all his extra people to me from his Glacia estate. Evander could easily come from Ronan's ranch.

"Sir Anant retired to his estate near the sea," Aiden said.

"Right. Just Assana and Evander, then. Hurry."

Mada and Morrigan cleared the way for us, opening the door to the house, then pulling a cot from the corner of the solarium for me and Ansgar to set Ronan on. I'd kept one around after a battle with a dragon had ended in seven people in need of healing. We'd set up a make-shift infirmary. It had been in my mind to create a permanent one somewhere and now I kicked myself for putting it off.

Assana rushed in as Ansgar and I lifted Ronan's legs onto the cot. I finally got to see the extent of his injuries.

He had a gash on his head where he'd been knocked unconscious. Given how I'd felt today, I assumed that had been what had woken me. When I'd felt what had seemed like random fear, that had actually been Ronan waking in the dungeon. So little time passed between when I'd first felt the fear and when I'd rescued him. But his injuries were still many.

He had metal devices attached to each one of his fingers. His shirt had been removed and I could see he'd been beaten and cut on. His chest and back were a riot of cuts and bruises. I wondered if the two guards had participated in the beating and didn't feel at all sad they were both dead. But the worst wound was the cut that started on his forehead, bisected his left eye, and trailed down his cheek. It bled freely.

Assana started working immediately, assessing the damage and staunching bleeding with her magic. Cuts knit back together; bruises faded. By the time Evander arrived, all that was left was healing the eye and the fingers.

"Carefully," Evander said, as they removed the metal devices. "We don't want the blood to rush into them too quickly."

Assana nodded. "My uncle explained the procedure to me, but I've never done it. Have you?"

"Aye. A few times."

I paced as I watched them work.

"What are those?" I asked.

"Thumbscrews," Ansgar said, clenching his fist. "They break the fingers. If they're tight enough, they can crush the bone to dust. When that happens, there is no fixing them."

"If his fingers are crushed, he won't be able to hold his sword," I said, fear lancing through me. Not that I cared about it. But I knew he would care.

"It usually takes a while to get the screws that tight," he said. "Judging by how his hands look, I'm not so concerned about them. I'm more worried about the eye."

"They'll be able to save it," I said.

"Calynn," Mada said, gently. "They're not even trying."

"They need to try," I said, starting toward them. But Morrigan and Mada caught me and pulled me back. I fought against them. Even with all my training, I couldn't overcome them both. They were bigger than me. Mada had been training for the better part of a century. And I wasn't in my right mind to properly fight. "They need to try," I yelled. "He said she wouldn't do permanent damage. Everything she does can be fixed."

"She doesn't do permanent damage to her toys," Ansgar said. "He is no longer her toy. He belongs to you now."

Ronan had been right. Mab hadn't come after me at all in the past few months. She had been planning something the whole time. Something I should have anticipated. I fell to my knees as the Queen's threat returned to me. *Next time, I* will *break him. If only because I now know how important he is to you.*

***

Triage. That's what Evander explained to me later, when they'd done all they could. Assana had started with the most important thing first, stopping the rapid blood loss. Then, when Evander had arrived, they'd tackled the next most important injury. His fingers. They could save his fingers. They would never have been able to save the eye.

I had him brought upstairs to our bed. Evander advised against moving him, but I wanted him in a place I felt safe. I would have preferred his house, now part of the Fréimhe. But for now, our bedroom in Winter was the safest place I could think of.

His breathing was even. Evander had given him a dose of something to help him remain asleep and in no pain. I sat in a chair next to the bed—my knees pulled up, arms wrapped around them—watching the steady rise and fall of his chest.

The red, sticky magic still burned inside me, regardless of the fact that I knew Ronan would be okay. Except his eye. For the first time since the Ancient Mother told me what my destiny would be, I wanted to do it. I wanted to kill the Queens. Both of them.

If Mab had thought this would break me, she was wrong.

Yet, even as I wanted to bring them to their knees for what they'd done to this world, for what Mab had done to Ronan, I remembered what would happen if I killed them. The destruction of the whole world.

In the moment in Mab's dungeon, I would have done it easily. If I'd needed to kill her to get him out of there, I didn't care the black hole dream was worst when I killed them separately. Fuck all the worlds.

Now that he was safe, the desire to make her pay was still there, but not at the cost of everyone.

I unfolded myself from the chair and went to the table in the corner of my room, gathering what I needed to make a cup of coffee. Making the perfect cup of pour-over coffee was like a ritual, each step important and carefully carried out. I used my magic to heat the water, let the ground bloom, and rinsed the filter. Once the pot was warmed, I poured the water slowly over the coffee grounds, ensuring I soaked them all thoroughly. Then I watched as the water dripped into the carafe, the smell of fresh coffee filling the air, a smell that should have made me feel calm.

When it was done, I poured it into my cup, lifting it to my nose, my shaking hands making the cup rattle on the saucer. I breathed in the aroma that usually eased any tension I'd been feeling.

But today was different.

Today, Ronan had been taken because of me. He'd lost his eye because of me. He'd been tortured, again because of me.

I set the cup down without taking a sip.

CHAPTER 36

I walked through the house and made my way back to the Fréimhe and the rowan tree. Everything looked a little darker, like everything was cast in shadows. I could feel the red magic boiling within me, and I released it into the Sidhe with a scream. As it flowed out of me, it tore pieces of me away, pieces I wasn't certain I could live without.

It found the sources of imbalance permeating the Sidhe, encapsulating them, surrounding them, and pulling them away from wherever they were. I stood by the rowan tree and the magic began to flow back toward me, bringing all the imbalance with it, leaving the Sidhe scrubbed clean and unbroken.

Some people were hurt because the imbalance lived within them. But all people were still alive. No one died. Everything was quiet.

The magic found me again, bringing all the poison from the Sidhe into me, and I was consumed with it. I felt like I was burning up, like I was on fire. Parts of me turned to ash, and I realized it was not my body, but my magic that was disintegrating. But I was my magic, so where did that leave me?

I woke and for a minute I didn't know where I was or who I was or what was happening. My hand on Ronan's chest grounded me in the present. I was in my bed at my Winter estate. I had not cured the Sidhe with my magic. It had been a dream.

But who sent the dream?

My previous ones had been from the Ancient Mother, who had urged me to act now, think later, or from something older wanting me to consider my actions before I threw the Sidhe into chaos.

This dream had felt different.

I was still considering it when Ronan woke.

"How do you feel?" I asked, shoving thoughts of the dream aside.

"Like I can't see out of my left eye." He hadn't moved, laying on his back, staring up at the ceiling. Of course, I lay on his left side, so he'd have to move quite a bit in order to look at me.

I winced. "I didn't get to you fast enough."

"You got there faster than she thought you would. I think she believed she'd have a couple days at least. She didn't expect you to open a Way directly into her dungeon."

"I didn't. I opened the Way directly to you. I didn't know where I was going to end up."

He groaned. "Calynn."

I sat up, looking down at his beautiful, scarred face. "Don't start. You were in danger. You were hurt. What did you expect me to do? I brought Morrigan with me."

They had been able to save the eye itself, but not the sight. It had been cut, the pupil no longer a circle, but an odd teardrop shape that dipped into the emerald green of his iris.

"Bringing one slightly unhinged person with you is not what I would call being prudent," he said, his good eye catching me in its gaze. "You could have walked directly into a trap. If she'd anticipated you, she could have killed you the moment you stepped into the dungeon."

I ran my fingers through his hair. "I don't think you understand. The rage. Ronan. If she had killed you, I would have burned this whole world to ashes and felt no remorse. I've been struggling with what I have to do, the lives that might—that *will* be lost. But in those moments when I felt your pain, all I could think of was getting you back. By whatever means necessary. Even if it meant killing every living soul in every single world."

He sat up as well so he could hold my face between his hands. "I do understand. How do you think I've felt since the moment you stood on my porch?"

I kissed him, pressing my lips and my body against him, soaking up the feeling of him, solid and steady. He would be okay. Evander and Assana had assured me his hands would be basically back to normal within a day or two. The rest of the wounds had been mostly caused to drain him of blood before they started some more serious torture, giving him less of a chance to heal himself. His face had been cut with a hot knife, partially cauterizing the wound as it was cut so it would be impossible to heal. He might regain some sight over the next few days as the swelling went down. But likely no more than shadows.

Ronan's stomach growled, drawing my attention from the kiss.

"You need to eat," I said, getting out of the bed and going to the table where someone, likely my housekeeper Ethna or Quinn, had laid out a spread of food for us.

Ronan followed me.

"What's this?" He motioned to the abandoned mug on the table.

"I made coffee last night to try to calm myself. When I was done, I realized I didn't want to drink it."

"That's a first."

"Have I ever told you about the perfect cup of coffee?"

He shook his head as I handed him a plate loaded with food. I pushed him into a chair and returned to the table to start the process again for that perfect cup.

"When I was fifteen, Arial and I were already best friends. I spent more time at her house than with any foster family I'd been put with. I stayed over one night, and in the morning, I went down to breakfast. Arial and her mom were sitting at the dining table already with this huge stack of pancakes with butter and real maple syrup. And coffee. This really amazing stuff from Guatemala." I huffed a laugh. "I remember being worried they were trying to give me a nice morning before they told me to leave. Then I saw the folder in front of Arial's mom. Candice was her name. I sat down and she said she'd filled out adoption paperwork, but she wanted to make sure it was what I wanted before she filed it."

I wiped my cheek, looking at the wetness on my fingers. When had I started crying?

"It was the perfect morning. For one moment, I had a home. Shortly after that, Candice received her schizophrenia diagnosis, and we decided together she wouldn't submit the paperwork until it was under control. Unfortunately, she never got it under control." I took a deep breath before continuing. "Ever since, coffee has always brought me back a tiny sliver of that morning. That moment of hope and family and home. But last night, I realized something."

I turned back toward him, cup in hand. I breathed in the steam like I always did, then set the cup on the table behind me. "There is no home without you."

He held out his hand, and I went to him, sinking onto his lap as our lips came together once again. Then I rested my forehead against his, our breath mingling in the space between us.

"We should come up with a codeword," I said.

He chuckled and his stomach rumbled again. I picked up a grape off the plate and held it out to him.

SP NEESON

"What for?" he asked before allowing me to slip the grape between his lips.

"I knew when you were taken. I felt your fear. But I'd thought it was a nightmare. If we have a codeword, we can send it to the other if we really need help. I can open a Way to wherever you are, and I'll be there. Since you have access to my magic, you should be able to do the same. I'll talk to the Guardian about it later."

"What would you like the codeword to be?" he asked as he allowed me to feed him another grape.

"What about red? It's one syllable. Fast to say. And Code Red usually means some kind of emergency."

He nodded, accepting another piece of fruit, a small chunk of pineapple this time.

We sat there together for a long time, eating. I had a bit as well, but mostly I fed him. His arms stayed wrapped around me, letting me feel his presence, since that was what I needed most, to know he was okay.

Soon, I would need to answer Mab's assault with one of my own. But right now, I needed to know my anam cara was with me.

CHAPTER 37

The dream returned the next night. That red magic leaving me in a rush, soaking into the Sidhe and stripping it of all the imbalance but leaving it whole and unbroken. I was the only thing that broke.

When I woke, my heart pounded and my fingernails were stained red, almost as though the magic was trying to flood out of me without my permission.

I got out of bed, pacing the room, trying to regain control of myself and the magic swirling within me.

Ronan had woken when I got up and watched me. He didn't ask what was wrong. I knew he could feel it.

"What can I do?" he said.

"I don't know," I said. "It wants me to use it. Two nights in a row, I've had this dream. I think it's from the magic itself. It seems to be saying if I use it, I can erase all the imbalance in the Sidhe without destroying the realm."

"At what cost?"

I turned to him, catching the look in his one good eye. He knew what the cost would be.

"You can't do it," he said simply. "The cost is too high."

"Is it though? How is one person's life worth more than the whole rest of the world's?"

He got out of bed without answering and took my hand, drawing me to the window, looking out over my lands and the people there.

"I could show you the same thing in Summer and in the human world. Or the Fréimhe. Whatever. People living without fear. Actually living."

"Anyone could have done that."

"No one did. No one except you." He turned me to face him. "You are the leader we need, Calynn."

"But I have to destroy everything. Doesn't that make me the villain? People are going to die because of me."

"People are going to *live* because of you."

I paced away again, shaking my head. Then I went to my closet or wardrobe or whatever and found pants and a shirt, quickly getting changed. Ronan pulled clothes on, too.

"Where are we going?"

"To the ranch. I want to talk to the Ancient Mother."

We both stepped into our boots, and I bent to lace mine up while Ronan did the same.

"Can you do that?" he asked.

I nodded. "The rowan tree is her tree. I just need to ask the dragon for assistance."

I strapped my sword to my hip, noticing as Ronan reached for his, and hesitated. We'd found it where he'd been taken. Linden had taken it off him and left it to be found later. It was supposed to be what alerted me to Ronan's kidnapping.

"Put it on," I said.

He didn't look at me, staring at the weapon that had been almost an extension of his own body. "I can't use it. My depth perception is all wrong now."

"You'll figure it out. Probably not today, but eventually. You won't if you don't keep trying."

He gave a decisive nod and strapped the sword to his side, where it always was, his hand resting on the hilt. He'd never needed to look to see where it was. But I could feel his hesitation, the worry he wouldn't be able to do what he needed now he couldn't see out of one eye.

When we were both ready, I went downstairs. Quinn rushed toward me. "Do you want something to eat or some coffee?"

"Not yet. I'm going to the ranch. Maybe there. Later."

She nodded, following along behind me. We went to the stand of trees where I'd created the Ways and stepped from Winter into what had become the Fréimhe. I stalked from the Way to the rowan tree where the golden dragon slept, smoke drifting from her nostrils to tangle in the branches above her. She lifted her head when I got close.

"I need to see her. Will you take me?"

She stood and stretched her front legs forward, arching her back and spreading her leathery wings before folding them again and looking at me expectantly.

"I'll be back soon," I said without looking over my shoulder. I placed a hand on the dragon, and we walked into the tree trunk like I had done the first time.

Now that March was upon us, the landscape looked like a beautiful spring field, covered in wildflowers. The little house sat with smoke drifting from its chimney. I wasn't hesitant this time. I went right to it, opening the door and letting myself inside. The single room was empty of all but two chairs facing an empty fireplace. In one sat the Ancient Mother, covered as usual in her cloak with the deep hood.

"What, no creature comforts to try to manipulate me today?" I asked, striding toward the unoccupied chair. "No coffee to try to convince me you're interested in me as a person?"

"It did no good last time. Why would I bother this time?"

Her voice sounded weaker than it had before. Almost like she was having trouble breathing.

"You're dying, aren't you?"

"Me. The Sidhe. I have lived six thousand years. It is long past time."

"I had a dream last night and the night before," I said, sitting down. "The red magic wants to scrub the world clean of the imbalance."

"Of course it does."

"It told me no one would die."

Her nod was barely visible with the hood hiding her head. "That is true. But it would destroy you."

"Why is that important? I'm just one person."

"You are the only person living who can take this mantle from me."

"Couldn't you just keep holding it for a while longer until someone else could take it?" But even as I asked, I knew the answer. She had the same length of time left as the Sidhe had. Possibly less. "Your magic is broken, isn't it?"

She lifted her hands to the hood, pushing it back. This time, they didn't change color. The nailbeds were stained red. As the hood fell off, I saw the red, spiky lines covering her face.

My heart raced.

"It was you, wasn't it?" I said. "You caused the imbalance. Your magic broke, and you didn't let go."

She turned silver eyes to me, so similar to my own except for the red staining what should have been the whites of her eyes. Within them, I could see regret mixed with defiance.

"You said six thousand, but the daoine sidhe should only live to be three thousand. What happened three thousand years ago?"

The regret and defiance were replaced in an instant with an overwhelming grief. Even three thousand years later, whatever had happened still haunted her.

"My anam cara died."

I never thought hearts could actually skip beats. The way it was always described before, it had seemed like something to do with being in love. But my heart stopped and restarted at the very idea I could lose Ronan. I felt that red magic come to me, invading me before I pushed it away. I could so easily become like the Ancient Mother. And if I did while wearing the Ancient Mother's mantle, I too, would break the magic in the realm.

"Why?" I asked. "Why did you hold on instead of letting go?"

"The world was in shambles. The Queens were in their twilight years. New Queens had yet to be born. Summer and Winter were at war for no other reason than they were different. I had to hold everything together."

"But your magic was broken."

"My heart was broken," she snapped. "My magic did not break until much later."

"Magic comes from the heart. If your heart is broken, your magic is broken. I've been here for months, and I know that." I stood, incensed. "How could you not see that? You were supposed to protect the magic in the realm and instead you broke it." I stopped as something occurred to me. "You did the wrong thing for the right reasons."

"What is that?"

"That's what everyone has been doing. The wrong thing for the right reasons. My father. You. Mab. Titania. All of you. You're trying to help, but you're just making things worse until it altered everything, including the people in power." I paced away, thinking furiously. "The red magic caused the imbalance in the first place. You let it consume you and didn't let go when you should. Now, it wants me to use it to fix what it broke, but it can't. It's just another wrong thing. People would survive, but nothing would be fixed."

"The red magic is a natural part of the Sidhe. It is the magic that holds fae to their bargains. It is meant to devour that which had been corrupted, but it has become corrupted itself."

I shuddered as I remembered Barden's broken bargain. My magic had torn his away because he'd broken the bargain with me. "If I take the Ancient Mother's mantle, and someone breaks a bargain..."

She nodded. "You will feel it. Every time. It did not always feel as it does today. It used to feel sickly sweet, like something to give you a toothache. Now, it just feels rotten."

I stopped pacing and turned to her. "The mantles are broken."

"Yes. All three. This is another responsibility you must take on."

I considered the path magic that had allowed me to heal the scars in Kai's magic. Before he'd become an assassin, Mab had hurt his magic to try to draw his latent magic out. It hadn't worked.

"If I heal the Ancient Mother's mantle, will it make that red magic not feel so rotten?"

"I do not know the answer to that question. I can only hope the answer is yes."

I closed my eyes and took a breath. Hope. It wasn't much to hold on to. It wasn't much to base all my future plans on. But it was all I had.

"You told me the only way to save the Sidhe is to kill the Queens, to remove them from power. But I have to remove you from power as well, don't I?"

She nodded slowly.

"Do I need to kill you? Or can I just take the mantle?"

"You can just take it. It belongs to you. They all belong to you."

"If I don't have to kill you, I don't have to kill them."

She looked at me condescendingly. "Mantle or not, they will not simply step aside to allow you the thrones. You must kill them for there to be no question who rules the Sidhe."

"You let me worry about that. Last question. If I'm supposed to be the Ancient Mother, and I don't have to kill you to take the mantle, why didn't you just give it to me when I was here the first time?"

"You mean the time when you were acting like a stupid child?"

"No. I mean the time when you were trying to manipulate me into doing what you wanted. You know what, I think I have my answer. Hand over the mantle."

"If you want it, you must remove it yourself."

I held out my hand, knowing instinctively the same way I gave people access to their magic would help me lift the mantle from her. I could feel it as soon as our hands touched. It draped over her magic, giving it strength and breadth and allowing her magic to be used without her needing to think about it. Constantly putting more magic into the world and taking it back as the balance shifted. I could feel her lifting it off herself and passing it over. It settled down over my own magic as though that is where it belonged, but it was heavy, and my body buckled under the weight of it. When I came out of the magic, I was kneeling on the floor, her hand still clasped in mine.

I gasped as I felt the full weight of the mantle, making me both stronger and weaker at the same time. I knew the weakness would become more strength as I got used to the weight, but for now, it was just heavy.

Finally, I stood.

The Ancient Mother was no longer the Ancient Mother. Now she was just another daoine sidhe, one much older than any other I had met.

"You won't be here much longer, will you?"

She shook her head. "Already I am fading, my magic returning to the Sidhe."

"The tree will remain."

"Indeed."

I turned to leave the cabin, but her voice stopped me. "You will do the right thing, Calynn. The right thing for the right reasons."

I left the cabin and returned to the Fréimhe, hoping she was right.

CHAPTER 38

Ronan was waiting for me when I returned from the Ancient Mother's magic. Or, I guess, not the Ancient Mother's. Since I was now the Ancient Mother.

He was joined by Quinn, Ansgar, and Mada, along with a few other guards who were usually posted near the house and the tree. Somehow, they all knew. Their eyes widened fractionally before everyone started to kneel.

"Don't you dare," I said, pointing.

"But you're—" Quinn said.

I glared hard at everyone. "Don't."

The guards who didn't know me well froze, eyes wide with uncertainty. But no one dropped to their knees. Thank fuck.

Ronan came down off the porch and I noted he held the railing a little tighter than he normally would have. Actually, he normally wouldn't have held it at all.

"Are you all right?" he asked quietly when he reached me.

I nodded. "Feels a little heavy, but it's fine. Not really looking forward to taking the other two. Speaking of which, we need to have a meeting. The lieutenants, Kai, Gavyn, Quinn, Aiden, Rhys, Cacey, and Idelisa."

"Give me an hour and I'll have everyone ready. Here?"

"Yes."

I went inside to wait. I sat at the dining table, at the head of it, like the leader should. Quinn came in next, counting chairs and asking Aelwyd, the brownie who usually took care of this house, to find a few more. She bustled about in the kitchen making coffee and getting out snacks.

I wasn't sure this was the kind of conversation that called for snacks, but when she set a steaming mug of coffee in front of me without forcing me to drink a full glass of water first, I was grateful.

As I waited, I considered how I felt different from before. I could feel the world through the mantle. It almost felt like an extension of myself. I knew where the land connected to another place that fed our magic. I knew where the sea kissed the shores, connecting our world to the other worlds. I felt the pinpoints where our world connected to the human world, allowing magic to trickle out. I understood the difference between Summer and Winter—two sides of the same coin—and where the Space Between and the Fréimhe connected them. Already, I could feel my magic healing the mantle where it had been frayed from the constant imbalance in the Sidhe.

It was all a little overwhelming.

The table filled. Kai and Gavyn took the next two seats to my left. Mada and Ansgar sat on my right, leaving the seat immediately next to me empty. Ansgar wasn't technically a lieutenant, but I wasn't about to send him away. Everyone else came in, found a spot, and waited expectantly. I was surprised when Morrigan came in and found a seat, but I didn't send her away either. The last one to arrive was Ronan, who sat in the seat everyone had left for him at my right hand.

I took a deep breath. "It's time you all heard what's going to happen. I've been tasked with removing the Queens from power, taking over the whole of the Sidhe until new queens can be born and raised to take on the roles. As a result of the Queens' removal, the Sidhe, as it stands today, will be destroyed."

A few people gasped. No one from my original inner circle. And, interestingly, not Morrigan.

"Will you need to kill them?" Kai asked, his dark voice making some at the table wince.

"I thought I would. I was told I would. But now, I'm not so sure. The thing is, I need to dethrone them both at the same time or else the whole Sidhe will swing too far out of balance."

"Are you certain you will not kill them?" Morrigan asked in a deceptively conversational tone. "After what they have done to our home, do they not deserve a death sentence? Have their magic return to the Sidhe so it may be reborn into something new?"

I locked eyes with her. "They did the wrong thing. Over and over, they did the wrong things, and it changed them into something horrible. But they did it because they thought it was the only way."

"How do you know this?" she demanded.

"Because the imbalance didn't start with them. It started with the Ancient Mother. They were just trying to correct what was already happening. In fact, they were made queens of a realm that was already broken."

Everyone around the table grew silent. I scrubbed my hands over my face, suddenly tired. For the last three months, ever since I'd learned what my destiny was, I'd been trying to find a way around killing the queens. I hadn't wanted to kill anyone. Now, I knew how to take the mantles from them without killing them, and it didn't change anything. The Sidhe would still be destroyed.

"My problem is, in order to dethrone them at the same time, I need them in the same place. I can't exactly ask them to come over for a chat.

They'll know something's up. So how do I get them and me in the same place at the same time so I can do it?"

No one said anything for a long moment. I noticed Kai and Gavyn exchange a look loaded with meaning. Then Kai nodded.

"You could take their sons hostage," he said.

If everyone was quiet before, now they stopped breathing.

"Are you sure about this?" I asked.

"We discussed it. You want to do this without additional loss of life. You want to keep our mothers alive. You have shown me often since the time I met you that you are worthy of my respect and loyalty. I have convinced Gavyn of the same. We will help you if you think this is a good way."

"You think it'll work? That they'll believe I've done this?"

They both nodded.

"They have seen neither of us since you gave us access to our latent magic," Gavyn said. "What is more, it is something they would do. It makes sense."

My mind screamed at me, asking: is this another wrong thing for the right reasons? Or is this just strategy? It was true. They would absolutely kidnap someone if they thought it would further their goals. Fuck. Mab had already done it when she took Ronan. Without this plan, I would never be able to call both of them to the same place. They would know I was up to something. So how else would I get to them?

"What day is it?" I asked.

"March nineteenth," Ronan said.

I'd run out of time. The Equinox was in less than two days.

I nodded, feeling the weight of the Ancient Mother's mantle a little heavier now. "We'll do it. It's time to end this."

***

I sent a message to both Queens with the time and place where I would bring Kai and Gavyn. Then I discussed strategy with Ronan and my cousins.

"How many people do you plan to bring with you?" Kai said.

My brows lowered in confusion. I'd been intending for it to be just the four of us. But then Ronan said, "At least a hundred."

"Wait. What? A hundred?"

"Yes. Fifty Winter and fifty Summer."

Kai and Gavyn were nodding.

"That's ridiculous," I said. "You want this to turn into some kind of fight? We show up with that kind of force, and they're going to need to answer back."

"They will show up with a similar force," Ronan said. "I guarantee it. They're going to come with everyone they can spare. And as many people as possible to personally hurt you."

It felt like my heart dropped in my chest. "My parents."

He nodded. Behind him, Gavyn and Kai looked solemn. They agreed. And they knew the Queens better than anyone. Maybe this was the right path?

"Let's pretend I agree to this plan," I said. "And I'm not saying I do. How am I supposed to get to them with all the other people around?"

"You have been practicing shadow-walking with the best assassin in the Sidhe," Kai pointed out. "You will sneak up to them."

"So I just bring all my people onto a battle field then disappear? No one's going to question that?"

Gavyn shrugged. "Once the fighting begins, no one will notice a single person disappearing from view for some time."

My stomach dropped at the idea of fighting, but I had to agree. If the Queens refused to come to me, it would provide the perfect distraction.

"Fine. But nobody comes who doesn't want to come."

Ronan nodded and my cousins left.

"Shouldn't you be getting the people ready for tomorrow?" I asked when Ronan lingered.

"I will. But something is troubling you."

"I just don't know if I like this plan." I paced the length of the living room and dining room from the back door to the kitchen and back.

"It's a good plan. Maybe that's why you don't like it."

I shot him a quelling look that did nothing to make him stop smirking at me.

"I just don't like the idea of putting people in harm's way. I've been putting this off for so long because I didn't want to destroy the Sidhe. I don't want people to die because of something I'm going to do. Yet, here I am, dragging people with me into a fight I'm not even sure I should be fighting."

He caught my hand as I paced past him, tugging me to a stop.

"How about this? We'll get the people ready, fifty Winter and fifty Summer. But we can also ask your spy cousin if he can check on both Queens. See how many people they're planning to bring with them. If they're bringing fewer people, you can bring fewer people."

I let out a long breath. "Fewer people would be better, but I'd still rather not have to bring any. That would make me feel better. I shouldn't have put this off for so long. I kept procrastinating and now I feel like I need to do something immediately, but I'm still not sure what the right thing to do is."

It didn't help that deep down, this felt like the wrong play, and I was going to regret this plan.

CHAPTER 39

I stepped onto the battlefield and could feel in my bones this was a mistake. Or maybe I felt it in my magic. Whatever the case, I immediately wanted to turn around and go back. But the Equinox was tomorrow. I needed to have this finished before the imbalance became permanent.

The battlefield was a place within the Space Between, the spot where Summer, Winter, and the Fréimhe met. Apparently, back when Summer and Winter had been fighting thousands of years ago, they'd used this battlefield. There had already been a Way here from both Lumina and Glacia. I created one from the ranch with a little help from the Guardian who seemed just as displeased with this plan as I was.

Both Queens had brought an army, just as Ronan, Kai, and Gavyn had predicted. Gavyn and Kai had done the spy thing and found out how many people they were bringing. I thought they had fewer people than they would have wanted, but their armies were still a little bigger than my own.

I mentioned this.

"You have not been to either city recently," Kai said from his place hidden in the light Gavyn bent around them. "They are empty of people. You have taken in many, and those who do not wish to take up your hospitality have retired to their own estates throughout the Sidhe. When the Queen's sent out the call, few people responded."

Yet, included in the few who responded were both my parents.

They came to me now while the Queens hung back with their armies. I watched them approach.

"Daughter," Queran said as he came within speaking range.

"Queran. Eilidh." She flinched at the sound of her name.

"The Queens request the return of their chief assassin and marshal of their guard," he said. "Return them now and there will be no need for a fight."

I arched an eyebrow at him. I guessed the Queens were still not telling anyone who Kai and Gavyn really were, even though I had written it in the letters. I was glad I had sent the letters with pixies who dropped them and left before the Queens could try to kill them for the knowledge they may have.

"I asked them here for an exchange. Not a fight. Yet they brought armies with them."

"So did you," Queran pointed out.

"I only brought people with me because I was advised they would. My advisors turned out to be right."

Queran's gaze shot to Ronan. "And if they were wrong?"

"I'd send all my people away."

Queran turned his attention back to me and scoffed. "Do not be ridiculous. You would no more send them away than the Queens would. You have an army at your back. This makes you powerful. But not powerful enough to defeat the Queens."

I guessed he didn't feel the magic of the Ancient Mother's mantle on me. I wondered why. How could all my people sense it immediately, but those who stood against me couldn't sense it at all? Was it because they were deliberately ignoring it? Just as they had deliberately ignored the rest of my power? Or were they affected so much by the imbalance they simply couldn't see it?

"I do not even see your prisoners," Eilidh said. "You must return them to the Queens or else they will kill you and take them from you."

"I don't have to do anything. They didn't come here in good faith. We made no bargains. I just said if they met me here and didn't try to harm me or any of my people, I would bring the assassin and the marshal. I did what I said I would do. I brought them. Whether or not you can see them is irrelevant. The fact is, the armies tell me they came here with intent to harm me. So, I'm not going to show them where... my prisoners are." I took a breath. "I'm going to give you this one last chance. Stand with me. Give me your trust and support. And know, this is the last chance I'm ever going to give you."

Eilidh looked nervous. She glanced between me and Queran. I could tell she was torn. But I had no sympathy. So many people had put their faith in me without knowing anything about me. For some reason, my parents couldn't do the same.

"You do not need to walk this path, my heart," she finally said, her tone pleading.

Queran remained silent.

They would probably both support me if they had any faith in me at all. But they didn't. Like my enemies for the past five months, they underestimated me.

Even though the Queens no longer did.

"Yes, I do, Eilidh. It's time to rebalance the Sidhe. You can tell the Queens I will give over the assassin and the marshal to them and to them alone. If they want them, they can come to me and try to take them."

"You are going to drive them to attack," Eilidh said, her voice barely above a whisper.

"They don't have to. If they approach, just the two of them, I'll send my people back. I give you my word."

Calynn. Ronan tried to warn me this could backfire. I already knew it could. But if we could end this without fighting, it was worth the chance.

Before my parents could answer, the ground rumbled and I wondered if I was too late. Was the Sidhe going to be destroyed by an earthquake?

But it wasn't an earthquake. It was another army. This one filled with gigantic creatures that looked like mountains, other tall creatures wearing red hats, tiny creatures that looked like blue flames, rangy black dogs with glowing red eyes.

And at the front of the army was a friend.

"Deegan!" I said, smiling. He grinned back at me.

"Greetings, Princess Calynn. It was my sincerest wish to accept your invitation those weeks ago, but my queen required my presence. She has requested an introduction."

He gestured to an even larger buggane striding next to him. I wasn't sure how someone could be bigger than Deegan, but his queen was. She was dressed for battle with a leather loincloth similar to the one Deegan wore and leather straps across her massive body, holding various weapons. The spikes on her back and arms were all buffed, so they shimmered in the morning sunlight. Her tusks had chains hanging from them and looked deadly sharp.

"Princess Calynn of the Winter and the Summer daoine sidhe," Deegan said, "may I have the privilege of introducing the queen of the bugganes, Uny?"

"Good morning, Uny, Queen of the bugganes," I said, bending in a slight bow.

She matched my movement.

"Good morning, young Princess. The wyldfae heard rumblings of a battle for the Winter and the Summer courts. My Deegan tells me you have caused quite a shift in Summer and assured me the same would hold true in Winter."

I gave a little shrug. "I do what I can."

"He tells me you are the Stag's champion. Now I stand before you, I see you are more than that still."

So she could see I was the Ancient Mother.

"The wyldfae wish to pledge our loyalty to you. We will be friends on this battlefield."

My eyebrows shot up. "Forgive my ignorance, Your Majesty, but you can speak for all the wyldfae?"

"In this matter, those who have come with me have allowed me to speak for them. Some have no desire to fight and have sought shelter among the daoine sidhe estates throughout the realm. But many of us are bloodthirsty and long for the chance to adjust the imbalance that has plagued the Sidhe for the last three thousand years."

I nodded to her and turned back to my parents. "Are you going to give the Queens my message?"

"You cannot think to have the wyldfae fight in this," Queran said.

"Why not? This is their home as much as it is ours. Do they not have the right to fight for it, just as we do?"

"This isn't a fight for our home," Eilidh said. "This is a fight between you and the Queens."

"They're the same thing." I sighed. "Look. The deal stands. If they come up to me, just the two of them, I'll tell my people to fall back."

"What about the wyldfae?" Queran asked.

"They're not my people, just my friends. But I'll ask them to fall back as well."

Queran and Eilidh turned and went back to the Queens.

"What do you think they'll do?" I asked.

"They will not approach," Kai said from his hidden place.

Uny and Deegan looked in his direction but made no other movements.

"Not now that you have another army at your back," Ronan agreed.

Sure enough, a few minutes after Queran and Eilidh returned to the
Queens, their armies shifted, readying for the first attack.

Ronan and Deegan called directions, readying our armies.

"You do not wish to fight the Queens?" Uny asked.

I shook my head. "I don't want my people fighting their armies. I don't
want my people to get hurt."

"It is ever thus in a war. People get hurt. People die. This is the way of
things."

"If the Queens would do the right thing, there wouldn't need to be a
war at all. The trouble is, they think they *are* doing the right thing."

"We can all justify our own actions," she said. "Otherwise, why would
we do the things we do?"

We stood in silence for a moment as we watched the armies across from
us prepare.

"I do not believe you intend to stand here and watch the battle. What
is your plan, tiny princess?"

"I have two allies with me you can't see. Together, we're going to
disappear and go to the Queens directly."

"The battle is a subterfuge."

I nodded.

"You mean to dethrone them."

I nodded again.

"My people will cause a beautiful distraction for you."

I turned toward her. She was grinning, relishing the idea of a fight. I found myself smiling back in response.

CHAPTER 40

I t turned out battles were very loud. Much louder than I ever could
have imagined. Swords clashed. People screamed. The armor people
wore wasn't quiet either. You could hear as each person moved, rustling
and clanking on the battlefield. Magic filled the air so thick I could taste
it, metallic and hot on my tongue.

I watched in horror as the armies met and began fighting. So many
people fell in those first few minutes, I wanted to call a retreat immediately. I caused this. I caused this destruction and death, exactly the
opposite of what I had been working toward since I first learned what
my destiny was.

But Kai and Gavyn just stuck to the plan and shrouded me in light
and shadows, making me disappear. They came with me through the
battle. I'd made Ronan stay behind, telling him it would be easier to slip
through the crowds with only three of us.

We both knew the truth. I didn't want him anywhere near Mab after
what she'd done to him. I knew neither Queen would hurt their sons. I
was the only one in danger in this plan.

So we slipped through the fighting toward the Queens, unseen. We
had to be careful as we moved because we were still actually there physically. Just because people couldn't see us, didn't mean a stray arrow or
sword wouldn't be able to strike us. And that completely ignored what
would happen if someone bumped into us.

We finally got close enough that I could see the Queens, but they were too far away from each other for me to do what I needed.

"I need them closer," I said. "I can't take their mantles at the same time unless they're practically right next to each other."

"What would you have us do?" Gavyn asked.

I thought for a minute. "If you guys go closer, reveal yourselves, and I'll reveal myself. They'll maybe come toward me."

"If you do that, you will leave yourself open to attack," Kai said.

"I know. But I'll only drop the shadow magic for a couple of seconds. Then I'll pull it back up. They'll come toward where they saw me last to try to attack me directly."

"They have others who might try to attack you," Gavyn pointed out. "My father, for one."

"And Deardriu for another," Kai said.

"It's a risk, but I need them together."

I took up the shadow magic Kai had been using. I hadn't had a chance yet to ask Gavyn to help me learn to bend the light around me. The shadows would have to be enough. I looked up to where the sun had crept higher in the sky. I'd be fine for only about another fifteen minutes before it got too high for me to hide with shadow magic.

"Hurry," I said.

They left my side. I watched for them to reveal themselves to their mothers, waiting so I could do the same right when they did. I kept an eye on the sun, but it wasn't exactly like I could slow it down. I had a huge amount of magic, but it didn't extend that far.

At least, I didn't think it did.

Kai and Gavyn dropped their magics at the same moment, catching both Queens' attention before pulling the shadows or light back around themselves. As soon as they did, I dropped mine, letting the Queens see where I was before pulling the shadows back around me like a wispy blanket.

The sun crept higher, and it became more difficult to keep the shadows around me.

But it had worked. Mab and Titania started toward where they'd seen me last.

A buzzing started in my ears, distracting me. I shook my head to try to clear it, but it didn't help.

The Queens stalked closer. I wasn't sure where Kai and Gavyn had ended up. They were still wrapped in the magic that hid them from sight. Had they returned to me? But if they had, surely they would let me know.

The buzzing grew louder. I wasn't sure what it meant, but I had a feeling it was nothing good.

My shadows slipped, and I knew people could see me again. I drew my sword. The Queens were only about twenty feet away from me, gathering magic to them. I did the same, readying to take their mantles. As I did, I reached out my magic, ready to grab them as soon as they were close enough, and I felt something was wrong. It was hard to focus on exactly what I was feeling because of the buzzing, but after a second, I realized I couldn't just take their mantles the way I had taken the Ancient Mother's. They had corrupted the magic so thoroughly the mantles were fused to them.

Then, with a flash, the buzzing stopped, drawing my attention away from the Queens.

"Calynn!" I heard a shout, confused as to why Rhys was calling my name. He wasn't supposed to be on this battlefield at all.

But as I had the thought, he flew through the air in front of me. I felt the magic he had used, the gale of wind, stronger than any air strike I'd felt from the battle raging around us. Just as he passed in front of me, I felt the magic that had been buzzing in my head—the magic intended to slice me in two—strike him instead. He fell to the ground with a thud, and I saw blood. So much blood.

"No," I whispered. Or screamed.

A blast of magic pushed out, shoving people within a hundred-foot radius away from us. I realized distantly the magic had come from me. I didn't know what happened after that because the only thing I could see was Rhys and his broken, bloody body.

CHAPTER 41

The battle was over. I didn't know if we had retreated or if they had. All I knew was Rhys was still alive, but barely. Kai had returned us to the ranch, where the area outside the back door had been set up as a field hospital. Assana came over immediately from the person she had been helping before. She took one look at Rhys and shook her head.

She knelt next to us and did something that stopped the bleeding.

"That is all I can do for him," she said quietly. "I must help someone who stands a chance of survival. He is beyond help now."

"No! You're wrong. I'll make a bargain. Any bargain. Just fix it."

Someone put their hand on my shoulder. Ronan. Tears streamed down my face, soaking Rhys, who lay in my arms.

Assana moved away.

"Deardriu had been able to focus on you in the moment you revealed yourself," Kai said. "Gavyn and I could not return to you fast enough. When she released her strike, the boy must have felt it. It was his mother's magic, after all."

"His mother did this to him?" I asked, my heart breaking anew.

"Yes."

Rhys opened his eyes, returning to consciousness, though I could see it was a struggle.

"You stupid little fool," I said. "Why did you do that? Huh? You weren't supposed to be in the fight. Why did you have to—" My voice broke, and I couldn't say any more.

"It was the right thing to do," he said, his voice thin. "You wouldn't let Ronan go with you. Someone had to. You're the hero. You can't die."

I shook my head. "I'm not the hero in this story, Rhys. I don't even know if I'm the hero in my own story."

His lips tilted up in the barest hint of a smile. "You're the hero in mine."

He slipped into unconsciousness again and I sobbed. I couldn't help it and I didn't care. Gathering him close, I reached for his magic with my own, trying to do something, but my magic wasn't made to help this kind of wound. I was able to heal the magic that had been torn asunder, but his body was beyond my skills. And it was his body that was dying.

"There is one who might help," Niall said, drawing my attention to her.

"Who?" I asked, desperation making my voice sharp.

"Keilah. The dragon priestess. She has more magic than anyone else in the whole realm. If anyone could save him, it would be her."

"Why would she help me?"

"My research has led me to understand she helps any who seek her. The only problem is, you have to know where to find her."

"I know." Morrigan stepped forward. "My mother knew, and she passed the knowledge to me. I will take him."

"Are you sure?" I asked, hating myself for asking. But I needed to know. "He's your enemy's son."

"I know who he is," she said. Her gaze caught mine in a calm assurance, the gray of her eyes dark and stormy. "He is the ally of my ally. Friend of my friend. I will take him."

I nodded. "Take him, then." I leaned down. "And you," I said, unsure if he could even hear me. "Hold on. I expect you to come back to me."

Morrigan took him, heaving his almost lifeless body over her shoulder, though he had to be heavy, and she was slight. Then she opened a Way and was gone.

I forced myself to stand, though every part of my body protested. My lieutenants stood nearby, along with Uny.

"Casualties?" I asked.

Sorcha answered first. "Only three from my regiment. But about half are wounded."

"Five casualties," Airleas said. "About thirty percent wounded."

"Two casualties from Winter," Andras said. "Also about thirty percent wounded."

"Ten." Uny said. "And sixty percent wounded."

I looked at Gavyn and Kai.

"The Queens suffered similar numbers," Kai answered. "They could fight again, but your people are evenly matched. I do not foresee another battle fairing well for any side."

I nodded. It was what I had already expected to hear.

The sun had reached its zenith and began the slow descent to the western horizon.

"What are our next steps, Your Highness?" Sorcha asked.

I flinched at the title. I'd always hated it, but no more than I did at this moment. My people sat around me on the ground, some bleeding, some dying, many wounded. All hurt because I had led them into a stupid plan I hadn't really believed in.

I looked at the sun again.

It mocked me as we crept second by second closer to the Equinox.

"I'll let you know when I figure it out."

***

I don't know how long I sat outside in a state of shock and grief. I might have slept. I might have just sat on the ground with all the other people who had been wounded. I could feel, through the Ancient Mother's mantle, whenever someone died. Their magic flowed out of them and back into the Sidhe, and it felt like a sigh of relief and a scream of anger at the same time.

Then, suddenly, I knew it was time to get up and move. I went into the house and took my seat at the head of the dining table. Without thinking about it, I knew Ronan, Mada, Sorcha, Andras, and Airleas had come with me. Kai and Gavyn were already waiting. Uny joined us as well, with Deegan following a step behind her.

"What time is it?" I asked.

Everyone looked at each other, confused by the question.

"Is it midnight? Is it the Equinox?"

"Yes," Ronan replied. "Midnight struck the moment you stood up to come into the house."

Of course it had. Because today was the day I was supposed to do what I needed to do. If only I knew exactly what that was. I recalled the feeling of the mantles fused to the Queens' magic. How was I supposed to take them? The answer was close. I could feel it through the Ancient Mother's mantle, trying to tell me what it was I was missing.

I knew one thing for certain.

"We will not be returning to battle," I said.

Ronan sighed with relief. Sorcha grimaced and looked like she wanted to argue, but held her tongue.

"I won't be the cause of any more death. Not that way, anyway."

"What will you do instead?" Uny asked.

I released a breath, dropping my head into my hands. "I don't fucking know. Why did it have to be me?"

Everyone was quiet, letting my question linger in the air.

"You give the people hope," Uny's rumbling voice spoke into the silence.

I laughed, a humorless sound. "Hope. What even is that?"

"The wyldfae have felt this storm brewing for many centuries. We felt it and despaired. But then you arrived, and we felt the shift in the world."

I looked up at her.

"It was as though the Sidhe itself rejoiced. It is tired. It needs the renewal you represent."

"Renewal? Don't you mean the destruction? Because that's what's going to happen. Once I take the Queens' mantles, the Sidhe will be destroyed. I'm not the hero here. I'm the villain."

"I have heard you are glamour blind, yes?" Uny asked.

I nodded.

"You believe you are the villain. You believe you will destroy the Sidhe. That does not make these things true. You of all people, should know this."

Something shifted inside me, like a puzzle piece sliding into place. Uny made a good point. It was something I'd often thought. Just because someone believes something to be true didn't mean it *was* true. I'd heard false statements a number of times in my life that had not had the discordant sound of a lie. The person had believed the statement, so it sounded like the truth.

I thought of how, when someone died, I could feel almost a sigh of relief. I remembered something the Guardian of the Space Between once told me. Whenever I closed a Way, a guardian died, their magic returned to the Sidhe. I had felt uneasy about that, but the Guardian had assured me it was a good thing. No Way had been closed in a very long time, so many of the smaller guardians wanted to be given back to the magic. They couldn't because they needed to defend the Ways.

"I need to speak to everyone," I said, standing.

I went out the back door. Lights had been set up around the yard where people lay getting healed and eating. A few people slept. When I came out of the house, every eye looked at me and I was uncomfortably aware of the attention.

I swallowed and took a steadying breath.

"I want to apologize to you all. I led you into a battle that should never have happened. It had been a good plan, but it was wrong. I understand if you decide you no longer want to stand with me. I'll hold no grudge against any of you for that choice."

For a moment, no one moved or said anything. I could feel Ronan, my lieutenants, the Queen of the bugganes, and my cousins at my back. Then someone stood up. Everyone turned to face him in the dim light.

It was Ansgar.

"If you need proof you are the right leader for us, I might remind you that you are the Ancient Mother. You have healed the magic that had been broken in many of us. You treat us all with consideration and respect. In the few short months I've been with you, I have gained access to my latent magic and been able to bring my relationship out of the shadows. I have felt comfortable in my home in a way I haven't before. I have been unafraid to laugh with my fellow guards, to be happy. We didn't follow you because we thought you would win. We followed you because we thought you were right. You allow us to be by your side out of loyalty alone, where any other person in power would have us pledge a fealty of thirty years. I cannot speak for anyone else, but I will stand with you until time ends."

Before he finished speaking, other people had already begun to stand. When he was finished, everyone who was able was standing with him. Standing with me. I could feel their belief in me. Their hope for a better future.

Another puzzle piece clicked into place, and I knew what I needed to do.

CHAPTER 42

The second time my people and I stepped onto the battlefield, I felt a lot more confident than I had the first time.

"Are you sure about this?" Ronan asked. "It could go terribly wrong."

I nodded. "It could. It's a terrible idea. My worst yet." I turned to him with a grin. "That's how I know it's going to work."

"Let me come with you this time."

The memory of Rhys, bloody and broken, flashed through my mind, wiping the smile from my face.

"No. You can't. They know how much you mean to me."

"Then you should know how much you mean to me," he countered.

"I do. But this whole thing started because the Ancient Mother was heartbroken when her anam cara died." I placed my hand on his cheek, tracing my thumb over the new scar. "The only ones going forward are me, Kai, and Gavyn. They won't hurt their..." I glanced around at the other people, who probably couldn't hear us. But just in case, I said, "They won't hurt them."

"That just leaves you. They will try to kill you."

"I know. But this is how it has to be. This is my fight. Not theirs." I gestured to the people behind us. "They're just here to prove a point."

I noticed movement from the Queens' camps and was about to start my walk toward them when Ronan grabbed my arm and pulled me back, turning me and capturing my lips in a fierce kiss. I held the back of his neck, digging my fingers in a way that must have been painful, but he gripped me back just as hard.

When he broke the kiss, he touched his forehead to mine, his eyes still closed. "Please don't die," he said.

I huffed a small laugh. "I promise, I'll try not to."

Then I let him go. I turned and walked away, noting my parents were coming out to meet me, like they had before. Kai and Gavyn walked with me into the space between the three armies. They hid in the light and shadows, completely invisible to everyone.

"Are you certain you should not bring someone they can see with you?" Gavyn asked.

"I'm certain the only person who should be next to me is Ronan. And you know what will happen if I bring him with me."

"My mother will kill him the moment she can," Kai said. "She does not like it when her toys find new homes. Especially ones in which they are content."

I didn't like how he called Ronan one of Mab's toys, but I understood that's how she thought of them. I reached the middle of the battlefield just as my parents did.

"I won't talk to anyone but the Queens," I said. "No more emissaries. I'm here. Unarmed. They can come talk to me themselves."

Eilidh and Queren exchanged a look. "They will not agree to this."

"I thought not. What if I sweetened the deal?"

At the word *deal*, Kai and Gavyn dropped their camouflage and let everyone see them. Eilidh and Queran stumbled backward a step.

"They'll come to me and talk to me like adults instead of hiding behind their armies like children."

"Do you not do something similar with your army behind you?" Queran asked.

I raised my hand. At my signal, every single one of my people laid down their weapons.

"Do you surrender?" Queran asked.

"No," I said, rolling my eyes. "I want to talk to the Queens." I said each word slowly, like I was speaking to a couple of idiots, because it seemed like I was. "My people have no weapons. I have no weapon. I brought... the Dark and Gavyn. I didn't come here to fight. I came here for something else entirely and I will see this through. Send Mab and Titania to me. Tell them to stop hiding and face me. Unless they're scared."

Eilidh paled. "My heart, do not say such things."

I tilted my head to one side. "But they're true. If they won't come out to face me, they must be scared of me." I waved a hand at them, shooing them away. "I'll wait here. Go get the Queens."

Queran's jaw tightened. He didn't like being dismissed. I didn't care.

After another second, they turned and went back to the encampments, disappearing among the soldiers.

"Will they come?" I asked, without turning away from the armies.

"They must," Kai said. "If they do not, they will be seen as scared, and their people will lose some of their fear. They can no longer control their people without fear."

My heart beat a heavy rhythm in my chest. I wasn't anxious, but I wasn't exactly calm, either. I kept checking where the sun sat in the sky, watching as it climbed. Instinct told me it was just about time.

Finally, after what seemed like forever, I saw movement and Mab and Titania stepped out from among their people.

Mab offered me a sneer as she got closer, which was definitely the truth about how she felt. Titania looked at me with a concerned smile, but it was a lie.

"You truly are full of yourself, child." Mab said when she came to a stop in front of me.

"You brought us here," Titania said. "No battle. And you have brought back our people. I can only imagine you wish to come to some sort of ceasefire."

"Not at all."

"Then what?" Mab asked. "I can simply order the Dark to kill you and it will all be over."

"No, Mother," Kai said. "You cannot order me to do so."

Mab looked as though he'd just slapped her. Titania paled and her eyes grew wide as she looked between Mab, Kai, and Gavyn.

"And you?" she asked in a whisper. "Has she managed to turn you against me?"

"No, Mother," Gavyn replied. "But nor will I move my hand against her. She is not what you think."

I knew as soon as the moment arrived. I reached out and took hold of both Queens' wrists. They tried to pull away, but then they felt the red, sticky magic latch onto them and they both froze. For the first time, when I called to that magic, it didn't feel like tar. The Ancient Mother's mantle had been healed and now, the red magic felt more like syrup, sweet enough to cause a toothache and to make me sick if I used too much, but not that awful tar feeling sliding under my skin.

"Queen Mab and Queen Titania," I said, as I let that red magic slip further into them. "I charge you with neglect of duty. Under your care, the Winter and Summer Sidhe have fallen out of balance." The red magic continued to seep between the magic that made them who they were and the mantle of power that made them Queens. "Queen Mab, you felt the imbalance and believed it needed to be corrected through violence and fear. Queen Titania, you felt the imbalance as well and believed it needed to be corrected through lies and subterfuge. You were wrong."

After my initial contact, both Queens had focused on my words instead of what I was doing and now they looked confused, glancing at each other, then back to me.

"Who are you to speak thus to us?" Titania asked. This time, there was no reproach in her voice. She asked out of curiosity, and I knew she understood I had the authority to level these charges.

"I am the one with support from my people, freely given. I am the one who has taken the time to learn the magic of the Sidhe. The Stag's champion, friend of the wyldfae."

"You have been busy to accomplish all that in a few short months," Mab said.

"I am also the new Ancient Mother and you are no longer the Queens."

It was time. High noon on the spring Equinox. The midpoint between Winter and Summer. The Space Between.

The Ancient Mother had been wrong. I never needed to kill them. It would have just been another wrong thing for the right reason. What I had needed was the reminder to stop thinking like a human. Death did not mean the same in the Sidhe as it meant in the human world. So long as the red magic didn't consume it, the magic would always be reborn, renewed, and many parts of the Sidhe were in desperate need of renewal.

I had also needed the support of my friends, freely given, to remind me I was the leader they'd been hoping for. That they wanted me to lead them.

And I had needed to hold the Ancient Mother's mantle and heal it. Because Mab and Titania had corrupted their mantles so completely, they were fused together. I needed that red magic I'd hated in order to be able to do this.

I cut their mantles away from each of them, lifting them off and toward me. Time stood still for a long breath, then the mantles settled over my first one.

Distantly, I was aware that all three of us fell to the ground. I couldn't see what was happening with the Queens as I was crushed under the combined weight of their mantles of power, my own magic already beginning the work of healing them. I couldn't breathe. I couldn't stand. The first mantle had been heavy. I'd barely been able to manage the weight of it. Adding two more left me wondering if I would ever be able to stand again.

If anyone had wanted to kill me, they would have had no trouble in that moment as I struggled to adjust. I could barely keep myself on my hands and knees, my head dropped toward my elbows, falling closer and closer to the ground. I might have been screaming if I'd had the breath to do so.

Then I felt a hand on my shoulder. The weight eased slightly. Someone's voice came to me as though through a long tunnel. I could hear him calling my name. I felt my body being lifted, and I wondered how anyone could lift me. I was so heavy. Then I thought nothing at all.

CHAPTER 43

For a while, I floated through the blackness. I remembered this place from the time I had been unconscious and had met Ronan here; I'd called it the void. This time, I floated alone.

Through the mantles, I felt the Sidhe fracturing into pieces. The Ancient Mother's mantle worked to stabilize the Sidhe even as the Winter and Summer mantles took everything apart. Some pieces disappeared, breaking off entirely, the magic from those areas flowing back into the realm, ready to be renewed and reshaped into something different. All the magic was at my disposal, or rather, at the disposal of the mantles of power that continued to work even while I was unconscious, the magic rushing out of me in an intense river, acting on its own.

The thing that had scared me the most—the death of so many people—never happened. The daoine sidhe who had retreated to their estates held their spot against the destruction and many others made their way to those safe places.

There was some death, but it was only those who had allowed the imbalance to affect them too deeply. And even most people who had were just left crippled and not dead.

Through it all, I felt the strength of a person sitting next to me. As I felt his strength through the darkness, I realized others offered theirs as well. I began putting names to the people. Ronan. Quinn. Aiden. Arial. Kai. Gavyn. Mada. Ansgar. Niall. Andras. Sorcha. Airleas. Ryleigh. Deegan.

On and on the names went. Every person I had helped. Some who had bargains with me. Many who didn't. They helped me because they wanted to, because they thought what I had done was the right thing for the Sidhe and for our people.

As I floated in that dark void, I realized I wasn't alone. A woman had come into the void and was looking at me curiously.

She looked mostly human, though I wasn't sure if she was wearing a crown or if it was actually the shape of her head. Her blue dress was covered in living flowers, butterflies, dragonflies, and other insects, the full skirt moving with life. Her skin was so pale white, it had a faint tint of blue and I wasn't sure if it was a reflection from the dark blue of the dress or the veins beneath her skin. Her dress showed off an impressive chest without being obscene and also allowed me to see a deep jagged scar beginning at her left shoulder and disappeared into the fabric.

"So you are the one the trees whispered about," she said. "I admit, you are not what I had expected."

"Who are you?" I asked.

"I suppose, with your lack of education, you are not able to hazard a guess."

"You suppose right. Look. I just got rid of the last asshole who wouldn't leave my dreams alone. You're not going to start that up again, are you?"

She laughed. "Oh, you are a bold one. I hoped I would like you. I am so glad I do. I am called Keilah."

I'd heard that name before. "The dragon priestess. Did Morrigan find you? Is Rhys with you? Is he okay?" The questions rushed out of me, my heart speeding as I waited for her answer.

"Peace, child. Your friend found me and requested my aid. The boy was grievously injured, but he will live. Though he must stay with me for some time before he can make his way back to you."

"As long as he can find his way home, eventually. So, why are you here?"

"I wanted to introduce myself. It is my duty to assist the Ancient Mother in any way I am able."

"Why didn't you help the last one when she broke the magic here?"

Keilah sighed. "I tried. Over and over, I tried. She refused my assistance. She refused to see reason. Blinded by her pain."

"Couldn't you have done something? Taken her mantle away?"

"This is not my world. I am here as an instructor, as an aide. I must not interfere unless asked directly. Already I pushed the bounds of my task when I sent you the dreams of the black hole."

"You sent those?"

She nodded. "A warning of what would happen if you chose the wrong path."

"I figured that's what it was. I just didn't know where they came from."

"As the Ancient Mother, you may call on me. If you find yourself here, in the void, I can come to you and offer counsel. It would be best if you found me in person, but alas, I do not see that being a possibility in the near future. Too much must be rebuilt."

"Will you do something for me, then?" I asked. "Will you tell Rhys we're waiting for him to come back?"

"I will tell him, though I am certain he already knows it."

She faded away, going back to wherever she came from and leaving me alone once again. Any time I wanted to talk to her, I would simply think about her, and she would appear. It made the void less lonely. But I wanted to go back to my friends.

"It will be a painful journey back," she said. "And while you travel it, you will no longer be in the void, so I will not be able to visit you."

"How do I do it?"

She gestured to me, and it seemed like she was getting further away. "You are already doing it."

I moved out of the void and suddenly could feel little more than pain. My body felt too small to contain all the magic living within me now, and my skin felt stretched tight. Slowly, I adjusted to the feeling and could finally understand what was going on around me.

The first sense to return was touch. I could feel my body lying in a bed. My bed. In my house in the Fréimhe.

Hearing came back next. I could hear when people were in the room with me. I learned the sound of each person's breathing. Sometimes I would hear conversations. Usually, one person asking another if there had been any change in my condition. The answer always a sad no.

Sight returned to me, and I was left wondering if my eyes had been open the entire time. I hadn't opened my eyes to see what was around me. I was just suddenly able to see Aiden, curled on my pillow, Quinn sitting on a chair beside my bed. They switched, and Ronan returned. Later, Ronan left and Arial took his place.

I was conscious in a way that didn't let others know I was conscious. Unable to move under the weight of the mantles, I worried I'd never be able to move under them. Eventually, two new queens would be born. Thanks to the Ancient Mother's mantle, I already knew the queens would be born on the upcoming Fall Equinox. But babies could not bear the weight of these mantles. I wouldn't be able to shift them from me to the new Queens until their thirtieth birthdays.

I couldn't tell how long I stayed like that. Seeing, hearing, feeling what was going on around me without being able to participate.

Ronan was in the room. It wasn't the first time I'd noticed. It wasn't the first time he'd talked to me. He said, "I miss you, little changeling. Even your risk taking. You are strong enough. Come back to us. We need you. Now more than ever." He pressed my hand, held between both his, to his forehead and whispered, "I need you."

Then he laid a gentle kiss on my knuckles before laying my hand back down on the bed and moving to stand. I was able to grip him and keep him there.

He stared at me for a long time before trying to disengage our fingers once more, as though he was testing if he had imagined the hold. I was able to still hold him in place, and he dropped to his knees beside the bed.

"Thank the Sidhe. You return."

CHAPTER 44

My semi-conscious state continued for a while longer. Whenever I had visitors—which was always—my friends would talk to me, reading to me or telling me about the things that were happening.

Slowly, my body adjusted to the weight of the mantles. By the time I was able to move and speak again, almost three months had passed. I had lost weight and muscle mass, but I was awake.

On my first day out of bed, Ronan helped me downstairs, where I found Arial, Quinn, and Niall waiting for me.

"You look like shit," Arial said with a huge grin and tears in her eyes.

"I feel like shit," I said, my voice still hoarse from disuse.

I hated how weak I felt, but I allowed Ronan to lead me to the couch and I sat down, exhausted. Ronan pressed a kiss to the top of my head. He'd gotten used to the blindness in his one eye. And Killian, the dwarf, had been teaching him how to see with magic.

"I'll leave you with your friends. Just call if you need me."

Quinn hovered nearby and pressed a glass of water into my hands as soon as Ronan was out of the way.

"We're still doing this?" I asked.

"I have your coffee right here," she said. "But you're to drink that first, then eat something."

My stomach made its interest in food known.

"Put the coffee down," I said. "I'll drink the water first. And bring me something to eat, I guess."

Quinn smiled and I could see the relief on her face. She set the mug down, but before she went to get me something to eat, she leaned down and hugged me.

"I'm glad you're all right," she said. "Not because you're our leader. Because you're my friend."

I cleared my throat. "Get out of here," I said. But I didn't let her go right away.

She went to the kitchen and Arial took a seat right next to me, pressing into my side as though she needed to feel I was okay.

I looked at where Niall was sitting in the chair Ronan liked. She still wasn't exactly comfortable with friends, but she was getting better.

"Wanna spar?" I asked her. "I bet you could beat me this time."

She laughed. "Maybe later. I'll let you eat first." She took a deep breath. "This is something I never thought I'd say, but I was worried about you."

Quinn brought me a thin broth on a tray with a steaming roll I knew had come from my Winter estate.

"Okay, guys. Come on. I'm not dead. Tell me what's been happening."

My statement broke the air of caution that had hung around us, and my friends started chatting. I ate and listened to their stories. Some I'd heard while semi-conscious. Others I hadn't. I interrupted to ask questions, but even if I'd heard the story before, I let them continue.

After I ate, I drank the water, then reached for my coffee, still steaming, and brought the cup to my lips. I inhaled the steam, breathing in the rich scent before drinking the brew. It tasted like home.

As we chatted, other people came in to say hello. No more than one or two at a time. I wondered who was outside, ensuring they didn't overwhelm me, but I didn't ask. My heart ached every time the door opened and Rhys didn't come bounding inside with his mischievous smile and unending energy.

Later in the evening, after I'd eaten a second time, Killian arrived with a large leather sack. I hadn't yet removed the magic from in front of his eyes, but I knew I would be able to do it as soon as I could travel out to his home in the mountains. He would need to be in a comfortable place so he could adjust to vision again slowly.

"Your Majesty," he said as he came into the living room and bowed to me.

"Killian, you know you don't need to do that."

He stood again with a smile. "Today, I do. I have a gift for you." He reached into his bag and pulled out a bundle wrapped in a soft cloth.

"You've already given me a sword," I said.

"This is not a weapon, Your Majesty. This is a far more important symbol for a Queen who means to show the worlds she is to be reckoned with."

He handed me the bundle and I could feel the weight of it and the magic humming within it. I carefully unwrapped it, revealing a tall crown wrought in silver and gold. Gems sparkled within it, rubies red like blood, sapphires such a dark blue they were almost black, and emeralds the deep green of Ronan's eyes. In the very front was a huge diamond sparkling like the snow in sunshine.

"It's perfect, Killian. How did a dwarf from Winter make something with such obvious Summer touches?"

He smiled. "I know many people, Your Majesty. I am not the only one who had input in this piece. I am merely the engineer."

"Well, it's beautiful. But, what's it for?"

Everyone exchanged an amused look, even Arial.

"It's for the ceremony, Calynn," Arial said.

"The Summer Solstice is in a few days," Niall said. "Kai and Gavyn figured we would start with the challenges like usual, except everyone who wants to can participate. From pucas to pixies. They thought you would like that."

"Of course. But what ceremony?"

"On the Solstice, after the challenges are over," Quinn continued, "you're to be crowned Queen of Summer. We'll do another ceremony in six months when you're crowned the Queen of Winter."

"Why do we need a ceremony? I'm already both."

"Your people want to celebrate you," Killian said.

I sighed. I couldn't have done what I had without the people who had stood with me. I rolled my eyes. "If that's what everyone wants."

***

The morning of the Summer Solstice, and the last day of the challenges, I woke early. The previous two days of had gone well. People had fun competing. No one was afraid to take part in an event and fail because everyone knew there would be no punishment. It was simply a test of strength. It could be used to figure out where people landed in a hierarchy of magic, but for this year, it was just a way to show off in front of other people.

In the evenings, there had been parties. Everyone had laughed and danced together whether they were pixie, buggane, or daoine sidhe. Whether they were half-human, fully fae, or even a human changeling.

I was feeling strong enough that I could walk without assistance. Though Ronan insisted on accompanying me pretty much everywhere unless someone else was going to come with me, usually Quinn. This morning, before the final challenge, I went with Ronan to a building I hadn't been to yet. It had been retrofitted into a jail.

At the end of the battle, Kai and Gavyn had brought the Queens back to the ranch where they lay, unconscious for a number of days. As the Sidhe broke apart, some of their followers had fled, others had been captured by my people and brought here. The result was I had a number of prisoners who had just been waiting for me to pass judgment on them.

Both former queens, around ten followers each, and my parents.

I entered the building and everyone inside turned to look at me.

"So you have come to see us at last," Titania said with a sneer. She looked me up and down and clearly found me wanting.

It didn't bother me. I was the one holding her in jail, after all.

"You are weak," Mab said. "You will not hold the crown long before someone takes it from your head. You must rule with strength in order to keep what you have stolen."

"That thinking is exactly why you lost the mantle. You don't understand the magic, and that is the Ancient Mother's fault. She should have taught you what it means to be Queen. What your responsibilities are. What you can and cannot do. Who can and cannot take the mantle from you."

I could feel Queran's eyes on me as he listened to what I said. No one had taught him, either.

"You're right," I continued. "You do need to rule with strength. But strength doesn't mean beating people—torturing them—for disobeying or simply because you feel like it. You need to rule with compassion and mercy as well as strength. Something you failed to do."

They watched me with a kind of confused indifference. They didn't care about what I had to say, convinced they had done what they needed to do. Maybe they had. Maybe there was no other way for them. But there was another way for me.

"I'm willing to let everyone go. I'll release you right now. But first, I want a vow that you will not stand against me or mine."

Everyone looked to the former queens, who continued to glare at me. No one took me up on my offer.

I shrugged and turned to leave.

"Wait!" Eilidh called.

I stopped but didn't turn.

"I will swear."

I took a deep breath and turned to her. "I told you before, it was your last chance to stand with me. That's not what I'm offering here."

"I understand." Tears streamed down her face, and I could feel the regret come off her in waves. "I still swear not to do harm to you or to your people."

I nodded to the guard who was in charge of the prisoners. Queran stepped forward.

"I made a mistake," he said. "I should have stood with you instead of my sister. I too, vow to do no harm."

I had expected it, especially after Eilidh had made the vow. It still hurt that it took me winning for him to believe in me.

I didn't wait around to see them released.

***

The last day of the Solstice challenges was supposed to be a fun one. People showing off their creativity. The story of how I'd created a diamond and given it to Mab had made the rounds and other people created things, giving them to me at the end. I rolled my eyes but smiled through it all. When it was over, I went back to the house to get ready for the ceremony.

Arial was there to do my hair. Quinn was there to help with everything else. After a shower, I sat down to allow them to start their work. My heart pounded in my chest, anxiety making me tremble.

It was stupid. I was already Queen. And Ancient Mother. This was just a formality. A ceremony for the people. It didn't actually mean anything.

"It's going to be okay, little changeling," Ronan said from behind me. He caught my eye in the mirror. "You will enrapture everyone."

"And if I don't?"

Even though other people were in the room, he gave me a smile, a real one I could see on his lips and in his eyes.

"You already have."

Someone knocked on the door and he let Bidina and Agata into the room. The two brownies carried a large garment between them.

"What's this?" I asked the seamstresses.

"When we heard about the ceremony, we worked together to create this," Agata said.

Ronan looked at me again and sent me a thought that he was going to leave me to it, closing the door softly behind him.

Quinn and Arial worked their magic first, then Agata brought the dress over. I didn't get to see it before she was pulling it over my head, settling it around my body. It fit perfectly, as I knew it would. She laced up the back, and I got my first glimpse of it.

The top was white, blending into a green that darkened to almost black at the bottom of the loose skirt. The bodice was strapless and would show off a lot of my chest and therefore the antler necklace I wore, a gift from the White Hart. Gold and silver embroidery covered the dress in snowflakes and suns, flowers and trees. Then there was the living aspect. At the bottom of the dress, where it was darkest, black flowers bloomed with silver centres, a symbol of Summer in the colors of Winter.

"It's perfect," I said.

"Not yet," Agata said, stepping aside as Bidina brought forward a bundle of black.

She started by strapping a belt around my waist, an embroidered leather scabbard attached to it. Agata passed me my sword and it fit in the scabbard like the brownies had taken its measurements as well. They probably had.

Agata looked me over with her discerning eye. Bidina did as well. I passed some kind of test because they both nodded, then Bidina picked up another piece and held it out to me. My worn leather jacket, freshly oiled, patched up from when Gavyn stabbed me. New embroidery had been added to the roses Bidina had embroidered on the back the first time she'd patched it. Pure white snowflakes over the shoulders, bright red flames licking up from the bottom.

"It's beautiful," I said.

Bidina held it open, and I shrugged it on over the dress. Miraculously, the two garments complemented each other. The red embroidery looked vibrant next to the green in the dress. The black leather balanced the black bottom of the skirt.

"How—Why?"

"You are representing our world, Your Majesty," Agata said. "You must look like the Queen you are, but you must also look like yourself. And this jacket reminds people of the battles you have fought and won."

"Are those flowers real?" Arial asked, pointing at the ones along the bottom of my skirt.

"Yes and no," Agata said. "They are magic."

"Of course they are," she said.

"There is one more thing," Bidina said. "Quinn mentioned new boots."

It had been something I'd talked to her about before. New ones, so she didn't have to shine up my old ones every time I needed to go somewhere fancy.

Bidina set the boots in front of me. The same red embroidery in the jacket and scabbard decorated the sides of the boots. I stepped into them, and they already felt incredibly comfortable.

I laced the boots—something Quinn always said I should let her do, but I insisted on doing myself. When I straightened, Arial held the crown Killian had gifted me.

"May I?" she asked.

I sat down in the chair where she had painstakingly created my hairstyle and she placed the crown on my head. I felt the weight of it, but it was something I could handle.

I stood again and turned to my friends. "Well?"

Arial wasn't breathing. Quinn had her hands clasped and tears welled in her eyes.

"I love you, Calynn," Arial finally said. "And I've known you for a long time. Today is the first day I thought of you as a Queen."

My face heated, and I looked away, trying to hide the blush I knew everyone saw.

We made our way downstairs, where Ronan waited for me just outside the front door.

"What do you think?" I asked him as I came outside.

"You are ravishing as always, my Queen," he said, taking my hand and bowing over it to place a gentle kiss on the back.

I lifted my eyebrow at him. "Everyone knows you're my consort. Do you always have to be so formal?"

A brief and rare smile lit his face for a moment. He was getting better at sharing them with me around other people. "Yes."

The ceremony would take place by the rowan tree. Tables and chairs had already been set up, food and drink loaded onto them for the party afterward. The dragon snoozed at the base of the tree. I knew she wasn't truly asleep, but most people would think so to look at her, smoke drifting softly up from her nostrils, tangling in the branches and the leaves above her.

I took a seat and reached for a steaming carafe, heated by a small flame in a holder beneath. Quinn slapped my hand away.

"You're lucky no one's here yet," she said, taking the carafe and pouring the coffee into my cup. "You're Queen. You don't do menial things like pour coffee."

"I can lift it myself, though, right? To take a drink?"

"Of course, Your Majesty."

I snorted but took the cup from her, sipping it as people began to filter into the area.

My cousins arrived, fingers linked together. I'd known they needed to meet each other, but I had been surprised by how hard and fast they'd fallen for each other. Even more surprising was that they were already expecting two children. The Ancient Mother's mantle told me the children would be the future queens.

They came to me, sitting at the table with me. Quinn came forward and poured them each a cup of coffee.

I told them their mothers didn't make the vow, so they would remain in jail. They understood.

As the sun began to dip below the horizon, the three of us stood together.

The front yard was crowded with people. Everyone from Summer who stayed with me, a few people from Winter, and even some of the wyldfae. As we made our way to the tree, all eyes turned to me.

For the first thirty years of my life, I had been alone, disliked, and set aside by everyone I met, except for Arial. Having this many people look at me, even though they liked me, felt uncomfortable.

We stopped in front of the tree and all the people. The dragon looked up, and I placed a hand on her head. She rumbled beneath my touch in happiness.

Gavyn met my eyes, a question in his gaze, asking if I was ready. I nodded.

"Welcome, my fellow Summer people," he began, turning toward the waiting crowd. "Some of you may know my role among the old Summer court. I was Titania's marshal and her chief spy. I gave up that role when Calynn helped me." His eyes strayed to Kai, standing next to him, then back to the crowd. "Few people know the extent of my connection to the Summer court, however. You see, Titania is my mother."

The crowd murmured, but Gavyn didn't pause to let the statement settle.

"Calynn knew this. Yet, though I swore I would never turn against my mother, and she understood our connection, she helped me anyway." He turned to me. "Because it was the right thing to do. I do not get the power to choose who leads the Summer people. Thanks to you, I do get to decide who I choose to follow."

He started to drop to his knees, but I caught his shirt in my fists.

"Don't you dare," I said.

His eyes sparkled with amusement. "You are unlike any ruler, cousin. I can't wait to see what trouble you cause next."

The End

If you enjoyed *Hope in the Inferno*, please consider leaving a review. Reviews help indie authors like me gain exposure which helps sell books. Which helps me create more books.

Did you love Ronan as much as I do? If so, you can sign up to my newsletter to get a collection of scenes written from his point of view called *The Other Side of the Fire*. Find a link to the collection on my website: www.18streetpress.com

Have you read Niall's story yet? Find out how she and Calynn go from enemies to sisters in *Out of the Embers*, available now. Keep reading for a peek at the first chapter.

OUT OF THE EMBERS

R onan came down the stairs, and I made sure my glamour was in place before moving to intercept him. He didn't notice me right away, focused ahead on where he was going. Calynn and her entourage spent so little time at her Winter estate where I'd basically been kept prisoner for the last two weeks. Now was the first chance I had to enact my plan.

I moved forward—dressed in Calynn's clothes, with glamour turning my eyes from blue to silver—and walked right into him, exaggerating my stumble as I started to fall.

As I'd hoped would happen, Ronan caught me.

"Oh, Ronan. I didn't see you there."

He set me back on my feet with a polite smile. "No harm done."

His hands were already sliding away from my arms. I thought he would want her more than that; the way he was always looking at her certainly made it seem like he would. I thought he would take advantage of her practically throwing herself at him. But I had to catch his hand before he could let me go.

"Ronan," I said. "Let's not fight this anymore."

The smile immediately left his face, and I knew he wasn't fooled. Where had I miscalculated? My gift for glamour was better than most of the fae's. He should not be able to tell the difference between me and Calynn.

"My lady, I am going to do you a favor and pretend this didn't happen. You should change back into your normal clothes before anyone else sees you trying to impersonate the princess."

"But I am—"

He held up a hand, cutting me off. "Don't." He pulled his other hand out of my grasp.

I released the glamour from my eyes, letting them fade slowly from the silver that was Calynn's natural eye color to my entirely human blue. I wasn't exactly supposed to be using magic, though using glamour here didn't seem to be much of an issue. It was the only glamour I'd needed since I wore her clothes, stolen from her room, and other than our eyes, we were identical, a by-product of our connection as changelings who were switched with one another.

I frowned at Ronan. "I was careful. You shouldn't have been able to tell."

"And you shouldn't be trying to pass yourself off as the princess. What are you thinking?"

I couldn't say anything that wouldn't get me in trouble, so I just straightened my shoulders and said nothing.

Eventually, Ronan shook his head. "Be on your way. I must be on mine."

I watched his retreating back until he turned a corner and was gone. Then I went outside. He shouldn't have been able to tell I wasn't Calynn. My glamour had been perfect. Of course, there was the difference in our magics. But magic permeated everything in the Sidhe. It was impossible to separate what belonged to a person versus what belonged to the world unless you concentrated.

I wasn't paying particular attention to where I was going. I should have stopped to change. Anyone who saw me would question why I was wearing Calynn's clothes, especially since I didn't feel comfortable returning the glamour to my eyes. If Ronan could figure out I wasn't Calynn, who else might?

I wandered for a while, lost in my thoughts. When I came back to the present, I found myself just beyond the eastern border of Calynn's property. I was at the edge of a forested area and knew better than to enter it without knowing anything about it. I'm not made of magic like the fae, but I can use it. While I had more access to magic than the average human, I was certainly no match for some—a lot—of the creatures who lived here.

Then I heard a small cry.

I hesitated. Someone could be trying to trick me, to lure me out of a place of safety in order to attack. But the cry sounded like a wounded bird. My heart urged me to go, ensure the creature wasn't injured, while my head told me to stay. The forest was a dangerous place.

The cry came again, and I decided. I stepped into the forest, toward the sound, careful to keep the property behind me visible through the trees. It wasn't far when I found the little bird on the ground. It was from the finch family with a red breast, black head, and black wings. And it was a baby. It must have fallen out of the tree. I found the nest quickly, the cheeping of the fallen one's siblings guiding me. I crouched next to the baby.

"Well, hello, little one." I reached down and carefully scooped the baby into my hand. "You remind me of a friend of mine. He also tried to fly before he was ready. He got there eventually, though. You will, too."

I lifted him toward his nest above my head. He wiggled around and I got him into his home just as the mother returned with breakfast.

"Everyone is safe," I told the mother. She didn't pay me any attention as she disappeared into the nest. I turned back to the property and started toward the house. Now I had calmed a bit, I could figure out my next move.

I wanted to cause Calynn pain. After everything I had endured in her absence these last twenty-nine years, she deserved to feel a little of what I felt. And since she spent the majority of her time away from her Winter estate, I only had a few more hours to plot something new.

***

After changing out of Calynn's clothes and into a lovely blue day dress that matched my eyes, I made my way to the library. I paused outside the door, considering the character I needed to play. A woman, ruled by passion, intent on ensuring she can be with her lover against all odds.

I threw the door open and swept through, a look of terror on my face. I took half a second to appreciate the startled expressions of Calynn and her house manager Cacey as I paused, framed by the door.

"Ronan and I want to be together," I said, rushing the words out as though I couldn't keep them in any longer.

They stared at me for a long moment and then Cacey began gathering up some papers that had been spread on the desk.

"Perhaps I should leave you," he said.

Calynn nodded. "Come back in about an hour."

"Shall I fetch Ronan?"

"That shouldn't be necessary."

Cacey stood with the papers and gave Calynn a shallow bow before he left the room, barely acknowledging me as he moved past. I didn't let the annoyance show on my face, but I noted his disrespect.

Calynn pointed her pencil toward me. "Come in and close the door."

I did and flipped my hair over my shoulder as I sat in the chair Cacey had just vacated.

"Now. You want to run that by me again?"

She didn't look particularly concerned as she spun the pencil between both hands. Indignant anger rushed through me. Did she think I was so beneath her notice that nothing I did would harm her? Did she think me so unworthy of love that no one could possibly want me?

"We slept together this afternoon. He loves me and I love him and we want to be together."

She set the pencil down and leaned back in her chair, regarding me. She looked at me for so long that I fought not to fidget under her scrutiny. I reminded myself of the part I was playing: I was a woman who wanted a man, willing to do whatever it took to get what she wanted. I was desperate to be in the arms of my lover.

Finally, she leaned forward again. "Okay, let's pretend for a minute that I *can't* tell you're lying. We can also pretend Ronan didn't already tell me exactly what happened this afternoon. Do you know how difficult it is for a full fae to fall in love, not just have some love for a moment, but actually *fall in love* with a human? Setting aside our differences in magic, there's the lifespan to consider. Daoine sidhe live to be three thousand years old. You're going to live around three hundred years if you remain in the Sidhe. Now, I'm not saying it's impossible, especially given how long you've lived in the Sidhe, but it's extremely unlikely."

My mouth dropped open.

"You—he—how—"

The door opened again, and Ronan entered the library. He closed the door softly behind him and genuine terror flooded me when I noticed the violent anger in his eyes. It was quite possible I had taken this too far.

"I said it wouldn't be necessary to call you in," Calynn said as Ronan strode past me to stand next to her.

"If someone is telling lies about me, I deserve the chance to defend myself."

"You think I would ever believe what she said was true?" Calynn stood so the two of them were close together.

I maintained my composure, but inside, I called myself every kind of fool. They never showed their intimacy in public. I had thought he had feelings for her, but not that those feelings were reciprocated. It was as clear as glass—now they were in this private setting—I had severely misjudged their relationship.

"Have you been with anyone since you've been with me?" Calynn asked quietly. I could tell she asked for his benefit and not because she thought he had.

"I haven't been with anyone but you for the past six months."

"We've only known each other for three months."

"I know."

One of his hands traced her cheek and my frustration bubbled up as he leaned down and kissed her. It wasn't a long kiss, but I could see the affection they shared. They didn't even care that I was watching. In fact, I wondered if the show was partly *because* I was watching.

I crossed my arms over my chest and looked away. From the corner of my eye, I saw Calynn resume her seat and regard me. Ronan took up a spot right behind her.

I refused to acknowledge them.

"Come on, Nialas. Stop acting like a petulant child for not getting your way."

I glared back at her.

"You tried a move. You lost. Get over it. Obviously, you were trying to separate me from Ronan. I have a few guesses as to why. You want to enlighten me on which one is right?"

I thought furiously for a moment. What could I say that she might believe?

"I didn't know you were together. He's not a noble after all. And I find him beautiful. I just hoped to be with him. Even if he thought I was you."

"Try again."

"Excuse me?"

"The truth, Nialas. Or get the fuck out of my office."

My eyes widened before I could school my expression. How could she possibly know I was lying?

She sat back again, completely relaxed. Like nothing I did could possibly bother her. Like I was nothing of consequence.

"I'm told it's called glamour blind and is the reason fae changelings were outlawed. Whatever. I know when people are lying. I can even see through glamour. It's probably also why you're so *good* at it, given our connection. And lying, for that matter. But you can't lie to me."

I stared. I couldn't think. How could I accomplish anything if I couldn't lie or hide behind my glamour? How did she know I had glamour? It was forbidden for humans to use magic in the Sidhe. While I'd noticed a lack of punishment for my own use of it here, I had thought it was because no one had been paying attention.

"Look," she said, spreading her hands in an open gesture. "It's just us. I won't punish you for whatever you say. I swear. Tell me the truth."

I glanced at Ronan and noted Calynn's "just us" included him. They were more intimate than I could have ever imagined. I wondered how close they actually were and if it was something I could use. For now, she had sworn she wouldn't punish me for whatever I said. It was my chance to say some things I'd always wanted to say.

"I hate you," I said, and I didn't fight to contain the loathing dripping from my voice. "I hate how you have everything I ever wanted and you don't care about any of it. I hate how you have the loyalty of your friends, yet no one even looks at me. I'm invisible here, even though I look exactly like you. Even though I am your sister in everything but blood. My whole life you have been set up as a paragon which I could never live up to. You represent everything I despise about the Sidhe. And I wanted to hurt you."

As I spoke, I watched as Calynn began to smile. The smile continued to grow the more I talked, and it caused the rage to grow within me. She couldn't even take my declaration seriously. But when I finished, I noticed her hand had come out in a gesture to stop Ronan from drawing his sword. He took me seriously. The fiery anger in his eyes matched the anger in me and I was nervous he might ignore Calynn's gesture and cut me down where I sat.

"Your honesty is refreshing, *sister*. In exchange, let me offer my own. I don't hate you, Nialas. I pity you. Not for any of the reasons you just stated, but because you let your anger rule you instead of seeing what's right in front of you."

"And what is that?"

She shrugged. "Could be a lot of things. From me? I want to give you an opportunity, but you probably won't accept it."

Whatever opportunity she could offer me, I was certain I didn't want it. I didn't need her handouts or leftovers. I sat silently, not willing to entertain the unspoken offer.

She twitched her head in a gesture toward the door. "Go. We're done for now. You don't want to hear anything more from me, anyway."

I stood with all the regal bearing I could call to me, chin lifted, shoulders back, and swept toward the door. Before I could open it, Calynn called out.

"Oh. One more thing, Nialas." She stood and came around her desk to stand next to me, moving with a steady confidence that needed no augmentation of style. "The people here are under my protection. All of them. You will not attempt to seduce anyone who is unwilling again. You may express interest, and if it is not reciprocated, you will *back off*. Immediately. In addition, you will not use anyone who is under my protection to try to exact some childish idea of revenge against me. Do I make myself clear?"

I'd lived my entire life among predators, people who could kill me with little more than a thought. Calynn had never struck me as dangerous before—so much smaller than everyone else, so much more laid back—until this moment.

"I understand."

Her inhuman silver eyes searched me for a long time, and I actually felt a sense of relief that she could hear lies because she would be certain I told the truth.

Then the fierce look faded, and she sighed.

"I don't want us to be enemies. I've got enough of those. I brought you here for a reason. Maybe we can never be friends, but hopefully we can find a way to co-exist?"

I was about to say of course we could, but she would be able to hear the lie. Instead, I went against my nature and told her the truth. "I don't know."

ACKNOWLEDGEMENTS

Phew! I am in kind of a state of shock right now that this book is finished. This series is finished. When I started it back in 2016, I had no idea I would be indie publishing it with such a wonderful reception, so I'd like to first thank you, the reader. As a writer, you never know if people will make it this far in your story and I'm so happy that you stuck with me to the end. You have no idea how grateful I am.

But there's a bunch of others I need to thank, so here goes.

To my Team Hikes and Games: Krys, Steph, Jenn, Meagan, and Kim. You're always there ready to help me celebrate and to commiserate (except for Krys, who likes to remind me that I did this to myself, but then what are sisters for?). You answer my polls and help me figure out what's not working and what is, so thank you for your unflinching support.

To my critique group, even though you didn't help me critique this book, you have helped me with so much. Especially Ashely, without whom there would be no spicy scenes in any of my books.

Thank you to my editor, Tracy. You always ask the hard questions and I both hate and love you for it (mostly love).

Thank you to all my writing friends at Blood and Pulp, The Creative Academy for Writers, and Author Ever After. If you are an aspiring writer and want a free piece of advice, it would be this: find a writing community. The support and friendship I have found in mine have been invaluable.

Last but not least, thank you to Sean and Ryan for all of your patience and tolerance when I'm spending too much time at my laptop. Love you guys.

About the Author

SP Neeson's recipes for books always include a little bit of twisted tropes, a handful of found families, and a dash of swearing and spice.

She also writes contemporary romance under the pen name Sarah Neeson where you can find more delicious stories but in a contemporary setting.

When she's not writing, she can be found having fun with her family or hanging out with her angora goats.

And yes, the u in "favourite" means she's Canadian.

Follow Sarah on Facebook and Instagram @sarahneesonwrites

Also By

By SP Neeson

Glamour Blind Trilogy (in four parts) – optimal reading order

Truth in the Smoke

Destiny in the Flames

Out of the Embers

Hope in the Inferno

By Sarah Neeson

The Blue Vista Crew Series

Why Not Both?

40013304R00203